Paving the
New Road

Books by Sulari Gentill

The Rowland Sinclair Series
A Few Right Thinking Men
A Decline in Prophets
Miles off Course
Paving the New Road
Gentlemen Formerly Dressed
A Murder Unmentioned
Give the Devil His Due

The Hero Trilogy
Chasing Odysseus
Trying War
The Blood of Wolves

Paving the New Road

A Rowland Sinclair Mystery

Sulari Gentill

Poisoned Pen Press

Originally published in 2012 by Pantera Press
Copyright © 2012, 2018 by Sulari Gentill

First US Edition 2018

10 9 8 7 6 5 4 3 2 1

Library of Congress Catalog Number: 2017946809

ISBN: 9781464206894   Hardcover
      9781464206917   Trade Paperback
      9781464206917   Ebook

Poisoned Pen Press
4014 N. Goldwater Blvd., #201
Scottsdale, AZ 85251
www.poisonedpenpress.com
info@poisonedpenpress.com

Printed in the United States of America

Prologue

"No! For God's sake, no! Rowland Sinclair cannot be trusted." Freddie Middlemiss was adamant and furious. His lips puckered and pressed into a disconsolate line. "The man's a disgrace. We still can't be sure he's not a bloody Red." He stubbed out his cigarette, agitated. "If I had my way, we'd shoot him and be done with it!"

"What Charles is suggesting may be tantamount to shooting him," Maguire observed. It was hard to tell if the surgeon was necessarily unhappy with the proposition.

Senator Charles Hardy pushed his fingertips together as he considered the warning. The select meeting of loyalists waited for his response in the private meeting room of the Riverine Club. A dozen men sat around the polished board table, ashtrays and scotch within easy reach. The air was heavy, a smoky, conspiratorial fog. It was a testament to Hardy's growing influence that the venerable men in attendance had travelled to Wagga Wagga at such short notice, and that they had done so without the knowledge of Wilfred Sinclair.

A throat was cleared. Frederick Hinton tapped the table impatiently, his chin dimpling as he dropped it into his fleshy jowls. Sir Adrian Knox mopped at his brow with a handkerchief as if he were searching for the judge's wig under which his balding crown was so often hidden. Even Goldfinch pulled restlessly at his moustache. Only Maguire remained rigid, unmoving.

"I believe Rowland was cleared of suspicion," Hardy said finally. "And the Sinclairs have always been true to King and country."

A general murmur of agreement.

"There is not a man here who would doubt Wilfred," Middlemiss returned. "He's a decent chap, but Rowland is another matter entirely. I doubt even Wilfred trusts him."

"Rowland has skills that could be very useful," Hardy said, sensing the mood was against him. It would take a great deal to convince these men to act against Wilfred Sinclair. "Rowland is fluent in French, Spanish, and, most importantly, German. Not to mention the fact that the very associations which cause some of you to doubt his loyalty may make him privy to valuable information."

Frederick Hinton's round face puffed. "Surely you are not suggesting that we should endorse his enlisting the Reds to help…"

"No, of course not," Hardy said hastily. "But his ability to move among the vermin may be useful. Let us remember, gentlemen, why we need to place a man in Germany."

"We have not forgotten, Charles." Knox pointed at the Senator. "It's why we need a man we can trust, who is unimpeachable. It's why Wilfred is our man…whether or not he speaks German."

"One should also remember that the ability to speak German didn't really help Peter Bothwell in the end," Goldfinch added.

Hardy pulled the unlit pipe from his mouth. He spoke carefully. "You may be right, gentlemen. But let us not deceive ourselves—this operation is not without risk and Wilfred is both very valuable to and inextricably connected with our movement."

"What are you saying, Hardy?"

"I am simply making the observation that if things were to go wrong, Wilfred is inseparable from this organisation…he is closely linked to every man at this table. Rowland Sinclair, on the other hand, is a known renegade—there was that business last year between him and Campbell, and then that nonsense with the Theosophical Society. No one will doubt that he was acting of his own accord."

Hardy's proposal was considered. The Senator waited.

It was Maguire who first broke the pensive silence. "Wilfred won't like it. He won't allow it."

"He could be made to appreciate the wisdom of it if we were resolved. We really can't risk a good man like Wilfred."

"And how do you expect to get Rowland Sinclair to agree?" Maguire asked. "You have hardly endeared yourself to him."

Hardy did not flinch. "Leave young Sinclair to me. I'll make him see the sense of taking his brother's place. Needless to say, I shall have to speak to him before Wilfred suspects our purpose."

Maguire folded his arms, tilting back in his chair. "Wilfred will not take kindly to this plan of yours, Charles."

"I suppose he won't," Hardy replied. "Regardless, it will keep Wilfred out of harm's way."

"By putting his brother directly in it."

Middlemiss snorted loudly. "Wilfred may thank us for it. Rowland's been little more than an embarrassment for years."

Maguire's beard moved with the clench of his jaw. "Rowland Sinclair is his only surviving brother. You're a fool if you think Wilfred will tolerate any proposal to send Rowland into danger!"

"Steady on, Maguire," Knox protested. "All we're doing is replacing Bothwell."

"And may I remind you, Sir Adrian, that Peter Bothwell is dead."

The room fell again into an uneasy silence as the inescapable fact settled on the consciences of the Old Guard leadership.

Hardy's voice was brittle. "All the more reason we should send Rowland Sinclair."

Chapter One

ERIC CAMPBELL NOW IN LONDON. FASCISM URGED FOR N.S.W.

LONDON, March 7

Mr. Eric Campbell told a press representative he was seeing Sir Oswald Mosley regarding organising Fascism in New South Wales. He proposes to visit Italy, Germany and Poland. Mr. Campbell added the time was never so opportune as now for Fascism in New South Wales. Not only Lang and his Communist friends need watching, but the Stevens Government was paving the way to Socialism and Communism.

—*The Townsville Daily Bulletin*, 1933

It was a particularly inconvenient time to call.

The smoke was thick and the blaze in real danger of getting away. A misshapen, one-eared greyhound barked madly at the flames as it tried to warn its master of the peril.

"Lenin! Calm down!" Rowland Sinclair relinquished his shovel reluctantly. No doubt it would be another irate neighbour demanding to know why he was trying to set the street alight.

"Who is it this time, Mary?" he asked the housekeeper, who had personally ventured into the gardens of Woodlands House to bring him the message. He patted his thigh to call his dog to heel beside him.

Mary Brown sighed, conveying all manner of frustration, disapproval, and concern in a simple exhalation of breath. She had been employed at the Sydney residence of the Sinclairs since well before its current master was born, and although she had run Rowland's household for several years, she did not condone his lifestyle. Of course she would never utter what it was not her place to say…and so she sighed again. "A Senator Charles Hardy, Master Rowly," she said, addressing him with the title she had used since he was a child. "The Senator is most insistent that he speak with you now."

"Hardy?" Rowland stopped, frowning as he unrolled his sleeves and rebuttoned his waistcoat. He and the Senator were hardly friends. Why would he call unannounced? "Ask the Senator to wait in my studio, please, Mary. I'll be along directly."

"What is it, Rowly?" Edna shouted over the crackling roar of the fire. The young sculptress for whom they had built the small inferno tossed an armload of split logs into the flames. She wore overalls, as she always did when she was working. Her auburn hair was caught back from her face beneath a headscarf and her cheeks were streaked with smoky residue. Rowland paused to enjoy the dishevelled picture of her. There was something particularly enchanting about such a beautiful creature, being so at home in overalls and soot.

"Rowly…?" Edna prompted, rolling her eyes. She had become accustomed to how easily men were distracted in her company…or by it.

"Just an unexpected visitor," Rowland said finally.

"Who?" Edna persisted. She knew him too well to dismiss the hard glint in his dark blue eyes, and she was too curious by nature to let it pass.

"Senator Hardy, apparently."

Milton Isaacs looked up from his book. The poet had taken refuge in the gazebo upwind of the fire, unwilling to risk his immaculate cream jacket in the smoke. "And they were enemies: they met beside the dying embers of an altar-place," he said loudly, looking pointedly at the fire.

"Byron," Rowland shouted back at him. Milton's posture as a poet was the ill-gotten product of his talent for quoting the works of English bards at will. That the words were not the creation of his own poetic inspiration was a detail that escaped most people…except Rowland Sinclair, who felt obliged to make the attribution his friend so conveniently omitted.

Milton snorted contemptuously as if it were Byron who had, in fact, stolen *his* words.

Clyde Watson Jones leaned on his own shovel, a wary eye still on the fire. He was not the eldest of them by many years, but his face was already mellowed, weathered but comfortable, like a well-worn pair of boots. The time he'd spent in the luxury of Woodlands House under Rowland's generous patronage had not erased the map of care etched by years on the wallaby, scrounging for work and dignity. "What would Hardy want with you, mate?"

Rowland's face darkened further. "I'm sure I'll find out." His last encounter with Charles Hardy had been anything but pleasant. The Senator had essentially accused him of treason… some cockeyed notion that Rowland Sinclair, the youngest brother of Wilfred Sinclair—that bastion of conservative respectability—was a Communist spy, a traitor to King and country. Rowland might have found it funny, if it had not seemed that his brother was standing with the accusers.

Retrieving his jacket from the garden seat on which he had tossed it when they'd begun the task of digging a pit for Edna, he dragged it on. Edna reached up and straightened his tie, and used her sleeve to wipe a stray smudge of black from his cheek. Unfortunately, her sleeve was not itself pristine and her efforts were less than successful.

Rowland smiled as he attempted to rectify the extra soot she had left on his person. It was just cursory…let Hardy take him as he found him, cinders and all.

He entered the house through the conservatory. Lenin padded quietly after him.

Rowland's studio, in which Hardy waited, had once been the grand mansion's main parlour. It was a large room with high, ornate ceilings and ample light afforded by bay windows. It was this light that made it an excellent studio space. That using it in such a way stamped his stewardship of Woodlands House absolutely did not displease Rowland either.

Charles Hardy was standing before the larger-than-life portrait of Rowland's late father, the pastoralist Henry Sinclair. His gaze, however, was on the painting that graced the opposite wall—a nude of Edna seated in the armchair which Rowland now invited his guest to take.

The Senator smiled broadly. "Just admiring your father's portrait…a fine, loyal Australian, a real Briton," he said as he approached Rowland with his hand outstretched.

Rowland accepted the handshake cautiously. Aside from the fact that he doubted Hardy had been concentrating on his father's portrait, the Senator was no more than thirty-five. It was unlikely he'd known Henry Sinclair, who had died in 1920.

"Of course, I didn't have the pleasure of meeting him personally…but I knew him well by reputation. A man to be reckoned with, I'm told. He was taken too early, as I suppose the best men are."

Rowland glanced at the glowering likeness in oil, and said nothing. He had been fifteen when his father died.

In the silence, Hardy's eyes fell upon the greyhound. The dog ignored him and stretched out at Rowland's feet. "Good Lord! Your dog?"

Rowland nodded.

"What do you call him?"

"Lenin."

Hardy changed the subject. "Been barbequing, I see."

Eager to ascertain the purpose of Hardy's unexpected visit, Rowland offered the Senator a drink. He allowed Hardy to make small talk for the minimum time that courtesy would allow before asking quite bluntly, "What can I do for you, Senator Hardy?"

"Please…Charles," Hardy said. He studied Rowland over his glass of whisky. "Look, Sinclair, I'd like to bury the hatchet, as it were. I misjudged you. I admit it and I apologise."

Rowland watched him suspiciously. "Thank you."

"Good…good…no hard feelings, then." Hardy didn't wait for Rowland to reply, and Rowland didn't make any attempt to do so.

The politician glanced back at the portrait of Henry Sinclair. "I should have known that despite your unusual social connections, the Sinclairs have always been King's men. Your father would have brought you up with love of country and Empire." He paused in his rhetoric. "I was hoping that I could rely on that now."

"Rely on it for what, exactly?" Rowland knew full well Hardy had not called merely to apologise.

"I hoped to enlist your help on a matter of national security."

Admittedly, Rowland's interest was piqued. "National security? Are you sure it's not Wilfred you'd like to talk to?" It was Wilfred who now wielded the power of the Sinclairs— influence born of wealth and political connections. Rowland had instead claimed the role of black sheep, a part which suited him and which he thought he played rather well. That the Senator would seek his help on any matter, let alone one of national security, was, at the very least, a little surprising.

Hardy sipped his scotch and let the silence settle dramatically before he answered. "No, it's you…Can I depend on you, Sinclair? Can your country, your fellow Australians, depend on you?"

Rowland raised a single brow. Hardy had always had a predilection for theatre. "What do you want, Senator Hardy?"

"I really must insist you call me Charles," Hardy said, placing down his drink. He leaned forward with his elbows on his knees. "I need your word as a gentleman, Rowland, that what I am about to tell you will not go outside these walls."

Rowland nodded impatiently.

"I understand that you are acquainted with Eric Campbell."

"I believe he is a mutual acquaintance," Rowland replied. He wasn't going to allow Hardy to deny his own involvement with the fascist group.

Colonel Eric Campbell was the commander of the New Guard, a right-wing movement of citizens which had once sought to overthrow the New South Wales government of Jack Lang, who they decried as a Communist-coddler. Over a year ago now, Rowland had infiltrated the movement for his own reasons and, in the process, come to know Eric Campbell and the machinations of the New Guard quite well. But the whole affair had ended rather badly, destroying his reputation in certain quarters, enhancing it in others.

Hardy studied him piercingly. "The Riverina Movement was not a part of the New Guard," he said tersely, defensively.

Rowland did not withdraw. Led by Hardy himself, the Riverina Movement was to Rowland's mind not so different from the New Guard. Indeed, Campbell and Hardy had been tentative allies against what they regarded as a common evil. Of course, now Charles Hardy was a respectable member of His Majesty's parliament and Campbell considered an extremist crackpot...in some circles, at least.

"What is Colonel Campbell up to, then?"

"Abroad...he's abroad," Hardy replied, "on an educational tour of Europe. Right now he's in Britain consorting with Sir Oswald Mosley. In a couple of weeks he'll be in Germany meeting members of the Reichstag—perhaps even Hitler himself—making contacts and allegiances with, we believe, the intent of bringing European fascism to Australia."

Rowland laughed. "Last year you were all sure Stalin had his eye on New South Wales—now it's Hitler and Mussolini?"

Hardy waited until Rowland's grin subsided. "This is not a matter for jest, Sinclair. Surely you are aware of the changes Hitler has already brought about in Germany. She is no longer a democracy. Hitler's latest manifesto speaks of Lebensraum… room to live. His agenda has become expansionist."

Rowland frowned. Germany did indeed disturb him. Only the previous year he had taken his friends there in search of the avant-garde, bohemian Berlin which had nurtured and inspired so many artists. But things had changed. Many of the painters and sculptors he had known and admired were under attack, their work labelled as degenerate. Rowland had called on his old friend, Jankel Adler at the Art Academy, to find the revered painter persecuted and in fear of his life. Adler had since fled to Paris. It was hard to believe that such things could happen in the modern world. Clyde and Milton kept him apprised of what they learned through their links in the Communist Party.

"And what has this got to do with me?"

"I'd like you to go to Germany."

Rowland choked on his drink. "You what?"

Hardy opened a leather briefcase and took from it a cardboard file of documents. "You are a scholar of languages, I believe—you speak German like a native."

"The natives might disagree."

"You also speak French, Spanish, and Italian."

"I've not had call to do so recently," Rowland said carefully, wondering what exactly the file held.

Hardy sat back in his chair. He frowned. "I wonder if you might have read about Peter Bothwell?"

Slowly, Rowland nodded. The Sydney papers had reported the death of Bothwell, a grazier from Cootamundra. He had drowned, though the reported details had been noticeably vague. Bothwell had been in Germany at the time of his death. "Yes, I did read something. Did you know him?"

"I'm godfather to his boys." Hardy sighed. "Indeed, Peter and I have…had been friends for many years. We served together.

You couldn't find a better chap or a more loyal Australian."

"My commiserations." Rowland wondered where the Senator was leading.

"The fact is, Rowly, Peter wasn't in Germany on holiday. We'd placed him there to wait for Campbell's arrival. He was a vital part of our operation to keep an eye on Campbell."

Now Rowland was intrigued. "The Federal Government sent this chap Bothwell to Germany?"

Hardy shook his head. "No, this was never official." He dropped the file onto the occasional table beside him as he tried to explain. "Let's just say Peter Bothwell was sent to Germany by men who have our country's, and arguably the Empire's, interests at heart…who are concerned to ensure that Eric Campbell's star does not rise the way Hitler's has in recent years."

"I see…but what has this got to do with me?"

"We have another man in Campbell's party…travelling with him—a little like a spy."

"A lot like a spy, I'd say."

"Blanshard is Campbell's interpreter. He speaks both Italian and German—and a couple of other languages besides. He will be assisted by other operatives in Italy, but Peter was to be his contact once Campbell arrived in Germany. With Peter's passing, Blanshard is isolated."

"So bring him back."

"That would be suspicious and he is the last man we have left within the New Guard. If we lose him, we'll have no idea what Campbell's up to."

"And you want me to go to Germany to do what, exactly?"

"We would like you to assist Blanshard, see what you can find out about Campbell's connections to the Nazi government." Hardy paused before adding, "*I* would like you to look into Peter Bothwell's death."

Rowland put down his drink. "I'm not a detective, Senator Hardy."

"No, but you do speak German and you are familiar with the country." He handed the cardboard file over to Rowland. "I'd like you to read this. It contains all the communication received on the matter of Peter's death, as well as newspaper clippings, letters from Peter himself…that sort of thing. You read it and tell me if you think his sudden demise isn't suspicious."

"You want me to swoop in like some Colonial Sherlock Holmes and solve the case?" Rowland didn't bother to hide that he thought the proposition ridiculous.

"I want you to find out what you can while you're assisting Blanshard in making sure Campbell doesn't bring Nazism back here."

"I wonder why you think I'd be interested in—let alone humanly capable of—doing what you want?"

"Because you more than anyone know how dangerous Campbell can be…the fanaticism he is able to incite. I believe the New Guard nearly killed you once."

"If I recall, Senator Hardy, the good men of your Riverina Movement seemed keen to shoot me too."

Hardy looked at him blankly and Rowland wondered if it were possible that the man was unaware of the excesses of the mobs he had incited to violence.

Hardy sat forward. "Look Sinclair, do me the indulgence of hearing me out."

Rowland raised his glass. "Be my guest."

"I assume you are aware of the organisations of patriotic men who have the defence of democracy and our way of life as their purpose."

"I am aware of a number of organisations who claim that is their purpose," Rowland said carefully.

"And you are aware of your brother's involvement with the Old Guard?"

Rowland stiffened. The Old Guard was the vehicle of the establishment, a clandestine conservative militia, the leadership of which included Wilfred Sinclair. Beyond that, he knew little about the movement. "What has Wil got to do with this?"

"The Old Guard is becoming increasingly uneasy with Campbell's attempts to forge allegiances with the European fascists. Our information is that he proposes to float a political party...to work within the democratic system to wrest power from it."

Rowland nodded. The parallels to the German Chancellor's recent rise to power were unmistakable. He frowned. "Our? You've been recruited to the Old Guard?"

"In times of need, like-minded men will join forces," Hardy replied. "The underlying tenets of the Riverina Movement were never at odds with those of the Old Guard."

Rowland shrugged. So Hardy was now with the Old Guard...it was inevitable, he supposed. He was a Senator.

"The Old Guard is concerned enough about recent developments to have installed a man within Campbell's inner circle and to have sent Peter Bothwell to Germany to ensure that he didn't receive too warm a welcome." Hardy spoke slowly now, ensuring his next words had maximum effect. "Now that Peter is dead, Wilfred himself will go to Germany in his place."

Rowland sat up. "Wil?"

Hardy sat back, noting with satisfaction Rowland's alarm. "Of course I was struck by the similarities between Wilfred and Peter—both good men with loving wives and fine young sons. Wilfred has two boys, I believe?"

"Yes."

Hardy spoke urgently now. "Wilfred is prepared to go to Germany, Rowland. In fact, he'll leave within the week. Your brother is a capable man, but he does not have your flair for languages and he does have a family."

"Why hasn't Wilfred mentioned this to me?" Rowland said, his eyes moving to the framed photograph of his young nephews which stood among the others on the mantel.

"Perhaps he doesn't trust you."

Rowland knew full well that Charles Hardy was playing him, but he couldn't prevent his response. "I doubt that's the case," he said coldly.

"You must understand, Rowly, Wilfred's in a difficult position. This is a matter of national import. The Old Guard are necessarily cautious men. If you'd seen service, they would have proof of your loyalty, but unfortunately…"

Rowland glared furiously at Hardy.

"Perhaps if you were to assume this task for your brother, for your country and fellow countrymen…well, your loyalty would be beyond question, regardless of your associations."

"I'm not a fool, Hardy," Rowland said, his eyes flashing dangerously. "And I'm not interested in proving myself to the Old Guard."

"Of course, if you went, Wilfred would not need to." Hardy looked over at the picture of Wilfred's sons, leading Rowland's eyes and mind to the same.

"Is Wilfred aware you're here?" Rowland asked.

Hardy shook his head. "Rescuing you has become something of a habit for your brother. I expect he will object most strenuously to your going anywhere outside the bounds of his protection."

Rowland's eyes darkened. Hardy watched closely, clearly gauging the effect of his words.

Rowland rubbed his face, aware that he was reacting just as Hardy intended, and irritated that he could be so easily and obviously manipulated. He stood and walked over to the mantelpiece.

"Peter Bothwell's younger son is barely two years old. He won't even remember his father." Hardy pressed his advantage. "Our only chance to prevent Wilfred from doing this is for you to go in his place. Surely, man, you're aware of Campbell's extremism, his ambition…"

Rowland picked up the picture of Wilfred's boys. "Fine," he said quietly. "I'll go."

Chapter Two

"A DEMOCRAT"
NO FASCISM OR RULE BY
COMMISSION
PREMIER'S DECLARATION
(FROM OUR SPECIAL REPORTER.)

WELLINGTON, Friday

Mr. Stevens declared that he was not an extremist. "I claim to be a democrat," he said. "I would like to see our democratic institutions preserved. There are some who want to wreck our democratic institutions. On the one hand, there are those who want to socialise them by political domination by the Trades Hall bosses. There are a few people who talk about Fascism, and who want to govern this country by a commission."

A voice: Such as Eric Campbell.

The Premier: I do not know Eric Campbell, but if he or anybody else talks about ruling this country by Fascism or commission I will deal with him. (Cheers.)

—*The Sydney Morning Herald*, 1933

It was dark by the time Charles Hardy left Woodlands House.

"I'll be back tomorrow," he said as he shook Rowland's hand. "There are several matters we need to organize, and of course I'll need to introduce you to Smithy. I'm so glad to have you on board, Rowly."

Rowland walked him to the car and chauffeur who had waited all this time in the sweeping drive of the Woollahra mansion.

He checked his watch, noting that the smoke had cleared. His houseguests had obviously managed to get the fire under control without him.

Returning through the house he found them sitting about the glowing pit. The fuel had burned down to a large mound of radiant charcoal. It was pleasant in the cool of the early April evening. Edna made room for him beside her on the garden chair. "You've been a while, Rowly…What did the Senator say?"

"Did you get the fire up to the heat you wanted?" he asked, looking towards the pit.

Edna nodded. "A couple of smaller pieces exploded a while ago, but I think we've got the temperature right, finally. We just have to wait and watch now."

"Which gives you plenty of time to tell us what Hardy wanted with you," Milton said. "What's going on, Rowly?"

Clyde agreed. "You look a bit worried, mate."

So Rowland told them what Charles Hardy had asked of him, and why he had reluctantly agreed. For the most part they listened in silence.

"I can at the very least speak German. I can't imagine why they would consider sending spies over there who can't speak the language."

Clyde shook his head. "I always thought that the Old Guard and Campbell were essentially on the same side."

"It seems that even with Lang's demise, Campbell's not willing to leave things to democracy," Rowland replied. "This chap

Hitler's sudden rise has the Old Guard worried that Campbell may try to emulate him here."

"So what exactly do they want you to do over there?"

"Apparently, the Old Guard has some chap called Blanshard travelling with Campbell. He's been working to undermine Campbell's attempts to make real alliances with the British and European Blackshirts."

"How?"

"As far as I can tell, he's been creating quiet obstacles… making sure that Campbell doesn't get to meetings, or that he makes some kind of social faux pas. Campbell doesn't seem to speak anything but English, and a bit of grammar school Latin and French, so they're expecting it to become easier once the good Colonel is relying on Blanshard to translate."

"So why do they need you?"

"It seems there are some things Blanshard can't do alone. He needs another operative on hand to make sure that things go wrong whenever it looks like important contacts are being made."

"And they want you to be that operative in Germany, to replace this dead chap, Bothwell?"

Rowland nodded. "Bothwell was supposed to assist Blanshard. He'd been in Germany for a few weeks establishing contacts and so on, when he died. Fortunately, the fascist sightseeing tour isn't due to reach Germany until May, so they want to replace Bothwell as soon as possible. Of course, Hardy seems to think there was something suspicious about Bothwell's death, so he wants me to look into that as well…"

"And try not to get killed yourself, I presume," Clyde muttered.

Rowland smiled. "That's not his priority, but it'd be helpful, I should think."

"So when do we sail?" Edna asked sweetly.

"We? No…"

"We're coming, Rowly," Clyde said in a way that made

Rowland realise that the matter had been discussed. He should have known that at least one of them would have been eavesdropping.

"But don't tell Rosie," Clyde added sheepishly. "She won't understand."

"She won't need to," Rowland said firmly. Rosalina Martinelli was Clyde's sweetheart. "I'm not dragging you all with me. It's too dangerous."

"Exactly." Milton flicked a cinder off his lapel. "You're walking into God-knows-what and you can't trust Hardy or his fascist cronies. Us, you can trust. We're not letting you go alone, mate."

"Look, I appreciate…" Rowland started.

"Tell Hardy that we know all about his little plan." Milton fished a pewter flask from his jacket. "Sending us with you is the only way to ensure we keep quiet."

"It'll be dangerous…"

"More so if there's no one watching your back, Rowly."

Rowland met Milton's eye. "Germany is hostile to people like you right now, Milt."

Milton smiled. "The Germans have never liked poets, you know…it's not really a poetic language—too many slurping noises."

Despite himself, Rowland laughed. "Goethe might disagree."

Edna put her hand on his knee. "You can't go on your own, Rowly."

"I'm not a child, Ed."

"Neither was Mr. Bothwell, I expect. He might be alive if he'd taken someone with him." Edna stood suddenly and poked at her firepit with a stick. "When do we sail?"

Rowland sighed. "Not sailing. As it turns out, Hardy wants me in Germany as soon as possible. A boat is too slow…I'm flying."

"You're what?"

Rowland grinned, unable to disguise his enthusiasm for that part of Hardy's plan. Obviously his friends had stopped eavesdropping before Hardy gave him these particular details. "Hardy's managed to convince Kingsford Smith to take a passenger to Europe."

"Kingsford Smith! You can't be serious."

Clyde laughed. "No wonder you agreed to go. Well, Smithy will just have to take four passengers."

"I don't know…"

Clyde pressed his shoulder. "Look, Rowly, we understand why you have to go. We're not going to try to talk you out of it…but face it, mate, Hardy's using you." He moved to take the place Edna had vacated. He spoke calmly, sensibly, in a way that was very typical of Clyde. "You tell the good Senator that you're not going without insurance, without us. If he wants you to go, he'll make it work."

Rowland dressed hastily, checking his watch as he knotted his tie. It was nearly three in the afternoon. He might have time for breakfast before Hardy arrived.

He had slept late. The residents of Woodlands House had spent most of the previous night keeping watch over Edna's pit fire and continuing to argue over who exactly would be going to Germany. In the early hours of the morning Rowland had been worn down by either cogent argument or fatigue…he wasn't sure which. He wondered how Hardy would take the news that Rowland Sinclair was taking a Communist painter, a Jewish poet, and an unpredictable sculptress to Germany. Admittedly, he was rather looking forward to the Senator's reaction.

Mary Brown was answering the door just as he hurtled down the staircase. Inwardly, Rowland cursed—Hardy was early.

But it wasn't Charles Hardy.

Briefly, Rowland was startled, though he knew he should have expected this.

Wilfred Sinclair entered. Silently he removed his hat and handed it to Mary, who all but curtseyed. His blue eyes were livid. They glared at Rowland over the gold-framed rims of his bifocals.

Rowland was taller than his brother, but he had never felt so in Wilfred's presence. Wilfred Sinclair had a stature that was much more than physical.

"Wil…" Rowland started awkwardly.

Wilfred didn't bother with the niceties.

"A word," he said, as he strode into the library.

Rowland braced himself and followed.

The library at Woodlands had, to him, always been a place of censure. It was to this room that Henry Sinclair had summoned his son to vent his displeasure and impose his will. Wilfred, too, seemed to prefer the library for the purpose of bringing Rowland into line, however futile that purpose had now become.

Decorated and furnished exactly as it had been when their father was the master, the library was an island of conservative, masculine style in a house that had, under Rowland's reign, become artistically idiosyncratic. Perhaps that was why Wilfred felt most comfortable there.

For a time, Wilfred said nothing, pacing angrily about the room. And then, "What the devil do you think you're doing, Rowly?"

"Look, Wil, I'm sorry I didn't speak to you first, but Hardy—"

Wilfred ignited before he could finish. "You are not to have any part of this insane plan of Hardy's. Do you understand, Rowly? I forbid it!"

"You what? I'm a grown man, Wil."

"Then act like one. Use your common sense, Rowly. This is not a game."

"I know that." Rowland was beginning to flare himself.

"Not so long ago, Charles Hardy accused you of treason,

for God's sake. Now you're going to drop everything because he asks you to go to Germany? Don't be such a bloody fool!"

"I'm not doing this for Hardy," Rowland said quietly.

Wilfred stopped. He sighed, sitting down in the studded leather armchair.

Rowland took the seat opposite and waited.

Wilfred took off his glasses and polished them with a handkerchief, regaining his composure. "Rowly, you don't have to prove anything to me."

"I know," Rowland replied, though he was glad to hear it from Wilfred. "You have a family, Wil, and I can speak German."

"You want to work for Hardy?" Wilfred asked. "You've always claimed to find the Old Guard abhorrent."

"I have no interest in the Old Guard," Rowland said. "Or in working for Hardy...And, though I don't mind working against Campbell and his fascist legions, I'm going only so you don't have to."

Wilfred's mouth twitched. He nearly laughed. "*You* are trying to protect *me*?"

Rowland frowned. Wilfred made him feel like an idiot, a precocious child. "You have a family and I can speak German," he repeated irritably.

Wilfred met his eye. "Rowly, don't you see that they're exploiting you? You're disposable. If you get into trouble over there, they'll disown you, deny that you ever had anything to do with them."

Rowland nodded. "Yes, that's what Milt said."

Wilfred stiffened. "You told that bludging Bolshevik..."

"He overheard. But, yes, I told him as well. How else was I going to explain why I'm going to Germany a few days after Hardy visits out of the blue?"

Wilfred exploded again. "You have no concept of how dangerous and sensitive this is, do you, Rowly? This is not some jaunt designed for the amusement of your unemployed Communist friends!"

"That's a pity—they're coming with me."

"What?"

Admittedly, explaining how exactly he came to invite his friends to accompany him to Europe was difficult. Wilfred was incredulous.

"What possible use would they be? Aside from the fact that they're flaming Reds, they can barely speak the King's English, let alone any other civilised language."

"Actually, Ed's fluent in French, Milton speaks Yiddish, and Clyde has picked up a bit of Italian." The last claim was grossly exaggerated. Clyde had been seeing Rosalina Martinelli for a couple of weeks and now seemed able to apologise in Italian, but that was about it. "Anyway, they're not coming as translators; they're coming so I have more than your Old Guard to rely on."

Wilfred groaned. "I should have you committed!" He pointed at his brother. "I'm going to have you committed!"

Rowland smiled.

Wilfred shook his head. "You're out of my reach in Germany, Rowly. You do realise that? I won't be able to help you."

"I realise that. Look, Wil…we don't know that Bothwell's death was untoward. Perhaps there is no real danger. I'll be careful."

"Campbell knows you."

"He knows you too. I won't need to approach him directly, Wil. The idea is to give the man you have travelling with Campbell someone with whom to work. If the good Colonel does happen to see me, the last thing he'll think is that I'm spying on him for the Old Guard."

"And why's that?"

"Well, word is that I'm a Communist."

Wilfred extracted a cigarette from the case in his pocket, and lit it. He smoked sullenly, simmering. "This is bloody preposterous…Hardy's gone too far this time…."

"It's only for a couple of months, Wil." Rowland ran his

hand distractedly through his dark hair. "As much as I hate to agree with your lot, I think Campbell could be dangerous if he gains momentum. If he has the success that this Hitler fellow has…"

Wilfred turned away in exasperation. "Hardy knew just how to get to you, didn't he?"

Rowland said nothing as he waited for his brother to face him again.

It was a moment before Wilfred did so. He smiled faintly. "At least we seem to be standing on the same side, for once."

Rowland laughed. "It's a little disconcerting."

Wilfred tossed his cigarette into the smoking stand. His face became stern again. "I want you to tell Hardy that you've changed your mind. That you will not go."

"I'm sorry, Wil." Rowland shook his head.

The Sinclairs argued for some time after that. It was heated, but not vindictive. Now that Rowland was convinced he would be protecting his brother by going to Germany in his stead, it was, it seemed, impossible to make him stand down. The elder Sinclair demanded, ordered, and reasoned, to no effect. The exchange was interrupted eventually by a tentative knock on the library door.

"Senator Hardy to see Master Rowly, Mr. Sinclair." Mary Brown automatically deferred to Wilfred when he was in the house.

"Send him in here, Mary," Wilfred said tensely. "Rowly, I'd like to have a word with Hardy alone, if you don't mind."

"For God's sake, Wil…"

"Rowly…"

"Fine." Rowland relented. It seemed only fair that Hardy should have to deal with Wilfred for a while. Rowland was, in any case, hungry. He could find something to eat while Wilfred shouted at the Senator.

Chapter Three

SOUTHERN CROSS RUMOURS DENIED KINGSFORD SMITH INDIGNANT DELIBERATE AND MALICIOUS LIES

SYDNEY, May 17

Indignant denials were given by Squadron-Leader Kingsford Smith before the Air Inquiry Committee today, to rumours that the forced landing of the Southern Cross had been premeditated and arranged as a publicity "stunt". He said that such rumours "were absolute, deliberate, and malicious lies".

—*The Brisbane Courier*, 1929

Rowland decided to take a breakfast of sorts in the conservatory. He settled for scones and bread and butter, rather than try to convince his housekeeper that it was not sinful to eat eggs and bacon at four in the afternoon.

Edna was already there, cleaning up some of the successful firings from the night before. She wore a man's shirt—which

Rowland suspected might once have been his—over her dress as she worked with various brushes and picks to clean off the ash and polish the clay's blackened surface. Lenin sprawled at her feet.

"What do you think?" Edna asked, holding up what appeared to be a large bulbous terracotta vase with multiple breasts.

"Can't have too much of a good thing, I suppose," he murmured, resisting the urge to handle it. Edna's work always seemed to invite touch but on this occasion he feared it would appear somewhat lewd.

The sculptress rolled her eyes. "It's based on the ancient goddesses...fertility, Earth..."

"Uh huh, that's exactly what I was thinking."

Mary Brown wheeled in a silver service of tea, scones, and fresh sandwiches. She glanced at Edna's vase and sighed indignantly.

"Thank you, Mary," Rowland said, winking at Edna, and piling several sandwiches onto a Royal Doulton bread-and-butter plate.

"Oh, breakfast!" Edna piped enthusiastically, eliciting another sigh from the housekeeper. Wiping her hands on the stolen shirt, the sculptress stepped over Lenin to the oaken traymobile. She heaped jam and cream onto both halves of a split scone and gave one to the greyhound, as Mary Brown made a disapproving exit. Lenin grunted happily, accepting the morsel and looking adoringly at his benefactor.

"Have you told Senator Hardy about our refinement of his plans?" Edna wiped the cream off Lenin's nose with a starched linen napkin.

"I believe Wil may be bringing him up to speed now."

"Wilfred's here? Oh, dear. Was he very cross?"

"Yes, but I gather he's rather more livid with Hardy than with me."

Edna smiled. "Good. So, are we still flying to Germany?"

"I expect we are. Are you sure you don't want to change your mind, Ed? Aside from anything else, flying is not the safest way to travel…they still haven't found Bert Hinkler."

"He was trying to break some silly record," she said, pouring tea for both of them. "He'll probably walk out of the African jungle sometime soon…" She handed Rowland an excessively sugared cup of tea. "A single man travelling alone will make people wonder, Rowly. Together, we are just tourists."

At this juncture Charles Hardy strode briskly into the room. "Good afternoon, Miss Higgins."

"Senator Hardy." Edna looked up. "How nice to see you again. How is Mrs. Hardy?"

"Alice is well, thank you, Miss Higgins…I don't mind if I do," he added, as she offered him tea.

"Where's Wil?" Rowland asked, as Hardy became visibly distracted by Edna's vase.

"He's making telephone calls. Wilfred has some reservations about your involvement…but I'm sure he'll come to see that I'm right."

Rowland gave his attention to the sandwiches. "I really wouldn't count on it."

"He mentioned that you have some notion about taking Miss Higgins and two other gentlemen with you."

"You could call it a notion."

"It's not possible, Sinclair."

"It is, if you want him to go and us to keep quiet," Milton announced, as he and Clyde walked into the conservatory.

Hardy turned stiffly, casting disdainful eyes over the poet's deep purple jacket and spotted cravat. They had, of course, met only a month before, but then Hardy had believed Milton to be a business associate of Rowland's. He had since been made aware of the petty criminality of the poet's past and the Communist allegiance of his present. "If you don't mind my saying, Mr. Isaacs, that's a very reckless threat."

"Not a threat," Milton replied blithely. "It's a statement of fact."

"We will hardly agree to send known Communists on a mission of such importance."

"Why not? We Communists are just as disturbed by Campbell's ambitions as you are. If Campbell models himself on Europe, believe me, Senator, life will be more difficult for us than you."

Hardy stared at him, stunned by both the man's affront and his logic.

"He's right, Charles," Rowland said calmly.

"You want me to send a Communist, particularly one of Mr. Isaac's heritage, to Germany. Don't you see how ludicrous that is?

"Call him Smith and he could pass as a Protestant," Clyde snorted. "And we're hardly going to announce our party memberships—we're not fools."

"No! It's out of the question!"

"Senator Hardy, sir," Clyde said, helping himself to tea. "If Rowly were to suddenly disappear, leaving us in charge of his home, you can imagine that questions would be asked. There'd be rumours. We'd be forced to tell people where they could find him, lest it be concluded we'd done him in."

Rowland smiled faintly.

Hardy's contemplation was sullen. "And why do you gentlemen wish to go to Germany?" The question was accusatory.

Milton took a seat and looked directly at Hardy. "The thing is, old mate, our Rowly's not a Communist. If he was, we wouldn't need to keep an eye on him."

"You see, we don't completely trust you, Senator Hardy," Edna said sweetly.

"What's more, the housekeeper, although one of the proletarian classes, is a bit of an old dragon when Rowly's not here," Milton continued gravely. "She scares us."

"Why, that's outrageous!" the Senator declared, affronted.

"I'm afraid she can be rather set in her ways." Rowland

glanced over his shoulder to make sure Mary Brown wasn't within earshot.

"I was referring to the implication that I am not to be trusted," Hardy snapped. "I'm a Senator, for God's sake—I will not stand here and be insulted."

"Then sit down," Milton muttered.

"We don't mean to offend you, Senator Hardy." Edna took a seat beside Rowland on the wicker settee. "But you must understand that we simply will not allow Rowly to go on his own. We'll make a terrible fuss."

Hardy turned to Rowland in exasperation. "Sinclair, surely you're not—"

"It might seem more natural if I travel with a party," Rowland said, as he handed the plate of scones to Clyde.

Hardy eyed them all intently. He walked over to the window and gazed out onto the remains of the firepit in the otherwise immaculate gardens of Woodlands House. He sighed loudly and returned to place his teacup on the table.

"Desperate times, strange bedfellows," he said, offering Milton his hand.

Milton accepted the handshake. "I trust you sleep soundly, Senator Hardy."

The dance floor was lively: a rhythmic kaleidoscope of couples moving to the slick tempo of a twenty-piece orchestra. To the blast of brass and bounce of strings, they swung. The night spot was stylish, risqué but not quite scandalous. The affluence of its patrons gave it a de facto respectability that eluded less opulent sly groggeries.

Elaborate chandeliers hung from the ceiling roses. The round tables which surrounded the parquet dance floor were draped with crisp white linen. Waiters delivered trays of drinks from one of several bars within the club, to the dancers at pause and to the committed drinkers.

Edna laughed in Rowland's arms as the number finished.

"Shall we have a drink, Rowly? Poor Clyde looks a bit lonely. Perhaps I should dance with him."

"I think he might prefer to drink," Rowland said, as he allowed her to lead him back to their table. Clyde was neither a proficient nor an eager dancer. Indeed, Rowland suspected that Clyde had not invited Rosalina Martinelli to accompany them that night so that he would not feel obliged to dance with her.

"Where's Milt got to?" Edna asked, as Rowland called for drinks.

"He's performing," Clyde muttered tossing his head towards the crowded floor.

They noticed the poet now, taking far more than his fair share of space with flamboyant moves that invited applause. He danced with a glittering and noticeably intemperate blonde.

"Who's that?" Rowland asked.

"Said her name was Dulcie." Clyde grinned. "She and Milt seem...acquainted."

Rowland watched Dulcie entwine herself about Milton as the music slowed into a sultry foxtrot. "We've got a few minutes—he may as well make the most of them."

They had all been a little surprised when Sir Charles Kingsford Smith had suggested they meet at The 400 Club. The man was, after all, a national hero—so they had expected to be summoned to some utterly respectable establishment that would admit only Rowland.

The past days had been consumed by the Old Guard, by suspicion and conspiracy, plans and warnings, and so they had jumped at the opportunity to relax and enjoy the hedonistic pleasures of the exclusive club, arriving well before the appointed time.

"Sinclair! Blimey...fancy runnin' into you 'ere."

Rowland turned sharply.

A sallow man approached their table smiling broadly. He was dressed in a dinner suit like all the gentlemen present, but on him it seemed a disguise. His face was angular, shrewd; his eyes twitched constantly around the crowd. Several men followed him.

Inwardly, Rowland groaned. It was Jeffs. Called The Jew, he was a gangster, a violent ruffian who specialised in sly groggeries and extortion, and who may or may not have been Semitic. He owned and ran Darlinghurst's 50-50 Club, an establishment which, like The 400, plied sly grog and promised wanton pleasure, but did so without any pretence of refinement or basic hygiene. Rowland had once inherited a half-share in the 50-50 from a beloved but disreputable uncle, and though he had managed to extricate himself from the partnership, Jeffs seemed intent on maintaining some sort of familiarity.

"Mr. Jeffs," he said as The Jew extended his hand.

Quietly, Clyde took Edna onto the dance floor, so that Rowland would not be forced to introduce her. Jeffs was not someone any of them wanted to know, but it would be dangerous to snub him.

"Enjoyin' yerself, Sinclair? Top joint, don't yer think?"

"Indeed."

"I'm thinkin' of acquirin' the place. Cater to a better class of criminal." He laughed loudly, slapping Rowland on the back in acknowledgement of a shared joke.

"It certainly looks as though it could be a good investment, Mr. Jeffs."

Jeffs waved at a table on the other end of the room. A stout woman, wearing a fur and enough jewels to be noticeable from across the dance floor, waved back. She sat beside a barrel-chested man in a dark suit. "I met Tilly and Jim 'ere for a drink to check the place out," Jeffs said. "Come on, Sinclair, I'll introduce yer…never met a gentleman who didn't have need of Tilly's services from time t' time."

"I'm afraid I have a meeting myself," Rowland said hastily. He already knew more underworld figures than he cared to without adding Tilly Devine, the notorious madam, and her thug of a husband to the list.

"Come on, Sinclair," Jeffs cajoled. "I'm certain Tilly'll take a real shine to yer."

Rowland glanced at his watch. "Regrettably, Mr. Jeffs, I really must leave it till another time."

Jeffs' tone hardened. "Tilly might be offended…She's a lady, yer know…"

"Rowly!" Milton strode up to stand beside him. "We're going to be late." He nodded at Jeffs. "Hello, Phil. You don't mind if I drag Rowly off, do you? We've got a prior."

Jeffs considered them both icily. Rowland kept his eyes on the gangster's hands. He'd had personal experience of how suddenly Jeffs' hands could move for a concealed razor, how quickly that razor could end up pressed against your face.

Then Jeffs seemed to accept that he was not being slighted.

His face relaxed. "Another time, Sinclair. Next time yer come, tell the blokes at the door that yer a friend of The Jew… I'll own the joint by then."

"I'll do that, Mr. Jeffs."

The 400 Club offered discreet dining rooms for patrons who required privacy. It was in one of these opulently decorated rooms that the residents of Woodlands House first met Sir Charles Kingsford Smith.

It was difficult to tell whether it was the airman's person or reputation which cut such a dashing figure. Both were larger than life. Even his voice seemed loud.

"Sir Charles," Rowland said, offering his hand as Hardy introduced them. "It's an honour, sir."

"You can drop the 'sir'…it's Smithy." Kingsford Smith looked piercingly at Rowland. His expression was not necessarily warm.

Rowland had been prepared for this. Eric Campbell was Kingsford Smith's solicitor, perhaps his friend. The airman was a member of Campbell's New Guard and rumour had it that Rowland Sinclair had attempted to assassinate its Commander.

Of course, that was not quite true, but then the truth would probably not endear him to Kingsford Smith, either.

Indeed, if it had not been for the fact that Kingsford Smith was once again on the verge of bankruptcy, and that he was desperate to prove the viability of an aerial mail route between England and Australia, he almost certainly would not have considered Hardy's proposition. Even so, it was essential that they keep the true reason for the journey from him.

Kingsford Smith led with a jibe, an undisguised challenge. "You have a rather interesting reputation, Sinclair."

Rowland's face was unreadable, but there was nothing in his voice that sounded like any sort of retreat. "I might. I don't pay a lot of attention."

"Why not?"

Hardy muttered something about drinks, keen to diffuse the tension.

Rowland shrugged. "Reputations are easily lost—there's not a lot one can do about what people choose to believe. I take a man as I find him."

Kingsford Smith stared as the words hit their mark. The airman's own reputation had been all but destroyed for a time—probably quite unjustly—by what had become known as the Coffee Royal Affair. Rescuers had died in what the media had labelled a publicity stunt staged by Smithy and his co-pilot. The public had turned against the pair almost overnight and Kingsford Smith had gone from Australian hero to the worst kind of scoundrel.

"Fair enough, Sinclair." The airman nodded thoughtfully. "Let's you and me start with a clean slate, then."

"I would appreciate that, sir…Smithy."

And so, over exorbitantly expensive and illegal drinks, they became acquainted. Smithy, as he insisted they all address him, was gregarious, a booming optimist with ready tales of death-defying courage.

"Once you fly, you'll never be happy with the ground again," he promised them.

Hardy looked dubious. "Never took to it myself...a few too many near-misses," he muttered, his lips pressed around the mouthpiece of a cold pipe. Having been gassed in the war, Hardy was unable to smoke but clearly he had adopted the pipe as some kind of oral habit.

Rowland watched quietly while his friends regaled the legendary airman with questions. Kingsford Smith was exuberant, reassuring in his confidence that man was meant to fly.

Although he was as fascinated by the famous aviator as the others, Rowland held back a little, observing Kingsford Smith. His fingers itched to extract the leather-bound artist's notebook from his jacket and draw the man, capture the animation of the large face made familiar through the front pages of every newspaper in the country...the easy smile, the weathered brow, the slightly mad glint in his eye as he talked of flight.

"How long will it take us to reach Germany?" Edna asked.

"Well, considering this a passenger flight," Kingsford Smith replied, "I'd say about fourteen days." He winked at Edna. "If it was just me and the boys we'd be able to do it much faster, but I wouldn't expect a lady to put up with the inconveniences and indignities of a long-distance flight...so we'll hop."

Rowland heard this with relief. He wasn't that keen on inconveniences and indignities himself.

"Fourteen days!" Edna was incredulous. "All the way across the world in fourteen days. Why, that's unbelievable!"

"Of course, the Old Bus is rather less comfortable than a liner." Kingsford Smith grinned proudly, nevertheless. "But she certainly doesn't dilly-dally."

With the passing of time and the consumption of liquor, the gathering became quite festive. Milton began to speak of their intended "expedition" in terms that were almost Homeric. Rowland laughed and Clyde snorted, but Kingsford Smith matched the poet's hyperbole, and one may have been forgiven for thinking that Rowland Sinclair and his friends were setting out to discover the New World.

Even Senator Charles Hardy seemed to relax, exchanging war stories and comparing tattoos with Kingsford Smith.

"A toast—we should have a toast," Hardy announced, rising a little unsteadily to his feet.

"Allow me," Milton insisted, pushing the Senator down as he stood.

"Here we go," Clyde murmured.

Milton raised his glass to Kingsford Smith and delivered the tribute with the deep sincerity of a slightly inebriated man. "Better than all treasures, that in books are found, thy skill to poet were,"—at this point he bowed slightly—"Thou scorner of the ground!"

The aviator was visibly moved. "You, sir, have a gift!" He turned to Rowland to support the sentiment. "Have you ever known anyone to put a thought so well as this very, very insightful gentleman?"

Rowland lifted his glass. "Only Shelley, perhaps."

Chapter Four

AIR MAIL
AUSTRALIA AND ENGLAND
ANOTHER COMPANY

Australian National Airways, Limited, is in the process of voluntary liquidation. Mr. C. T. P. Ulm, joint managing director with Sir Charles Kingsford Smith, stated last night that a new company was being formed, to be known as British International Airlines, Limited.

This company, he said, would have for its immediate object the tendering for Government air service contracts, and, particularly, for the section of the Australia-England service between Darwin and Singapore.

Mr. Ulm stated that, on commercial routes, triple-engined aeroplanes should be used. The company would tender for the new service with triple-engined planes, which would be such that they would be able to fly with safety with one engine out of action.

Mr. Ulm also stated that the new company would be wholly Australian, employing Australian capital and Australian administrators, pilots, and mechanics. He hoped that it would be possible to construct most of the equipment in Australia.

—*The Sydney Morning Herald*, 1933

Rowland could not take his eyes off her. He knew he was staring like some love-struck fool but it was beyond his control.

Milton nudged him. "Rowly, mate, you're leering. It's unseemly."

"Bloody hell...she's gorgeous, Milt."

"Surely you've seen her before." Milton laughed.

"Not up close," Rowland murmured. "She's magnificent... crying shame we can't tell anyone."

The *Southern Cross* waited before them on the runway. The Fokker F.VII had appeared so often in the newspapers that the cigar-shaped fuselage and massive wingspan were familiar to most Australians, but newsprint failed to show the true blue-and-white paintwork. In colour, the celebrated plane seemed to be a part of the nation's standard, a flagship of Australian identity and pride.

They would be taking off after dark. The Old Guard was operating with its customary secrecy. Two dozen motor cars stood ready to light the runway with their headlamps. Among them was Wilfred's dark green Rolls-Royce Continental.

At some point in the last couple of days, Wilfred had come to a grudging acceptance that his brother would go to Germany in his stead. He remained furious and Rowland was in no doubt that Hardy would learn what it meant to cross Wilfred Sinclair.

Hardy had, through channels which may or may not have been official, obtained all the papers and passports they would require. Rowland was, if truth be told, intrigued by the flamboyant Senator. Officially, Hardy did seem to be involved with intelligence and national security, though his role was vague, and might well have been a manifestation of his patriotic fervour. That he was now aligned with the Old Guard was not surprising. The Riverina Movement, which had hailed him as their anointed, had lost a lot of its zeal once the controversial premier, Jack Lang, had been removed from office. The Old Guard had probably welcomed the popular Senator as one of their own, a right-thinking man...but Rowland wondered if a man of Hardy's past fame could resign himself to being a mere foot soldier in the clandestine army of the establishment.

At Rowland's suggestion, it was decided that they would pose as art dealers. Art was a language they could all speak. Rowland's documents named him as Robert John Negus of Melbourne. Milton, with his hair cropped short, and divested of his recently cultivated Leninesque goatee, was taking the name of Albert Greenway; and Edna had been allocated the part of his sister, Millicent. It was an extra precaution. Edna's auburn hair and green eyes would belie whatever hint of Jewish heritage existed in Milton's features. Clyde had been given the documents of a Sydney art collector named Joseph Aloysius Ryan. And so they were disguised, on paper at least.

"Perhaps you should go talk to her, mate." Milton nodded towards the smartly dressed blonde in a white stole who stood by one of the motor cars. "She looks a bit glum."

Rowland groaned. He wasn't entirely sure why Lucy Bennett was there at all, let alone looking as though she was sending her sweetheart to war. "I don't want to encourage her," he muttered.

"What on Earth is she doing here?"

"My sister-in-law, Kate," Rowland replied tightly, "seems to have given Miss Bennett the impression that I am an appropriate catch, and that persistence will win the day."

Milton laughed. "It might be the only time anyone considers you appropriate, Rowly. She appears to be waving at you."

Rowland looked and saw that, indeed, she was. She increased the vigour of her wave as she noticed him turn. Rowland sighed. Continuing to ignore Lucy Bennett would be difficult, not to mention impolite. He set his face and walked briskly over to attend to the demands of courtesy.

Lucy was not alone. By her side was an elderly gentleman who bore himself with a military rigidity. Rowland had met the man before in his brother's company.

"Miss Bennett, what an unexpected pleasure. Colonel Bennett, how do you do, sir?"

Morris Bennett beamed and slapped him on the back. "Well, son, are you ready?" He nodded towards Lucy. "I'm afraid Lucy would not stop weeping and carrying on until I allowed her to come along…not really protocol, but, all things considered, I didn't think you'd mind."

"Pater!" Lucy gasped.

Rowland glanced at her. A mortified blush was spreading upwards from her neck. He felt a bit sorry for her.

"How I envied your father his sons," Morris Bennett continued, ignoring his daughter. "The good Lord saw fit to bless me with four girls. Four!" He looked at the sky resentfully. "And each one sillier than the last!"

Lucy Bennett looked like she might cry.

"Believe me, Colonel Bennett, my father wasn't always so pleased with his sons," Rowland said, smiling briefly at Lucy.

She burst into tears. It took him by surprise. For a moment he just stared at her.

"Come now, Lucy, pull yourself together, old girl," Bennett said irritably. "I'm afraid Lucy seems to have formed quite an attachment to you, Sinclair. Lucy! That's enough now!"

Silently, Rowland handed Lucy Bennett his handkerchief, wondering how on Earth she could have formed such an attachment. He hadn't seen her in months and even then he had paid her only the minimum attention that good manners would allow. She began to cry quite desperately now.

Bennett rolled his eyes. "Perhaps we should go and sit in the car." He shook Rowland's hand. "Well, son, good luck." He looked at his sobbing daughter and shook his head. "When you get back, you best come and see me, and we can sort out the formalities."

"Formalities?"

"Come on then, Lucy." Bennett shuffled her away firmly. "You're making rather a spectacle of yourself, my girl…."

Rowland stared after them. Lucy gave him a teary wave as she climbed into the backseat of her father's Armstrong Siddeley.

Responding with only the barest of nods, Rowland wondered uncomfortably what she was expecting, and, suspiciously, how exactly those expectations were created. He might have thought to clarify the matter with her then and there, if Wilfred had not beckoned him over.

"I say, Wil, what exactly has your wife been telling the Bennett girl?" Rowland demanded, accusingly.

"Who?…Oh…Lucy. For pity's sake, Rowly, now is not the time to worry about courting." Wilfred handed his brother an envelope. "A copy of the letter I have already sent to the Deutsche Bank in Munich. It will allow you to access whatever funds you may require."

"Hardy's already taken care of…"

"Yes, I'm sure he has. You need to watch your back, Rowly… If things go wrong, Hardy will make sure there's nothing to connect you and your friends to the Old Guard. If you need it, the funds are there."

Rowland slipped the envelope into his breast pocket. "If things get awkward, we'll leave, Wil."

"See that you do." Wilfred glanced at the Old Guard motorcade waiting to light the runway and lowered his voice. "Rowly, there has been a suggestion that Peter Bothwell was betrayed by someone within our ranks." He frowned, shaking his head. "It's probably just loose speculation…there's no reason to believe Peter's death was not the accident it seemed…but you watch your back."

Rowland nodded. He wondered about Bothwell, grazier-cum-spy. "Did you know the poor blighter, Wil?"

"Yes, of course…He was a good man, excellent soldier." He regarded Rowland with his traditional severity. "Don't you get cocky, Rowly. Peter spoke German, and he served in the Special Forces during the war. He was no wide-eyed novice."

"I'll be all right, Wil. I'll be careful."

Wilfred sighed. "Ernie's in the car…I thought he might like to see you off. Don't tell him where you're going."

Rowland smiled. His brother's elder son missed nothing. The six-year-old quite possibly already knew exactly where his uncle was going and why. "I won't tell him."

Ernest Sinclair was understandably excited by the goings-on. He offered Rowland his hand like a gentleman, though he jumped up and down on the spot as his uncle shook it. He pulled Rowland down and whispered in his ear. "That's the *Southern Cross*, Uncle Rowly."

"I believe it is, Ernie."

"Are you trying to break a record?"

"Not this time."

"Then what are you doing?"

"We're just going on a little holiday. You'll look after Lenin for me, won't you?"

"Of course...But you've just got back from holiday. Isn't it time you settled down, Uncle Rowly?"

Rowland glanced at Wilfred, who tried to restrain a smile. "I'll think about it, Ernie."

The wicker armchair creaked as Rowland sat down. It had been bolted to the floor of the *Southern Cross*, as had three others, in preparation for the passengers who would make this trip. The Fokker F.VII was a long-distance craft. While she had been designed to carry up to a dozen passengers, under Kingsford Smith's stewardship, she had been pushing the edges of aerial endurance and speed. Her interiors were a little rudimentary.

Regardless, Rowland could only look about in awe.

Edna glanced over at him, her eyes bright.

Tommy Pethybridge emerged to see that all was well outside the cockpit. Kingsford Smith's co-pilot was apparently usually his engineer. He was an extraordinarily enthusiastic fellow, delighted at the chance to fly with the man who was clearly his idol. Unable to contain his exuberance, Pethybridge positively crowed in a manner that was quite endearing...in the beginning, at least. As they waited for the ferry tanks to fill, he spoke to them with inordinate joy of the more mundane practical matters: of what not to touch, what to expect, where they would land and the duration of each hop. With great pride and ceremony, he familiarised them with the plane and emphasised that they were to stay out of the way while the great Smithy did "what God had created him to do." Finally, Pethybridge presented them with legal documents which indemnified Kingsford Smith Air Services Ltd, in the event of any accident.

Edna was curious. It was no secret that Kingsford Smith's Australian National Airways had only recently failed, its assets sold by receivers, leaving the bankrupt airman with only the *Southern Cross* to his name.

"New company," Rowland whispered. "I suspect the right-thinking men of the Old Guard may be funding it…I can't imagine why else Smithy would be asking so few questions."

"Oh." Edna giggled, pointing out the Campbell & Campbell letterhead. The waiver had been prepared by Eric Campbell's own firm.

Rowland smiled. Of course. In his experience, anything which involved the New Guard would necessarily become farcical. It was oddly comforting.

There were two other crewmen, McKinnon and Lambert, a navigator and a radio man, who would make the journey with them. Both were young men, excited to be flying with the famous Smithy. They conducted final checks very loudly, glancing often at Edna to ensure she was appropriately impressed by their aerial knowledge.

Kingsford Smith popped his head back to announce that he was about to warm up the engines. Rowland smiled, noting the Felix the Cat badge on his flying helmet. It seemed an odd standard for a grown man. Having already been shown the cockpit, Rowland had seen the picture of the American actress Nellie Stewart, which had famously been on every flight with the airman. There was also a horseshoe and various other knickknacks. He could only guess that Kingsford Smith was superstitious.

Each of the three engines gunned in turn. The laminated plywood of the *Southern Cross'* body shook as the noise rose in a bone-rattling crescendo. Edna looked a little alarmed. Rowland handed her the large bag of chocolates they had picked up from Mark Foy's the day before. Edna feared nothing, but occasionally she required sweets.

Through the small window, Rowland could make out the row of lights created by the headlamps of the Old Guard motorcade.

When the *Southern Cross* began to move, it became very obvious why the chairs had been bolted to the floor. Weighted with extra passengers and crew, as well as enough fuel to see them easily to Darwin, she waddled like a hobbled bird down the runway. Clyde crossed himself. Edna ate chocolate. Milton recited loudly, though his undoubtedly appropriated words were lost in the deafening scream of the *Southern Cross'* motors.

The Fokker bounced once and then finally she left the ground. Pushed back into his chair by the force of the takeoff, Rowland felt exhilarated, taken completely by the wonder of it. They were flying…in something that seemed far more rudimentary and loosely engineered than his car. They were sitting on garden furniture, for God's sake. And yet, they were flying.

Spontaneously, they broke into applause. From the cockpit, Pethybridge whooped in response. As the plane gained altitude, Rowland reached over and took the bag of sweets from Edna. "You'll make yourself sick," he said as she protested. "We're fine, Ed…Smithy is the world's best pilot."

Edna closed her eyes and exhaled as she gathered herself.

In time, they became accustomed to the noise, and to the vibration of the craft. Somehow Edna managed to curl up in the wicker armchair and sleep. Clyde sprawled out in his chair, his limbs hanging loosely as his body slumped into fitful dozing. Rowland and Milton remained wakeful. McKinnon explained a little about how one navigated the *Southern Cross* at night, using compass, stars, and basic geography. The sun rose behind the plane's right wing.

And then the noise stopped.

"What the—?"

McKinnon moved towards the cockpit. "The engines have cut out."

"Shouldn't we have landed first?" Milton demanded, as the *Southern Cross* began to drop.

"That would have been ideal," Lambert agreed.

Edna was jolted awake still bewildered by sleep. "Rowly... what—?" She stood.

Rowland pulled her down again. "We should stay out of the way, Ed," he said, taking his cue from the crew who seemed concerned, but not panicked.

The engine choked and spluttered and coughed into life. The plane began to claw upwards, and then the engine died again. Now they began to plummet out of control. Edna screamed. For a minute the swearing was unrestrained. Rowland was aware that he'd pulled Edna into his arms but, plunging to Earth as they were, it did not seem improper.

From the cockpit they could hear shouting as the pilots struggled with the controls. The Fokker resisted and bucked. Everything but the bolted wicker chairs was thrown about the cabin. And then the *Southern Cross* raised her nose, and slowly eased into a hesitant glide.

"What happened?" Rowland asked over his shoulder as he helped Clyde to his feet.

"We've lost the engines," McKinnon replied. "Smithy's trying to find someplace to land so we can work out what went wrong and hopefully get her back up."

"I'll settle for just getting her down at the moment," Milton muttered.

Fortunately they were quite close to Darwin now and barren unpopulated stretches were not scarce. Voices rose in the cockpit, now audible without the competition of the engines.

"What's going on?" Edna asked, her knuckles white on the arms of the wicker chair.

"Smithy's refusing to dump fuel." Clyde stood closest to the cockpit where the airmen argued. "McKinnon and Lambert think he should, but Smithy reckons it's not necessary." Clyde leaned against the door to listen. "He says he's not going to carry the can for some hairbrained rescue again."

"So he's going to let us explode!" Edna was outraged and suddenly terrified.

"I'm sure he'll do what he can to avoid that, Ed." Rowland spoke with deceptive calm. "I'm sure he's done this hundreds of times…If anyone knows what he's doing, it's Smithy."

Clyde nodded, still eavesdropping. "Pethybridge seems to agree with Smithy…"

"So what do we do?" Milton squinted out of the window.

"I think we'd better hang onto these chairs," Rowland said, pushing Edna firmly back into hers. "It might get a bit bumpy."

The *Southern Cross* continued to descend, to glide to Earth. McKinnon and Lambert were either convinced by Kingsford Smith's confidence, or had simply given up, for they returned to the cabin and instructed their passengers to brace themselves.

Clyde crossed himself again.

"Would you stop that?" Milton said irritably. "It's too late to become devout now."

"I've still got time," Clyde muttered.

"Catholics," Milton returned in disgust.

The *Southern Cross* made contact with the ground, skipping once before her wheels stayed against the hard sand on which Kingsford Smith had brought her down. Inside the cabin the occupants held grimly to the groaning wicker as the plywood body rattled and shook. When the plane finally came to a stop, the relieved passengers cheered and applauded while McKinnon and Lambert looked on amused.

Kingsford Smith came out of the cockpit and bowed. His eyes glinted and his wide mouth stretched into a smug grin.

"Best pop out and check what went wrong with the Old Bus," he said. "You folks feel free to stretch your legs…but don't go far. It's probably just the push rods…We'll have her fixed in no time."

And so they clambered out onto what seemed to Rowland to be the flattest land on the planet. Red earth stretched out in a vast occasionally tussocked plain. It was already uncomfortably warm, though the sun had only just risen over the horizon. Immediately, Rowland was struck by the colours, the shades of ground and gold, the immense, watchful blue of the sky.

As tempted as he was to join the men as they poked about the motors discussing rods and torque, he could not take his eyes from the plain, from the way the light fell on the ancient face of this land. He pulled the notebook from his jacket, watching Edna as she bent to touch the ochre soil.

He drew quickly, making written notes to remind himself of the colour or sense that he could not reproduce with simple graphite. He was caught by the strangeness of the sculptress here, the incongruity of her creamy skin, her elegant dress and pretty shoes in a land that seemed to devour the delicate. And yet there was something in the way her hair seemed to blend with the red and gold of the landscape, the way she pressed her hands into the dirt, that seemed to belong here too. She noticed his gaze and held up her ochre palms. "Just look at these colours, Rowly…the ground is so hard, like it's been fired by the sun. I feel like I'm inside the Earth's kiln."

Rowland smiled. "Sounds a little uncomfortable." But he knew what she meant. It felt somehow like the Earth was created here, like this was the first place.

"Righto…shall we start her up?" Kingsford Smith jumped down from the wing.

Rowland was startled. They'd been tinkering with the motors for only a few minutes. He'd expected that anything serious enough to completely compromise the engines would take a while to repair. It was almost more disturbing that it did not.

"It was just a push rod," Pethybridge said, as he followed Kingsford Smith into the craft.

And so they all did likewise. Any lingering doubts that the plane would function were allayed when the engines roared on cue.

"What if this happens while we're over water?" Edna whispered.

Rowland squeezed her hand wordlessly. The sculptress had a point.

Chapter Five

AUTHOR'S PREFERENCES
Mr. Somerset Maugham
Interviewed

Mr. William Somerset Maugham, the famous author and playwright, who is visiting Sydney, made some interesting observations in an interview yesterday regarding Russia, and on modern literature.

Mr. Maugham was sent to Russia by the British Government in 1917, and he was there during the two revolutions which occurred that year. He is of the opinion that if the Allies had handled the situation properly by giving support to the Provisional Government and combatted the unreliability of one or two members of that Government and the outpouring of German money, the situation might have been saved.

"After the armistice, I resumed the most agreeable occupation of a man of letters," said Mr. Maugham. "In Russia I worked from 9 a.m. till 10 p.m., and I only then realised how jolly it is to be a writer. You have your freedom; you can work when you like, and you are not at anybody's beck and call. Though you have much less money than is made in many other vocations, and you are exposed to the slings and arrows of the critics, it is a delightful life. All you require are some blank sheets of paper and a fountain pen." The interviewer suggested that perhaps brains were also necessary, but Mr. Maugham insisted that as far as play-writing was concerned it didn't require brains, but only a certain knack. "I think this knack is only a natural sense of logic," continued Mr. Maugham. "Much nonsense is talked about the technique of the drama, but so far as I can see, the whole mystery of it is to get a good story and to stick to it like death."

—*The Sydney Morning Herald*, 1921

They stopped in Darwin long enough to bathe and eat, while the Fokker was refuelled. Wilfred had somehow organised for fresh clothes to be awaiting them at every stop to minimise what they would need to take on board. He had instructed his English tailors by telegram to ensure that trunks of appropriate attire would meet them in Munich.

Milton was a little put-out by the traditional nature of the suits which had been supplied by a local tailor under instructions from Rowland's very conservative brother. The poet's personal style was flamboyant, occasionally adventurous, as he felt befitted a man of literary sensibilities. He had a penchant for unusual colours and extravagant neckwear.

"I'm sure we can find you something more to your taste in Europe," Rowland offered, as the poet complained that the dark grey three-piece suit made him look like an undertaker.

Clyde snorted. "Could always rob some gypsies, I suppose."

"Stop grumbling, Milt," Edna chided, as she adjusted his tie. "You'd hardly expect Wilfred to order cravats and velvet jackets." She giggled. "How would he explain it?"

Rowland smiled. The thought amused him.

The airmen joined them for a drink or several before the next leg, which would take them on to Singapore. Kingsford Smith was in excellent spirits and Pethybridge an enthusiastic chorus. And so they drank gin and tonic water in a small bar near the airport and toasted the *Southern Cross*. McKinnon and Lambert flirted outrageously with Edna, who enjoyed the game, while Kingsford Smith talked of his plan to develop a motor car based on his beloved aeroplane.

"I say, that's not a bad idea." Milton nodded thoughtfully over his glass. "I don't suppose you're looking for investors?"

Clyde groaned. "The suit's gone to his head."

Kingsford Smith seemed to accept that Milton was a man of means, however, and regaled him with the potential of the venture.

"My capital's tied up at the moment." Milton sighed, as if he was, in fact, burdened with capital. "I do know some chaps who might be interested, though."

"He means you, Rowly," Clyde murmured. "The bloody fool's going to commit your fortune to this bloody aero-car cross-breed."

Rowland laughed. "I'll have to squander it somehow... might as well have an aero-car to show for it. Will it have wings, do you suppose?"

When the *Southern Cross* left Darwin for Singapore, her passengers were slightly less than sober. Perhaps for this reason they were not unduly alarmed that their pilots were in a similar state. Even so, the leg was uneventful. The winds were with them and they made good time, arriving tired and crumpled into the tropical heat. They were duly met by the Australian High Commissioner to the island and made discreetly welcome.

Leaving the valiant Fokker to be refuelled, they checked into the Colonial splendour of the Raffles Hotel under the false names on the passports that Hardy had requisitioned for them. Kingsford Smith and the pilots were, of course, recognisable, even in Singapore, and signed their own names with a flourish. They did not appear to notice the subterfuge beside them. Briefly, Rowland did wonder what explanation Hardy had given for the fact that the *Southern Cross'* passengers were travelling incognito. But perhaps he had not given an explanation at all; perhaps he had just given money.

The suites, like the rest of the hotel, were lavish invocations of the British Raj—teakwood floors and handmade carpets underfoot; majestic ornate plasterwork above; furniture that hinted at the East in a style that befitted the glory of the Empire. A barber was sent up as they bathed and dressed for the evening.

Rowland regarded his own reflection a little dubiously as he deftly manipulated a bow tie. He wasn't really sure about the evening attire which had been left for them in the suite. White dinner jackets were not entirely new. They had become quite popular in Australia after some visiting duke had adopted the trend, but Rowland had never worn one before. He'd always considered the style unnecessarily loud, and whatever visiting Englishmen may have thought, Sydney was not the tropics. Still, they were in Singapore, and he was supposedly an art dealer.

Milton was much more pleased with his reflection, but then, he usually was. They had all been provided with the white-jacketed dinner suits with slight variations in style. Rowland did wonder who had made these particular selections—some expatriate Old Guardsmen, no doubt. He was, if truth be told, rather impressed with the Old Guard's efficient attention to detail.

Milton sported a black-and-gold cummerbund rather than the white waistcoat. Rowland found it somewhat garish, but Milton was obviously satisfied. Indeed, the poet fished a tropical flower from one of the suite's many vases and fashioned a boutonniere to complete the florid ensemble.

Clyde cursed, perspiring already with the humidity as he fumbled with cuff links. Feeling the heat himself, Rowland opened the doors that led out to the balcony, allowing the salted sea breeze to refresh the room. The sky churned and rumbled, dark with the promise of a tropical storm. The air was heavy and tasted of rain. Rowland watched, glad that they were not still in the air.

Edna waltzed into the suite after a perfunctory knock. She wore an evening gown of green Chinese brocade, which deepened the colour of her eyes. The dress hugged her figure and the straight, tight skirt was split on one side almost to the hip. A boa fashioned entirely from peacock feathers draped over her bare arms. For a moment, Rowland forgot to breathe. Clyde whistled. "You couldn't wear that in Sydney."

Edna turned for effect. "Isn't it exotic? I've never had anything quite like it. It's such a shame we'll have to leave it behind."

Rowland swallowed. "I'll have it sent back to Sydney, if you like, Ed."

Edna beamed at him. "Yes, please. I wonder who chose it for me? It doesn't look like something Wilfred would select."

Rowland smiled. "It is a little risqué for Wil."

"Aren't you boys ready yet?" Edna pushed him away to help Clyde with his cuff links. "I'm famished. What time are we booked for dinner?"

"Not till eight, I'm afraid," Rowland said apologetically. "We could have a drink at the bar in the meantime...I'm sure they'll have some sort of hors d'oeuvres to keep you from expiring."

The Long Bar at Raffles was as elegantly extravagant as the rest of the hotel. Decorated in the style of a Malayan plantation, it had an air of intrepid refinement. It was all but empty when they arrived—a few couples enjoying drinks before dinner and two gentlemen sitting at the bar. The first was quite elderly, distinguished and distinctly British, the second, younger and handsome, his smile very wide. He raised his glass as they walked in and signalled the barman. Both men stood, obviously expecting the party of Australians to join them.

Clyde looked enquiringly at Rowland. "Friends of yours?"

Rowland shook his head. "Never laid eyes on them before."

The younger gentleman spoke to Edna first, betraying an American origin to his accent. "You look simply gorgeous, my dear. I just couldn't resist that gown...I can't tell you what a relief it is that you are equal to it."

Edna extended her hand. "I don't believe we've been introduced…"

He took her hand and kissed it. "Forgive me, darling. Gerald Haxton at your service." He put his arm around the other man and drew him forward. "And this excellent gentleman is William Somerset Maugham. You must be Miss Millicent Greenway, an exquisite, blushing pearl from the Antipodes."

Edna was flustered. She was not yet accustomed to her new name, and she was very familiar with the one he introduced.

"Somerset Maugham? The playwright?"

Maugham bowed. He spoke quietly, stammering. "The same."

Edna glanced at Rowland. Why had William Somerset Maugham and his American friend chosen her gown?

"Perhaps we should all have a drink," Haxton suggested.

"At least one," Milton agreed.

On cue the barman placed a tray of cocktails before them.

"Singapore Slings," Haxton announced, handing a glass to Edna. "Gin, cherry heering, Benedictine, and fresh pineapple juice—quite possibly this country's greatest contribution to civilisation."

"Gentlemen…" Rowland began.

"Mr. Negus, can't tell you how pleased we are to make your acquaintance." Haxton, then Maugham, shook his hand. "How is your dear brother?"

"Wilfred?" Rowland said uncertainly.

"Indeed. He wired us that you'd be coming. Asked us to look out for you…see that you had everything you needed."

Still a little bewildered, Rowland introduced Milton and Clyde as Albert Greenway and Joseph Ryan, though it became clear that the introductions were unnecessary. Haxton and Maugham clearly knew of both their pseudonyms and actual names.

"How is it that you gentlemen are acquainted with my brother?" Rowland asked finally.

"Willy met him during the Great War. Fine officer, by all accounts. They've kept in touch on and off since…and collaborated occasionally."

"Wilfred writes plays?" Rowland felt the conversation taking a somewhat surreal turn.

"Good Lord, no!" Maugham spat out despite his stammer.

Haxton surveyed the room before he went on. "Perhaps you are familiar with a collection of stories Willy wrote some years ago—*Ashenden*?"

"I'm afraid not," Rowland replied awkwardly.

"The British Agent," Milton said, as he made quick work of his gin cocktail. He raised one brow and spoke with theatrical gravity. "'There's just one thing I think you ought to know before you take on this job. And don't forget it. If you do well, you'll get no thanks and if you get into trouble, you'll get no help. Does that suit you?'"

"By George, you know it!" Haxton exclaimed, beaming at the poet.

"A collection of stories about a well-groomed spy, I believe."

"Yes, exactly." Haxton nodded emphatically. He slurped his sling, wiped the froth from his upper lip and sighed in satisfaction before continuing. "Willy has quite the reputation for using personal experience in his work, if you get my meaning. Shall we indulge in another round?"

Rowland had not yet tried his own drink, but another tray of gin-slings appeared almost immediately.

Rowland turned to Maugham, who had, he noticed, said very little. "Are you saying you were a spy, Mr. Maugham, or that Wilfred was a spy?"

Haxton moved in. He threw his arm around Rowland's shoulders, lowering his voice. "Willy doesn't say much," he said. "The darned stammer, you know."

Maugham stood watching them, quietly sipping his drink.

Haxton overheard Edna talking to the barman about food, and became immediately distracted, ordering mooncakes and other eastern delicacies with a gin-sling in each hand.

Rowland shook his head, more than a little bemused by the whole exchange.

A tap on the shoulder caught his attention, and William Somerset Maugham motioned him away from the bar. "Shall we walk?" he said carefully.

Glancing just momentarily at his friends, who were now engrossed in tasting canapés and sweetmeats under Haxton's guidance, Rowland accompanied the renowned playwright onto the wide verandah. Maugham took a slim gold case from his breast pocket and offered Rowland a cigarette. He lit one himself when Rowland declined.

"I had expected to see Wilfred here, but then he wired me a few days ago that you would be coming instead. I understand that you intend to conduct some sort of intelligence operation in Germany. He's concerned that you may be out of your depth." Maugham spoke slowly but smoothly. The stammer was now barely noticeable. "Your brother hoped that I might talk some sense into you, or at least give you some advice."

Rowland smiled. He was intrigued by Maugham and his sudden wish—and ability— to converse.

It had started to rain. On the verandah the air smelled sweet and the breeze breathed cool relief.

Maugham drew on his cigarette. "You are wondering about my stammer, I expect. It has not for some time been as debilitating as commonly believed."

"Clearly."

"I have always found the ability to observe quietly very useful," Maugham reflected. "An impediment such as mine is an interesting thing…often mistaken for an impediment of the mind rather than the voice. I find it leads men to be less inhibited and circumspect in my presence. Perhaps they believe I cannot understand, or that if I could, I would not in any case be able to repeat it."

Rowland nodded. "I can see how that would be useful for an intelligence agent."

Maugham smiled slightly. "No less useful for a writer, my boy. We are first and foremost observers of the world. I believe you are something of an artist?"

Rowland was surprised that Maugham would be aware of such a thing. Wilfred still treated his brother's determination to paint like some unfortunate habit that would hopefully be outgrown. "Something of one."

"Well, then, you know what I mean. You will learn a lot more if you wait for something to be revealed rather than if you actively try to uncover it. It's also a much safer way to proceed."

Rowland leaned on the balustrade, watching as lightning lit the sky and flashed the hotel's wet courtyard into colourless clarity. "Are you working with the Old Guard, Mr. Maugham?"

"No. But there are certain courtesies extended between gentlemen of the Empire."

"Gentlemen?"

Maugham smiled, exhaling perfect rings of smoke. "In 1917, I was sent to Russia to prevent the Bolshevik Revolution… though regrettably my efforts didn't meet with success. Regardless, this sort of work is best done by gentlemen."

"Because spying ought to be done politely?" Rowland ventured, amused.

"Because it ought to be done dispassionately…and there is nothing as devoid of passion as the English gentleman."

"I'm Australian," Rowland replied.

"Yes…it's unfortunate." Maugham sighed heavily. "I knew Peter Bothwell during the Great War."

"I see. Was he working in intelligence?"

"I'm afraid that sort of information is classified, Mr. Negus." He straightened, his lower lip jutting just beyond his moustache. "Although Gerry Haxton is no longer welcome in Britain, I am still an Englishman and His Majesty's servant."

Rowland sharpened to the aside. "Why is Haxton not welcome in England?"

"He was deported…for, I believe, an act that was described

as 'not buggery'...Apparently he was undesirable, though there are many men who would disagree—which I suppose is what began his trouble in the first place."

"Oh." Rowland swigged his gin-sling in the awkward silence, wishing to God he had not asked.

Maugham smiled. "Gerry can be quite forward and, occasionally, indiscriminate with his attentions. He seems to have taken quite a shine to Miss Greenway, but you really don't need to worry. His interest could not be more platonic."

"Right...thank you. But Miss Greenway is not...she can do as she pleases."

"I see. It seems a pity."

"Quite."

When Rowland and Maugham returned to the Long Bar, the cocktails had done their work: Gerald Haxton was wearing Edna's boa around his neck and Milton's boutonniere behind his ear while belting out a French love song. Edna sat at the bar, laughing. Milton, who was not used to being upstaged in such a manner, watched uneasily.

"Rowly!" Clyde was clearly glad to see their return.

"Robbie," Maugham corrected. "You will have to get used to your aliases if you hope to carry this off."

"Yes...Robbie." Clyde jerked his head towards Haxton. "It might be time to..."

"Gerry—I believe it's high time we chuffed off to dinner, don't you think?" Maugham spoke loudly over the din, with the stammer making a reappearance.

Gerald Haxton stopped singing, grinning affably. "Willy! Where did you and Mr. Negus get to? I was beginning to get rather jealous."

"Dinner," Rowland said tensely. "We should go to dinner. Would you gentlemen care to join us?"

"Au contraire," Haxton insisted brightly. "You shall all join us! Come along." He offered his arm to Edna and proceeded to lead them from the bar. "Have you enjoyed curry before, my dear? Raffles is famous for its tiffin curry. Traditionally eaten at luncheon, of course, but I'll have a word. You really must try it…heats the blood…"

Chapter Six

GOSSIP

THERE is an interesting extract from a letter from Mr. Cuthbert Wells, in Singapore, to his daughter in Adelaide, relating to the wedding of the popular Adelaide girl, Miss Alison Thomas, now Mrs. Charles C. T. Sharp. Mr. Wells was in a quandary about the frocking, but he tackled the subject nobly. "I felt greatly honoured when Mrs. Thomas ásked me if I would give Alison away at the wedding. I was up very early and down at the hotel at 7.15. Mrs. Thomas, Sharp, and a Mrs. Millar went off first to the cathedral at 7.30 a.m., and Alison and I followed in my car, the former looking very charming in silk georgette dress of a pinky dove grey color with a close-fitting little straw hat (cloche?) with a feather. Only the archdeacon, Graham White, was there beside ourselves, and the ceremony was soon smoothly over. We all—six of us—had a cheerful breakfast at Raffles Hotel, and I was at the office at 9 a.m., while the bridal couple caught the Plancius at 10 a.m. en route to Brastagi, Sumatra, for the honeymoon.

—*The Mail*, 1932

Rowland lay on the chaise, laughing. He had abandoned his dinner jacket, and his tie hung loosely around his neck. Edna sat on the rolled arm of the lounge trying to poke the feathers back into her boa. Clyde and Milton had also relinquished their jackets. The poet stood in the middle of the room singing French-sounding nonsense in a quite remarkably accurate impersonation of Haxton. Clyde was drinking like a man trying hard to forget.

Dinner had been a mildly alarming affair. Raffles, it seemed, was accustomed to Haxton. The waiters and maître d' barely reacted to the Americans' extraordinary antics. While the occasional diner tskked disapprovingly, most seemed to consider it part of Raffles' exotic charm, some form of spontaneous floor show.

Maugham had, in the presence of his companion, retreated into an aloof but dignified reserve. Haxton had compensated by becoming increasingly loud and flamboyant. Champagne had accompanied dinner, and by the end of the evening the American did not confine his flirting to Edna. Rowland and Milton were more amused than anything else, but Clyde reacted with noticeable panic and so became the focus of Haxton's attentions.

"He was fun, though, wasn't he?" Edna said smiling.

"No." Clyde was blunt.

"Oh, Clyde." Edna reached over and patted his knee. "You mustn't take him seriously. Gerry's quite sweet beneath all that nonsense. He has lovely taste in gowns."

"Just let the poor chap drink, Ed." Rowland put his hands behind his head. "Clyde's had rather a shock."

"Do Mr. Maugham and Gerry actually live here?" Edna asked brightly.

"Some of the time, I believe," Rowland replied. "Maugham has a villa in France. Apparently Haxton's been deported from Britain for some sort of misbehaviour, but of course the French are more understanding…"

Edna shoved him playfully. Her mother had been French. "Mama always said the English were frightful hypocrites."

"Can we please talk about something else?" Clyde begged tersely.

"Yes," Milton agreed, taking an armchair opposite the chaise and looking directly at Rowland. "Why did Maugham whisk you away, for instance?"

Rowland's brow rose. "He wanted to tell me about Bothwell, I suppose."

"What about him?"

"I'm not entirely sure. Maugham hinted that Bothwell was in some form of intelligence work during the war."

"Hinted?"

"Well, he didn't say explicitly, but I'm quite sure that's what he meant. I suppose if Bothwell was working for the British Secret Service, it might be treason—or some such thing—to just come out and tell me."

"But Maugham wrote a book."

"Yes…perhaps I should read it."

Milton sat back, playing with a peacock feather that had come loose from Edna's boa and ended up in his collar. "It makes sense, though…Perhaps that's why the Old Guard sent Bothwell on this caper, in the first place. He'd spied before."

"Maybe."

"What about Wilfred?" Edna asked, sliding down to share the chaise with Rowland. "Do you think he was an agent too?"

Rowland laughed. The idea was ridiculous.

"He was going to do this if you didn't," Milton reminded him.

Rowland sat up. He pushed the hair back from his face. "You're right, he was."

"And he met Maugham during the war. Where exactly was Wilfred posted?"

Rowland shrugged. "France…Wil's never spoken to me about the war. I wouldn't have a clue what he actually did over there."

Edna giggled. "Can you imagine what Wilfred would make of Gerald Haxton?"

Milton grunted. "He'd barely have noticed—the upper classes are full of chaps like Haxton."

Rowland smiled. "I've known a few," he admitted.

The oppressive humidity of the previous evening had dissipated in the deluge overnight, and so the morning was fresh, the air still warm but no longer cloying. With the first light of day, Edna had attempted to drag them all out of bed "to take in the sights." Only Rowland could be persuaded to leave the superlative comfort of his bed, though he did so reluctantly. Fortunately, they were due back at the airport that morning and so Edna's sightseeing would be necessarily limited to a walk on the beach before breakfast.

Although it was early, the paved boulevards of the European sector of the island were busy. Locals pushed carts, laden with produce or trinkets, along Beach Road. Bare-chested men in sarongs swept steps and paths while turbaned traders set up for the day's business. Edna marvelled at the strength and endurance of the rickshaw pullers, who dragged white-suited businessmen at a run, negotiating a road shared with motor cars and bullock drays.

"It's a shame we can't stay longer, Rowly," Edna said, as she paused to photograph the Colonial splendour of the buildings which lined the thoroughfare.

Rowland smiled. "We can come back, Ed." He held out his hand for hers. "Come on, we'd better return to Raffles."

"Robbie!"

Rowland turned towards the voice.

Maugham and Haxton emerged from the teahouse behind them, dressed almost identically in pale suits and broad-brimmed straw hats. Rowland was mildly surprised to see Haxton. He had expected that the American would be somewhat unwell after his consumption the evening before.

Haxton kissed Edna's hand and slapped Rowland heartily on the back. "Well, this is a lucky chance. I had expected I'd have to chase you to the airport."

"Chase me? Why?"

"Willy wanted me to make sure you had this." He handed Rowland an envelope.

Edna glanced at Rowland and coaxed Haxton away. "Gerry, you must let me take a picture of you...over here...in front of this palm tree."

"What is this, Mr. Maugham?" Rowland asked, studying the envelope as Haxton moved out of earshot under Edna's direction.

"A letter of introduction to an old acquaintance." Again the stammer was barely noticeable.

"In Germany?"

"Yes." Maugham started walking back towards Raffles, motioning for the Australian to follow. Rowland glanced back to see Edna arm in arm with Haxton at the window of some boutique. He fell into step beside the playwright.

"Peter Bothwell was staying with an old chum of his in Munich—Alois Richter. Of course, Richter has no idea what he was really doing in Germany."

"I see."

"All of Bothwell's papers and whatnot are still at Richter's villa...the address is on the envelope. The letter introduces a Mr. Robert Negus, a dear and trusted cousin of Bothwell's widow. It gives you the authority to take charge of the poor fellow's personal effects and chattels, and return them to her."

Rowland slipped the envelope into his inner breast pocket. It didn't seem unreasonable, but he was uneasy.

"Alois Richter has already received a telegram informing him to expect you," Maugham said, stopping to light a cigarette.

Rowland frowned. "Why didn't Wil give me the letter himself before I left Sydney?"

"I hadn't written it then, I suppose. In any case, these instructions are from Senator Hardy, my boy."

"Rowly, wait!" Edna caught up with them and unburdened a large parcel into Rowland's arms. Haxton was just behind her and similarly laden with purchases.

The sculptress smiled triumphantly. "We found the most divine Indian fabric, Rowly...sari, I think they call it. Yards and yards of the most glorious, vibrant silk."

Rowland glanced at his watch, charmed as he always was by Edna's unbridled enthusiasm for small things. "We'd better hurry if we're going to arrange for it to be sent back to Sydney."

"Sydney? Oh, no—it's not for me, Rowly." She turned to Haxton, who beamed from beneath his dark moustache. "Gerry just had to have it."

They took breakfast on the verandah at Raffles, sipping tea and enjoying a civilised repast in the cooling movement of a sea breeze from Indochina. Clyde sat between Edna and Rowland, where he was protected from Gerald Haxton. The American was either completely enchanted by Clyde or just amused by his discomfort, and continued to lavish the poor man with compliments and invitations that could be taken amiss. Maugham ignored his personal secretary's eloquent zeal for the visibly mortified Australian, retreating into a kind of indulgent reserve.

Milton had enhanced his conservative suit with a black and gold cravat, which Rowland suspected had been fashioned from the cummerbund the poet had worn the evening before. One of the peacock feathers from Edna's boa had also found its way into Milton's hatband.

"It was a good idea to bring them," Maugham said quietly to Rowland, while the rest of the party flirted and performed and chatted merrily.

"I do beg your pardon?" Rowland was a little startled.

"Your friends, my boy." Maugham put down his tea and whispered again. "They're eye-catching. You're much less likely to be noticed among them." He nodded approvingly. "That was well thought-out."

Rowland smiled as Milton stood to steal poetry once again, and Edna bestowed a glance upon Haxton that would have enslaved most other men. Eye-catching was an apt description. Even Clyde was noticeable for the fact that he was trying so hard to escape notice. Indeed, Rowland suspected Edna was flirting with particular dedication in a vain, but loyal, attempt to distract Haxton's attentions from Clyde. The whole scene was typical, ludicrous, and yes, eye-catching.

In time they shook hands and took their leave of William Somerset Maugham and Gerald Haxton. It was time to get on.

Kingsford Smith and his crew were already at the airport when they arrived. They looked as though they, too, may have enjoyed a gin-sling or several the evening before. Rowland thought it better not to enquire too closely, all things considered.

Singapore was to be their longest stopover. The *Southern Cross* would land a number of times before she crossed the Alps into Vienna. In Ceylon, they lay down for a few hours beneath mosquito nets at the Galle Face Hotel and left before dawn; in Karachi, they slept briefly in the Colonial splendour of the Killarney Hotel; and in Baghdad, Edna drowsed on Rowland's shoulder as they waited for the Fokker to be refuelled.

At each stop they had been met by men who were connected with either Charles Hardy or Wilfred Sinclair, who had advice, warnings, and instructions.

In Bagdad they received the news that Bert Hinkler's body had been found in the Italian Alps after he'd been missing for over three months. They paused to farewell him with some local brew that was both sweet and potent. To Rowland and his houseguests, who knew Hinkler as a hero, the passing was sad, but to the airmen, he was a friend, a brother-in-arms. They mourned him truly. No one spoke of the fact that they were about to fly a route not unlike that which had brought Hinkler to his end.

Chapter Seven

HINKLER'S BODY FOUND

May 1: The body of Squadron-Leader Bert Hinkler, the Australian airman, was found on Friday on a desolate plateau in the Apennine Mountains between Florence and Arezzo, in Italy. Hinkler disappeared on January 7th, the first day of an attempted flight from England to Australia. Apparently, the plane had run out of fuel, smashed itself against a mountainside 4,600 feet above sea level, and burst into flames. The tanks were empty. Hinkler must have died instantly, for he had terrible head injuries.

—*Portland Guardian*, 1933

The *Southern Cross* made an unremarkable landing just outside Vienna. Nothing failed mechanically and the airfield, although small, was even, and adequate for a pilot of Kingsford Smith's skill. The company was to part here.

Kingsford Smith and his crew would take the Fokker F.VII on to London, where they would deliver several bags of mail, ostensibly proving the viability of a mail route between Britain and Australia.

"Well, Sinclair, good luck." Kingsford Smith shook Rowland's hand as the *Southern Cross* was being prepared to fly again. For the first time Rowland sensed a curiosity in the airman as to their purpose in Europe. "I suppose you'll be back in

Sydney in a few months so we can teach you to fly that Gipsy of yours."

Rowland sighed. There was a beautiful de Havilland Gipsy Moth stored in a shed on Oaklea, the Sinclairs' property at Yass. Since the moment the Gipsy had come into his possession Rowland had been determined to pilot her himself. He had signed on months before to the flying school that Kingsford Smith would soon open. Of course, now he would have to delay the lessons till his return, but nothing so far had dampened his enthusiasm for the sport. "You'll see me," he said. "You can count on it."

"Senator Hardy didn't really mention what you were doing here." Kingsford Smith pressed a cigarette tightly between his lips.

"We're buying art."

"Art?"

Rowland tried to sound like he knew what he was talking about. "Yes…Good time to invest…the Depression, you see…"

Kingsford Smith nodded slowly. "So, why the hurry?"

Rowland smiled. "A Rubens, actually…It's been in a private collection for decades but the owner needs to liquidate quickly…debts, or some such thing. We wanted to get here before other collectors got wind of it."

"What has the good Senator Hardy got to do with it? I wouldn't have thought he was an art collector."

Rowland searched quickly for a plausible response. Kingsford Smith knew full well that the Senator had smoothed their way with passports and papers. The airman might also have noticed that his passengers were travelling, on record, under assumed names. Rowland decided to take a punt that Kingsford Smith was not himself a saint. "We are making purchases for a number of powerful investors while we're here," he said carefully. "Senator Hardy is one of them. Sometimes there can be issues with Customs, foreign laws, that sort of thing."

Kingsford Smith grinned suddenly. He winked at Rowland and slapped him on the back. "I see. Well, never let it be said that Smithy hasn't helped out the Australian entrepreneur. Had the odd stoush with Customs myself."

Rowland laughed, relieved. "You understand that our purpose here is something that needs to be treated with…discretion."

"Yes, of course…mum's the word."

And so, with Kingsford Smith convinced that they were involved in some sort of minor smuggling operation, they said farewell. Edna kissed each airman for luck and Kingsford Smith added her scarf to the collection of charms in the cockpit. And the *Southern Cross* and the men who flew her soared once again into the sky.

The Wien-Bahnhof, Vienna's major railway station, was crowded, bustling with travellers and merchants. Bakers with baskets passed warm pastries to passengers through carriage windows, as smartly dressed travellers promenaded on the platform. Beggars lurked in the shadowed spaces of the station and brown-shirted members of the Sturmabteilung, otherwise known as the SA, wandered in loud, arrogant groups. Rowland watched as they strutted, bullying railway workers. He shook his head. Common thugs cloaked in the dubious legitimacy of the SA uniform.

Rowland organised their passages upon the Orient Express to Munich. Trunks of clothing and necessities had already been loaded onto the train. The trunks had, of course, been stocked and packed by someone else. They were now conscious of appearing like art collectors on a purchasing tour of Europe and boarding without luggage would have seemed odd to anyone who noticed. In a small guesthouse near the station, they had washed and changed. One did not travel and dine on the Orient Express without being appropriately attired.

Though the journey to Munich would be one of hours rather than days, Rowland booked sleeping cabins in the first-class carriage. They were tired, having only snatched sleep for several days now, and they would need privacy. Each of them would have to become accustomed to new names—their own and each other's. They would have to ensure they told a consistent story of their recent history, their association, their business.

"Oi!" Milton reached out and grabbed a small boy by the shoulder. The child was swarthy and ragged, with eyes that glittered resentfully as Milton restrained him. "Little blighter had his hand in your pocket...Robbie," he said, hesitating slightly as he used Rowland's alias. "Hand it over, you thieving scamp."

The boy kept his fist tightly closed and berated Milton bitterly in some foreign language.

"Not so tight, you'll hurt him," Edna said, looking sympathetically at the thin, dirty pickpocket. "What did he say, Robbie?"

Rowland shrugged. "I don't know. I think it's Romany...I'm pretty sure it wasn't 'Welcome to Vienna,' though."

The child spoke again, but this time in Bavarian, addressing Rowland directly and finishing with what seemed like a hiss.

Rowland paused for a moment, mildly astounded, and grinned despite himself. "That, I understood...but I can't repeat it in the presence of Ed."

"What's your name, sweetheart?" Edna asked, bending down.

"Schlampen." The boy glared at her.

"Schlampen," Edna said smiling. "How do you do, Schlampen?"

Rowland tried hard not to laugh. "I don't think that's his name, Ed. In fact, I wouldn't repeat it."

Clyde chuckled. "Belligerent little blighter, isn't he?"

Edna took the boy's clenched fist, but gently. "What did you take, little boy?"

He opened his hand. Coins. Australian coins.

A whistle warned that the Orient Express was preparing to pull away.

Rowland glanced back at the train. "Let him go. It's just a couple of shillings."

Reluctantly, Milton released the boy, who did not linger, fleeing with the coins still clutched in his hand.

"We'd better get moving—the train leaves in…" Milton stared at his bare wrist, where a watch should have been. Cursing, he looked around for the young pickpocket, who was by then well and truly gone. "Damn it. If I get my hands on that—"

Rowland checked his own watch as the final whistle sounded and the air became moist with squealing steam. "We don't have time to hunt the boy down. We'll have to get you another in Munich."

For a moment Milton resisted but the theft had been well timed, and they had little option. They ran for the train now and boarded, breathless, just seconds before it pulled out.

Their assigned compartment had been converted for the day into a carpeted sitting room; the seats upholstered in burgundy velvet on either side of a central table. Luggage racks and other fittings were brass and the walls, panelled cedar. It was a cosy fit with the four of them, but, although Rowland had booked three double sleeping cabins to accommodate them, they did have many matters they needed to discuss.

Edna and Milton squabbled briefly for a place beside the window. Milton won, and Rowland gave up the facing seat to Edna.

The window framed a passing vista of snow-capped mountains, swathed in hills of radiant yellow and deep green. Rowland watched, almost mesmerised. The colours were more intense here than at home. Perhaps it was the broadness of the Australian continent that muted its shades, faded them somehow. Here the colours seemed to be thicker, undiluted. A landscape made for the brush of Van Gogh. "Would you look at that," he murmured, as the band of yellow widened into a golden sea.

Clyde prodded him. "Don't tell me you want to paint it."

Rowland laughed. He had long given up trying to paint landscapes. Both his talent and his interest had always been in portrait work, and not even the magnificence through the window could intrigue him as more than a backdrop.

"What's making the fields appear so yellow?" Edna asked.

"Dandelions," Rowland replied, remembering from previous visits, when he had walked in those fields. "Rather a lot of them."

Milton was unable to refrain. "Ten thousand saw I at a glance, tossing their heads in sprightly dance."

"I think you'll find that Wordsworth was talking about daffodils, not dandelions."

As the train churned through the Austrian countryside towards the German border, they decided brief personal histories consistent with their new identities. Edna was prone to embroider the story, and for a while they debated the efficacy of the elaborate lie over the simple one. The sculptress and Milton were adamant that plausibility lay in detail, while Clyde demanded something he could remember. In the end it was decided that they could be creative with those aspects that did not require Clyde to remember them, and a satisfactory agreement was reached.

Edna rested her head on Rowland's shoulder as the gentle rhythmic lurch of the moving train rocked her towards sleep.

"How are we going to find Campbell?" Clyde asked.

"We don't want to find him," Rowland yawned. "He'd quite probably recognise us all. And he'll most certainly recognise me."

"So what are we supposed to do?"

"Apparently, this chap Blanshard, Campbell's interpreter, will get in touch with us at the Vier Jahreszeiten."

"The fear of what?" Clyde murmured.

Rowland smiled. "The Vier Jahreszeiten—The Four Seasons. It's a hotel. Until then, we visit galleries, talk to artists, generally carry on like art collectors and see if we can't find out more about what happened to Peter Bothwell."

"And Campbell has no idea that Blanshard is an Old Guard spy?" Milton asked, playing with the dark moustache he had kept when he sacrificed his goatee for their time in Germany. It was now just long enough to twist.

Rowland shrugged. "We have no way of knowing. I can only presume that if Blanshard is still with him, then Campbell is still in the dark."

"And if not?"

"Things will get a bit awkward, I expect."

It was early in the evening when the Orient Express stopped in Munich before continuing on to Strasbourg and Paris. It was cold, the sky dark with cloud, and the day misted with a light but steady drizzle.

Rowland offered Edna his hand as she alighted. The sculptress was still not completely awake, having roused only moments before. Indeed, they had all slept through most of the journey, forgoing their turn in the dining carriage in the interests of rest. Rowland's last memory was of the simple lines and rural colour. The ornate, architectural grandeur of the Munich *bahnhof* was disorienting in contrast.

The railway platform buzzed and whistled with celebration. A band played folk tunes and the brown-shirted men of the SA were present in force. The general noise was punctuated with shouts of "Heil Hitler!"

Edna started. "Is he here?" she asked, casting her eyes around.

"Who?"

"Mr. Hitler…they keep 'heiling' him."

"No…I think they use his name to greet anybody," Rowland explained.

"Really? Well, that's a bit silly," Edna said, as she looked out into the crowd to observe that he spoke the truth.

"It is, a bit," Rowland agreed. He glanced around at the banners and posters which festooned the station. "But you probably shouldn't say so too loudly."

When another train pulled in, the jubilation rose into a roar of approbation and the Brownshirts began to chant "Heil!" in a pounding rhythm. It was focussed upon a small group alighting the train on the opposite platform. Fleetingly, Rowland wondered if it was, in fact, the Chancellor, and then his ear, having become attuned, picked up snippets of excited conversation.

"Who is it?" Milton asked, as Rowland now strained to see the party from the other train.

Rowland motioned towards a large, stocky man who emerged from the carriage with his chest thrust out at the world. The Brownshirts exploded into applause. Rowland glanced uneasily at Milton. "Apparently that's Röhm. He's head of the SA...the Brownshirts."

Edna grabbed Rowland's hand. "Let's get out of here," she whispered.

Chapter Eight

HITLER'S LATEST COUP. TRADE UNIONS UNDER NAZI CONTROL

LONDON, May 2

The Nazis simultaneously assumed control of the trade unions throughout Germany today, inaugurating Herr Hitler's campaign to break Social Democracy's hold on the workers and to mould them to his will.

"Politics of hate" will not be tolerated. Communist journals must submit to Government control and distribution. Provocative leaflets are banned.

Herr Hitler's blow at the Socialist trade unions, which have a membership of more than 5,000,000, was executed with ruthless efficiency. Police and Brown Shirts occupied all the trade union buildings, workmen's banks, and co-operative stores, and arrested 50 leaders, including the secretary of the Trade Union Federation, Herr Leipert, an ex-Minister of Labour (Herr Wissel) and three editors.

The raid was organised by Dr. Ley, President of the Prussian State Council, who describes it as the second phase of the national revival. "Marxism has been pretending to be dead," he said, "but we are not going to be deceived."

—*The Sydney Morning Herald*, 1933

Maximilianstrasse, through the centre of Munich, was the city's busiest boulevard. Here among the fashionable boutiques and clubs, behind a magnificent gothic façade, stood the Hotel Vier Jahreszeiten. Built in the previous century under royal command, it was easily Munich's premier hotel.

Rowland led the way into the wood-panelled foyer, checking them all into two of the hotel's best suites, while his companions waited under a domed ceiling of coloured glass. Milton and Edna, posing as brother and sister—Albert and Millicent Greenway—would share the Ludwig suite, while Rowland and Clyde—as Robert Negus and Joseph Ryan—took the rooms named for Hindenburg.

Although he was equally comfortable with the Bavarian dialect, Rowland was careful to use only the High German spoken in Berlin, and by most foreigners. Already, he'd caught the loose words of hotel staff, who assumed their Bavarian dialect would not be understood.

The hotel was busy. It seemed there was to be a rally of some sort soon, and the Vier Jahreszeiten was brimming with Nazi officialdom and tourists. As the meeting place of the German supremacist Thule movement, the hotel had a proud association with the inception of the Third Reich.

They were shown to the suites, each of which overlooked Maximilianstrasse, and was opulently furnished in Baroque style. Extra trunks had already been delivered to the rooms and unpacked. Again Rowland marvelled at the global efficiency of the Old Guard.

He and Clyde were in the suite's sitting room when Milton and Edna rejoined them, dressed to go down for dinner. Rowland looked up from the newspaper, clearly perturbed.

"What's news, Rowly?" Milton asked.

Rowland dropped the newspaper on the low marble side table. "The trade unions have been dissolved."

"Which ones?" Milton asked, appalled. Both he and Clyde were active unionists back in Australia.

"All of them," Rowland replied. "Union offices were demolished yesterday and, today, all the unions were dissolved."

Clyde picked up the paper, though he couldn't read it. "Can the government do that?"

"Apparently they did."

Milton cursed. "Just like that? No...that's crazy...they wouldn't just..."

Rowland took the paper back from Clyde, shaking his head incredulously. He scanned the article and paraphrased. "It's been done, Milt. Any man found to be a trade unionist is apparently being arrested."

"We'll have to do something...we can't let the fascists—" Milton said, outraged.

"Calm down, Milt. We're not in Sydney, mate. We can't just petition parliament with our concerns."

Milt sat down, slapping the chair's arm in frustration. "Someone's got to say something!"

Edna looked at the poet with concern. She sat down beside him. "Milt, darling, this is not our country."

"But..."

"We must be careful. You can't walk around Munich decrying the German government. God knows what they'd do if they found out why Rowly was really here."

Rowland rubbed his brow thoughtfully. It wasn't just the dissolution of the unions; there was so much in the newspaper that disturbed him. Even when New South Wales appeared on the brink of civil war, the rhetoric had not seemed so extreme. "Perhaps you fellows should take Ed home. I can book passages on the next ship."

Edna rolled her eyes. "Don't be ridiculous, Rowly."

Clyde looked out the window at the bustling boulevard below. "We have all the more reason to make sure Campbell doesn't bring this insanity back home."

Rowland met Milton's eye. "The SA seems to be going after anybody who's out of step with the National Socialists."

Milton sighed. "I get your meaning, Rowly. Clyde's right… all the more reason we should make sure Campbell doesn't make powerful friends." He smiled sadly. "Don't worry, mate, I'll remember why we're here."

They did not dine at the Vier Jahreszeiten that evening. There were many Nazi leaders patronising the hotel and Rowland thought it best that they allow themselves time to adjust, before breaking bread in the company of fascists.

He took them instead to a different part of Munich—the jazz and cabaret district which he had frequented years ago when he had travelled across from Oxford. There was something alluringly unwholesome about the area, a refuge of things which had become clandestine, and those things which had always been so. Women for purchase congregated on corners posing against streetlamps as they waited for the men who came like moths towards the glow of their cigarettes. In the shadows, merchants of the black market traded the foreign goods which had been banned under the Nazi Government.

To Rowland's disappointment, many of the cabarets for which the district was known had now been closed, but they did find a small, smoky restaurant that served food and beer and boasted a three-man swing band on a rough stage. It was a bustling, crowded venue and it looked as though they would not get places at one of the extended communal tables, until Rowland paid a group of long-haired young men to give up theirs. The food was simple: sausage, bread, and pickled cabbage. The fine Bavarian beer was served in massive tankards. In dinner suits, they were possibly overdressed, but the gathering was eclectic enough that they passed without attracting too much attention.

Rowland noticed that the conversations here were not so firmly in support of the government. Occasionally he heard the sentiment of contempt, and the salute of "Heil Hitler!" was rare and halfhearted.

They ate and drank. As it became late, the night spot became only more crowded and busy. Milton and Rowland danced with Edna, and she danced with many men besides. And then, with no warning, the band stopped and disappeared through a door behind the stage. An almost spherical man in traditional costume replaced them, playing German folk music on an accordion. On the dance floor, Rowland was bewildered, but he and Edna followed the other couples into a slow polka.

It was only a few minutes till the brown-shirted officers of the SA made their entrance. Tables were cleared for them and the round man with the accordion continued to play.

One of the SA men was arguing with the night spot's owner. Rowland cut across the floor with Edna to listen—not an easy feat during a polka. He could only get close enough to hear the Brownshirt shout *"Juden!"* while the proprietor shook his head emphatically and pointed to the accordion player. He realised then. Rowland pulled Edna close and whispered in her ear. "The band members, they're Jewish."

Her eyes widened. "Surely that's not illegal?"

"I don't think so," Rowland replied. "I think they're just trying to start trouble." He glanced at the floor full of apparently sedate polka dancers. "Perhaps we should find Milt."

Milton was working his way through another stein of beer. He hailed them merrily as they approached the table. "Robbie, I hope you've been treating my sister as a gentleman should."

Rowland smiled. "I've tried, but she won't stop flirting with me."

Milton swung an arm around his shoulders. "Sadly, mate, it's not just you. We're thinking a nunnery might do the trick."

"I want to go." Edna glanced at the SA men, who were now gathered at the bar, drinking. "Can we go?"

Clyde looked down at the beer he had only just started drinking. "Right now?"

Milton drained his stein. "Yes, very well. This music is getting on my nerves, anyway."

They weren't the only ones to leave at that time and so they had to walk a fair way on a night that was sharp and clear and cold before they found a motor cab to take them back to the Vier Jahreszeiten.

In the privacy of the Ludwig suite, Rowland handed Edna a glass of sherry. "Drink this, Ed. You look chilled to the bone."

The sculptress took the glass in both hands. She did feel cold, but she wasn't sure it was anything to do with the chill of the night air.

Milton watched her thoughtfully. "You remember last year, when Campbell's thugs were running around Sydney belting every Communist they could find?"

Edna nodded.

"And when Hardy's mob tried to tar and feather me?"

"Yes, of course."

"Well, the SA is no different, Ed. Cowardly thugs doing the bidding of their fascist masters."

Edna shuddered. "I don't know, Milt. I think they might be different."

Milton shook his head. "That's because they're speaking German...all that slurping makes them sound more sinister. But they're little different to the New Guard...and they won't win."

Alois Richter's villa was on Schellingstrasse, near the centre of Munich. Most of the buildings were multi-storey blocks—commercial concerns and apartments. The motor cab driver was at pains to point out number 50, which once housed the offices of the Nazi Party. Rowland translated for the others.

Eventually the motor cab pulled into the gated driveway of a grand villa among the commercial premises. Window boxes overflowing with geraniums gave it away as a residence among the businesses which occupied Schellingstrasse. The building had stark, simple lines, its façade inlaid with plaques featuring woodland scenes. The door was flanked with classical columns, and the grounds were neat and compact.

Richter was expecting them—well, Robert Negus, at least. He glanced at the letter of introduction which Somerset Maugham had provided Rowland, and welcomed them all warmly. Richter himself was an interesting figure. Small and slim, he greeted them wearing a deep green, shawl-collared smoking jacket and a purple fez. The hair visible at the base of the fez was improbably black and the skin around his eyes was creased with years and laughter. He carried a black Scottish terrier in his arms, which made shaking hands a little difficult.

Rowland addressed him in High German at first, but Richter spoke English, and graciously elected to do so. He complimented Milton on the cummerbund-cum-cravat the poet had once again chosen to wear. He gushed over Edna in both English and German and demanded they all come in, showing them into an elegant sitting room, furnished in a florid Victorian style. There he placed the Scottish terrier onto the silk-upholstered couch and made sure the creature was comfortable.

"Tea, Frau Schuler, we must have tea," Richter shouted into a hallway.

He turned, beaming, his smile fading as his eyes moved systematically over each of the men. He walked slowly around Rowland, who was beginning to feel quite awkward. Finally Richter snorted. "English tailors," he said, peering closely at Rowland's lapel. "One of the better ones, of course, but still unimaginative, conservative. With your height you could wear the double-breasted jacket…Why is a young man like you wearing a waistcoat?"

Milton grinned, delighted. Clyde fiddled nervously with his tie.

"Are you a tailor, Mr. Richter?" Edna asked, walking across the room to an old manual sewing machine displayed in the corner.

"My first machine," Richter said proudly. "Just a relic now, of course, but she has been with me since the beginning."

A greying matron with an operatic bearing entered wheeling

a traymobile laden with tea and cake, which she set out on the low marble-topped table in the centre of the room.

"Sit, sit," Richter invited, motioning them towards chairs. "Frau Schuler has been with me from the beginning too. She has looked after this poor widower since the war."

"Your wife died during the war?" Edna asked softly.

Richter's voice thickened. "*Gott hab sie selig*. I was the soldier, but it was my darling wife and our beautiful daughter who died."

"Oh, how dreadful, how very sad."

Richter smiled at the sculptress.

"He who has not tasted bitter does not know what is sweet," he said, with resigned sorrow. "It was a long time ago now, *Leibchen*. Fourteen years. I began again. Poured my grief into every stitch, every seam. Now I have five factories, over a hundred workers." Richter paused to feed a bit of cake to the terrier, crooning as it gagged on the cream.

"You have done rather well," Edna said quietly, deciding to pour the tea as Frau Schuler had left and Richter's hands were full. She found a little room on the end of the couch occupied by the terrier and perched there as she poured. "You must be a very fine tailor, Mr. Richter."

He waved away the compliment. "The tailoring is my business, its success is God's." He heaved the terrier onto his lap and sat beside Edna, inviting her to stroke his dog. "But *Dankechön*, Fräulein," he added, "for that acknowledgment, which, sadly, I do not get from my peers."

"Jealousy and quivering strife therein a portion claim," Milton contributed, nodding knowingly.

"You speak like a poet, Mr. Greenway," Richter said, delighted.

"Wordsworth, to be precise," Rowland muttered.

Richter misheard him. "Yes, your words have worth and insight, Mr. Greenway. The clothing industry can be very vicious and unkind."

Milton smiled, accepting the accolade triumphantly.

Edna leaned over to Richter and whispered. "I'm sure they must just be envious."

Richter laughed. "Envy eats nothing but its own heart...And business has been good under the Nazis. Germany is booming again...not since before the war have we been so prosperous."

Rowland noticed the framed picture of Richter shaking hands with a man in uniform, just below the large portrait of Adolf Hitler that seemed to hang in both public buildings and private homes. "You do business with the National Socialist Party, Mr. Richter?"

"We supply many uniforms to the Reich," Richter replied. "If not for Hugo Boss and his inferior products, we would have the contract solely." He lifted his dog onto Edna's lap and proffered his arm to Rowland. "Feel that fabric, Herr Negus. See how well the sleeve sits, note the invisible stitching." He threw his hands up in disgust. "Hugo Boss uses cheap thread and his buttons are insecure. For this reason, he undercuts. I just hope the officers of the SS are proficient with needle and thread, for they will be refixing their buttons!"

"I'm sure they'll return the contract to you as soon as they realise, Mr. Richter." Edna attempted to soothe the irate tailor. "I know I hate sewing buttons."

Richter sniffed. "Perhaps I do not want that contract anymore. Hideous design!" He shook his head. "Entirely black... no colour, no style whatsoever. Now, if we had taken the red of the armband and used it for a jacket, that would have been a uniform...but, no! Himmler wants black. Pah! Of course Hugo tells him it is the height of couture...simpering *Schwein!*"

For several moments there was silence as the Australian men searched for an appropriate response and Edna patted the indifferent dog.

The pause seemed to jolt Richter out of his invective. "I apologise. You did not come to hear of disreputable tailors. You are here on a mission more sombre, and one which saddens me deeply. My most heartfelt commiserations, Mr. Negus."

"Thank you, Mr. Richter."

"It was a great shock, you know," Richter said. "To see Peter again after all these years and then…" He bit his lip and did not go on.

"What exactly happened?" Rowland asked. "We have not been told a great deal."

"You do not know?" Richter looked at him, shocked and grieved. "It was terrible, just terrible…a tragic miscalculation, you see. Peter was not used to how cold the water can be here. The Starnberg is a glacial lake and, as warm as the day may seem, the water can cause a body to cramp and sink."

Rowland spoke gently, for the man was obviously becoming distressed. "He drowned in a glacial lake?"

"Yes, the Starnberger Sea…it is about fifteen miles from here. I have a house quite near Berg Castle, where I holiday at times. Peter had joined me there, but I was forced to return to attend to a problem at the factory."

"He went swimming?" Clyde prompted.

Richter sighed. "So it seems. I have a copy of the police report somewhere." He stood and began to rummage through the papers stacked neatly on the sideboard.

He paused to study Rowland. "And you, young man, did you know Peter well?"

Rowland elected for a half-truth. "I'm afraid I didn't know him at all, Mr. Richter. Mrs. Bothwell is a cousin of my mother's…and as I was coming to Munich anyway…"

"Oh, I see. And what is your business here, Mr. Negus?" He paused to smile at Edna. "What brings you and your so-charming companions to Munich?"

"We are art dealers—here to buy paintings. It is a good time to buy."

Richter seemed to accept this readily. "Yes, a great deal of art has become available lately…Jews selling up to leave." He frowned as if the situation did not entirely meet with his approval. "Ah, here it is!" He handed Rowland a large sealed envelope. It was quite heavy. "I believe some of Peter's personal possessions are in there too. The rest of his belongings have been repacked into his trunk."

"Perhaps you could arrange for them to be sent to our hotel," Rowland began, as he took a calling card from his pocket. "We're staying at the Vier Jahreszeiten."

"The Vier Jahreszeiten!" Richter exclaimed. "Well, that will not do! The place is crawling with Brownshirts…ill-bred thugs, not the kind of men with whom a gentleman such as yourself would choose to share accommodations."

"Thank you for your concern, Mr. Richter, but the hotel is very comfortable."

"No, it will not do!" Richter was adamant. "You must stay here. There is much room here…I will tell Mrs. Schuler."

"We couldn't possibly impose," Rowland protested.

"No, you must stay…See, Stasi has already fallen in love with Miss Greenway." Richter pointed to the dog who, aside from the barest movement of its ear, looked as though it might have expired. "If you take her away, he will pine!"

Rowland laughed. "Miss Greenway seems to have that effect, but we have business associates who will look for us at the hotel."

Richter sighed. "Ah, of course. Forgive me…I am a stupid, lonely man trying to stave off old age by playing with young people."

"We would much rather stay with you and Stasi, Mr. Richter," Edna scooped the dog into her arms. "I don't care much for the SA either."

Chapter Nine

BOOKS AND PUBLICATIONS
MULLENS FOR GIFTS

ROBERTSON AND MULLENS LTD
THE LEADING BOOKSELLERS,
STATIONERS LIBRARIANS
MULLENS FOR GOOD BOOKS
SUGGESTIONS FOR GIFTS

HORSE NONSENSE, by authors of "1066" and "Now All This": 1/6 each (5d.)

WEEK-END BOOK, a social anthology: 9/ (5d.)

KING EDWARD AND HIS TIMES, by Andre Maurois: 16/6 (9d.)

DISRAELI and BYRON, by A Maurois, cheap edition: 7/ each (5d.)

MY STRUGGLE, the Autobiography of Adolf Hitler: 21/ (1/)

FLAT OUT, by G. E. T. Eyston, motor racing: 9/(5d.)

FOR EVER ENGLAND, by General Seely: 8/6 (6d.)

—*The Argus*, 1933

"Poor old bloke should face facts and bury that wretched hound," Clyde murmured, as they strolled down Schellingstrasse.

Edna shoved him, though she laughed. "Stasi is just a little lazy."

"Lazy!" Clyde guffawed. "I've seen fur stoles show more signs of life!"

"Mr. Richter loves him, Clyde. Stasi keeps him company."

"I suppose. Gotta admit, the hat had me worried for a while, but Richter's not a bad bloke really."

Rowland agreed. Richter had been a warm and generous host. He had shown them examples of the uniforms that his factories made for the Reich, pointing out the modifications that would be made if he were to have his way. Opening his best wine, he had pressed upon Rowland the keys to his house on the edge of Lake Starnberg, should they wish to use it.

"Perhaps we should have agreed to stay with him," Edna sighed. "I don't think Mrs. Schuler is great company."

"We need to be at the Vier Jahreszeiten for this chap Blanshard to contact us," Rowland said, trying to stem Edna's compassion with practicalities. He suspected that Richter reminded Edna of her own father, who had a similar proclivity for ridiculous headgear.

They had, after taking an extended and lavish luncheon with Richter, decided to explore a little before returning to the hotel. And so they strolled down Schellingstrasse, enjoying the Gothic façades and Baroque architecture of Munich.

"Richter's correct about one thing," Clyde said, casting his eyes about the busy street, which was bustling with business and smartly dressed shoppers. "The Germans seem to be doing well under the National Socialists. I haven't seen a beggar since we arrived."

Rowland realised he was right. Perhaps they were not looking in the right places, but the streets seemed devoid of the homeless and destitute who haunted many parts of Sydney. "It does seem positive."

"Depends who you are, I expect," Milton said, nodding

towards a boarded shopfront. Its windows had been broken, vandalised. On the door was scrawled the word *"Juden"* in white paint. He thrust his hands into his pockets, his eyes hard.

Rowland stared silently at the abandoned premises. That the fascist government of Germany victimised Communists was no surprise, but the hostility towards Jews was harder to understand. It seemed to him bizarre and arbitrary. He glanced up at the sign above the shop. "Blumberg für Mensch"...a Jewish tailor...at one time, at least. Perhaps this, too, was why business was so good for men like Richter, who were allowed to prosper unmolested.

Edna entwined her arm in Milton's and, quiet now, they walked on.

Rowland's face was dark. Silently he berated himself for allowing his friends to come. He could have refused. Why didn't he refuse? As much as Milton was probably the most untraditional Jew in the world, he was still Jewish. To expect him to witness this and hold his tongue was too much.

"Stop flogging yourself, Rowly." Clyde and Rowland had fallen a few steps behind the others.

Rowland did not reply.

"Milt was determined to come...not just for you. We'd heard rumours through the Party—he wanted to see for himself."

"So now he's seen."

"And we're even gladder we came, Rowly. It's important we don't let Campbell take this home."

"This would never happen back home," Rowland murmured, with more optimism than conviction.

Clyde shrugged. "I hope not. I hope it's just that the Germans are stupid or mad...but maybe they're not, Rowly. Maybe, just maybe, Campbell could replicate this back home. If Lang hadn't been sacked, how many more men would have joined Campbell and the New Guard?"

"But Lang was sacked," Rowland replied. "All the hysteria seems to have subsided, thank God."

Clyde extracted cigarette papers and a tobacco tin from his pocket. "You know what I think, Rowly?" he said as he tipped tobacco along a paper and rolled a cigarette. "I reckon that Campbell picked the wrong enemy. If Lang hadn't been sacked, he'd still have an army, still be leading a revolution. Over here, he might just learn how to choose a new villain and create a new rallying point." Clyde pointed his cigarette at a poster in a baker's window. He couldn't read it, but the sinister depiction of a misshapen money-lender with his foot on the neck of a weeping woman made its message obvious.

Rowland cursed.

Clyde lit his cigarette. "You know, I've seen a very similar drawing…on a New Guard poster, except it was Lang who was stepping on some hapless woman. As I said, Campbell just picked the wrong villain…he hasn't got anybody to unite his fascist masses against anymore."

Rowland glanced at Milton and Edna ahead of them. Milton was laughing now as the sculptress pulled him towards some shop.

He turned back to Clyde. "You make a lot of sense."

Clyde grinned. "I tend to. You'd do well to remember that, old mate."

Rowland laughed. "I shall try. I say, where did they go?"

"That shop, I think."

The business was a photographic studio: Hoffman's. Clyde and Rowland entered to find Edna trying to talk to the young, blond assistant with the half-dozen words of German in her vocabulary. For a while they simply watched as the sculptress engaged in pantomime to ask whether Hoffman's would develop the film she had shot. Milton stood beside her, obviously amused and no help whatsoever. Eventually, Rowland intervened, introducing himself and his companions in High German. "My friend would like to have some photographs developed, if that is a service your business provides."

The shop assistant smiled warmly and responded. "I'm

afraid we don't, Herr Negus. Herr Hoffman provides a complete studio service. He is our beloved Chancellor's personal photographer, you see. We develop only our own pictures."

Rowland translated for Edna, who was visibly disappointed. "We shall have to wait till we get home."

"I could develop the photographs for Fräulein Greenway on my day off, if you like," the shop assistant volunteered. "I would hate to have to wait, myself. I know I'm impatient, but I usually do my own developing, you see, so I find waiting a trial."

Rowland passed the offer on to Edna, who accepted gratefully.

A conversation followed, for the sculptress had a talent for making friends which transcended language, and Rowland was, in any case, on hand to interpret. It was agreed that Edna would bring in her rolls of film, which the shop assistant, who introduced herself as Eva, would develop when next she had a chance. Eva was friendly and unreserved. She and Edna talked enthusiastically about photography, and the latest cameras and techniques. Her laugh was natural and easy.

Rowland gave Eva the card of Robert Negus the art dealer, on which he wrote the name of the Vier Jahreszeiten, where they could be reached. "*Dankeschön*, Fräulein Eva. We will see you again soon."

"I will look forward to it, Herr Negus," she replied, looking up at him with large china-blue eyes. "I am very pleased to make your acquaintance…all of you."

Rowland smiled. "And we you, Fräulein."

When they finally returned to the Vier Jahreszeiten later that evening, there was a message waiting for Robert Negus.

Rowland opened the envelope as Milton tried to replicate gin-slings from the contents of the Ludwig suite's drinks cabinet. It seemed that the poet had developed a fondness for Raffles' signature cocktail.

"Is that from Mr. Blanshard, Rowly?" Edna asked, as she rummaged for the rolls of film she intended to have developed.

"Indeed, it is," Rowland confirmed. "I'm to meet him tomorrow morning at the Königsplatz."

"How will you know him?"

"I won't. Apparently, I'm to carry a copy of last week's *Der Stürmer*, and he'll find me."

"Just you, then?" Clyde grimaced as he tried the concoction Milton presented to him.

"At this stage it's easier to be discreet on my own." He glanced at Milton, who was phoning down to the reception desk in search of pineapple.

Clyde chuckled. Edna flopped down on the settee beside Rowland.

"What's the Stirmer?" she asked.

"*Der Stürmer.*" Rowland sighed. "It's a filthy rag, put out by some deranged idiot. I don't particularly like the idea of even carrying it around."

"Well, where are you going to get a copy?"

"They're everywhere, Ed. Sadly, *Der Stürmer* is rather popular these days."

Milton handed him a glass and sat down opposite. "Don't worry about it, mate, just do what you have to." He sipped the frothy cocktail of his own making, his face breaking into a broad and triumphant grin. "I must say, I'm a genius."

Tentatively, Rowland tried the drink he'd been handed. It didn't taste anything like the Singapore cocktail. He winced as it went down. "Good Lord, what did you use instead of pineapple?"

"Crème de menthe and peach schnapps...shall I mix you another?"

"I suspect the one might be enough to kill me."

Rowland awoke the next morning with a headache. It didn't surprise him. The evening had somehow turned into a series of attempts to replicate the gin-sling without pineapple. At the time it had seemed like a good idea.

He and Clyde had stumbled back to their own suite in the early hours of the morning. Now it was nearly nine. He was due at the Königsplatz by ten.

Rowland showered and shaved quickly. A bleary-eyed Clyde emerged as he was searching for an appropriate tie.

"Is it morning already?" Clyde groaned. Clearly the previous evening's consumption had been generic in its effect. "He's bloody well poisoned us," he complained.

Rowland smiled, pointing to the tray of coffee he'd just had sent up. "That'll help...or you could just go back to bed."

"No," Clyde sighed, reaching for the pot. "It'd hardly do for us all to be asleep while you go off to meet a spy."

The conversation was interrupted by a knock. Rowland answered the door, as Clyde was still undressed.

"Good morning, Robbie!" Perhaps it was the after-effects of the alcohol, but Edna seemed dazzling that morning. Fresh, and so beautiful it was almost hard to look at her. Rowland stood back to let her in.

"I thought I had better make sure you were up," she said, as he shut the door. She smiled. "You didn't look so well when you left last night...oh Clyde, you poor thing!"

Having realised it was just Edna, Clyde returned to the coffee pot in his pyjamas. He grunted and poured.

"You look pretty, Ed," Rowland murmured, as he knotted his tie in the sitting room mirror.

"Why thank you, Rowly," Edna said, twirling to display the fullness of her skirt. "It's a little exciting having a wardrobe full of clothes I've never seen before."

"How's Milt this morning?" Clyde asked.

"He was waxing his moustache when I left," Edna replied, shaking her head and giggling. "He should be along in a minute."

Rowland checked his watch. "I'd better get going. Are you going out? Shall I meet you all back here for lunch?"

Edna nodded. "Yes, do. I thought that since we're supposed to be art dealers, the boys and I should be seen at a few galleries."

"That's not a bad idea," Rowland admitted. "I wish I could join you." He thought for a moment, and then said, "Perhaps you should buy a few things. We'll be rather unconvincing dealers if we don't actually buy or sell anything."

"You want us to buy art?" Clyde asked incredulously.

"Only if it's good. We don't want people to think we're bad art dealers."

"No, that wouldn't do at all," Edna agreed.

And so Rowland left his friends to purchase art, while he set out to meet Alastair Blanshard, who, as an Old Guard plant, had infiltrated Eric Campbell's inner circle. He paused to collect an old copy of *Der Stürmer* from the reception desk on the pretext that he had missed an edition. He slipped the paper into his jacket without looking at it.

He walked to the Königsplatz, and took a seat on the park bench on the grassed square adjacent to the Museum of Classical Art, in accordance with Blanshard's instructions. He checked his watch. Still twenty minutes to ten. For a while he sat watching the plaza, the movements of people, of motor cars and horse-drawn vehicles, the children who played on the grass and the bullying presence of the Brownshirts. Almost without thinking he pulled the leather-bound notebook from his jacket to record what he saw. The square was surrounded by buildings inspired by classical architecture—Corinthian columns and iconic plaques on all sides—but Rowland wasn't interested in the buildings. He sketched quickly, his eye drawn, as it always was, to faces and figures. With strong, stern lines he captured the ruthless arrogance of the SA patrol and then, with a softer hand, the faces of the boys who gazed admiringly at them. He had lost himself in trying to catch the wistful eyes of a young woman casting coins into a fountain when a man sat wordlessly on the bench beside him.

Rowland glanced up. Dressed in tweeds, with a shock of

thick red hair and aged about forty-five, the man opened a silver case and silently offered him a cigarette.

Rowland declined in German.

The man glanced down at the paper now on the bench between them. "Mr. Negus?" he asked. He looked disgruntled.

Rowland nodded.

The man sighed and cursed under his breath. "Alastair Blanshard," he said finally. "How old are you?"

A little startled by the question, Rowland did not reply immediately.

"Well?"

"I'm twenty-eight…but I'm not sure what that—"

Blanshard swore—quite extravagantly, though his expression was so controlled that anyone watching might have thought them discussing the weather, and he nodded in a manner that was quite contrary to his words. "What the bloody hell do those fools think they're doing? I ask for an experienced man and they send me some novice who—" he paused to glance at Rowland's notebook, "who likes to draw pictures, for God's sake!"

Rowland did not react visibly. "I am who they've sent, Mr. Blanshard. What can I do to help you?"

Blanshard cursed again while smiling congenially, and then he asked, "Do you mind if I glance through your newspaper?"

"Be my guest," Rowland muttered, a little disconcerted by the divergence between Blanshard's gestures and what he was saying. He decided it was best to just not look at the man.

Blanshard unfolded *Der Stürmer* and spent the next several minutes studying it. Unsure of what else to do, Rowland went back to his sketch. The meeting was not going as he had expected.

Eventually, Blanshard refolded the paper and returned it to the bench between them. "You'll find an itinerary in the paper," he said, lighting a cigarette. He kept his eyes focussed on the plaza. "Campbell has a meeting with Göring at the Braune

Haus the day after tomorrow…the details are all there. The meeting must not happen, or it must not go well."

"What exactly do you want me to do?"

"Something very dangerous, Mr. Negus, which is why I can't believe that they have sent me an untried man!"

Rowland was getting somewhat fed up with Blanshard's dissatisfaction.

"Suppose you just tell me what has to be done, Mr. Blanshard."

Blanshard drew so heavily on his cigarette that Rowland half-expected to see the stick disappear entirely. "Among the National Socialists, Hermann Göring's star is rising. If Campbell manages to ingratiate himself with the man, it could be dangerous, indeed. I have done what I can to stop the meeting but my hands are tied on this. Göring speaks English, so Campbell has no need of a translator."

Rowland waited silently until Blanshard continued.

"Ideally, we would like Göring himself to cancel, or simply fail to attend the meeting."

"How on Earth am I supposed to get Göring to cancel a meeting?" Rowland interrupted. Surely Blanshard didn't expect him to kidnap a minister of the Nazi cabinet.

"We have one chance." Blanshard stubbed out his cigarette and lit another immediately. "Göring has a younger brother, who is currently in Munich. Albert Göring is, we believe, a dissident, opposed to the National Socialist Government of which his brother is a part. According to our intelligence, he hates Adolf Hitler and has been actively working against the Third Reich."

"But…?" Rowland pre-empted the qualification.

"But we can't be sure. He is Hermann Göring's brother, after all, and we have no evidence of any falling out between the two. Indeed, their relationship appears to be warm."

"I see."

Once more Blanshard swore, while smiling pleasantly. "I

was expecting someone I could send to talk to Albert Göring. Someone of at least the calibre of Bothwell, who could convince Albert to persuade his brother to cancel the meeting."

Rowland shrugged. "I speak German, Mr. Blanshard, both High and Bavarian. You can send me."

"You do not seem to understand the danger, Mr. Negus. We have no way of knowing what Albert will do…no guarantee that he will not simply turn you in to the Nazis as a spy or an insurgent. If you fail to convince him to manipulate his brother to assist us, it is quite likely that you will be arrested and shot."

For a moment Rowland said nothing as the words settled between them.

"And if this meeting goes ahead?"

"Campbell could make a very powerful ally. I have already heard some of the Nazis call him Australia's Hitler."

Rowland smiled. "The Germans can call him whatever they want…I doubt Australians will call him anything that remotely resembles Hitler."

Blanshard tapped the ash from his cigarette, subtly checking the area around them. There was no one too nearby. "Have you read *Mein Kampf*, Mr. Negus?"

"Hitler's manifesto?" Rowland shrugged. "Only partially… I'm afraid I find fascist insanity more tedious than amusing."

"As much as you dismiss it, Mr. Negus, there were many men who were seduced by its ideas. It has sold a quarter of a million copies already, and now every newlywed couple in Germany receives some kind of nuptial edition."

Rowland laughed. "Sounds like an intriguing wedding night, Mr. Blanshard."

Blanshard refused to share his flippancy. "Eric Campbell has begun drafting his own manifesto, which he plans to release on his return. It will set out what he sees as the path for Australia, much as *Mein Kampf* set Germany's road. Campbell already considers that there are similarities between himself and Mr. Hitler. Any encouragement by the hierarchy of the Reich could easily see Campbell's view become more extreme."

Rowland frowned uneasily as he remembered Clyde's earlier insight on Campbell's choice of foe. Campbell could well be looking for a new enemy. "Very well, Mr. Blanshard. I'll try."

Blanshard swore at him, though again his face revealed nothing to anyone out of earshot, anyone but Rowland. "You'll have to do more than try, Mr. Negus," Blanshard said tightly. "An experienced man would know how to judge Albert Göring—to assess his chances and proceed accordingly. I bloody well hope you're up to this."

Rowland exhaled. "I'll bloody well have to be," he said abruptly.

Chapter Ten

MR. ERIC CAMPBELL AND THE NAZIS
PROTESTS AGAINST HIS ADDRESS TO UNIVERSITY STUDENTS

SYDNEY, October 17

In the Legislative Assembly today, Mr. Heffron (Lab.) directed the attention of the Minister for Education (Mr. Drummond) to a speech made by Mr. Eric Campbell, leader of the New Guard. Mr. Heffron asked, "Has the Minister's attention been drawn to a statement in the press reporting a speech of Mr. Eric Campbell, delivered to a meeting of undergraduates at the University, in which he is reported to have said that if there was a great Nazi demonstration in Sydney today, the University would be represented by its most distinguished professors; and, further, that the racial hatred in Germany today was due to the cleverness of the Jews?"

—The Advertiser, 1933

Rowland walked slowly back towards the Vier Jahreszeiten, his collar turned up and his hands thrust deep into the pockets of his overcoat. The weather had closed in suddenly and it was now overcast and cold. As much as he'd concluded that Blanshard was unnecessarily alarmist, Rowland was understandably preoccupied. He might not have even noticed her had she not run into him.

"*Entschuldigung sie, bitte*...Fräulein Eva? Hello." Rowland's speech slipped automatically into German.

"Herr Negus." The young woman they'd encountered at Hoffman's studio clutched his arm to regain her balance. "I'm so sorry...I wasn't watching..."

"You're crying," Rowland said, startled, as he noticed the tears still wet on her cheek. "Did I hurt you?"

"No, no, I'm not." She blushed. "I've had a little disappointment, you see." She turned her face away from him as she tried to wipe her eyes with the back of her hand.

Rowland passed her his handkerchief and waited until she'd composed herself. "Is it anything I can help you with, Fräulein?"

Eva laughed. "You are kind, Herr Negus, but no. Unless, of course, you have a dachshund in your pocket?"

"A dachshund?" Rowland smiled. "Do you have a particular reason for needing a dachshund?"

"Oh, I don't suppose I need a dachshund, but I would like one more than anything in the world. I had hoped a certain person would make me a present of one...but he has not." Her eyes brimmed again.

"I'm sorry for that," Rowland said, amused and somehow touched by her childlike desperation for a puppy. "I, too, like dogs."

"Oh...do you own a dog, Herr Negus?"

"At home, yes."

Eva smiled. It lit her face. "A dachshund?"

Rowland laughed. "No, Len pretends to be a greyhound."

She slapped his arm playfully and giggled. "You must think me silly, Herr Negus," she said wistfully.

Rowland regarded her kindly. "Not at all. If I should come across a dachshund, I shall keep you in mind, Fräulein Eva, but in the meantime would you care to join me for lunch at my hotel?"

She gasped excitedly and then stopped. "I am afraid Herr Wolf would not approve of my dining with another gentleman. He would not deem it proper."

"We won't be alone—my friends, whom you met yesterday, will be joining us. I'm sure your Herr Wolf would have no objection…if you would care to join us, that is."

Eva clasped her hands together. "Oh, yes, I would, please. Herr Hoffman, my employer, is closing the shop for a week, so he has let me go home early. I am free to do as I please just as soon as I post these." She pulled a sheaf of envelopes from her bag to show him.

"I'd best walk you to the post office, then," he said, offering her his arm.

The others had not yet returned when Rowland and his guest arrived at the Vier Jahreszeiten. And so he took the young lady to wait in the hotel's famous Walterspiel Restaurant.

"Will you have something to drink?" Rowland asked as he called for the waiter.

Eva hesitated.

"You are old enough to drink, aren't you?" he asked, looking at her carefully. She was wearing rather a lot of makeup…perhaps she was younger than she looked.

"I was twenty-one on my last birthday," she replied. "May I have champagne?"

"Of course." Rowland smiled, relieved that he hadn't accidentally invited a child to lunch. He asked a waiter to bring a bottle of the hotel's best.

Eva took a cigarette from the case in her handbag and moved so that Rowland could light it. As she leaned towards him, he glimpsed the scar on her neck.

Perhaps sensing he'd noticed it, Eva moved her hand to

cover the penny-sized dent in the skin of her throat. "You don't smoke, Herr Negus?"

"No, I don't."

"Herr Wolf doesn't smoke either. He doesn't approve of this bad habit of mine."

"I see."

Eva's eyes moistened again. "Perhaps that is why I see him so little…" She shook her head. "No, I am being silly. He has so many demands upon him…I must just learn to be patient, to share him."

Rowland was struck by the loneliness in her voice. "Perhaps, if Herr Wolf is currently unavailable, you will be able to join us on occasion," he said. "I should like to take my companions to the lakes for a few days. I spent some time at Königsee years ago…I have heard that Starnberger See, near here, is quite as beautiful."

Eva cheered visibly at the invitation and spoke happily of swimming in the Starnberger See with her sisters.

"Will you go soon?" Her eyes shone hopefully. "I do not have to return to Hoffman's for a week, and Herr Wolf is too busy to see me. I will be miserable if I do not find a distraction."

"I suppose we could go soon," Rowland said awkwardly. "I have a spot of business I must attend to, but perhaps we could all set off in a day or two."

"Oh, yes, please…that would be wonderful. I can't tell you how long it's been since I've had such an outing."

"I'll organise something and be in touch," Rowland promised. "Where can I reach you?"

Eva's face fell so dramatically that Rowland was startled.

"It's better if I contact you," she said hastily. "Shall I phone you here tomorrow evening?"

Rowland was admittedly caught a little off guard. "I suppose I could organise something by then," he said, though he was not at all sure that was the case.

Impulsively, Eva took his hand. "Thank you, Herr Negus.

I'm sure I would die of loneliness if I had to spend the next week just wishing Herr Wolf would call."

"Well, that would indeed be unfortunate, Fräulein Eva."

Eva smiled, looking at him with undisguised warmth and gratitude as she chatted of little things.

Rowland listened quietly. He found her easy company, girlish and open. There was something lost about Eva that elicited his sympathy. She spoke passionately of photography, but otherwise her thoughts were of clothes and parties and of how much she would like a puppy. And she did seem to like champagne.

Edna, Clyde, and Milton also brought a guest to lunch. Edna introduced him enthusiastically when they arrived. "Rowly, darling, I have brought you the most extraordinary... Why, hello Eva. How lovely to see you again."

Rowland translated quickly, possibly unnecessarily, for the welcome of the sculptress' words was apparent in her tone.

Edna returned then to introducing the gentleman who stood somewhat stiffly by her side: Hans von Eidelsöhn. It seemed they had met at a nearby gallery where von Eidelsöhn's work was hung. Rowland offered the artist his hand. The artist bowed as he took it. He seemed about thirty, but there was an intensity to his face, a gravitas in his demeanour. He addressed Rowland in English. "Mr. Negus, how do you do? Fräulein Greenway has said much of you."

"How do you do, Mr. von Eidelsöhn." He introduced Eva in German.

"I must say, Mr. Negus, you speak German very well," von Eidelsöhn noted, after greeting Eva.

"Oh, Robbie can speak just about anything," Edna said, as she sat down. "It's handy, you know. We travel so much in search of undiscovered masterpieces."

Rowland smiled. Apparently the sculptress had settled into the role of art dealer. He had never known Edna to do anything with half her heart.

Von Eidelsöhn shifted uncomfortably. "I do not create

masterpieces," he said. "For who can say such a thing exists? I create pieces which, like the world, have no meaning."

"Of course, Hans," Edna said brightly. "Champagne?" She beamed as the waiter rushed over to charge her glass. "You're clairvoyant, Robbie. We must celebrate our discovery of Mr. von Eidelsöhn."

"He's a Dadaist," Clyde whispered into Rowland's ear as the gentlemen sat and Milton called for more champagne.

Rowland's left brow rose slightly. Dada was a movement born of the human horror of the Great War, its adherents rejecting society and all its traditions. Their artwork was unconventional, to say the least. It often offended the general public, and it infuriated the Nazis. He glanced at Edna and she met his eye and laughed.

Milton and Clyde sat in the generous armchairs of the Hindenberg suite, papers spread out on the coffee table between them. They looked up as Rowland walked in, after seeing Eva home.

"What are you chaps reading?" Rowland asked, removing his coat and hanging it and his hat on the hooks by the door.

"We're not actually reading anything," Milton said, raising his glass. "Clyde got it into his head that we should have a look at that police report Richter gave us."

Rowland sat down. "It's in German."

"Yes, we worked that out."

Rowland picked up the police report and scanned it. "It says that Bothwell drowned while swimming at dusk in the Starnberger See…"

"So it was an accident. Hardy's imagining things," said Clyde.

Rowland frowned. "It does seem a bizarre time to go for a swim." He stopped, scrutinising the report again for a moment before he added, "And without swimming trunks."

"What?"

"Says here, he was naked. His clothes were neatly folded on the bank, but he was naked."

Clyde folded his arms. "That's odd."

"And rather cold, I would imagine."

"If you're alone..." Milton murmured. He upended the envelope and let the contents fall out onto the table: a platinum signet ring bearing a Masonic rule and compass, and a watch. "These must be Bothwell's."

Rowland picked up the watch. A Rolex. An inscription on the back identified it as a wedding gift from Bothwell's wife. He shook his head, turning it over to look at the face. The glass was misted. Rowland tried to wind it, but the winder seemed to have seized. "Look at this," he said, handing the watch to Clyde.

Clyde held it up to the light, and then, after using a pocket knife to open the case, he examined the workings. "It's rusted."

"That's rather peculiar, don't you think?" Rowland said. "That Bothwell would fold his clothes on the bank and wear his watch swimming."

Clyde agreed. "You would have thought the police would notice that."

Rowland looked again at the police report. "They didn't."

"There are two reasons why he might not have taken off his watch, Rowly," Milton cautioned. "Maybe someone killed him, or perhaps the poor bloke had his own problems."

"But, in either case, why would he take off his clothes?" Clyde said, as he put the watch back together.

Rowland rubbed his hair. "We might just see if we can find out what Bothwell was doing when he died. He was staying at Richter's house. We'll start with him...after I talk to Göring?"

"Who's Göring?"

Rowland told them then of his meeting with Blanshard and what the Old Guard agent wished him to do.

For a moment they both gaped at him. "Rowly, you did tell him to go to hell, didn't you?"

"No, I said I'd do it."

"Are you insane?" Clyde slammed down his drink. "You're going to walk up to the brother of one of Hitler's henchmen and tell him you're a spy, and then ask for his help?"

Rowland replied calmly. "Apparently, Albert Göring is not a Nazi. According to Blanshard, he despises Hitler and has been speaking out against the regime. They think he might be sympathetic."

"And if they're wrong?"

"I'm not asking Albert Göring to betray his country…just to help me stop Nazism from infecting mine."

Clyde dropped his head into his hands. "Oh, Rowly."

Reaching into his jacket, Rowland pulled out the copy of *Der Stürmer* he had taken to his meeting with Blanshard. He tossed it onto the table between his friends. "Look at that," he said quietly. "You don't need to read German to understand the illustrations. And that's just the tip of it."

As Clyde and Milton bent over *Der Stürmer*, both incredulous of and repelled by the depictions of Jews in its caricatures, Rowland translated the vile headlines. And he recounted Blanshard's concern over Campbell's proposed manuscript.

"Australia's got no problem with Jews," Milton said angrily. "The flaming Governor General's a Jew. We aren't like the Germans…there's no way we'd buy into this."

Rowland ran a hand through his hair. "I don't know, Milt. Perhaps Campbell won't use the Jews…perhaps he'll decide to blame the Catholics, or the trade unions or the artists. For all we know, he could decide the Chinese are responsible for the bloody Depression."

"I don't think the Nazis like any of them, either." Clyde pulled away from the open newspaper. "Von Eidelsöhn says they've been rounding up artists and union men into re-education camps."

"Re-education?"

"Teaching them how to be good little fascists, I suppose."

Rowland said nothing, as he waited for Clyde and Milton

to realise that approaching Albert Göring was worth the risk.

"You're determined to do this, Rowly?" Clyde asked finally.

"I think I should."

Milton stood. "Then we'd better take some precautions."

"What do you mean?"

"If Albert Göring decides to report you, then presumably the Nazis will try to arrest you…if they can find you."

"Go on."

"We leave here. Go somewhere where we won't be so easily found."

Clyde agreed. "We don't need to check out of the hotel, just not be here, in case things go wrong."

Rowland sat back. "I think I may be ahead of you. We're going to stay by the Starnberger See for a couple of days."

"Since when?"

"Since I mentioned the idea to Eva this morning." He smiled apologetically. "She cornered me into promising, I'm afraid…I wasn't actually thinking about hiding, just going to the lake."

Milton grinned. "Sounds like she's set her cap for you, Rowly."

Rowland laughed. "No, I believe the poor girl's just dreadfully lonely. In fact, I suspect she's involved with a married man. He doesn't seem to have a lot of time for her."

Clyde raised his brow. "There's no reason she shouldn't come, I suppose. If we do need to leave Germany in a hurry, she can just return to Munich. Still, Rowly, getting involved may not be a good idea."

"As opposed to everything else we're doing?"

Clyde sighed. "You have a point."

"Are you thinking about using Richter's villa on this lake?" Milton asked.

Rowland nodded. "I have the keys but I'll mention it tomorrow when I speak to him about Bothwell's movements. I recall he said it had a telephone, so Blanshard will be able to reach us if he needs me to do anything further."

"Or to warn us to run," Milton added ominously.

Chapter Eleven

THE GERMAN PROBLEM
HITLER AND HIS CONSORTS

BY PROFESSOR A. H. CHARTERIS

January 30, 1933, is the beginning of the year one in the Third German Reich—an era born of political intrigue, on which light is thrown by recent information from Europe.

Captain Hermann Goering is Minister without portfolio in charge of Aviation for the Reich and now, according to the recent advices, Premier in Prussia. Alone among the German Nazis, he is reputed to command the respect and friendship of Mussolini, whom he is at present visiting in Rome. A Bavarian by birth, he has just turned forty. During the war he served in the German flying corps, and was leader of the "Richthofen Circus" famous on the Somme. After the war, such was his love of flying, he entered the Air Services of Denmark and of Sweden.

In 1922 he attended some classes at the University of Munich, where he met Hitler, took part in the Putsch, and escaped, with wounds, to live for a time in exile at first in Austria and afterwards in Italy. In 1925 he returned to Sweden, and it was there, in 1927, that he was called home to Germany to join the great Hitler undertaking. He was elected to the Reichstag in 1928. He is the strong silent man of the Hitler movement. Blessed with what the Germans call a "cold head", he never loses his temper, however furiously the heathen may rage.

—The Sydney Morning Herald, 1933

Edna drew her legs up onto the couch, wrapping her arms about her shins and resting her chin on her knees. "I'd best come with you."

"You'd what?" Rowland looked up, startled.

The sculptress had knocked on his door that morning at some ungodly hour. He'd still been asleep. She had called down for tea and coffee and pastries, while he'd showered and dressed, and for a while they'd shared breakfast without speaking of what he was about to do.

She knew, of course. Milton had told her when she'd eventually returned after dining with Von Eidelsöhn.

"I'd better come with you…when you call on Herr Göring."

"Absolutely not!"

She held up the information that Blanshard had secreted in the copy of *Der Stürmer*. "It says here that the Görings are aristocrats of sorts…or that they think they are."

"Yes, but…"

She smiled knowingly at him. "Men, particularly gentlemen, are more likely to act heroically in the presence of a lady, Rowly."

He shook his head. "No. It's too dangerous."

"You're just proving my point."

"You will not talk me into this, Ed."

She reached out and grabbed his hand. "Rowly, darling, I am in no less danger waiting for you than with you. Take me. I can help you convince him."

For a fleeting moment Rowland wavered, because her hand felt so natural in his and he found it hard to refuse her anything. "No…I've already put you in harm's way. It's not—"

"Take her, Rowly." Clyde walked in, in his robe and slippers. "She could be right. We all know Ed can get you to do just about anything she wants. Perhaps she'll be able to do the same to poor Albert."

"You can't be serious!" Rowland said, aghast that cautious Clyde would side with Edna on this.

"He's not going to attack her, Rowly. You'll be there, for one thing."

"And if he decides to call the police?"

"If he does, then we're all in a bit of bother anyway, regardless of whether Ed is with you or not. We're hardly going to leave you here, are we?" Clyde yawned and rubbed his head. "The moment you walk out of there, we all have to disappear for a while, anyway. If you think Göring would prefer to talk to you alone, then speak German…but Ed makes sense. Let her remind him to be heroic."

The private hotel in Ludwigstrasse was small, but clearly catered to men of consequence and wealth. Surrounded by a hedge of pine trees, it spoke of elegance and discretion. The staff were present but unobtrusive and the appointments tastefully lavish. It was here that Albert Göring stayed when he was in Munich.

Rowland had decided that the easiest way to gain a private audience with Göring was to simply check into the hotel, and take whatever opportunity arose. Edna's presence allowed them to pose as young newlyweds honeymooning in Munich. They checked in as M. and Mme. Marcel of Paris. Once again taking her role to heart, Edna decided to speak exclusively in French. She told the impressively multilingual hotel manager all about her wedding as Rowland requested a room on the uppermost floor where, according to Blanshard's information, Göring also had his suite.

"The honeymoon suite is situated on the ground floor, Monsieur Marcel. It has an exquisite private courtyard attached. The rooms on the top floor are also very comfortable but—"

"My wife has a preference for views from a height," Rowland interrupted. "I like to give her whatever she wants."

"Oh, darling, you are sweet," Edna crooned, reaching up to kiss his cheek, allowing her lips to linger and sliding her hand under his jacket in a manner that left the manager in no doubt as to why Rowland was happy to indulge her.

"Well, if Madame insists." He moved quickly to assign the room they requested and promptly remove them from the foyer before the scandalous display was repeated.

A bottle of champagne was delivered immediately to the suite, with the manager's compliments.

The moment they were alone, Edna fell into the chair, giggling. Rowland smiled. "You're incorrigible, Ed. I thought he was going to ask us to leave."

"We're married, Rowly...not to mention French."

"That much was clear."

Edna removed her gloves. "He was a bit stuffy, wasn't he? Didn't seem the least bit interested in my wedding."

"I can't imagine why." Rowland sat down beside her. "Are you ready?"

"Do you suppose he's in?"

"Only one way to find out. I believe his suite's at the end of the hallway."

Edna took a deep breath. "Let's go."

The man who opened the door to the suite at the hall's end was dark featured. What hair remained in the fringe encircling his head was black. He was smartly dressed, his suit the latest double-breasted cut, and his moustache was waxed to two pert points.

"Herr Göring?" Rowland asked, extending his hand.

"The same," Göring replied, accepting the handshake cautiously. "Do I know you?"

"Rowland Sinclair, Herr Göring."

Edna glanced at him sharply, startled by his use of his real name. He took her hand reassuringly and continued. "This is Fräulein Edna Higgins. We haven't met before, but I was hoping we might talk."

Göring stared at them for a moment, and then he stood back. "You, I might turn away, but Fräulein Higgins is a rare find. Come in, come in."

He invited them to sit and spoke to Edna, as he inserted a cigarette into a short Bakelite cigarette-holder. "You are an actress. You would like to be a star."

Of course, as he was speaking German, Edna had no idea what he was saying. She told him so in French.

Göring smiled and repeated himself in fluent French.

Edna returned his smile warmly. "Yes, I am an actress… Well, I have been, but I'm not a star, by any means."

"Not yet, my dear, but with the right part, you shall be." He placed a finger under her chin and turned her face to profile. "Why, you are exquisite from every angle!"

"*Merci beaucoup*, Monsieur Göring," Edna said, a little confused. "Are you an actor?"

"I'm a filmmaker, *ma chère*, but you know that…it is why you are here."

"I'm afraid it isn't," Rowland interrupted, now also speaking French.

Göring's eyes narrowed. "Who exactly are you? Why have you come here?"

"I am given to understand, Monsieur Göring, that you have been outspoken in your opposition to the Reich and to Chancellor Hitler?" Rowland kept his gaze on Göring's.

Göring stiffened. "Are you a Nazi? Has that obnoxious idiot Röhm sent you to intimidate me? I assure you, it will not work."

"No, sir, we are not Nazis. The contrary, in fact. We are trying to prevent the spread of the Nazi regime."

"What do you want, Monsieur Sinclair?"

"I want you to persuade your brother to cancel a meeting."

"A meeting? What meeting?"

"Tomorrow, your brother, Hermann, has an appointment with Colonel Eric Campbell from Australia. He must *not* meet him."

"Why? Is this man dangerous?"

"Not to your brother, Monsieur Göring, but to Australia, he could be very dangerous."

Göring pulled back. "What has this got to do with Hermann?"

"Colonel Campbell is a great admirer of Adolf Hitler," Rowland replied, watching the man intently. "He is here to learn from the Reich…to bring its ideals back to Australia."

"And you think he will stop just because he does not meet with Hermann?" Göring snorted.

"Probably not. But if he does not have the chance to make an ally of your brother, perhaps he will not take the same road."

Göring studied Rowland thoughtfully, absently twirling the end of his moustache. "Tell me about this Campbell. What kind of man is he?"

Evenly, and as fairly as he was able, Rowland recounted what he knew of the New Guard Commander, the radical right-wing organisation that Campbell led and what they had already tried to do. Edna interrupted when she thought that Rowland was being too fair, with an invective about the lengths to which Campbell was willing to go. She told Göring of Australia's Fascist Legion, and of how they operated as cloaked and hooded thugs to silence the enemies of the New Guard with violence.

Once Edna began, it was difficult to pull her back and Göring was a close and quiet audience. Her voice became strained and tearful as she spoke of how the Legion had branded Milton with the word "Red" and then nearly beaten Rowland to death.

Rowland let her go. He had not realised how angry she still was over what the New Guard's henchmen had done.

"And the Jews?" Göring asked when she had finished. "What is this Monsieur Campbell's stance on the Jews?"

"I don't know," Rowland admitted. "I have never heard him utter anything anti-Semitic."

Göring rubbed his chin. "My brother, Hermann, was not anti-Semitic either until he got involved with Hitler." He sighed. "All that we have, all that we are, we owe to Hermann's Jewish godfather. Without his generosity we would not have known a roof over our heads as children!" Albert Göring shook his head. "But you are asking me to deceive my brother…to betray him."

Rowland said nothing. It was what he was asking.

"Do you have a brother, Monsieur Sinclair?"

"Yes."

"Are you friends, your brother and you?"

"Not always."

"Would you undermine your own brother like this?"

Rowland shrugged. "Often Wil has accused me of doing just that, Monsieur…I do what I must, as does he, I suppose. Sometimes we stand together; at other times we are opposed. On the issue of Campbell, we are together."

For a while Göring smoked wordlessly.

Rowland broke the silence. "You are opposed to your brother's involvement with the Nazis, Monsieur, that is no secret. At the moment Eric Campbell's putsch for power has stalled. All I want to do is ensure that he and his supporters do not regain momentum."

"How do I know you are telling me the truth? You are asking me to trust the word of a stranger. How do I know that you are not working with Röhm or Himmler to discredit Hermann through me?"

Rowland hesitated, flustered. "I don't know how you would know that, but I am not."

Göring smiled. "Did you hope to persuade me with a heart-felt plea?"

"Yes…I suppose I did."

Göring laughed. "Naivety in a spy. I like it. But it might get you killed." He looked hard at Rowland. "This is what we are going to do, Monsieur. I will call upon this man Campbell and I will talk to him. If he is the man you say, with the ambitions you speak of, then I will speak with my brother. If he is not, you should probably expect a visit from the police tomorrow."

Rowland exhaled slowly. "I cannot ask more."

"But I can ask more." Göring leaned forward. "And I do. If I find myself doing as you ask, then I will expect something in return."

"What exactly?"

"I do not know yet. I, too, am trying to save my homeland from the Nazis. I fear that one day just protecting our own countries will not be enough. There may come a time when I will need something from you."

Rowland met Göring's eyes. It seemed fair. "You have my word, Monsieur Göring."

Rowland shut the door. Edna was already pouring the champagne. She handed him a glass.

"What do you think, Rowly?"

"He's a decent chap. I just hope he can see through Campbell." Rowland went to the window. In the drive below he could just make out Albert Göring climbing into a light blue Mercedes saloon. The filmmaker was wasting no time.

"Why did you tell him our real names?" Edna asked, as she came to stand beside him.

He put his arm around her. "I'm sorry, Ed…I should have warned you somehow. It just occurred to me that if it all goes to hell and we need to get out of Germany, the passports we entered the country with say Robert Negus and Millicent Greenway."

Edna sipped her champagne, smiling. "You might make a spy after all, Rowly."

M. and Mme. Marcel checked out on the same day that they arrived. Edna resumed her role as the spoiled newlywed with aplomb, declaring that the hotel's top floor was just not high enough for her liking. "I want to know the whole world is below us when we make love, darling," she announced loudly as she played with the buttons on Rowland's waistcoat.

Rowland winced, apologised, and settled the account. The mortified manager did not try to persuade them to stay.

Edna maintained the charade in the taxi ride back to the Vier Jahreszeiten. For what reason, Rowland was unsure. Perhaps it amused her to publicly challenge his sense of decorum. To be truthful, he was rather enjoying the artifice, however forward and improper.

When the Marcels alighted at the Vier Jahreszeiten, the taxi driver was utterly convinced they were French.

Alastair Blanshard was waiting for them in the salon, as arranged. They joined him in a private booth in the corner from which they could see anyone who entered the bar. It was still too early for the midday rush and so they were almost alone.

"Well?" Blanshard asked, as soon as Rowland had introduced Edna.

"He's going to speak to Campbell," Rowland replied quietly. "If he concludes we are telling the truth, he'll do what he can. If not, he'll call the police."

Blanshard nodded. "Good show. Campbell will hear the name Göring and be more than eager to tell him how the New Guard isn't giving an inch to the Left…Still, it's a jolly good thing you're heading out of the city, just in case. I'll keep my ear to the ground and telephone as soon as I hear anything."

Alois Richter was delighted that they intended to use his villa.

"A woman from the village keeps it clean and aired even when I am not there," he said, when Rowland and Edna called in. "I'm sure you will be very comfortable." The tailor pulled out a map and told them of the walks and sights which surrounded the lake. "You must have a look at Berg Castle," he said, tapping the paper. "Built by Bavaria's beloved mad king…a romantic vision which I am sure Miss Higgins will enjoy."

Rowland then broached the subject of the rust and moisture in Bothwell's watch. Richter became visibly distressed. "This is terrible, Mr. Negus. You are saying that Peter's death might not have been an accident? Oh, my poor friend…"

"I don't know, Mr. Richter, but it does seem odd that he would wear his watch swimming. Did the investigating police not find it unusual?"

Richter removed his purple fez and stroked the half-dozen strands of hair that had been painstakingly grown to a length that would comb over the otherwise bare terrain on the top of his skull. "The police!" he spat. "Incompetent fools! Who knows who their masters are!" He paused to soothe Stasi, though the dog showed no signs of agitation—indeed, it showed no signs at all. "I thought that Peter might have been troubled, that he was keeping something from me." He sat down and, passing Stasi to Edna, he buried his face in his hands. "Oh, if only I had pressed him, talked to him, instead of coming back to Munich to deal with orders!"

"What makes you think he was troubled, Mr. Richter?"

"Telephone calls and meetings late at night." Richter hesitated and then whispered. "I thought perhaps money troubles…or a woman. I thought he would tell me, his old friend, in time, and so I didn't ask. I did not suspect his problems were so great."

"Who found Peter Bothwell?" Rowland asked.

"A patrol of boys from the Hitler Youth. They were hiking around the lake."

"I see."

"Your cousin, Mrs. Bothwell, will be made only more sad by this discovery, I think," Richter said sombrely. "I am afraid, Mr. Negus, you will return to her not only her husband's possessions, but more sorrow."

Rowland caught himself, remembering that he was supposed to be a distant relative, here only to collect Bothwell's effects. It would not do to sound like an investigator. He changed the subject. "We are grateful for your hospitality, Mr. Richter. We are all looking forward to a few days at Starnberger See."

Richter smiled. "You will be enchanted by the lake, young people. If I can get away, I will come down myself to have a meal with you, provided you can tolerate the company of a poor old man."

Edna draped the flaccid Stasi over her lap. "We will look forward to it." She smiled mischievously at Rowland. "But you must promise to bring Stasi…Robbie will teach him to fetch."

Richter beamed. "Of course, of course…Did you hear that, Stasi? Aren't you excited, my love?"

Rowland stroked the dog as it lay inert on Edna, primarily to check it was still breathing.

"So, my friends," Richter said, sitting back watching Stasi like a proud father, "when do you plan to leave?"

"Soon," Rowland replied. "I'll have to check the trains."

"Trains…no, no. You must take one of my automobiles. Can you drive? Will you need a chauffeur?"

"You're very kind, Herr Richter, but we couldn't—"

"Nonsense!" Richter would not hear no. Apparently, he had a stable of motor cars, though he rarely drove himself. When Rowland saw the brand new Mercedes-Benz 380S roadster, he relented.

Chapter Twelve

ALL THE FUN OF THE FAIR
The Surrealists' Leg Pull
BY M.J. MACNALLY

...Of course there are cults, societies, brotherhoods—
call them what you will—such as Dadaists, Symbolists,
Surrealists, Aesthetes, Parnassians, Symbolists, and a
hundred and one other names, who on the European side
are continually popping up, doing a stunt, and then fading
out in a blaze of fireworks...the same old stunts, cigar bands,
and matchboxes pasted on the canvas with girls covered
with spots carrying cabbages, raving about 'pattern' ...dear
old London 'falls' for it, just as it 'falls' for anything bizarre
or freakish. It is truly the home of the chestnut.

Here in Australia we are very lucky. We get very little
of this Continental hysteria. Occasionally an artistic 'con.
man' will come to light with a freakish landscape of the
'pattern' and 'design' he has seen in reproductions and,
getting hold of a group of moneyed people, will hypnotise
them into the belief that he is something new and a modern
John preaching in the wilderness. ...There was a group of
young men some years ago in Sydney who called themselves
"Dada-melodists," or some such name, and who set out to
produce pictures that were tone melodies. A colour would
represent a note and they had a scale of pigments, each with
its corresponding noise. While obvious notoriety seekers,
there was a certain amount of sincerity about them. One

was the son of a distinguished musician, and he it was who really started the affair and lectured on the system.

One day he arrived at the office of a newspaper and wanted some publicity. "Well," said the materialistic chief of staff, "what is it all about?" "It's like this," replied the artist. "You see this picture?" (producing an oil painting from under his coat). "Well, this is the light house at Kiama," which was red (it was really white). "This is the sea," which was pink. "This is the cliff, and this is the grass," which was blue, and the sky was magenta. "What does it all mean?" said the journalist. "Well, it is a tone melody," said the artist, "and it goes like this." He stood up, held out the picture, and actually whistled the landscape. When we had simmered down from uncontrollable laughter, we bowed him out. He got publicity, all right, but not in the way he expected.

—The Mail, 1936

And so Edna and Rowland returned to the Vier Jahreszeiten in Alois Richter's Mercedes. Although Rowland noticed a similarity in style and handling, it was a later model than his beloved 1927 S-Class. And, unlike that flamboyant yellow tourer which waited for Rowland in Sydney, Richter's motor was a discreet black hardtop, with a full swing axle—the very latest in modern engineering. Rowland enjoyed driving the 380S, though it did leave him feeling vaguely adulterous.

Milton and Clyde were, of course, able to be entirely enthusiastic about Richter's automobile without the burden of loyalty. Very soon, Clyde had disappeared beneath the lifted hood to examine the engine. Edna went up to the hotel suite to ensure the porters brought down the correct bags, which Rowland and Milton then packed into the trunk themselves, much to the disapproval of the concierge. The biggest bag was stuffed with canvasses, paints, and brushes.

"Where did these come from?" Rowland rummaged eagerly through the painting supplies.

"Von Eidelsöhn," Milton replied. "Thought you and Clyde might like to dip a brush while we're here. He was rather grateful that we purchased his work. Apparently, he hasn't been selling much since the Nazis took over."

Rowland still hadn't seen von Eidelsöhn's work. "These pieces you bought," he asked, "what are they like?"

Clyde snorted. "Mona Lisa with her hair bobbed, painted on the wrong side of a stretched canvas," he said tersely.

"The boy's a genius," Milton grinned. "He's created an insightful and laconic challenge to artistic traditionalism and idolatry. We also bought his sculpture of drought."

"Drought?"

"It's an empty bucket, Rowly," Clyde sighed. "A very expensive tin bucket."

Milton chuckled. "I'm sure Hardy and the Old Guard will be delighted with their new acquisitions."

The expenses of Robert Negus, and his party of art dealers were being met by an expense account funded by the New South Wales Graziers' Association.

"Von Eidelsöhn also paints some quite sane landscapes," Clyde muttered, "but Milt thought Hardy would relate to backwards-Mona Lisa."

The poet was unrepentant. "Just what the Australian Club needs to brighten up its panelled walls, I imagine. Never been in there, of course."

Rowland looked at Milton, laughing now. "You're trying to bankrupt the Graziers' Association with ridiculous artwork?"

"Bankrupt? No, Rowly, that's too ambitious. I'm just striking a blow for the worker."

Rowland leaned back on the Mercedes. "So where are they…von Eidelsöhn's pieces?"

"We shipped them directly to Hardy."

Rowland was still laughing when the doorman came out to advise that there was a telephone call for Robert Negus. He took the call in the foyer rather than return to his suite. It was, as he expected, Eva. He told her what had been planned, and arranged to collect her on their way through. Although she had phoned much earlier than expected, Eva seemed anxious that they depart as soon as possible.

The address she gave them was for an apartment in an older part of Munich.

Rowland pulled up at the building.

"I'll only be a minute," he said, as he opened the door.

"Just hope she doesn't want you to meet her parents first," Milton called after him.

Eva opened the door as soon as he knocked. The apartment behind her was a tastefully furnished family home. The walls were adorned with framed photographs of Eva and other young women who Rowland presumed were her sisters. The largest frame, however, held the brooding likeness of Germany's Chancellor. Eva was apparently the only one home. She had on her hat and gloves, and a small suitcase waited by the door. She didn't invite him in. "Shall we go? I do not want to make you late."

"Don't you have to let anyone know where you'll be?"

"They shall think I am with Herr Wolf," she said. "I do not want them to know he has no time for me."

Rowland hesitated. "Are you sure? I wouldn't want your… anyone to be worried about you."

"You are kind, Herr Negus, but you must not worry. I often go away with friends. My parents are in Berlin right now, but they would be happy to know that I am enjoying myself, for once, instead of waiting by the telephone." She looked at him anxiously. "Please do not say you have changed your mind."

Rowland reached in and picked up her bag. "Of course not, Fräulein Eva."

Her face relaxed and, beaming, she took the arm he offered.

It took a little over an hour to find Richter's villa near the town of Berg, by the Starnberger See. They approached through a screen of natural woodland; the light of late afternoon speared through pillars of grey-barked birch to give the leaves a gentle incandescence. The building was, if anything, more impressive than the one in which Richter lived in Munich. Classically Bavarian, its walls were white, and seamed with dark external timbers. Its steeply pitched roof was shingled. Every window sat above a window box which hosted a mass of spring blooms, and looked out upon the crystal waters of the lake. A fat horse with a braided tail was tethered to a tree.

Edna was delighted. "It's magical," she said stepping out of the car. She turned slowly, putting out her hand as if she was trying to catch one of the thin shafts of light.

"There's a castle in Berg, isn't there? Can you see it from here?" Rowland asked Eva.

She shook her head and pointed. "It's in that direction, but it's hidden by trees."

Rowland translated, though Edna seemed to have inferred the gist of it. She was disappointed.

"I love castles. It's a shame we don't have one or two at home."

Clyde rolled his eyes. "Just what New South Wales needs…"

Though Rowland did have a key, the door was opened by a taut-haired woman who introduced herself as Frau Engels. She explained that she lived in the village, where her husband worked in the post office, and so Herr Richter had been able to telephone and get a message to her. Of course, she came to the house immediately to light the fires and air the bedrooms, making sure she put extra blankets on the beds because the nights could still be very cold. She'd stocked the pantry, and cooked a hot meal, and she hoped they would be comfortable. And then she took a breath.

Rowland seized the pause to thank her and translate quickly before she started talking again. Which she did.

Frau Engels bustled them into the living room, directed the men to take their bags upstairs and explained that the cat was deaf, so there was no point shouting at it.

Rowland was not entirely sure why any of them would want to shout at the cat, but he translated faithfully. When they had finally been settled to her satisfaction, she began a verbose farewell, assuring them she would return to prepare breakfast the next day. Eventually she mounted the fat horse, and chattering to it now, rode off towards Berg.

"Bet the horse wishes it was deaf too," Milton said, as Edna picked up a small white cat. "Did she say what its name was?"

Rowland shook his head.

Edna held the feline up and looked into its eyes. "What are we going to call you, then, sweetheart?"

"It's deaf," Clyde murmured. "I don't suppose it matters."

They sat down to the meal of roast pork and dumplings which Frau Engels had prepared and set out, and talked easily of inconsequential matters. Rowland, necessarily, didn't say a great deal on his own account as he translated between Eva and the others. Edna and Milton had picked up a few German words, but Clyde could not yet tell one word from another, let alone remember what they meant.

With dinner over, they retired to the sitting room. Clyde and Rowland rearranged the furniture to place the large card table closer to the fire, and Milton set a record on the gramophone. Eva ran upstairs to fetch the photographs she had developed for Edna.

For a time they examined the pictures: images of the *Southern Cross* and its crew, Maugham and Haxton at Raffles, and Karachi. And Eva was understandably curious about their travels.

"It must have been an old film," Rowland said, as she exclaimed over the pictures. "We did this trip some time ago." It was a minor and probably unnecessary deception, but Rowland opted for caution.

Milton produced a pack of cards and, armed with sherry, they taught Eva to play poker. She took to the game and the sherry enthusiastically, although Rowland remained unable to impart the art of bluffing, and her cards were apparent in the rise and fall of her face. He advised her in German as they played, which might have been unfair if it had had any impact whatsoever on the way she played.

She sang along when the recording took her fancy, imitating the low husky tones of Dietrich and standing to act out the words.

All this time, over the chatter and the music, Rowland was vigilant for the phone. By now, Albert Göring would have met with Campbell, and Blanshard might have been able to glean how that meeting had gone. They would not be in the clear for another day, but if Göring had called the police, Blanshard might have heard by now. Rowland was acutely aware that now Edna was as implicated as he. If worst came to worst, he would not even be able to claim she had no idea of his purpose in coming to Germany.

"Come on, Robbie, dance with me," Edna said, dragging him to his feet as Marlene Dietrich crooned a German version of "Falling in Love Again" from the gramophone.

"You mustn't worry," she whispered, in the privacy of his arms. "Even if Mr. Göring calls the police, it will take them a while to figure out where we've gone. Only Mr. Richter knows, and they have no reason to ask him."

He smiled at her. "Did I look worried?"

She laughed. "Not really. You're too good a card player for that…I just know you."

Rowland changed direction so that they didn't dance into the sofa.

Edna pressed into him. "If Mr. Göring goes to the police, we'll simply say that he misunderstood us. After all, we were speaking in languages that were not our own." She looked up at Rowland, her manner so sincere and innocent that he was tempted to believe that she could talk them both out of arrest.

Rowland assumed he was the only one awake. Certainly there was no sign of life from the other rooms. He could, however, hear singing from the kitchen downstairs. Frau Engels had returned, as she had promised. He elected to slip unannounced into the small sunroom. It was too early in the morning for the sheer volume of the housekeeper's conversation.

He had been there only a few minutes when Eva came in on tiptoe. Startled, she clasped one hand over her mouth when she saw him. He put a finger on his lips and shut the door behind her.

"Good morning," he said quietly.

She giggled. "You're hiding, too, Herr Negus?"

Rowland smiled. "I thought I'd wait for the others before I went in to breakfast."

"Of course." She sat and picked up the notebook he'd put down. "You're an artist," she said studying the sketch of Edna. "Herr Wolf, too, is an artist. I must show you some of the paintings he has made for me."

"He's an artist? Does he exhibit?"

"No…not anymore. He is too busy."

Her eyes darkened and Rowland suspected that Herr Wolf was often "too busy."

"It's difficult to make a living from painting alone," he said, more out of sympathy than any real knowledge of what it took to make a living.

"Oh, Herr Wolf could make a living—I am sure of it," Eva said fervently. "He is an extraordinary artist…I'm sure everybody would buy his works if he chose to sell them. Why, I sometimes feel like I could walk into his pictures and swim in his lakes."

Rowland's left brow arched. So this chap Wolf painted landscapes. Rowland tried not to hold that against him.

"I shall show you one day," she said. "I'm sure you will agree that he is a very talented man."

"I'm sure."

Eva chewed her fingernail. "Fräulein Greenway," she said, as she gazed at his latest study of the sculptress. "She is very beautiful."

"I think so."

"Is she your sweetheart, Herr Negus?"

Rowland laughed. "No, I'm afraid not."

She handed him back his notebook. "Do you not wish it?"

Rowland stopped for a moment. He slipped the notebook back into his jacket. "It's not really up to me."

"Oh." She looked at him intently. "You and I are alike, I think. We are not seen by those we love most."

Rowland smiled. He liked Eva, but she was a trifle histrionic. "I think everyone should be up by now. Shall we go in to breakfast?'

Chapter Thirteen

NUDE CULT
Banned In Germany

BERLIN, Tuesday

Captain Göring has prohibited the nude cult, which has hundreds of thousands of adherents, as the greatest danger to culture and morality.

He declared it was killing women's natural modesty and men's respect for women. Public displays of the no clothes movement would not be tolerated.

—*The Canberra Times*, 1933

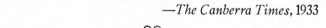

They stayed close to the house. Campbell was to meet with Hermann Göring at one o'clock. Until then they would not know if their plea to his brother had been successful.

The day was warm and Eva became quite impatient to go swimming. She begged like a child, but they could not risk missing the telephone call. When at one o'clock Blanshard still hadn't called, Eva decided that she would go on ahead alone, promising to stay on the shore just down from the house. Unable to explain why they all needed to stay, Rowland agreed. As much as Eva seemed childlike at times, she was an adult and it was broad daylight. As it was, Blanshard telephoned only minutes after she left.

The Old Guard agent apologised for not calling earlier. "I couldn't get away from Eric. He's a little despondent. It seems his meeting with Mr. Göring was cancelled at the very last moment."

Rowland breathed, relieved. "Well, that's capital. We can return to the Munich, then?"

"You could, but I won't need you for a few days at least. The Colonel and Mrs. Campbell are taking a tour with the BUF people."

"BUF?" Rowland smiled at Edna to let her know everything had gone well.

"British Union of Fascists…Mosley's mob. They're running this tour of Europe's fascist states. Anyway, Negus, you and your young lady have earned a couple of days' leave. Campbell won't be doing anything but meeting a few minor Nazis for a few days. You're at the Starnberger See, aren't you?…Enjoy yourself."

"Thank you, Blanshard, we might just do that. Before you go, could you tell me something?"

"Certainly."

"I don't suppose you know if Bothwell was involved with a woman over here?"

"He's married."

"Even so."

For a moment there was silence and then, "Perhaps…One of the Brits mentioned some woman called Nancy…a journalist from one of the American papers."

"The Brits?"

"We're not the only people with agents here, Negus. It was just gossip. I dismissed it. Why do you ask?"

"Just wondering what he was doing in that lake."

Rowland heard Blanshard sigh, and then swear. "This is Hardy's doing, isn't it? He's already wired me with his ridiculous theories…Got some bee in his bonnet about avenging Bothwell, or some such thing!"

"You must admit the circumstances of Bothwell's death are a little odd."

Again there was a pause. "That may well be, Mr. Negus, but you should remember that Munich is not Sydney. Even if you do find something—some sort of foul play—what the hell are you going to do with that information?"

"I'm sure the police…"

"The police have already determined that it was an accident. They may have reasons for doing so. Bothwell was not here playing tiddlywinks, boy! Digging into this won't bring the man back—but it will compromise your position here… Or have you forgotten why you're in Munich?"

"No, I haven't."

"Then don't worry about Bothwell, and stay low. I'll be in touch." The telephone was slammed down.

Rowland replaced the receiver in its cradle.

"It worked, didn't it, Rowly?" Edna said excitedly the moment the line was cut.

"Göring cancelled his meeting with Campbell."

Edna squeezed his arm, delighted and triumphant.

"We're spies!" she proclaimed, curtseying as Clyde and Milton applauded their congratulations.

Rowland laughed. "It's probably not entirely spy-like to shout that out, Ed."

She waved him away. "It's just us."

Reminded of that fact, Rowland took the opportunity to tell them of what Blanshard had revealed and his demand that they not investigate any further.

"So we're going to let it go?" Clyde prompted.

Rowland shrugged. "I'm curious now."

Clyde sighed.

"I'll be careful," Rowland offered. "But while we're here anyway…"

"Someone should look into it," Edna said quietly. "Mr. Bothwell was an Australian. Even if it will achieve nothing, someone should find out what happened."

"Bravo, Miss Higgins!" Milton put his arm around Edna and kissed her forehead. "If we discreetly apply our intellects to the riddle of Bothwell's untimely passing, the solution will show itself and justice will prevail."

Clyde groaned. Milton was an avid reader of Conan Doyle. So much so that he occasionally appropriated the persona of Sherlock Holmes…without acknowledgement, of course.

"It can't hurt to keep our eyes open," Rowland said, nudging Clyde. He glanced at his watch. "I'd better go find Eva. I feel a bit bad about letting her go on her own."

"I'll come with you," Clyde said, resigned. "I've been wanting to paint the lake anyway."

"Milt and I will organise a picnic basket and meet you in a little while," Edna volunteered. "It's such a glorious day, it will be lovely by the water."

That settled, Rowland and Clyde gathered easels and canvas and set out for the lake's edge.

They found Eva suddenly, catching sight of her stretching out on a towel as they came over a rise.

Clyde stopped. "Good Lord!"

Eva turned immediately, having heard his exclamation. She sat up and waved.

"Is she—?" Clyde started.

"Naked?" Rowland said, taking a deep breath. "Yes. I believe so." Of course they'd seen naked women before. Aside from anything else, they had both painted nudes. But this was a public place and a little unexpected.

Eva beckoned them over.

"You go," Clyde said, prodding Rowland. "Find out what happened to her clothes."

Rowland glanced back at Eva, who was waiting for them with her hands on her hips. "I suppose I'd better."

He walked down to where she stood. "Fräulein Eva," he said tipping his hat. "I hope we're not intruding."

Eva stretched out again. "Don't be silly, Herr Negus. I am just sunbathing. Do people not sunbathe where you come from?"

"They do…"

She laughed and wagged her finger at him. "Do not pretend to be shy. I saw your book of pictures…"

He smiled. "I'm an artist, Fräulein Eva. I often use models."

She glanced over at Clyde, who was focussing on setting up the easels. "Perhaps I could be your model. Herr Wolf has drawn me once or twice."

Rowland's brow rose. "Like this?"

Eva giggled.

He stood back and looked at her. She was completely natural and comfortable without a stitch of clothing. Her figure was athletic, surprisingly muscular, and she held herself with the confidence of a woman who was pleased with her body. His eyes moved to the lake which reflected the surrounding violet mountains in the polished glass of its surface, capturing the world and the sky in a mirror image. It was breathtaking in its way, but still just a landscape. Having Eva model for him might not be such a bad idea. Let Clyde paint the trees.

"Would you be comfortable over there?" He pointed out a protrusion of smooth rock.

"But it's much prettier over here with the lake behind me," she protested.

"I'm painting you," he said, fetching one of the easels. "The light is rather more important than the lake."

Eva spread out her towel and settled on the rock. Rowland allowed her to pose naturally. She reclined on her side, her head in the crook of her arm.

Clyde set up his easel beside Rowland's, but facing the other way, towards the lake. He had relaxed now. Somehow Eva seemed less naked as a model. Rowland had a talent and preference for nudes, so unclothed women had always been a feature of his studio. Often it had been Edna who sat for him, but occasionally he would use another subject. Indeed, Clyde had first met his own sweetheart, Rosalina, when she'd posed for Rowland.

They hadn't been working long when Edna and Milton joined them, lugging a massive basket filled from the contents of the well-stocked larder in Richter's lakehouse. Edna wore a green spotted sundress, fitted at the waist and sleeveless.

Rowland looked up and waved as she appeared at the small rise which fortuitously afforded some minor privacy.

"Over here, Millie." He used the alias without hesitation now. Edna stopped, startled, as she realised what Rowland was painting, but the pause was very brief. She left the basket and came down to peer over his shoulder at the beginnings of the work.

Milton seemed more amused than anything else. "I'm not sure Blanshard would consider this discreet, old boy."

Rowland laughed without lifting his eyes from the canvas. Clyde had procured a basic palette of colours, and so Rowland began with a tonal sketch in sepia, painting in the long lines of Eva's body and the shadows. Edna stood by him, intrigued. Rowland painted often, but as she was usually his model, she rarely saw how he worked at this stage. This early rendering was almost sculptural. He worked with shapes, pushing and moulding the paint about the linen surface until an impression of Eva seemed to jump from the canvas.

"May I see?" Eva begged, sitting up.

Rowland shrugged. She had moved now, anyway, and he was hungry. They might as well stop for a spot of lunch.

Eva came around the easel, still comfortably naked among them. Her face dropped as she studied what he had done.

"She says it doesn't look a thing like her," Rowland translated smiling, as he rummaged through the picnic hamper.

Edna laughed. "Don't worry, Eva darling." She patted the

picnic blanket beside her, as Eva slipped on a robe. "It will. Robbie's very talented."

Rowland translated, expanding so much on Edna's affirmation of his talent that it was obvious and she took back the original compliment.

They ate lazily in the sunshine, enjoying the languid company—the normalcy, of sorts.

"Shall we go swimming?" Edna suggested gazing at the expansive stillness of the water.

Rowland shook his head. "The Starnberger See is a glacial lake, Millie. I expect the water will be rather cold."

Edna lay back on the blanket, smiling. "I didn't mean you, Robbie. It's impossible to drag you away from a painting. I thought Clyde might—"

"No," Clyde said, slapping his hat back on his head as he stood to return to his easel. "And you're not going in, either…I don't want you messing up my view with splashing and whatnot."

Thus forbidden from swimming for the sake of art, Edna remained on the blanket, reading and chatting with Milton, who could not swim, and in any case, had no wish to do so.

It was only when he observed the silence that Rowland noticed that the poet and the sculptress had drifted off. Possibly it was the sight of his friends asleep that made him realise that Eva had been posing for rather a long time.

"*Entschuldigung sie, Fräulein,*" he said regretfully. "I'm so sorry…You must need to stretch."

Eva winced as she sat up and moved her arms gingerly. Rowland poured her a glass of wine, and offered her his hand. "You must tell me when you're getting uncomfortable." He helped her to stand and handed her the glass. "I get a little forgetful of other things when I'm painting."

"Can I see my painting?"

"It won't be finished for a while yet," Rowland stood back to allow her access to his easel. "I'll have to wait for the paint to dry a bit before I can continue. In fact, I may have to ask you to sit for me when we get back to Munich."

Eva wasn't listening. She stood before the canvas, squealing in delight and clapping her hands.

"You like it, then?" Rowland asked, laughing.

"Herr Negus, this is wonderful. You have made me blue!"

Rowland had indeed painted her figure in the palest grey-blue. Like an eggshell. Though her body was fit and strong, she had seemed to him from the first, fragile. There was a sadness and a desperation in her eyes. He had not captured that yet. At the moment she was just a vulnerable, almost translucent figure clinging to the rock.

"Blue is my favourite colour, but how could you have known that, Herr Negus?"

Rowland toyed with the idea of explaining why he had painted her so, but decided it was unnecessary. Eva liked blue. That was good enough.

Clyde turned to look at the painting. He whistled low.

"What do you think?" Rowland asked. This was somewhat of a departure from his usual style, and he respected Clyde's opinion.

Clyde stared for a moment, his brawny arms folded. "You used up all the blue."

Rowland grimaced. It had been a little inconsiderate. Clyde was trying to paint a lake, after all.

Clyde sighed. "It was worth it, mate."

Chapter Fourteen

ANOTHER HITLER BAN
Handshaking Forbidden

BERLIN, Saturday

Herr Hitler has banned handshaking and has issued an order that in future all officials in Germany must greet one another by raising the right arm, a system hitherto only used by Nazis.

—*Sunday Times*, 1933

Frau Engels looked at them suspiciously as she tethered her horse. "You have risen early, gentlemen," she said, her reproving gaze fixed unrelentingly upon them.

"Herr Greenway and I thought we might go for an early morning drive." Rowland was a little relieved the housekeeper had arrived before they left. At least Eva would have someone to talk to in his absence. "Our companions are still asleep. They will be glad to awaken to your fine cooking, Frau Engels."

The compliment seemed to soothe her a little. She shook her head. "I will not ask what you two young men are up to. I can only guess. My sons are about your age and they have turned me graveyard blond with their antics." She pointed at her white hair in its tight, efficient bun. "And here I am, cooking potato pancakes and cherry cake for breakfast…"

Rowland glanced at Milton. They knew by now that they would have to interrupt or the woman would never stop talking.

"If we depart straight away we might be able to get back for your excellent breakfast, Frau Engels, so we might just say good-bye right now.…"

Milton started the engine and though Frau Engels had not stopped talking, Rowland could at least now pretend not to hear her. He climbed into the Mercedes and waved as they drove out.

They set out for the place where, according to the police report Richter had given them, Peter Bothwell had drowned. Rowland was not sure why he wanted to see it. Surely, there would be nothing there now. Still, they were here. If nothing else, they could pay their respects.

He'd intended to go alone, but Milton, keen to sleuth, had insisted on accompanying him.

"Hello…what's this about?" Milton muttered, as they passed through the town of Berg. Though it was still early, the streets were lively.

Rowland craned his head out of the window as Milton slowed. "It's the SA," he said, identifying the brown-and-black uniform. Members were pasting posters on shop windows and distributing pamphlets. "Give me a second."

Swinging open his door, Rowland jogged over to the nearest poster. He was back in moments.

"What's going on?"

"A book-burning in Munich."

"A what?"

"A book-burning…like a witch-burning, except with books, I suppose. The SA is inviting the masses."

Milton shook his head. "So what books are they planning to burn?"

"The poster refers to books that are corrupting the nation."

"Sounds racy."

The road was now blocked by a gathering of Brownshirts, chanting against Jewish intellectualism. Rowland didn't bother to translate.

Milton gunned the engine, sounded the horn and moved the car forward, forcing the men to make way. The Storm-troopers shouted and cursed. Milton ignored them. As soon as the way was sufficiently clear, Milton accelerated.

The site of Peter Bothwell's death was on a more secluded part of the lake, away from the road and the villages. Milton parked Richter's Mercedes and they walked down to the water's edge. Rowland pointed out the pine tree described in the police report, under which Richter's clothes were found, neatly folded.

"What do you think, Rowly?"

Rowland looked out at the lake. There was barely a ripple in its surface. The spot was protected by trees but, unless there had been a full moon that night, it would have been very dark...and cold. He had noticed some Germans swimming in the Starnberger See, but they were locals. Bothwell had been Australian and it had been a month ago. "It seems an odd place and time to go bathing, Milt, even if it were a romantic tryst. I can think of things I'd much rather do with a woman."

Milton grinned. "Would have been too dark to paint, Rowly."

"That's not what I meant."

"Glad to hear it."

"It's a bit of a distance from the lakehouse." Rowland glanced at his watch. It had taken them twenty minutes to drive there. "Bothwell was on foot...It would have taken him rather more than an hour to walk. There're plenty of places near the house...Why would he come here?"

"The boy scouts, or whatever they were, who found him..." Milton started casting his eyes about for a walking track. "Where exactly did they see him?"

"The Hitler Youth. I'm not sure. The statements say they

were hiking around the lake and they came across a man's body floating face-down somewhere here."

Milton shook his head. "Poor little blighters…probably scared them senseless."

"To be honest," said Rowland, recalling the witness statements from the children, "they seemed to find it more exciting than anything else. They assumed the corpse had been with the *Gemeinschaft der Eigenen*. They were less than sympathetic, to tell you the truth."

"The Gemein-what?"

Rowland shifted uncomfortably. "*Gemeinschaft der Eigenen*. It's a men's movement—rather popular in the twenties, though not so much now. They like to think they're Spartan warriors."

"And what does that entail, exactly?"

"Well, as far as I can tell, they're rather keen on each other, and they run around the mountains naked, singing songs and being men."

"Sounds cold."

"Yes…very."

"Poor Bothwell. Kind of an ignoble end."

Rowland nodded. It was. He wondered if Bothwell's wife and boys would ever see the police report. If nothing else, that was a reason to find out what really happened.

"You! What is your business here?" The shout was in Bavarian but both Rowland and Milton turned towards it. At first they saw only one large man striding over from where they'd parked the car. And then five others joined him. They wore the brown-shirted uniforms of Nazi Stormtroopers—the SA.

Rowland was wary. It appeared they had been followed from Berg. The SA were brutish thugs, swelled with a sense of their own importance into bloated, volatile bullies.

"We are enjoying a view of the Starnberger See, *mein Herr*," he said calmly.

The Stormtroopers stood before them now. Their leader looked hard at Milton, lower jaw thrust out so that his chin protruded just a little from the fleshy flaps of his jowls. "Who are you?"

"Mr. Greenway is an Australian," Rowland said quickly. "He does not speak German. I am Robert Negus, also from Australia."

"Australia…never heard of it!" The Stormtroopers seemed to think that was funny.

Rowland said nothing, though he was becoming irritated.

"What is your business here?" The question was sharper now, a threat.

"We are taking in the view," Rowland repeated evenly.

"We do not like the look of you."

"We don't think you're very pretty either."

One of the Brownshirts laughed. The troop leader pushed Rowland backwards.

"Hey!" Milton flared, lunging for the man. The Brownshirt reacted quickly, pulling a truncheon from his belt and clouting Milton across the head. The poet stumbled, dazed.

"Stop!" Rowland reached out and grabbed the upraised arm before the truncheon could fall again. The other Brownshirts had now also pulled out their truncheons. "Would you like to see our papers, gentlemen?" Rowland forced deference. The Stormtroopers were spoiling for a fight and he and Milton were grossly outnumbered.

The Brownshirt pulled back. He smiled faintly. "Yes."

Rowland reached inside his jacket.

The truncheon came down on his shoulder, so hard that he fell to his knees.

"Rowly!" Milton forgot himself.

"Albert," Rowland said pointedly, through gritted teeth. "I'm all right."

The SA leader took the papers clutched in his hand and glanced at them. "I'm sorry, Herr Negus," he sneered, tossing them onto the ground before Rowland. "I thought you were reaching for a weapon."

The Stormtroopers circled them. Still on his knees, Rowland cursed quietly in English. "Entirely understandable, *mein Herr.*" His voice was furious though his words spoke of retreat.

For a while there was nothing but smirking silence and then the Brownshirt leader laughed. His comrades followed suit. "Enjoy your view, then, Herr Negus." He clicked his heels and raised his arm in the fascist salute. "Heil Hitler!" He looked at them expectantly.

"I'm afraid I can't raise my arm," Rowland said tightly.

The man rolled the truncheon slowly in his hands.

Milton raised his arm. "Heil Hitler!" he said loudly.

The Stormtroopers waited tensely for their leader's cue. Rowland braced for another attack and Milton's dark eyes glittered murderously as he held the Nazi salute.

The fat Brownshirt smiled slowly and turned away, stepping on Rowland's papers as he went.

The household was at breakfast when they returned, the table laden with pancakes and sausages and the dining room warm with the smell of fried potatoes and baking. Frau Engels, by the absence of her horse, seemed to have cooked and run.

"Oh, my God, what happened?" Edna gasped, jumping up from her seat on sight of them.

Despite the bloody gash above his right ear, Milton had managed to drive them back. Rowland was still not sure whether his shoulder was broken. Lowering himself gingerly into a chair, Milton told Edna and Clyde what had happened, while Rowland gave Eva an edited version in German.

Breakfast was forgotten. Clyde rummaged through the kitchen for some kind of first-aid kit. Among boxes of soap flakes and a bottle of kerosene, he found a basket containing iodine, various ointments, and gauze bandages.

Edna helped Rowland remove his jacket while Clyde dealt with Milton's head, using warm water and iodine.

"I don't understand," Eva lamented. "Why would the SA take issue with you and Herr Greenway?"

"They might have been put out that we ploughed through them in Berg," Rowland said, first in German and then English. "Perhaps they followed us."

Edna unbuttoned Rowland's shirt and gently slid it down so that they could have a look at his shoulder. It was already badly bruised, but the skin was not broken.

"We should call a doctor," she said, touching the area tenderly.

"Let's not." Rowland bit his lip and moved his arm. It was painful but not impossible and he could move his fingers now. "I don't think it's broken—just bruised."

"Shouldn't we at least call the police?"

"To make a complaint about the SA? I don't think it would be a particularly good idea…"

"I'll fetch some ice for your shoulder," Edna sighed. "There's an ice box on the back porch."

"I'd rather you put it in a drink."

"I'll second that," Milton said, pulling away from Clyde's ministrations.

Eva came closer as Edna left to find ice, staring at Rowland's shoulder in a way that made him feel quite naked. She put her hand to the scar on his upper arm. "What is that symbol, Herr Negus?" she asked. "The cat's eye…is it some fraternity?"

She seemed almost frightened now.

Rowland was bewildered. He translated for Clyde and Milton in the hope they could work out what she was talking about, and, grimacing, shifted his arm to look at the scar.

Clyde laughed suddenly. "It does look like an eye."

Rowland smiled and tried to explain to Eva that it wasn't some bizarre brand. He ran his finger around the shape that Eva thought was an eye. "I'm afraid that's the impression left by Fräulein Greenway's teeth."

Apparently, though he was speaking German, Clyde and

Milton could guess what he was saying. They were both laughing loudly now.

"Why would she bite you?" Eva asked horrified.

"She was trying to help." Rowland repeated the statement in English in the hope Clyde and Milton would stop laughing. Edna was still very sensitive about the incident which had occurred a world away from Munich and the excesses of the SA.

"Like when she shot you?" Clyde grinned.

"I don't think you'll survive much more of her help," Milton added.

Rowland elected not to translate, as Eva was clearly alarmed. Indeed, when Edna did return with the ice and an ice-pick still in her hand, the poor girl stepped hastily out of reach. Milton hooted gleefully, and Edna demanded to know what the matter was.

It was into this that Frau Engels walked with the boxes of groceries for which she had gone into Berg. The housekeeper added her voice to the mêlée of laughter and teasing and explanation and it was some minutes before there was any coherence at all in the room.

Finally, somehow, Rowland managed to convince Eva that Edna was not dangerous, and explain to Frau Engels what had happened to injure him and Milton. She had seen the SA in Berg and had much of her own to add on the subject.

Edna remembered then to tell them that Richter had called and that he would be joining them for luncheon, which was why Frau Engels had gone to Berg for supplies.

Frau Engels gave Rowland the same message in Bavarian, with an announcement of the menu which she would serve for luncheon as well as a description of how she would prepare it. All this as she fussed over their injuries and called on the good Lord to do something about the SA, who, it seemed, were throwing their weight about in Berg.

Eventually, Rowland decided that he'd best change, so that Richter didn't think he'd opened his house to street brawlers.

Edna's brow furrowed with concern, as he stood to go with a cloth packed with ice still pressed to his shoulder. "Do you need any help?"

That was too much for Milton.

Chapter Fifteen

CHALLENGE
TO PARIS
As World Fashion Centre
GERMAN HOPE

LONDON

One of the most interesting manifestations of the present
Nazi regime in Germany is the formation of an official
fashion bureau under the personal direction of the wife of
the Minister of Propaganda.

Under her direction, Germany will make an organised
attempt to capture world fashion supremacy, and usurp the
position of France as the present dictator of women's modes.

—*The Australian Women's Weekly*, 1933

Alois Richter arrived just after midday in a chauffeur-driven
Mercedes. He was dressed in a light pinstriped suit, complete
with spats, and had swapped his fez for a green Austrian felt hat
with a large red ostrich plume in its band. Stasi was, as usual,
in the tailor's arms.

"Miss Greenway," he said, craning his neck to kiss Edna on
both cheeks over the top of his dog, "you look truly enchanting,
my dear. My little country house suits you, I think."

"It is lovely, Mr. Richter." Edna took Stasi, who, according to Richer, was very excited to see her. "We are so very grateful for your hospitality."

"How good to see you again, Mr. Negus." Richter took Rowland's hand in both of his and shook it, warmly and vigorously. Rowland winced. "What is the matter Mr. Negus?" Richter asked, still shaking. "Are you unwell?"

"Not at all, Mr. Richter," Rowland replied, forcing himself not to pull his hand away. "I've injured my shoulder slightly."

Richter released Rowland. "*Eha*, my dear Mr. Negus. How terrible. What have you been doing? Have you seen a physician?"

"No, sir. It's just a bruise, really. Shall we go in? Mrs. Engels has prepared a veritable feast in your honour."

"Naturally, naturally."

They escorted Richter into the house, where Clyde and Milton waited with Eva. The tailor was delighted by the addition to their party and welcomed Eva in German. Noting the blackening bruise on Milton's face, he frowned. "You, too, are injured, Mr. Greenway. What have you and Mr. Negus been doing?"

"We had a rather unpleasant encounter with the SA," Milton said, as he poured drinks.

Richter sat down, sighing heavily. "I wish I could say that it shocks me," he said. "But it does not. You are not the first to have been innocent victims of those thugs. They wander the streets like schoolyard bullies. My good friend Franz was waylaid once because they didn't like his hat!"

Rowland couldn't help glancing at Richter's rather elaborate headgear. "They were here promoting some sort of book-burning in Munich."

Richter nodded. "I have seen the invitations. Please God, it will rain! But if not, they will burn the books."

"Which books, Mr. Richter?" asked Edna. "What could possibly be so frightening about a book that one would need to burn it?"

"Books are powerful items, Miss Greenway," Richter replied. "But this is more to do with public performance…the Nazis know how to put on a show."

Eva leaned over to Rowland. "What are they saying, Herr Negus?"

Reminded suddenly that Eva could not understand English, Rowland started to explain. "It's politics really—"

"Oh, I'm sorry," Eva interrupted. "Should I leave?"

"Leave?" Rowland looked at her, perplexed. "Of course not."

"I cannot understand what they are saying," she assured him.

"Which is why I was trying to translate," said Rowland.

Eva shook her head. "It has nothing to do with me," she said. "It is not becoming for a woman to interfere in the affairs of men." She stood before he could say anymore and, addressing them all, took her leave. "*Entschuldigung sie mir, bitte*. I shall see if Frau Engels would like help."

Rowland stared after her, a little stunned. It was a bizarrely archaic attitude to be held so determinedly by someone as young and otherwise uninhibited as Eva.

Richter was describing the pageantry of the rallies the Nazi Party held in the town of Nuremberg and had the complete attention of Edna and Milton. It was Clyde who noticed the abruptness of Eva's exit and the expression on Rowland's face.

"What's wrong with Eva?" he asked quietly.

Rowland shook his head. "She seems to think it's unladylike to discuss politics."

Clyde smiled. "Is that all?"

"Rather old-fashioned, don't you think?"

"Some would say well bred."

"I'd say it's a bit daft."

"That's just the company you've been keeping, mate." Clyde glanced at Edna. "You're beginning to believe it's the normal state of affairs." He paused. "Have you ever heard your brother's wife discussing politics?"

Rowland had to admit that Clyde had a point. Kate Sinclair's only political utterances were to concur with her husband's, and even that was done with softly spoken deference. On the other hand, he didn't think Kate Sinclair would sunbathe naked, either. Eva was intriguingly contradictory.

Richter had now moved back to their encounter with the SA, asking for details of the incident. Milton answered but he was vague in some respects. Rowland suspected that being forced to use the Nazi salute was more deeply humiliating to the poet than he had let on. He flexed the fingers of his right hand tentatively, aware that things might have become a great deal worse had Milton not submitted.

"You cannot intend to return to the Vier Jahreszeiten," Richter exclaimed. "It is crawling with Stormtroopers…in their ugly, badly styled brown shirts. No!" He slapped his thigh to emphasise the point. "You must all stay with me…you tell your business associates to find you in Schellingstrasse."

"We couldn't—" Rowland began.

Richter's face softened. "I would like the company. It would be my last gift to Peter to have you, his relative, in my home."

Rowland groaned inwardly, reluctant to accept the hospitality of a man they were deceiving.

Edna interjected. "Of course we'll stay with you, Mr. Richter. Robbie can let his business colleagues know where he may be reached." She leaned forward and rubbed his hand warmly. "It's lovely of you to extend such a kind invitation again."

In his joy, Richter lapsed into German. "*Das ist wunderbar, wunderbar!*"

Clyde turned to Rowland with a silent question.

Rowland shrugged, resigned. "The lady has spoken."

Following a luncheon of several courses, they drank coffee in the parlour, while Richter told them of King Ludwig of Bavaria, who had also drowned in the lake. Rowland did his best to bring Eva into the English conversation, translating everything and encouraging her to talk, but she remained quiet and reserved.

"I'm going to take a walk," he said standing. "Would you care to come, Fräulein Eva?" Perhaps a conversation in German would lift her spirits.

Richter smiled knowingly, and winked at Rowland.

The others did not react unduly. They, too, had noticed that the girl had become withdrawn. It was probably time Rowland paid her some attention. He had, after all, invited her.

Eva put on her hat hurriedly and accompanied him out. They took a path lined with wildflowers towards the lake's edge. The late afternoon sun was warm and mellow. Rowland offered Eva his left arm as any movement of his right was still painful.

"Is anything the matter, Fräulein Eva?" he asked. "You are very quiet this afternoon."

At first she would not look at him, and then the words burst out tearfully. "You will not be able to finish my painting, will you? With your injured arm? I hate the SA!"

Rowland nearly laughed, surprised that such a thing would trouble her so. There was something very childlike about Eva, an honest and open self-preoccupation. He found it amusing.

"Not at all," he said. "I can use my left hand as well as my right...sometimes better."

"Really?" she said, her eyes wide. "How can that be?"

"I was born left-handed. I learned to use my right hand when I was at school but I didn't forget how to use my left."

"So you will not abandon my painting?"

"No...I will finish it when we get back to Munich. When I am happy with it, you may have it, if you like."

Eva's eyes shone, and she beamed. "Naturally, yes, I would like it. I will give it to Herr Wolf to hang in his bedroom." She giggled. "Do you think it might keep him awake?"

"Quite possibly," Rowland murmured, wondering what Herr Wolf's wife would make of it. "But perhaps you shall find another gentleman to give it to…one who has more time for you."

"There is only Herr Wolf," she said earnestly. "I live only for him. Surely you understand, Herr Negus."

Rowland shook his head. "No, I'm not sure I do."

"You are in love with Fräulein Greenway…I see the way you look at her…always."

Rowland was caught off guard.

"She treats you like a brother," Eva said. Her voice was sympathetic but firm, as if she were explaining something he had somehow missed. "And still, you look at her as if she is the world itself. Could you stop loving Fräulein Greenway, Herr Negus?"

Rowland stopped. "Eva…"

Eva pressed into him, her arm entwined in his and her head against his shoulder as she whispered. "You see, I understand, Herr Negus. We are both enslaved to a love which is greater than us, beyond our will. We have no choice, you and I, whatever anguish it causes us. However much we may wish we did not love, the fact is that we do."

Rowland faltered, unsure of quite what to say. Eva seemed determined to cast him as a fellow romantic martyr. As melodramatically as she put them, her accusations were not entirely untrue. He bit his lip, embarrassed. He had not realised his feelings for Edna were so obvious.

"Have I offended you, Herr Negus?" Eva sounded frightened now. "I do not mean to. You have been so kind…I am too forward…improper. Herr Wolf has often said so."

"Damn!" Rowland's eyes were focussed over her shoulder. A half dozen Brownshirts walked briskly towards them. Tensely, Rowland pulled Eva behind him with his good arm.

The group slowed as it approached them. Rowland held off panic. It was not the same group from that morning. He held his ground. The troop leader stopped in front of them, studying them both openly. Eva clutched Rowland's arm and gazed back defiantly. The Brownshirt nodded slowly and then silently moved on.

They went back to the lakehouse after that, finding Edna standing on a stool while Richter modified the hem of her dress. "When you come back to Munich, I shall make you a gown," Richter promised. "A woman as beautiful as you, Miss Greenway, should not be buttoned into such dowdy, unimaginative styles. Do you like feathers, my dear? I think I shall use feathers…and the neckline shall be low, for your décolletage is exquisite! And a train…it must have a train…perhaps even a bustle."

"He's going to make her a chicken costume," Clyde whispered, as he handed Rowland a drink.

"Better her than us, old boy."

"Don't you worry," Clyde snorted. "If it looks as ridiculous as it sounds, Milt will want one too."

It was hard to know whether Edna was just being polite, or whether she really did like the idea of Richter's feathered creation. Eva, too, seemed cheered by the talk of frocks and told Richter of her various carnival costumes. Of course, Rowland didn't need to translate for Richter, who advised the young German woman of the fashions he predicted would prevail for the next year's festival. As the afternoon became evening, the visiting tailor stood reluctantly, to return to Munich. He told them again how happy he was to be able to repay his debt of friendship to Peter Bothwell through his young relative, and promised to prepare great things for their arrival.

After he'd gone they sat in the garden, enjoying the lake at sunset. When Eva retired, they talked of politics again, the SA and their intention to burn books to honour their Chancellor's strange, uncompromising sense of morality.

"They're probably printing another edition of *Das Kapital* just so they have enough books to burn," Milton said bitterly. "Bloody idiotic…Do they really think we'll become good little fascists because we don't have anything to read?"

"I'd like to go back to Munich the day after tomorrow," Rowland said tentatively. "I know we only just got here, but I'd like to see if we can't find this journalist liaison of Bothwell's before Blanshard and Campbell get back. What do you say?"

Clyde shrugged. "I can't paint anymore without blue anyway."

"Don't be so traditional, Clyde," Edna chided, smiling. "Hans would paint the lake and sky with red or yellow. You must let go of the rules."

"Hans?…Oh, von Eidelsöhn. He's an idiot. I like the rules."

Edna poked him. "Hans is an artistic genius."

"Often goes together."

Milton laughed. "We'd better go then, Rowly, before you're both forced to become Dadaists because you've run out of paint."

They spent the final day at the Starnberger See like holiday-makers. Eva managed to cajole Edna into going swimming with her. Milton had never learned to swim and both Rowland and Clyde flatly refused, preferring instead to watch and laugh as Edna shrieked in the icy water. Rowland tossed her a towel when she ran out blue and shivering, while Eva splashed and dived from the rocks. It was several minutes before Edna had warmed enough to talk.

"That was horrible," she stuttered. "Germans are utterly mad."

"Warned you," Milton said smugly, offering her steaming tea from a large Bakelite thermos which Frau Engels had packed in the picnic basket.

Edna pulled off her swimming cap, allowing her damp auburn tresses to fall loose before she grabbed the tea with both hands. "How can she not feel how cold the water is?" She glanced incredulously at Eva, who was stroking languidly to shore.

"You were a good sport to go in with her, Ed," Rowland murmured, as he lay back. "Completely daft, but a good sport."

Eva walked up to the picnic blanket, drying her hair with a towel. She laughed at Edna, and sat down. "*Kalt?*"

"*Sehr kalt,*" Edna replied, the triumphant smile fading from her lips as Eva launched into a more complex sentence.

"Eva thinks we should stay a few days longer," Rowland said lazily. "She's sure you'll become accustomed to the temperature of the water soon." He turned his head to respond in German. "I'm sorry, Fräulein, but we do need to get back."

Eva swallowed. "Life will be lonely and unbearable again."

Rowland didn't translate. "It can't be that bad, Eva."

"It is. In Munich, Herr Wolf is everywhere…I cannot stop thinking about him even for a moment." She rubbed her neck, anxiously fingering the scar on her throat.

Rowland propped himself up on one elbow. "What happened to your neck, Eva?" There was a strange public privacy to the fact that the others could not understand them.

She stared at him mutely for a moment. "It got too much last year. I was so lonely, and I knew that loving him was evil and wrong, that God would not forgive me, but I could not help it. I was so desperate and tired…I took my father's gun and shot myself."

Rowland sat up.

Though Edna understood nothing of what had been said, the anguish in Eva's voice and the horror on Rowland's face were enough. She placed her arm around Eva's shoulders.

"Oh, Eva," was all Rowland could manage.

She smiled, though she was crying now. "I did not do it properly, you see, and they found me in time. And Herr Wolf was so kind, so concerned. He said he loved me."

Clyde and Milton had moved away discreetly now, leaving Rowland and Edna with the distraught girl.

"Eva, if you are this unhappy, perhaps…"

She shook her head vigorously. "I have no choice. He is

everything to me. And yet I know I should not love him. I have given my soul to a monster and I will never have it back. Perhaps that is why I put the gun to my throat."

Rowland's face darkened. Eva was immature, but her pain was real. He handed her his handkerchief.

She wiped her face. "I am silly and selfish. Herr Wolf has other responsibilities. I am not the only one who loves him, who needs him."

Rowland shook his head, angry now. Adulterers were not uncommon, but how could this man carry on, knowing Eva was so emotionally fragile? It was indecent and cruel. She was only twenty-one, for pity's sake. "I think perhaps you should introduce me to this Herr Wolf of yours," he said finally.

She looked at him, shocked. "Oh, no, I couldn't do that. He wouldn't understand…he would not approve."

"I hardly think he's in any position to approve or not."

"But he is," Eva said firmly. "He is. I am sorry. I did not mean to make you think badly of him. I am lucky for whatever time he can spare me."

Rowland glanced at Edna, wishing she could speak German or Eva, English. Eva needed to talk to a woman; she needed to talk to Edna.

"Eva, you can't—"

"Enough!" Eva gave him back his sodden handkerchief. "I have spoiled our lovely day." She smiled with determination. "We will speak of my silliness no more." She stood and, committed now to proving all was well, plunged back into the water.

Edna moved to sit beside Rowland. Quietly he told her what Eva had said, angry and frustrated by her refusal to be helped.

Edna took his hand. "I'm so glad you invited her to come with us, Rowly," she whispered as they watched Clyde help Eva up onto the rocks. "Perhaps the company of real men will make her see sense."

Rowland shook his head. "I doubt it, Ed. She seems almost

obsessed with this fellow, Wolf. If I knew who he was, I'd deck the useless bastard."

"Oh, Rowly." Edna ruffled his hair fondly. "I don't think that would help. Eva's only twenty-one, but she is twenty-one. She's got to decide for herself."

Rowland's jaw tensed. "She's making rather a mess of it."

Chapter Sixteen

WEDDING "BARGAINS"
Hitler Scheme Popular

German registry offices presented on July 13 the appearance of shops besieged by bargain hunters on the opening day of the spring sales. And, in fact there were bargains going in plenty—no fewer than 300,000 of them. For July 15 was the last day of handing in applications for the Hitler marriage dowry.

This scheme—by giving loans of 300 to 1,000 marks to German couples about to marry—aims at bringing the German woman back into what the Hitler Government considers her right place, the home, and back to her right job—the bearing of children, writes the *'Daily Express'* Berlin correspondent. Long queues of excited young men and women were waiting from eight o'clock in the morning in the streets outside the registry offices, and the augmented staff were hardly able to cope with the bombardment of questions, the stacks of forms, and the number of instructions to put up the banns. The loan is given, not in cash, but in the form of certificates which will be accepted by furniture dealers and stores in payment for household requirements of different kinds and then cashed by the Government. It is to be repaid at the rate of 1 percent a month, but for every child born within the first eight years, a quarter of the loan will be remitted. Those couples who have four children will repay nothing at all. It is estimated that by the end of Hitler's four-year-plan no fewer than a million situations will have been vacated by women and filled by men. The cost of the scheme—estimated at £5,000,000 a year—will be met by a tax on all bachelors.

—*The Central Queensland Herald*, 1933

After the morning's revelations, they all paid particular and gentle attention to Eva, filling the hours with cards and music and dancing. Still, her gloom prevailed. Finally, Edna persuaded the unhappy girl to join her in taking photographs. After snapping the obligatory pictures of the lake, they had experimented with bizarre angles, climbing up on stools and on tables. For a while they lay on the floor, shooting Clyde upwards from his toes. The men learned to step over them, and Eva seemed to find solace or at least distraction through the lens.

They departed for Munich after breakfast the following morning. Rowland had telephoned Alois Richter to warn him that they were returning earlier than expected. The tailor had seemed glad to hear it.

Rowland's unfinished painting was packed carefully into Richter's Mercedes, along with Clyde's landscapes. They thanked Frau Engels and, armed with a basket of her ginger cake, left for the city.

They drove Eva home first.

She said her good-byes cheerfully enough at first, but ran back to the car suddenly to grab Edna's hands and speak to her in an outburst which was to the sculptress incomprehensible.

"Fräulein Millicent, you must marry Herr Negus. He loves you and he is free to love you. It is the duty of women to marry and raise beautiful children—you must not neglect it."

Rowland stopped, alarmed by the extraordinary plea and glad that Edna could not understand a word of it. He did not translate. It was endearing that Eva would make such an appeal on his behalf, but it was all rather awkward.

When she'd finally pulled away from Edna, Rowland walked Eva to her door. He decided to just pretend he'd not heard what she'd said. It seemed to him the path of least embarrassment to all concerned. Instead, he thanked her for her company and promised to finish her painting.

"Will you want me to sit for you again?" she asked quietly, like a child who'd misbehaved and hoped to be forgiven.

Rowland smiled, assuming she regretted her presumption in proposing for him. "I'll find you at Hoffman's," he said, knowing that she was nervous about him calling at her home. "Herr Richter's house is on the same street. Perhaps you could join us for dinner sometime."

The door to the apartment opened. A young woman with perfectly coiffed dark hair stood in the doorway. Her eyes were accusing and her arms folded reprovingly across her chest. Eva introduced her sister, Gretl. After a polite exchange, Rowland left them to it. As the door slammed shut he could hear the voices raised angrily behind it. He winced. Apparently Eva had some explaining to do.

"What was that all about?" Milton asked, as Rowland climbed back into the car. "What on Earth was she babbling to Ed about?"

Rowland shrugged. "Nothing sensible. Poor girl's still rather distraught about this Wolf chap."

"Love will find its way through paths where wolves would fear to prey," Milton replied sagely.

Clyde groaned.

"I'm afraid the old wolf in question has no problem preying on Eva," Rowland muttered. "That was Byron, by the way."

Edna sighed. "Poor Eva. She's too young to know what she's doing."

"You'd think her parents would put a stop to it," Clyde growled. "If any of my sisters had even smiled at a married man, my father would have had something to say about it, and my mother...Good Lord..." He shuddered.

Rowland smiled. They had met Mrs. Watson Jones a couple of months earlier. Clyde was not being dramatic.

"Perhaps her parents don't know," Milton suggested.

"Her sister seems to," Rowland said, recalling the resentful brunette who had greeted them at the door.

"How desperately lonely she must have been to shoot herself in the neck," Edna murmured, her hand moving unconsciously to her own throat.

Rowland frowned. "I suspect it was more that she was overcome by guilt. She seems to know this affair is wrong, but she can't bring herself to break it off."

"Bet she's Catholic," Milton snorted.

Clyde agreed. "We are rather fond of guilt. It's the bedrock of the church."

"She hasn't actually broken off the affair," Rowland reminded them.

"Definitely Catholic, then," Milton muttered.

Richter had spared neither money nor effort to make them feel welcome. The bedrooms had been aired, every vase filled with fresh flowers and he had purchased tickets to operas, plays, and concerts. Each meal was laid on like a banquet and one of the rooms had been cleared and equipped with easels in case Clyde and Rowland should wish to paint. The Australians were quite overwhelmed by the generosity and consideration of Richter's welcome.

In Milton, the German tailor found a man who truly appreciated his unusual sense of style, and, though slighter in build, the poet was soon the beneficiary of several items which more closely resembled his preferred mode of dress than the conservative suits organised by the Old Guard.

Richter had already begun work on the gown he'd promised Edna, and to Rowland's surprise it was indeed beautiful. An ivory chiffon creation, its hem was lined with soft ostrich plumes and just skimmed the ground. It would be the kind of dress that required a grand occasion.

Edna was speechless, quite moved by Richter's gesture, but he would not allow her to thank him. "My daughter would have been your age if she had not died. I think she would have been as beautiful as you. You must indulge me, for I was never able to make a gown for Helena."

Impulsively, Edna embraced him. "It's a beautiful gown, Herr Richter," she whispered into his ear. "Helena would have loved it too."

Amidst this hospitality, they were very soon at home, but despite the comforts and distractions of their situation Rowland had not forgotten Peter Bothwell.

Clyde called out to him from the sitting room as he was about to leave one morning. "Where are you going, Robbie?" They were careful now to use their pseudonyms if it was at all possible that they would be overheard by Frau Schuler or any of the other servants who tended Richter and his house.

Rowland checked the room and the adjoining hallway before replying. "The Bismarck," he said. "I'm told the expatriate journalists like to drink there."

"Would you like some company?" Clyde moved to put down the pen with which he'd been writing a letter.

"To whom are you writing?" Clyde had always been a reluctant correspondent.

"Rosie." Clyde smiled as he mentioned the pretty, somewhat emotional young woman who had once been Rowland's model, and who was now Clyde's sweetheart. "Eva got me thinking. I didn't want Rosie to think I'd forgotten her."

Inwardly, Rowland flinched, guilty that he was the cause of Clyde and Rosalina's separation so soon after the pair had begun courting. Rosalina Martinelli was, to his mind, difficult and a trifle hysterical, but it was clear that Clyde was completely besotted. He'd already written several times since they'd arrived, and when he spoke of his sweetheart, it was with helpless and grateful adoration. Clyde, it seemed, had become hopelessly enslaved. Still, Rowland was not about to dampen his friend's devotion. Clyde was the most faithful of men.

"You finish your letter, mate," he said. "I'll not be long." He put on his hat. "Where have the Greenways got to, by the way?"

"They stepped out with that Dada bloke, von Eidelsöhn, this morning, to see some new exhibition. He brought our Millie a tiara made out of cutlery…apparently he calls it *Silverware*."

"Good Lord. How much did she pay for that?" Rowland had already received two telegrams from the Graziers' Association demanding that they exercise fiscal restraint and cease squandering funds immediately.

Clyde hesitated. "It was a gift. A symbol of his deep admiration…carried on a bit, really."

Rowland nodded. It seemed von Eidelsöhn was about to become Edna's latest conquest. He reacted as he always did to Edna's liaisons, with studied and determined indifference. The sculptress was not his.

He left Clyde to his letter and walked from Schellingstrasse to the Königsplatz at the city's centre. Just a couple of blocks from there was the Bismarck Hotel, which the concierge at the Vier Jahreszeiten had assured him was the favoured drinking place of both British and Australian expatriates.

The bar had been fitted out to look like a traditional English pub, complete with kitsch knickknacks on the walls. It was already crowded. Patrons sat on bentwood chairs around the several small round tables and at the long wooden bar. Rowland ordered a gin and tonic, and stood by the bar, savouring the background of English conversation.

He had enquired of the German barman, who would only tell him that most of the foreign journalists came in at about three.

And so he waited, enjoying his drink and listening.

He first noticed the group to his left because of the laugh

that emanated from its centre. The group was a huddle of men, overlapping pinstriped shoulders, but the laugh was female. Somewhere in the masculine circle was a woman. He watched curiously, waiting for a break in the suited circumference. Eventually one of the men went to the bar.

Small—not much more than five feet tall—she balanced on the barstool with her legs crossed. Her face was round, her dark eyes striking on milky skin. Despite her height, she did not seem slight. Her figure curved in a tight skirt, and when she spoke it was confident and mischievous and without reserve. Rowland thought her beautiful.

"Would you care for another drink, Nancy?"

There was a general movement towards the main bar as several men sought to buy the young woman a drink. Rowland's interest, which had been piqued by her person, was sharpened by her name. Blanshard had said that the rumours concerned a woman called Nancy.

He was just contemplating how exactly he would approach her and ascertain whether she was in fact the Nancy he sought when she left her companions and took the stool beside him.

"Hello, there," she said, leaning on the bar. "I haven't seen you here before. Who are you with?"

"Robert Negus," Rowland said removing his hat. "Pleased to make your acquaintance, Miss…"

"Wake, Nancy Wake." She offered him her hand.

"I'm not with anyone, I'm afraid," he said, answering her initial question. "I came in on my own."

She laughed. The sound was loud and natural. "I meant who do you work for? I'm with the *Chicago Tribune*."

"Oh…I'm not a journalist." He looked at her quizzically. "If you don't mind my saying, Miss Wake, you don't sound American."

"Oh, I'm not. I'm Australian, really…English more recently, and Parisian." She smiled and winked. "The Americans don't mind—you can't read an accent, you know."

He returned her smile. "May I buy you a drink, Miss Wake?"

She looked at his glass. "I might have one of those."

Rowland signalled the barman and ordered another gin and tonic.

"None of the fellas seem to know you either, Mr. Negus," she said. "Most of the boys who come here are old hands. What are you doing here?"

Rowland's brow rose. Not only had she noticed him, she had asked about him. Nancy Wake was sharp.

"My cousin used to drink here," he said quietly. "He died suddenly, last month. I'm in Munich to collect some of his possessions."

She was clearly startled. "I'm sorry for your loss, Mr. Negus. What was your cousin's name? Perhaps I knew him."

Rowland tried not to watch her reaction too obviously. "Peter Bothwell."

Nancy put down her drink. "Put your hat back on, Mr. Negus. I think you and I should take a walk."

Rowland placed some money on the bar to pay for the drinks. "It would be a pleasure, Miss Wake."

He was aware of the disappointed and resentful scrutiny of Nancy Wake's colleagues as he accompanied her from the bar. He couldn't really blame them.

She took his arm and they strolled towards the Königsplatz like any other young couple.

"I knew Peter very well," she said. "We were very dear friends."

"How did you meet him, Miss Wake?" Rowland kept his voice casual.

"At the Bismarck," she said carefully. "I was devastated to hear of his death. I'll miss him a great deal."

"It would be easier to accept," Rowland ventured, "if the circumstances of his death were not so strange."

"*Monsieur Sinclair, bonjour!*"

Rowland turned startled. Albert Göring walked towards him, hand outstretched.

Chapter Seventeen

GERMANY HAS RAILED BACK TO BARBARISM
Nazi Policy Outrages Against Workers and Jews

...But the worst tragedies are those of the thousands of poor homes that have been broken up, and whose breadwinners are in the jails or the new concentration camps. I saw the flats of two trade union men after they had been raided. All the pictures and ornaments were smashed. The wife and mother sat amid the ruins in the grey hopelessness of despair. "We got through the war, and the blockade, and the inflation. ...I can't stand any more. ...I can't start again!" The senseless savagery of it!

And the stories from the countryside are worse. But the most astonishing thing about the whole situation is that so few Germans know what is happening except in their own district. The stranglehold on the Press is complete.

—*The Worker*, 1933

Rowland took Göring's hand, painfully aware that he was in the presence of two people each of whom knew him by a different name. By the look on her face, he was certain Nancy Wake understood French. He introduced her quickly.

"You are a lucky man," Göring said, slapping Rowland on the back. "So often in the company of beautiful young actresses."

Nancy glanced at Rowland suspiciously, but she said nothing.

The situation might have become more awkward if not for the growing noise from the Königsplatz. A large crowd had gathered, and cheering was punctuated by the harsh barked commands of the SA. "What's going on?" Rowland murmured, still speaking French.

Albert Göring clapped the hat back on his head. "Let's find out, shall we?" He strode towards the excited gathering, moving bystanders aside with an imperious tap of his walking stick. Rowland and Nancy followed.

They jostled their way to the front of the onlooking crowd. At first Rowland wasn't sure what he was witnessing. Several people were on their knees on the stones of the plaza, scrubbing with small brushes. Brownshirts stood over them, shouting orders and insults…"Bolshevik! Jew! Degenerate!"

"What is this? Who are these people?" Rowland asked Göring.

"They are Germans…from the so-called re-education camp."

Göring shouted at the Brownshirt captain in German. "What are you doing?"

The man sneered in reply. "Is it not obvious, *mein Herr*? The plaza needs cleaning."

A proportion of the crowd laughed.

"This is disgraceful, inhuman! I demand you stop at once!"

The Brownshirt turned his back pointedly.

Göring's face flushed furiously. "Very well, then," he said, stepping forward and kneeling next to an elderly man. "May I borrow your brush, *mein Herr*?" He took the scrubbing brush and proceeded to scour the ground. Onlookers began to snigger.

The SA captain screamed at Göring. "Get up! Get up now!" He pulled the truncheon from his belt.

Rowland tipped his hat to Nancy. "If you'll excuse me, Miss Wake," he said, as he moved in among the group of prisoners. He knelt beside a man who had momentarily stopped working to gape at Göring through cracked, wire-rimmed spectacles, and, taking his brush, began to scrub.

Göring laughed and called in French. "Well done, *mon ami!*"

Faced with two volunteers, the SA captain hesitated. The crowd's laughter was now with the dissidents.

Then Nancy was on her knees, too. She began to hum as she cleaned the stones. This proved too much for the Brownshirt, who bellowed for his men to arrest the intruders. A scuffle broke out as they dragged Nancy to her feet and restrained Rowland. The SA held back the crowd as the three were placed under arrest. The captain demanded their names.

Göring stood straight. His held up his hand to silence Nancy and Rowland, and extracted a card from his pocket.

"Yes, that is correct," he said, as the captain stared at the name. "Albert Göring."

"But Herr Göring…" the man stuttered, panicked now. "Surely there is some mistake…"

"Yes, the mistake is yours!" Göring roared. "I do not know under what authority you drag these fine Germans out to scrub the plaza, but I know that you cannot prevent me and my friends from assisting in the cleaning you claim is so necessary!"

Nancy clutched Rowland's arm. "What is he saying?" she asked.

Despite the fact that he was being held with one arm twisted behind his back, Rowland bent down towards her and translated quietly.

Nancy smiled, her eyes glistening. "Isn't he magnificent?"

Rowland nodded. "Smashing."

The Brownshirt captain was now almost pleading with Göring to walk away and avoid embarrassing his brother.

Göring insisted that if scrubbing was necessary then he would stay and lend a hand. It was all Rowland could do not to cheer. In the end there was nothing the man could do but abandon the orchestrated exercise in humiliation, to avoid falling foul of Reichsmarschall Hermann Göring.

As the crowd dispersed, some jeered Göring, annoyed that the spectacle had been cut short. One or two shouted that he was a Jew.

Göring slapped the dirt from the knees of his trousers.

"*Monsieur* Göring," Rowland started, reverting again to French.

Göring cut him short. "We have been on our knees together, *mon ami*. Now you will call me Albert."

Rowland rubbed the back of his neck, smiling. "Very well, Albert…shall we have a drink?"

Nancy cleared her throat.

"With Mademoiselle Wake, of course," Rowland amended.

Göring clapped him on the shoulder. "Yes, I believe a drink is called for…but you must let me select the venue." He twisted his moustache. "I know a place."

He took them to a run-down coffee house in a back street well away from the Königsplatz. The windows of the small eatery had been smashed and were partially boarded over, but it was open for business. Many of the patrons were recognisable as Jews by their orthodox attire, the long, spiralled locks and skullcaps. Others could have been anyone, but for the fact that they were patrons here.

The proprietor seemed familiar with Albert Göring and showed them to a table inside the little shop.

In the corner, two old men played chess on a bench.

When the wine was served, Rowland raised his glass. "It's an honour to know you, Albert."

Nancy agreed heartily and Göring smiled sadly. "I thank you for your help, my friends, but you must be careful. I am protected; you are not."

"Who were those people?" Rowland asked. "Why were they being humiliated?"

Göring drank deeply before he replied. "They were from Dachau...the re-education camp. Communists, trade unionists, Jews, Jehovah's Witnesses...the occasional alcoholic." He fitted a cigarette into his holder and lit it. "Hitler is going to teach them how to be German."

"I see."

Göring exhaled in disgust and slammed down his glass. "He's going to create a thousand-year Reich!" he said scornfully. "Man can't even grow a decent moustache...hangs under his nose like a limp brush!"

Nancy leaned towards the disgruntled German. "Your brother is..."

"Hermann is like many Germans," he said. "Willing to allow Hitler his little prejudices, tolerate the Chancellor's idiosyncrasies because inflation is under control and there is bread and sausage on the table. Hitler promises to restore prosperity and pride...for that we are willing to sacrifice the freedom and dignity of our neighbours!"

"No," Nancy said. "Surely people will come to their senses."

Göring shrugged. "Such is my hope." He looked at Rowland. "We will just have to do what we can to remind our countrymen of their senses."

Nancy did not broach the subject of his name until they had left Göring and were walking back to the Bismarck.

"And why exactly would you be using two different names, Mr. Negus?"

Rowland scrambled for a plausible story, any story. "Rowland Sinclair is my stage name."

"Your what?"

"My professional stage name. I'm an actor—that's why I was meeting with Mr. Göring. He's a filmmaker, you know."

Nancy's eyes narrowed. "You're an actor. Peter never mentioned that he had a cousin who was an actor."

"Well, he wouldn't. I'm afraid acting isn't really the done thing in my family." He smiled. "I believe they're all rather hoping I'll give it up and go into the law."

She studied him carefully. "Perform something."

"I beg your pardon?"

"You must have something you can perform...What did you do for Mr. Göring? How about it?" she challenged. "Surely an actor is not shy."

Rowland tried briefly to recall some suitable passage from *Hamlet* or *King Lear* but he could find nothing that he remembered well enough to pass as a thespian. "I wasn't auditioning for Mr. Göring...just meeting with him to discuss possibilities." Rowland lied so smoothly in the end that he was himself surprised. "A friend put me in touch."

"And did he give you a part?"

"Not yet, but hopefully he'll remember my name."

"You mean your stage name?"

"Yes...of course."

They had reached the Bismarck now. The young journalist glanced at her watch. She sighed, pulling a card from her purse and pressing it into his hand. "Very well, Mr. Negus. I have an appointment I must get ready for, so I will have to say goodbye. You may get in touch with me at the number on that card. I might just let you take me dancing one evening."

Rowland smiled, hoping she'd take his obvious relief as simple joy at the thought of taking her dancing. Perhaps it was. Nancy Wake was certainly beautiful. "Good evening, Miss Wake. It has been a very great pleasure to make your acquaintance."

She gazed into the deep blue of his eyes. Her own twinkled. "Perhaps you *are* an actor. Good evening, Mr. Negus."

Edna and Milton had returned by the time Rowland made his way back to Schellingstrasse. Richter, too, was at home and they were all assembled in the parlour, where Milton was displaying his latest purchase.

Rowland stared at the painting. It seemed to be a deformed duck walking on…well, he wasn't quite sure. "What is it?"

Milton smiled. "A substantial investment. I'll ship it out to the good Senator tomorrow morning."

"This Senator," Richter said, puckering as he cradled Stasi like a baby. "He is a client of yours?"

"Oh, yes," Milton replied. "He's quite the connoisseur. Recently developed an insatiable taste for modern art."

"Is this one of von Eidelsöhn's?" Rowland tilted his head to one side, in case a change of perspective would help. Perplexing though it was, he quite liked the painting…it was amusing, if nothing else.

"No…this was a chap called Miró. Von Eidelsöhn won't take our cheques anymore."

"Why?" Rowland asked, worried that the Old Guard had stopped payment on their previous purchases.

"Apparently he's in love with my sister," Milton replied, rolling his eyes at Edna. "He doesn't want to tarnish the purity of his admiration with something so base as money."

Edna smiled, curling her legs up into the armchair on which she sat. "Hans is so intense. I've never met anyone quite like him."

Rowland noticed then that her left wrist was bandaged.

"What happened?" he asked, taking her hand gently to inspect it.

"It's just a little burn," she replied. "Nothing really."

"She was welding," Milton said.

"Welding?"

"Hans has this wonderful welder that automatically feeds the fusing wire," Edna explained, the excitement bubbling quickly into her voice. "I'd heard of them but I'd never used one before…I usually cast, you know. It's the most amazing technology, but it takes a little getting used to." She laughed, embarrassed. "I'm afraid I fused the welding head to the sculpture a couple of times."

"Oh, dear." Rowland tried to look as though he knew what she was talking about. "You should be careful, though."

Edna smiled. "Don't worry, Robbie darling, it's far too late for my hands…they'll never look anything like a lady's should." She put out both hands to support her claim.

Rowland did not need to look. He knew Edna's hands—he had drawn them often. They were strong and sensitive, marked with several small scars from welding sparks, or pit fires or sharp edges, which the sculptress considered marks of her trade and showed off with a kind of professional pride. Her nails were short and rarely manicured and when she was working, the skin often became calloused. They were far from ladylike hands. To Rowland they were perfect.

"Thank goodness for gloves," he said.

"Dear Hans," Edna went on dreamily, "he was very understanding and patient. Once I got used to the technique, it opened my mind to so many possibilities for finer, more complex pieces than I've conceived before. Hans may seem solemn but it's only because he has a real vision for his work."

"Well, my dear, you must invite him to dine here," Richter said warmly. "He's obviously a man of impeccable taste, but we must meet him to decide if he's good enough for our Millicent."

"Do Dadaists have dinner?" Clyde muttered. "Surely dinner is just an archaic social tradition? Who can say if dinner really exists?"

Rowland laughed.

Edna laughed too. "You are becoming part of the artistic establishment, Joseph," she needled. "You'll be joining the Country Party next."

Clyde snorted.

They spent that evening quietly in the company of Richter

and Stasi. Rowland pulled out his notebook, drawing from memory as Clyde and Edna argued over whether the Modernist movement had gone too far. Their host discussed the problems he was having with the black uniform of the SS, which he maintained was a maudlin atrocity. "If Göring had retained the SS, my pleas for colour might not have fallen on deaf ears," he complained. "But Himmler is a boorish Prussian peasant."

Rowland contemplated the other Göring as he sketched a man kneeling in the plaza in the shadow of a Brownshirt. The filmmaker had surprised him with his open subversion of the regime in which his brother served. Rowland could not help but admire the man.

He didn't speak of the incident, however, until Richter and the servants had retired and they were alone.

Edna perched on the arm of his chair, looking curiously over his shoulder at the notebook. He looked up, distracted by the lingering scent of roses, the familiar smell of the sculptress' perfume.

"You're quiet, Rowly," she whispered. "Where were you today?"

Rowland stood and shut the door. He recounted the events of the day.

Edna clapped her hands softly as he told them of Göring's stand.

"So he's a good bloke?" Clyde said.

Rowland nodded.

"And this Nancy Wake…she's the woman Bothwell was involved with?"

Rowland dragged a hand through his hair. "She certainly knew him, but it might not have been anything improper. Albert appeared before I could find out."

"And now she thinks you're an actor?" Milton laughed. "Gotta hand it to you, mate, that's one way to impress a girl."

Rowland groaned. "I couldn't think of anything else to explain why Albert was calling me Rowland Sinclair instead of

Robert Negus. To be honest, I felt like a jolly fool. And I'm not sure she believed me."

"Do you think she had something to do with Bothwell's death?" Clyde asked.

Rowland shrugged. "I rather like her."

Clyde shook his head. "That doesn't mean anything, mate." He glanced at Milton, who was turning the Miró upside-down to see if it improved. "You've been known to display unfortunate lapses in judgement when choosing your friends."

Chapter Eighteen

HECKLING THE YOUNG MASTER

A certain Duke's son, very young, was finishing his campaign by addressing the electors near his father's estates, when at question time an old man at the back shocked everyone by asking, "Sonny, does yer mother know you're out?"

"Yes," shouted back the candidate with a show of anger, "and she'll know I'm 'in' tomorrow."

And she did.

The interjector proved to be the old gardener at home, whom the young man had paid one guinea to ask the question.

—The Advocate, 1933

Alastair Blanshard was not happy.

"You were given clear and specific instructions," he spat, staring at his newspaper. "You were to lie low."

Rowland was not entirely sure how Blanshard knew he had scrubbed the plaza with Göring, but it seemed he did.

"They called it off before I gave my name."

"And if it hadn't been called off? If you'd been arrested by the Nazis you would have been of no use to us whatsoever!" He flicked the paper angrily. "That's what those bloody fools get for sending me some idiot playboy."

Rowland stood. He wasn't about to let Blanshard dress him down like a child.

"Sit down!" Blanshard turned the page. "I'm not finished."

"I am."

"Sit down, Mr. Negus. I do not have time for your wounded feelings. I have a job for you."

For a moment, Rowland considered telling Blanshard what he could do with his job.

"This is not a game, Mr. Negus," Blanshard murmured. "You cannot take your ball and go home."

Rowland swore, but quietly, and he resumed his seat on the park bench.

"Campbell is supposed to deliver a speech tonight at this book-burning they've organised."

"A speech? What the hell could he possibly have to say?"

"He doesn't know himself…the speech has been written for him, in German. He's just going to read it."

"I see."

"I want you to be there."

"Why?"

"To stop it, of course."

"I suppose I could shout 'Fire!'" Rowland muttered.

"You're not funny, Mr. Negus."

"Well, what do you propose I do, Mr. Blanshard?"

"Campbell is scheduled to arrive at the Plaza at midnight. I will do everything I can to prevent him getting there, or at the least, getting there on time. If I am unsuccessful, he will throw a copy of *Das Kapital* onto the fire and go to the podium to address the crowd. It must not be a successful appearance. Do what you can."

Rowland shook his head in disbelief. "Fine," he said finally. "If Campbell shows up, I'll try to do something."

Blanshard folded his newspaper and lit a cigarette. "Do not get yourself arrested, Mr. Negus. There will be very little I can do for you."

Rowland sighed. "Believe me, Mr. Blanshard, I will do my best to avoid it." He stared out at the Königsplatz which was being prepared for the evening's event. The standards of the SA lined the square, the black and red of Nazi banners festooned all the surrounding buildings. "And if Campbell happens to see me? He knows who I am."

Again, Blanshard looked away as he spoke. "Get yourself to Hamburg and on the first ship out of here. You would be wise not to delay for any reason…Do you understand me, Mr. Negus?"

Rowland nodded slowly. They would have to be prepared, then.

Blanshard casually handed him the newspaper. "Page three."

Rowland opened the paper to the indicated page. A telegram had been inserted between the leaves.

ALASTAIR BLANSHARD
BUDGET ALREADY EXCEEDED STOP EXORBITANT
EXPENDITURE ON SPECULATIVE STOCK STOP CURTAIL
STOP
MUNROE

Rowland closed the paper and handed it back. "What the hell does that mean?"

"You, Mr. Negus, are the speculative stock."

"I see."

"We understand each other, Mr. Negus, don't we?"

"Perfectly."

"Good. I have more than enough to do without having to watch your wretched pocket money!"

Rowland simmered, but he did so wordlessly.

Blanshard shoved his paper under his arm. With only the barest of nods he walked away.

"Whoa, mate, what's the matter?" Clyde asked, startled as Rowland slammed the door so hard the windows rattled.

Milton selected a crystal decanter from Richter's Jacobean sideboard. "You look like you need a drink."

Rowland addressed the poet. "Did you buy anything today?"

"A sculpture," Milton replied, hesitantly. "Actually, it was a pile of old hats titled *Between Man and God.*"

"What did you pay for it?"

"Rather a lot."

"Good." Rowland took the drink Milton had poured him and raised his glass to the poet. "Well done."

"Righto, Rowly," Clyde said quietly, "what gives?"

Rowland told them of his latest meeting with Blanshard. He kept his voice to a virtual whisper, for though he knew Richter was out and the door was closed, Blanshard had made it amply clear that they could expect no help if they were exposed.

"The cheap bastards!" Milton was livid.

Clyde shook his head, pointing accusingly at Milton. "Look what you've done, you idiot."

Rowland shook his head and spoke in defence of the poet, as he fell into a seat. "The only thing that's keeping me from telling the whole flaming lot of them to sod off is the thought of Senator Hardy taking delivery of that deformed duck painting."

Milton bowed. "I aim to please."

"So what are we going to do about this book-burning, Rowly?" Clyde asked.

Rowland groaned. "Hope for rain."

Milton smiled. "We'll heckle."

Rowland sat up. "I beg your pardon?"

"Campbell's reading a speech. He doesn't speak German, and you do," Milton said, sitting on the occasional table opposite Rowland. "Heckle him and he won't have a clue how to respond. We could completely derail the speech."

"And how do you propose I do that without him recognising me and exposing us?"

"Good Lord, Rowly, I can't think of everything."

Rowland put down his drink, yanking the invitation to the orchestrated bonfire from beneath Milton. He stared at it. Heckling wasn't a bad idea, but for the fact that doing so would attract the attention of both Campbell and the SA organisers. It would be dangerous on many levels.

"You're not thinking about trying it, are you, Rowly?" Clyde asked, aghast.

Rowland bit his lower lip. He wondered how much time they'd have to get out of Munich if they were exposed…and how they would do so.

"Rowly?"

Rowland frowned. "We'll just play it by ear," he said. "Do what we can, without getting ourselves arrested…but we should be prepared to have to leave in a hurry."

Before Milton or Clyde could respond, they heard Edna's voice in the mansion's foyer. A few moments later the sculptress walked in on the arm of Alois Richter.

The elderly tailor had stepped out with her to one of the better hotels, where they had taken tea with Hans von Eidelsöhn. Richter had become quite paternal where the sculptress was concerned and Edna had decided to find his fatherly interest endearing rather than presumptuous. The lonely widower had elicited her compassion, and so she allowed him to fuss in a way her own father had never dared.

Of course, the men with whom she usually lived had already met von Eidelsöhn and in any case, they'd never felt it necessary to meet all of the sculptress' many suitors.

"Well, I must say, Mr. von Eidelsöhn is certainly an earnest young man," Richter said, settling into the settee with the drink Milton poured him. "Is he as revolutionary an artist as our Millicent claims?"

"More like civil disobedience than revolution, I would have thought," Rowland muttered.

Edna laughed as she sat on the arm of his chair. "You're just jealous…"

Milton and Clyde looked up sharply.

"Robbie wishes he'd discovered Hans himself," Edna told Richter. "I'm afraid we dealers can be rather competitive."

Rowland smiled. "Yes, that's it."

"Well, he is a very affable young man," Richter said. "Although I do think you'd be more suited to someone a little more cheerful, my dear."

Clyde laughed. "Gotta admit, he's a bit melancholy, Millie."

"He's a serious artist," Edna said loftily.

"Very serious." Rowland winked at Clyde.

Richter chuckled, tickling Stasi, who it appeared was not in the least ticklish. "Stop with your teasing, young men," he admonished. "I will not have you bully my Millie."

Edna smiled warmly at the tailor. "You are gallant, Mr. Richter." She glanced at her watch. "I might just duck out before lunch, if nobody minds. I won't be long."

"Where are you going, my dear?" Richter asked. "Shall I ring for the driver to take you?"

"No, please don't bother," Edna said standing and adjusting her hat. "I'm just going to walk down to Hoffman's studio with some film for Eva to develop." She turned to Rowland, the excitement plain in her face. "I've started shooting a series of artists with their work. I'm anxious to see how the pictures come out."

A thought occurred to Rowland. "I'll come with you, if you like."

"Yes, that is a good idea," Richter approved. "A young lady should not step out without an escort. After all, this is not Berlin."

Rowland waited until they were well outside the gates of Richter's mansion. "Look, Ed, I don't think you should leave your film with Eva."

"Whyever not?"

"Because it may be the last you see of it." Quickly Rowland told the sculptress of the task they'd been set. Edna looked up at him in shock.

"We should be prepared for the possibility that we may have to leave in rather a hurry."

"Oh, Rowly," she whispered. "How on Earth are we going to stop Colonel Campbell giving a speech?"

Rowland shook his head. "I'm not sure, Ed."

"He's reading a speech in German?"

"I expect it will be something simple…along the lines of '*Herr Hitler ist unsere Freund*'. Blanshard's worried that if he does well tonight, Nazi doors might open."

"But Campbell knows both you and me, and he might recognise Clyde, as well."

Rowland removed his hat to push back his hair. Edna was right. She had masqueraded as his fiancée when he'd infiltrated the New Guard the previous year, and hers was not a face a man would forget. Clyde had come to Campbell's house to drag Rowland out after Edna had shot him. It was indeed likely that the Colonel would remember him as well. Only Milton remained relatively unrecognisable. It all seemed impossible.

"Perhaps you should just tell Mr. Blanshard that we can't do it, Rowly."

This Rowland resisted, though he wasn't sure why he railed so against the idea of failing Blanshard. Perhaps he was becoming increasingly worried about what Campbell might bring back to Sydney, or perhaps it was simply Blanshard's repeated expectation that he was not up to the job.

"Herr Negus! Millicent!" Eva stuck her head out of Hoffman's shop as they approached. "*Grüss Gott*! How fine to see you…I was afraid you'd forgotten me."

"Not at all, Fräulein," Rowland said after he'd translated for Edna.

Edna took Eva's hand warmly. "Of course we wouldn't forget you."

"Do you have more film you'd like me to develop?" Eva was clearly eager to do Edna a kindness.

"No, not yet," Rowland replied immediately. It occurred to

him then that they did need some sort of reason for calling upon her, aside from Edna's negatives. "I was going to work on your painting this evening. I was hoping you might sit for me for an hour or two, if it's convenient."

Eva smiled. "I would love to, Herr Negus. You are staying on Schellingstrasse, are you not? Perhaps I could walk up after work? I finish at four today."

"That would do very well, I think," Rowland replied, pulling his notebook from his jacket and jotting down the address, which he tore out for Eva. "I would like to finish it for you."

Eva clapped her hands excitedly. "I cannot wait to see it finished…and it will be so nice to spend time with my Australian friends again."

With apologies, they took their leave of her to catch a motor cab into the centre of Munich. There they stopped at the Deutsche Bank and Rowland used the letter that Wilfred had given him before they left Sydney to extract a large amount of German currency, as well as pounds sterling. If they needed to leave in a hurry, they would also no longer be able to rely on the line of credit established for their aliases. He didn't expect they'd have time to stop at the bank, either.

"What are we going to tell Alois, if we have to go?" Edna asked quietly, staring at the small fortune stuffed into her handbag, which luckily was, by the dictates of fashion, large. It all seemed a little alarming now.

"This is only a precaution, Ed," Rowland replied. "Hopefully we won't need to use it. I'm sorry about Richter…he has been rather sporting. We'll leave him a note that we've been called away, and write once we're out of the country."

Edna sighed. "At least you'll be able to finish Eva's portrait."

Rowland nodded. As trivial as it seemed, he did want to finish the portrait. He had promised Eva that he would. "Just hope she isn't silly enough to give it to this Wolf chap."

"Don't make her too recognisable, in case she does," Edna advised. "You don't want poor Mrs. Wolf to walk into Hoffman's one day and recognise the naked girl on her bedroom wall."

Chapter Nineteen

NAZIS PUNISHED FOR VISITING LONDON

Strict disciplinary action has been taken against the two German Nazis who recently visited London in uniform, and who returned to Berlin by air, says a London newspaper.

The party tickets and the uniforms of the two men—Kurt Nitschke and Herbert Wessel—have been taken away from them, and they will be tried by a special disciplinary court of their organisation, the formidable S.S.—Hitler's bodyguard—for violating the party rule that members must on no account wear uniforms abroad. The young men were met in London on their arrival by officials of their organisation, who informed them of their fate. It is probable that they will be expelled from the party.

—The Mail, 1934

"Quick, in here!" Clyde's head appeared briefly through the crack in the door and disappeared again.

Rowland looked at Edna. She shrugged. They had arrived back at Richter's mansion to find that everybody appeared to have stepped out. And so they'd wandered up the stairs to the bedrooms to find a place to stash the money Rowland had withdrawn.

Rowland opened the door to the guestroom and then followed Edna in.

"Close the door," Clyde said, the moment Rowland entered the room.

Edna clamped a hand over her mouth.

Rowland stared.

Milton stood before them, his hands on his hips. He turned to show the black jodhpurs and knee-high boots to effect. "Well, what do you think?"

"That you've lost your mind." Rowland folded his arms, mystified as to why Milton would be in an SS uniform.

"Rowly, Rowly, Rowly…" Milton said sadly. "You're not really cut out for spying, are you, old chap?"

"What are you talking about?"

"Clyde and I have figured out how we're going to stop Campbell."

"Indeed." Rowland leaned back against the door. "Go on."

"I'm going to walk straight up to him and tell him to go back to his hotel."

"Have you been drinking?"

Milton smiled. "Yes, I have. While you and Ed were out doing God knows what, Clyde and I had a few drinks with old Richter." He directed Rowland and Edna to sit on the bed and took the club chair beside it. Clyde stayed by the closed door.

"You may recall that our host had been complaining about a certain black uniform that he would prefer to make a little less grim."

"Yes, the SS uniform…"

"Well, not exactly." Milton sat back and played with the twirled points of his moustache. "The uniform that Richter was hoping to modify belongs to a special unit of the SS…the *Leibstandarte Adolf Hitler*. Apparently they're the Chancellor's personal guard." Milton stood. "You will notice that my uniform is missing the red swastika armband." He bent forward so that they could more clearly see his collar. "See these little lightning bolt things? They're the insignia of the *Leibstandarte*."

"Where did you get this uniform?" Rowland asked.

"Richter has the contract to make them...He'd been hoping to convince some bloke called Dietrich—who's managed to wrest the unit from Himmler's control—to brighten up the uniform a bit...but he hasn't got very far. Anyway, there's a storeroom in the basement full of them, ready for shipping to Berlin. He showed us."

Edna nodded. "Alois showed me the other day...but what exactly are you planning to do, dressed like that?"

"Well, I'm not going fox-hunting."

Rowland was beginning to suspect where Milton was going.

"Campbell's never met Milt," Clyde said.

"Just what are you proposing?" Rowland looked from Clyde to Milton.

"According to Richter, this guard unit has only recently been formed and they're based in Berlin, separate from the ordinary SS. I figure the only way the blokes over here would be able to recognise a member of the *Leibstandarte* is by this uniform."

Clyde rolled his eyes and decided to cut to the point. "Milt plans to intercept Campbell as he gets to the Königsplatz and tell him that Hitler's in town."

Milton explained more clearly before Rowland could react. "The *Leibstandarte* is Hitler's personal guard. I'll speak to Campbell as an emissary of the Chancellor himself, who has decided that he wishes to meet the famous Australian fascist, Eric Campbell...but of course for security reasons it must be done secretly. I'll tell Campbell to go back to his hotel immediately and wait for Hitler to pop by."

"You're insane!" Rowland said incredulously. "Clyde, I can't believe you're going along with this!"

Clyde shrugged. "It's a better plan than trying to kidnap him, Rowly, which is our only other option."

Rowland shook his head. "Not even Campbell's going to believe a lone man, no matter what he's wearing, and the SA is hardly going to stand back and just let you take their guest speaker. Milt doesn't even speak German, for pity's sake!"

Milton was not deterred. "I've got that sorted out. You and Clyde come with me…hang back. You talk to the SA while I talk to Campbell. It'll be late and dark. If you don't get too close, he won't recognise you, and in this *Leibstandarte* uniform, the SA won't give us any trouble."

Rowland stared at him. "You're serious."

"I lifted three uniforms," Milton said. "We can return them tomorrow—Richter will never know."

"It's risky, Milt."

Milton grinned. "But you can see it, can't you, Rowly? You can see how it just may work."

Rowland said nothing for a moment. The ploy had its merits, but could they possibly get away with something so outrageous?

Edna stared at the three of them in alarm. "What if you get caught?"

"We'll say it's a lark," Milton said. "Some kind of elaborate joke…"

"Yes, I'm sure they'll be laughing when they shoot us," Clyde muttered. But it seemed that he, too, was in favour of Milton's plan.

Edna took a deep breath. "Don't you think Colonel Campbell will think it a bit odd that he's approached by a Nazi officer with an Australian accent?"

"I can have a German accent." Milton stood and recited the Lord's Prayer while maintaining the fascist salute.

Rowland grimaced. "You sound Irish."

Milton grinned. "Close enough." He sat down again. "Come on, Rowly, you managed to convince Campbell that you were a young fascist-in-the-making for months. I only have to pull off being German for ten minutes. He'll go back to his hotel to receive the Chancellor, we'll take off these ridiculous outfits and have a tale to dine out on for years."

Despite himself, Rowland smiled. "I'm not sure we'll be permitted to tell anybody, Milt."

Edna looked hard at Rowland. "You're going to do this, aren't you?" she accused.

"Campbell's so keen for an audience with the great man that it could just work."

Milton slapped Rowland on the back in triumph.

Edna frowned. "Well, what am I going to do?" She pointed her finger at Rowland. "I am not staying here."

Rowland laughed. Edna did not like to be left out of subterfuge. He'd suspected there was more to her caution than mere concern that they were about to embark on suicide in costume.

"Ed should come," Clyde said thoughtfully. "If things go wrong she can alert Wilfred, for what it's worth."

"If things go wrong," Rowland said, turning to Edna, "you buy a train ticket to Paris and send Wil a telegram from there."

They spent the remainder of that afternoon scripting what exactly Milton would say to Campbell. Rowland then coached the poet to ensure he sounded more German than Irish. Fortunately, Richter was away from the house and so their absence from the sitting room was barely noticed.

They secreted the money Rowland had withdrawn in the trunk of the Mercedes that Richter insisted they retain for their exclusive use. It occurred to Rowland that should they be forced to flee he might have to steal the motor car to aid their escape. He didn't particularly care for the idea. It seemed a poor way to treat one's host—particularly one who had been as generous and kind as Richter—but he supposed he could write and set matters to right once they had reached some sort of safety. He hoped it would not come to that.

Eva arrived promptly at half past four, bright and clearly excited. Strangely, Rowland was quite looking forward to spending a couple of hours painting. There were still several hours till midnight and dwelling on what they were about to attempt would probably not make it seem any less foolhardy.

Eva went ahead into the room which Richter had set up as a studio, while Rowland poured her a drink.

Clyde and Milton were passing the time at cards.

"Where's Millie?" Rowland asked, noting Edna's absence.

"She's downstairs with Richter," Clyde replied. "A dress-fitting, I think, for that ball gown he's making her." He shook his head. "Poor old bloke is going to be gutted when she goes," he said quietly.

Rowland nodded, glancing at the small blurry photo of Richter's wife and daughter which sat on the mantel. "He has taken rather a shine to her." The German tailor had all but adopted the sculptress, doting on her like an indulgent father. Edna, who had from the first been moved by the tragedy of his loss, raised no objection, and Rowland suspected that she had become genuinely very fond of him. Whenever it was that they would leave Munich, it would be a sad parting. "She can write, I suppose."

Rowland took the glass of sherry into the studio.

Eva reclined on the chaise already undressed. "I'm ready, Herr Negus. How do you want me?"

Rowland smiled. "You should really call me Robert, Eva. We've probably got past the formalities."

Eva rolled over onto her side. "Of course, Robert. This was how I was last time, I think…"

Rowland adjusted the painting on his easel. "Actually, I'm just painting your face now. You can get dressed if you like."

"Oh." Eva seemed a little nonplussed.

"I'm sorry, Eva, I should have said something earlier. I'll just step out so you can get dressed," he added, knowing even women who were comfortable modelling naked often required privacy for the act of getting dressed.

She laughed. "No, it's all right. We are, after all, on a first-name basis now."

He prepared his palette while she pulled on her slip and shimmied into a long, figure-hugging skirt.

"Are you going to the book-burning in Königsplatz this evening, Robert?" she asked casually, as she buttoned her blouse.

"No, I don't think so, Eva," Rowland lied, a little disconcerted by the question. Would they have to make sure they didn't run into Eva at the Königsplatz, in addition to everything else? "I don't suppose you're going?"

To his relief, she shook her head, beaming, stumbling over her words in the rush to tell him her good news. "I am having dinner with Herr Wolf this evening. He came into the shop not long after I saw you this morning. It was all I could do not to blurt out the surprise we have for him."

"The surprise?"

"The painting, of course, silly. Oh, Robert, will it be ready today? I could give it to him at dinner." She jumped a little, like a child anticipating some longed-for treat. "I have been waiting so long for him to have time for me. Are you not happy for me, Robert?"

He smiled, though he was worried about the girl's desperate infatuation. He could not see it ending well. "I'm afraid it won't be dry, Eva."

"Oh." Her face fell, disappointed. Then she cheered a little. "I will tell him I have a magnificent surprise for him and he won't be able to stay away."

Rowland pulled out a chair and placed it just before his easel. "Come and sit here, Eva," he said, as he dipped his brush in Pthalo blue.

Edna walked into the studio and gasped as she stopped behind Rowland. He was still working, although Eva had left over two hours before to prepare for her evening with Herr Wolf.

"What happened?" she demanded.

"Don't you like it?"

Edna scrutinised the portrait of Eva, lightly painted with soft strokes, a startling, gentle likeness. It was a nude but it was to the face of the subject that one was drawn. Her eyes gazed dreamily from the canvas, her fairness almost luminescent against the darkness of the background. There was a tender and romantic quality to the work. "It's lovely, Rowly, but where's the one you started by the lake? Didn't you finish it?"

Rowland rubbed his head. "Yes…it's on Clyde's easel." Both Clyde's easel and the canvas on it faced the wall.

"Then what's this?" Edna said, glancing back at the new portrait.

"I think I might have got rather carried away with the other one. I decided I'd better paint another piece for Eva."

"Didn't she like the first one?"

"She hasn't actually seen it…I came to my senses before I showed her and just started this one."

"Didn't you like it?"

"No, I did…I just think Eva is expecting something rather more traditional."

Edna couldn't resist any longer. She turned Clyde's easel around and stood back to view the canvas. "Oh, Rowly."

"What do you think?" Rowland asked tentatively. The painting was an experiment with a style quite outside his usual.

Edna didn't say anything for a while, as she studied the finished work. Rowland had rendered Eva's face in the same eggshell blue as he had painted her naked body. The lines were familiar. The almost reverential portrayal of her form, glorying in every curve, was distinctly Rowland Sinclair. He'd captured the cherubic roundness of her face but he'd washed out her features so they were mere hints of likeness. All but her eyes. In those he'd caught a kind of furtive, subjugated vibrancy and an overwhelming sense of desperation and hopelessness. To Edna, it was strange and beautiful and sad.

"You've never painted me this way, Rowly."

"I don't paint anybody the way I paint you," he replied quietly. He glanced at the canvas and laughed. "Perhaps I'm just trying to keep up with von Eidelsöhn."

Edna smiled. "I wouldn't think you'd need to do that. This looks just like Eva, but you wouldn't guess it if you didn't know. It's so heartbreaking…more like her than any of my photographs."

"Still," Rowland said, absently wiping his hands on his waistcoat, "I think she may prefer the other one."

"Perhaps." Edna turned to observe him critically. The canvas, it seemed, had not received all the paint. "You'd better get cleaned up…It's getting late."

Chapter Twenty

"German men and women! The age of arrogant Jewish intellectualism is now at an end!... You are doing the right thing at this midnight hour—to consign to the flames the unclean spirit of the past. This is a great, powerful, and symbolic act.

Out of these ashes the phoenix of a new age will arise... Oh Century! Oh Science! It is a joy to be alive!"

—Joseph Goebbels,
Reich Minister for Public Enlightenment and Propaganda,
speaking at the Berlin book-burning
May 10, 1933

The process of getting out of Richter's house and to the Königsplatz had been carefully planned. They had told Richter that they were attending a party thrown by one of the smaller galleries which exhibited work of interest. Earlier, when Richter had taken an afternoon nap, Clyde and Milton had stashed the uniforms of the *Leibstandarte* in the back of the Mercedes. At nine o'clock they shared a late supper with their host and at ten they wished him good night.

Many streets were deserted. It appeared the patriotic citizens of Munich had gone to Königsplatz to burn the un-German. Amidst a great deal of grunting and swearing, three fully grown men struggled into uniforms in the car and in the dark.

Edna inspected under the beam of a torch, smoothing lapels

and straightening ties. She sighed. "You all look disturbingly handsome," she admitted. "Quite frightening, but very handsome."

"Are you sure you lifted the right sizes, Milt?" Rowland grumbled. The high boots were uncomfortably tight.

Milton ignored him, trying to dry-shave in the rear-vision mirror. The flamboyant waxed moustache he had cultivated was both distinctive and distinctly unmilitary.

"Here, give me that razor before you hurt somebody," Clyde said, taking the blade and carefully finishing the shave in the light of Edna's torch. He did not remove the moustache entirely, but left the hair immediately below Milton's nose in the currently fashionable style favoured by both Germany's Chancellor and Eric Campbell.

"How do I look?" Milton asked, trying to squint into the rear-vision mirror.

Edna giggled. "A little silly, to be honest…but very fascist."

They managed to park the car quite close to the square. Fortunately, being a German automobile, it did not stand out the way Rowland's Mercedes had in Sydney. Judging from the noise, the SA had succeeded in summoning a large crowd for their bonfire, despite a last-minute concern that it would rain. A radio address by the Minister for Public Enlightenment and Propaganda, Joseph Goebbels, was being broadcast over a loudspeaker system, and there were cheers and a chanting. "Heil Hitler, Heil Hitler, Heil Hitler…"

Rowland glanced at his watch. Campbell was programmed to speak at precisely midnight and to arrive five minutes before that. They would need to time this perfectly so that they did not give anyone the opportunity to find them out. Fortunately, the National Socialists were fanatical about the punctuality of their events, programming everything to the minute.

That afternoon, Rowland had dispatched a telegram to Wilfred, informing him that he had used the account at Deutsche Bank. He hoped it would be enough to alert his brother that they could well need help quite soon. He didn't know what Wilfred could possibly do from Australia, but at the very least he could help Edna get home.

"Are you chaps sure?" he asked Clyde and Milton quietly, as they donned the greatcoats which would hide the uniforms until they were ready.

"I am," Milton replied without hesitation. "I'm afraid I'm beginning to take the Nazis a little personally."

"We knew what we were doing when we came, Rowly." Clyde dragged on a last cigarette before crushing the stub beneath the heel of his boot. "No point coming all the way over here just to watch Campbell bring this idiocy back home."

Edna's eyes shone in the scant light. She reached up and kissed each of them in turn. "Good luck," she said. "We'll meet back here by half past twelve, if all goes well."

Rowland put his arm around her. "You know where the money is, Ed. If anything goes wrong, don't do anything stupid—you just get out of here."

She smiled at him and for a moment he thought about kissing her…for no real reason and entirely inappropriately. Of drawing her into him and holding her in his arms. Perhaps it would be his last chance.

Milton pulled him away. "Come on, Rowly, we'd better get moving."

Rowland focussed again on the task at hand.

They had heard reports of the thousands who attended Nazi rallies, but the sheer number of people in the square surprised them nonetheless. It was as if the city had drained into Königsplatz. The atmosphere was festive, heightened by an almost religious fervour. Entire families stood cheering with armfuls of books ready to burn. Kerchiefed members of the Hitler Youth joined the SA in leading the demonstration.

They were not the only men there in black uniform. The SS was also present in force. From a distance they were only distinguishable from the uniforms Rowland, Clyde, and Milton wore by the presence of a red armband. Rowland could only hope that Germans were familiar enough with Nazi regalia to recognise the special authority that was signified by the lack of an armband.

The Australians fought their way through the crowd for several minutes before they could even see the flames of the massive bonfire at the square's centre, into which books were being tossed to a chant of "Burn... burn... *brennan sie alles...*"

There was an avenue of sorts cordoned off near the stage to allow the dignitaries and speakers to drive in without having to plough through the crowds. According to Blanshard's information, Campbell's car would arrive there at precisely five minutes to midnight.

They positioned themselves as close to the avenue as possible, finding a place in the shadows where they would be unnoticed. Edna stayed nearby, though they lost sight of her quickly in the crowd.

Rowland checked his watch again. It was five minutes to midnight. He signalled to Clyde and Milton and they removed the greatcoats and became, for all the world, members of the *Leibstandarte Adolf Hitler*. They walked purposefully towards the avenue, striding confidently like the men of rank they were supposed to be. A black Mercedes came down the avenue. As the automobile stopped, Milton strode directly to the back door before the SA chauffeur could open it. They had agreed that their best chance lay with Campbell never getting out of the vehicle.

"Look haughty," Rowland whispered to Clyde, as they prepared to do their part.

"Haughty?"

"Act as though everybody smells."

Rowland and Clyde intercepted the driver as he jumped out to open Campbell's door.

"Change of plans," Rowland told the man, using High German—the *Leibstandarte* was based in Berlin. "The

Chancellor wishes to meet with Herr Campbell…discreetly. You are to take him back to his hotel now."

The Stormtrooper was flustered. "Who are you?"

Rowland pointed to the insignia on his lapel. "*Leibstandarte,*" he snapped. "There must be no fuss. We do not want to alert the enemies of Germany of the Chancellor's movements."

Again the Brownshirt wavered. In the periphery of his vision Rowland could see a bloated SA officer striding towards him, with half a dozen Stormtroopers in tow.

Someone among the gathering shouted "*Leibstandarte*…It's the *Leibstandarte*…The Chancellor is coming…the Chancellor is here!" Women screamed and fainted. The crowd surged against the cordon in excitement. The SA moved to hold them back.

Rowland turned and barked at the SA officer who was approaching. "This was meant to be done quietly! This fool has alerted the people and compromised the Chancellor's security!"

The man glared at him. His face was pugnacious, scarred. Rowland had seen him once before, at the railway station when they first arrived in Munich.

"Röhm!" Rowland said, as if he knew him. "Your man is obstructing the work of the *Leibstandarte*. Do you no longer have control of this confounded rabble?"

Clyde stood beside him, his face stony, his nose wrinkled slightly. Milton was bent at the back window of the Mercedes, talking to Campbell and preventing him from alighting.

"Herr Campbell is scheduled to speak," Röhm said coldly.

"Am I to report back that Commander Röhm has overridden the express wishes of the Chancellor?" Rowland demanded, playing hard. Their only chance was to not allow Röhm the time to think. "There must be no delay."

"Why does the Chancellor wish to see Herr Campbell now?"

"That is not for me to know," Rowland sneered. "I do not question my orders. I carry them out!"

Röhm stared at the lapel of Rowland's uniform. He inhaled to bellow.

"*Entschuldigung*, Commander Röhm." Alastair Blanshard's head appeared out of the rear window of the stationary Mercedes. He spoke to Röhm in German. "All is well, *mein Herr*. Herr Campbell has been expecting a visit from the Chancellor. It is unfortunate that it should be now, but we understand the Chancellor is a busy man. Herr Campbell is honoured, and delighted to accommodate his request, if you are willing to make his apologies to the good people of Munich."

For a moment nothing was said. The screaming for the Chancellor grew louder, as people assumed Campbell's car contained their beloved leader. Rowland and Clyde kept their faces turned from the automobile. Clyde kept his nose wrinkled.

"You can tell Herr Campbell that the people of Munich will not notice his absence," Röhm spat at Blanshard. He motioned to the SA driver, who returned to his seat and put the car into reverse. The crowd cried out in protest and disappointment.

Rowland did not meet the eyes of either Clyde or Milton lest some tiny sign of mutual relief become recognisable.

Röhm was clearly unhappy. Vocally so. He cursed, shouting directly into Rowland's face. "You go back and tell that mayflower, Dietrich, that the SA stood with Hitler before he was even a party member!"

Rowland held his ground, his right brow rising as he smiled contemptuously. He ducked reflexively when the SA Commander's arm shot out in a fascist salute, swallowing a curse as Röhm clicked his heels and shouted "Heil Hitler!"

In the expectation that followed, Rowland decided that an enthusiastic return would be giving ground. The *Leibstandarte* held a privileged position as Hitler's personal guard...he needed to maintain a believable level of arrogance. He flapped his hand carelessly beside his head and muttered, "Heil Hitler!" before turning away. Milton and Clyde fell into step behind him.

"What the hell do we do now?" Clyde whispered.

"Just watch the bonfire for a while...until they stop watching us."

They stalked towards the blaze.

"You really pulled that fat bloke's tail, Rowly."

"It seems." Rowland glanced back at Röhm. "Hopefully enough to convince him that we are indeed from the *Leibstandarte*."

Milton laughed softly. "Almost feel sorry for Campbell… waiting for Hitler to come ask him to dance like some homely, forgotten debutante."

It was hot by the flames, which roared up in a multistorey furnace. Periodically the Stormtroopers would let a few citizens approach the inferno to throw in books and declare their animosity to the un-German works which they cast into destruction.

"My God!" Milton said, as a mis-aimed book landed near their feet. "That's Hemingway. They're burning Hemingway!"

They started now to note the titles which littered the fringe of the fire. Among the works of notable Communists such as Trotsky and Lenin were the works of Jews who had no connection with Communism whatsoever. Books by the renowned psychoanalyst Sigmund Freud were heaped upon the flames, and the words of the scientist Albert Einstein were also apparently dangerous to Germany.

Rowland placed a warning hand on Milton's shoulder as the poet spied Proust among the ashes. "It's not the only copy, Milt," he said, worried the other would attempt a rescue of the novel.

Milton swore.

They slipped into the crowd as the Hitler Youth led the people of Munich in singing "*Deutschland, Deutschland über alles.*"

Some of the cordons had now been breached as the crowd disintegrated into a kind of ordered chaos. Rowland watched as a small girl with golden curls hurled books into the fire screaming "Burn Jew!" while her father laughed approvingly. The more sedate parts of the crowd were now becoming caught up in the dark euphoria, rallied into a fury against what they were being told was un-German.

He glanced at Milton. The poet seemed bewildered, more than anything else.

They stood back as the crowd surged towards the stage, and used the movement to slip unnoticed in the other direction. Having abandoned their greatcoats earlier, they would have to return to the car as members of the *Leibstandarte*.

"Stop! I know you!"

Chapter Twenty-one

BONFIRE OF BOOKS
Nazis Clean Up In Germany
JEWS DERIDED

BERLIN, May 10

Berlin's greatest bonfire of books since the middle ages occurred in Opera Square at midnight. While searchlights played on the crowded square, university students led by Nazis committed 20,000 Marxist, pacifist, Jewish, and other "un German" books to the flames.

Thousands of students bearing torches escorted the condemned books.

They passed the books from hand to hand and then hurled them amid wild cheers onto the blazing pile. The flames luridly lighting the cathedral of the old Imperial Palace heightened the barbarity of the scene.

As the books were destroyed the authors' names were announced...The wildest applause greeted the destruction of works by Remarque, author of *All Quiet on the Western Front*...As Dr. Goebbels hurled works by Karl Marx into the flames he said: "I herewith bequeath to the fire all things contrary to German culture."

OTHER BOOK BURNINGS
Similar book burnings occurred in other German cities. In Munich 25,000 books were destroyed. The burning was

preceded by a patriotic demonstration at the university, where Herr Schemm, the Bavarian Minister of Education, said that all Germans should go down on their knees and thank Almighty God that they lived in an age which so reflected the fatherland's ever-increasing glory. The Nazi revolution, he said, would fit Germany more than ever to lead the world.

—*Barrier Miner*, 1933

The words were English, and shouted from behind them.

"Keep walking," Rowland murmured.

"Stop or I'll scream for help!"

They stopped. Rowland turned slowly. He squinted into the press of people to see who'd discovered them.

Nancy Wake walked angrily up to him.

"I knew it," she spat. "It's you! I couldn't believe it when I saw you just now in that…that uniform! But it's you."

"Miss Wake…"

"Don't you Miss Wake me…pretending to be a friend of Peter's. You're not even Australian, are you? You were just trying to get information for your superiors. You're a spy, aren't you? Good Lord! I'd been told the Nazis were spying on everybody…How dare you! I am a member of the free press! Were you spying on Mr. Göring, too, you two-faced, despicable…?" She reached up and slapped him.

Rowland blinked.

People were beginning to turn. Nancy continued to berate him. She did so in English but it was clear to the German-speaking crowd that she was immensely displeased. Rowland clutched for some way, any way, of silencing her.

He seized the journalist in his arms and kissed her on the lips, hard. For a moment she stopped shouting. Even after he'd pulled away, she gaped mutely, stunned. There were snickers in the surrounding crowd as the exchange was transformed into what appeared to be a lovers' tiff.

"Jesus, Mary, and Joseph," Clyde breathed, sure that Rowland had lost his mind.

"How dare you!" Nancy was suddenly in full voice again but now people laughed. An old woman shouted, "*Wieder schmusen ihr!*" and cackled. A couple of young men cheered.

Rowland caught Nancy's hand just as she was about to slap him again. He spoke loudly in German. "I'm sorry, darling...It won't happen again...She meant nothing."

It was probably fortunate that Nancy couldn't understand him. Nor the shouts encouraging her to forgive him. Holding tightly to her hand, Rowland proceeded to pull her away with him. She began to fight.

"Miss Wake," he said under his breath. "Would you stop before you get us all shot! I'll explain as soon as we can get out of here."

At first it seemed she would not desist, and then, still seething, she stopped struggling. Behind them there was laughter and even applause. It appeared that the errant Nazi officer had brought his foreign sweetheart under control. It was a testament to German manhood.

As the ceremony had not yet finished, the street in which they'd left the car was quiet. The occasional couple sat embracing in a vehicle, but they were disinterested in the uniformed men who accompanied a young woman.

Edna had not yet arrived when they reached the car. Rowland glanced at his watch. She still had a few minutes.

"Suppose you tell me what's going on, you insufferable cad!" Nancy demanded, hitting him again, this time with her bag.

Rowland opened the door and stood out of her reach, following only after she'd climbed into the relative privacy of the automobile. He removed his cap. Now that the immediate danger had passed, Clyde and Milton were trying hard not to laugh. He introduced them as Joseph Ryan and Albert Greenway.

"We're not spies, Miss Wake...well, not for the Nazis,

anyway. We're here trying to stop the spread of Nazism to Australia."

"By joining them?" she accused, looking pointedly at his uniform.

Rowland looked down. "Oh, these…No, they're just borrowed. Believe me, Miss Wake, I am spying on neither you nor Mr. Göring. I quite like the chap, for one thing."

"Whatever you were doing, you had no right to take the liberties you did in the square!" Nancy looked like she might hit him again.

"Yes…of course, you're right. And I apologise unreservedly." He kept a wary eye on her hand.

Nancy was not satisfied. "What on Earth did you think you were doing?"

"The only thing I could think of to prevent us from being shot."

"Why, that's ridiculous!"

Milton laughed. "Miss Wake's got a right to be upset, Robbie. A book-burning is hardly the most romantic venue. Dancing would have been more appropriate…or the theatre."

Rowland's mouth twitched upwards. It would not do to laugh at Miss Wake's indignation. Clyde reached over and clouted Milton on Rowland's behalf. There was nothing for it but to tell Nancy Wake what they were doing in the Königsplatz, masquerading as members of the *Leibstandarte*.

She listened with progressively less belligerence and then turned to Milton. "You just walked up to him and told him to go back? Why, that's extraordinary!"

Milton puffed. "You know, Miss Wake, I like to think that there is a tide in the affairs of men, which when taken at the flood, leads on to fortune." He winked. "I took that flood."

"That's not all he took," Rowland murmured, keeping his eyes on the road through the back window. "Shakespeare…" He relaxed suddenly. "There's Millie."

He stepped quickly out of the car to meet her and bundled her into the backseat between him and Nancy.

Edna was, of course, not a little surprised by the presence of the young journalist. Rowland introduced them.

"Miss Wake recognised me in the square," he explained. "We were forced to bring her with us."

"You weren't the one being forced!" Nancy corrected.

"You kidnapped her?" Edna stared at Rowland. "Why, that's not very polite."

Rowland groaned. They were joining forces.

"And where were you, dear sister?" Milton came to Rowland's aid. "Robbie was starting to worry…It's not safe for women out there—all sorts of blokes taking liberties."

"Oh, yes…I'm sorry," Edna said, heaving her large handbag onto Rowland's lap. It landed there with a thud.

"What in heaven's name have you got in here?" he asked.

"Did you know they were burning Hemingway…and H. G. Wells?" She opened her bag and took out a singed volume of *Farewell to Arms*. "I saved a few." She extracted several sooty books from the handbag, murmuring, "There's even a Proust in here."

Milton turned and, leaning over the front seat into the back, he kissed Edna on the forehead.

Clyde was less impressed. "Are you mad? If they'd caught you…"

Edna dismissed him with a wave of her hand. "What with the smoke, and the singing and the 'heiling,' nobody was paying any attention to me. I had to do something."

Nancy was quick to agree. "When you can do something, you must," she said vehemently.

Rowland glanced at Nancy hopefully. "So I'm forgiven?"

Edna looked up. "What did you do?"

"It would be ungallant to say."

The journalist met his eyes. "Since it was a matter of life and death, I will excuse you this time."

"I assure you it will never happen again," Rowland replied soberly.

Nancy Wake smiled. "There's no need to go quite that far, Mr. Negus."

They drove again to a secluded lane in the industrial part of Munich where they were unlikely to be noticed by passers-by. Edna and Nancy sat on the hood of the Mercedes, chatting as the men changed out of their uniforms within.

"They smell a bit smoky," Clyde said dubiously. "You don't suppose that Richter might notice?"

Milton shrugged. "Even if the old man notices, he's hardly going to imagine that they took themselves out to a book-burning."

They emerged from the car looking themselves, if a little crumpled. Nancy and Edna were laughing as they perched shivering on the warmth of the black hood.

"What's so funny, ladies?" Milton asked.

"Nancy was just telling me what exactly happened at the Königsplatz when she came across the three of you," Edna giggled. "Gracious, Rowly, I didn't know you had it in you."

Rowland started as she used his real name.

"Nancy knows what we're doing here, Rowly," Edna said calmly. "There's really no point in pretending with her." She smiled at the journalist.

Milton looked from Edna to Rowland. "You're bloody hopeless spies, the both of you," he said in disgust.

Rowland smiled. "Perhaps, but we did manage to stop Campbell speaking at the Königsplatz. And on that note, I think we should find somewhere to celebrate."

Clyde glanced at his watch. "What's going to be open at this time of night?"

"I know a place," Nancy volunteered. "It's a little rough, but it's open till dawn."

As none of them was inclined to sleep just yet, in the wake of what they had done, Nancy's suggestion was heartily adopted and they drove to the very outskirts of Munich, to a wine bar which seemed the only sign of life and light in a grimy street.

The place was full of journalists. The crowded room rang with a babble of competing Continental languages. The proprietor had obviously catered to his professional clientele. There was a telephone mounted on the back wall where patrons lined up to phone editors and relay news back to their home papers.

A swarthy gentleman played a Spanish guitar in a corner, as the woman beside him swayed and drank. The air was more congested here than it had been at the book-burning, as journalists discussed the state of Germany and smoked. In the background, the tap of a typewriter as someone met a deadline in the bar. Rowland ordered drinks and a platter of cheese and bread which they consumed as they toasted and talked.

Using their aliases, Nancy introduced them to a number of journalists she knew. Many were, like Nancy, foreign correspondents, freelancing in Germany. They all had ambitions of interviewing Germany's high-profile Chancellor. The world was watching the Third Reich, and Adolf Hitler sold papers.

Being mostly men, the journalists jostled to join them, to buy Edna and Nancy drinks and generally leave an impression. A Frenchman succeeded in persuading Edna to dance with him in the roughly four square feet of floor space available for the purpose. When she was asked, Nancy declared that a second couple would simply not fit and so the eligible men lined up to dance with Edna in succession, leaving Nancy free to talk to Rowland.

He asked her again about Peter Bothwell. "There were rumours that he was involved with a woman here."

"And you think that's me?"

"I had thought it a possibility."

"Don't be ridiculous," she said. "Peter was old enough to be my father."

"Then…"

"Peter and I met at the Bismarck. He was writing a book

about the Reich…not just Hitler but all his dubious lieutenants as well. He overheard me arguing with my editor on the phone one day." Nancy allowed Rowland to pour her another glass of wine. "I had written a piece about Commander Röhm and the perversion of the SA hierarchy. They source boys from one of the high schools in Munich…it's reprehensible." She sipped her wine before she went on. "Of course, the paper didn't want to publish it…they couldn't print the word 'homosexual,' apparently. Peter was interested in what I had on Röhm for his book. We became friends then…I'd let him know whenever I heard rumours or gossip and he did the same. He was charming and Australian and, with me, a thorough gentleman." She sighed sadly.

"I see." Rowland frowned. If Bothwell was gathering dirt on prominent Nazis, there could be any number of people who wished him dead. "I don't suppose you know if there was some other…"

"Woman?" She nodded. "There may have been. On occasion, Peter would smell of perfume. I ran into him once when he was buying flowers. Naturally, I teased him about it, but he said I was just being silly…as he would, I suppose."

"You know he was married?"

"Yes…that was the odd thing. He seemed so devoted to his family…showed me pictures of his boys. Peter was dearly looking forward to getting home to them."

"And you have no idea who this other woman might have been?"

Nancy's brow furrowed for a moment. "Perhaps she was an actress."

"Why do you say that?"

"Well, the day that Peter bought the flowers, he had tickets for the theatre: two. I thought he must be taking his mystery woman to a show, but he said the other ticket was for the friend he was staying with."

"But one would presume he wasn't bringing flowers to a man." Rowland nodded thoughtfully.

"Exactly." Nancy was emphatic. "That's when I wondered if he was besotted by some actress."

"You could be right. Do you remember the name of the show?"

"I'm afraid not…I do remember it was at the Kammerspiele in Maximilianstrasse. About six weeks ago now, I suppose."

Rowland smiled. "Thank you, Miss Wake…and for your assistance in the Königsplatz, however coerced. I do hope the experience was not too distressing."

She grimaced, though her eyes smiled. "It may take a few drinks but I'm certain I'll recover, Mr. Sinclair."

Chapter Twenty-two

WHISKERS
Their Significance in Relation to Human Psychology

BY C. J. DENNIS

...And this brings us to Germany, the natural home of hirsute grotesquery.

GERMAN EXAMPLES

From the "monkey frill" of Wagner to the "mutton chop" embellishments of Bismarck and his alleged master, Frederick, we come to those three outstanding wartime figures, ex-Kaiser Wilhelm, Von Tirpitz, and Hindenburg. With that elaborately-trained representation of the German eagle that reared arrogantly from his upper lip, the ex-Kaiser was a hoarding, advertising all the bombast, vanity, and childish fustian that his tragic acts later revealed. Behind his forked beard Von Tirpitz lurked, threatening but ineffective, even as his fleet lurked in the Kiel Canal. But those pendulous pothooks that drooped aggressively upon the Hindenburg cheeks were eloquent of savage obstinacy, of ruthless and ponderous persistence. They resembled nothing so much as a pair of strange, barbaric weapons designed for torture and brutal tenacity.

And so I am brought naturally to the comical moustache of Herr Adolph Hitler and to an abrupt end. For should I try to set down all the concentrated egotism and erratic mentality that even the printed effigy of that comic moustache suggests to me I should be here writing for a week.

—*The Courier Mail,* 1933

When Milton came down to a late breakfast, he was clean-shaven. The small brush-like moustache he'd worn for a few hours the night before had been removed and the uniforms returned to Richter's storeroom.

They had returned just before dawn. Their host and his household had been asleep, of course, and so they had entered quietly, and crept up to their beds and welcome sleep.

"Oh, I'm so glad you got rid of that thing, Bertie darling," Edna said, looking up from her tea.

"Did you not like my manly moustache, sister dear?"

Edna smiled sweetly. "It looked ridiculous."

Milton feigned dismay. "I thought you ladies would admire it."

"We don't."

Richter, who had last seen the poet sporting the waxed and twirled moustache favoured by the surrealists, agreed. "Once, men knew how to wear a moustache. It would arch over the entire mouth and join the sideburns, but alas…now it is the fashion to look as though the hair in your nose has grown too long…Pah!"

Milton sighed. He had, to be honest, become rather fond of the pliable highlight of his upper lip, in its original form. The unwaxed brush, on the other hand, had no style whatsoever. He was glad it was gone.

"So, young people," Richter said, taking a healthy slice of the cream-layered cake which, it seemed, was his customary breakfast. "What are your plans for this fine day?"

"I thought we might go to the theatre this evening." Rowland poured his third cup of coffee in an attempt to eradicate the fatigue of too little sleep. "One of the chaps last night was extolling the virtues of some show at the Kammerspiele. Do you know it, Mr. Richter?"

Richter shrugged. "Yes, it is a perfectly adequate theatre, I suppose, but it does not compare to the Nationaltheatre München. I believe the Bavarian Symphony is playing Wagner there tonight. I know the conductor…perhaps you would prefer…"

Clyde, who was standing at the sideboard behind Richter, turned with such a look of abject horror that Rowland was in no doubt that his friend did not wish to attend several hours of Wagner. Even so, Clyde felt the need to make his preference clear by signalling madly. Rowland resisted the urge to torture him by feigning interest.

"I did rather promise the chap that I would try to see this show—I wish I could remember what it was called. He's involved with the production somehow and it hasn't been selling well."

"Ah, my poor Mr. Negus." Richter lamented, patting Stasi feverishly as if the dog too might have been upset by the thought. "Condemned to attend a second-rate performance because you have befriended some incompetent producer. Surely there is some excuse you can give?"

"I'm hoping it won't be too bad." Rowland still had no idea of what play he had supposedly undertaken to patronise. He'd just have to find the theatre and ask what was showing. Richter didn't mention that he had seen a show there with Bothwell, but considering his opinion of the venue, it was probably not surprising. Rowland toyed with the idea of telling Richter everything and enlisting his aid in finding out how Peter Bothwell had died, but he dismissed it quickly. While Richter didn't seem as enamoured of Adolf Hitler as many Germans, he was still German, and knowingly harbouring spies would probably not be good for business. They would find a way to resolve this without involving their generous host.

The newspapers of the day all proclaimed the success of the book-burning the night before. Accounts varied in the strength of the doctrinal dogma they expounded, but it was not just *Der Stürmer* which reported that citizens had declared their Germanic pride by burning books that were against the national interest. Significantly, no mention was made of the last-minute cancellation of Eric Campbell's address. Perhaps, as Röhm had declared, Munich had not even noticed his absence.

Richter, for his part, did not seem particularly concerned one way or another. "It is mere puffery," he said. "A way of insulting Jews and Americans in the guise of patriotism. Germany will be great again but not because we burn books!"

It was nearly noon when Alois Richter took his leave to attend his offices in the city centre. It appeared Hugo Boss had undercut him once again, and the tailor was not willing to let the situation stand. And so he left his guests to their own devices.

Rowland intended to use the absence as an opportunity to seek out the Kammerspiele, which he had ascertained was located on Maximilianstrasse. He waited until he was sure Mrs. Engels was out of earshot before he told the others of his plans.

Edna grabbed her coat. "I'll come with you, Rowly."

"Me too," said Clyde, standing hastily.

Milton laughed. "He's afraid Richter will come back and take him to Wagner...Clyde prefers his music with lyrics."

Rowland tossed Clyde his hat. He wasn't a huge fan of symphonies himself. "It could be worse," he said sympathetically. "At least nobody expects you to dance."

"There is that." Clyde sighed. "They just take so flaming long, Rowly. Those bloody orchestras...Once they have the stage, they won't stop...Every time you think it's finally over, they get going yet again."

Rowland smiled. Richter had taken them to one symphony already. It had been Mozart, and, if he was honest, it had indeed dragged on. The experience had obviously traumatised Clyde.

"I suppose I'd better come too," Milton said, yawning. "There's a little gallery just off Maximilianstrasse which holds a collage that I think my dear friends in the Graziers' Association simply must have."

The boulevard was busy. There seemed to be a new injection of patriotism in the population. Even children screamed "Heil Hitler!" and saluted to all and sundry.

Rowland frowned as he saw a girl of no more than five mock an elderly Rabbi. The hatred displayed by children disturbed him more than anything else.

"Someone needs to give that brat a good clip around the ear," Clyde murmured.

Edna stopped suddenly, staring into the crowd on the opposite side of the street. "Look! It's Schlampen...the boy from the station." She stepped after him, waving and calling, "Schlampen! Schlampen!"

Rowland grabbed her around the waist and pulled her back, blanching as the oncoming traffic screeched rubber and blasted horns.

"Good Lord, Ed..."

Edna was still focussed across the road. "He's run off. Did you see him?"

"Afraid not." Rowland removed his hat and pushed the hair back off his forehead. "Ed, I would be very surprised if the boy's name is Schlampen...and you really can't shout that out in the main street of Munich."

Milton nodded towards a group of well-dressed young women who were standing at a shop window near where Edna thought she'd seen the young Romany boy. They were as a group glaring at the sculptress. "I fear you may have offended them."

"He said his name was Schlampen," Edna started.

"No—I believe that's just how he responded when you asked his name." Rowland smiled. "You truly don't want to call that out, Ed."

Edna inhaled. "The little…"

"Are you sure you saw him?" Rowland asked.

"Yes…but what would a little boy be doing here on his own?" she said, frowning. "Someone should be looking after him."

"He might not be on his own. Romanies are rather nomadic."

"I wonder if the little blighter's still got my watch," Milton growled. "If you see him again, Ed, don't shout insults…Let one of us know to catch the thieving vagabond."

They decided to walk further down Maximilianstrasse, well past the group of angry young women whom Edna had inadvertently insulted, before crossing.

The Kammerspiele had recently been made the municipal theatre of Munich. While it was neither as grand nor as illustrious as the neoclassical Baroque and Rococo structures which housed the state and national companies, the Schauspielhaus—as the theatre in Maximilianstrasse was called—was breathtaking on a lesser scale.

They searched the posters and bills for what was showing. They would need to find a play to patronise in order to give truth to the story Rowland had told Richter.

Rowland spoke to the girl in the ticketing booth. He used Bavarian, telling her of a show he'd been recommended which had been performed at the Kammerspiele in March.

"I am embarrassed to say, Fräulein, I have forgotten the name of the play entirely."

The young woman was blond and quite plump. She looked up at Rowland with bored brown eyes. "A play, you say? There was a production of *Macbeth* in March, *mein Herr*, but it closed early." She lowered her voice. "The reviews were very bad after Lady Macbeth disappeared."

"She disappeared?"

The girl smiled, pleased to have his interest. She whispered, "The producers were very upset…The understudy was not so good, you see. Fräulein Niemann, who played Lady Macbeth, just didn't come back one night and no one could find her. It is a mystery."

"Indeed. And what happened to the rest of the cast?"

She shrugged. "They returned to obscurity…The understudy sells cigarettes here during the evening shows."

"She hasn't found another part, then?" Rowland glanced at the current playbill.

The ticketing girl laughed unkindly. "Fräulein Kramer plays a cigarette girl very convincingly—it is her best work."

Rowland purchased tickets to *Romeo and Juliet* for that evening, before rejoining his friends.

"What are we coming back to see?" Clyde asked, taking the tickets.

"The cigarette girl," Rowland replied. "And *Romeo and Juliet.*" He looked at them sheepishly. "Just occurred to me it will be in German."

Clyde laughed. "Don't worry, mate—I've never understood Shakespeare in English. It might make more sense in German."

Alastair Blanshard was waiting at the Haus der Deutsche Kunst, a private gallery which boasted a dedication to the government-approved conservatism in its exhibits. He had left a message summoning Rowland to the gallery. To the servant who took the message, it seemed that Alois Richter's Australian houseguest was merely meeting another dealer to negotiate the purchase of yet another work.

When Rowland found him in the gallery, Blanshard was studying a classical work by someone with whom Rowland was entirely unfamiliar. The painting depicted a group of men standing in a heroic pose, fresh from victory in some medieval battle. The artist was technically proficient with figures, but the faces were expressionless and flat.

Rowland stood beside Blanshard.

"Not bad. Quite daring and well executed."

Rowland tilted his head to one side, squinting at the painting. "Do you think so? I find it rather dull."

"I was referring to last evening."

"Oh, yes. That. How is Colonel Campbell this morning?"

"Disappointed and exceedingly irritated, if you must know. In fact, he's considering writing to the Chancellor to complain."

Rowland smiled. "He's given up on becoming Hitler's best mate, then?"

"Not quite yet, I'm afraid. But he certainly has had the wind taken out of his sails."

Rowland laughed.

"Don't get cocky, Mr. Negus," Blanshard said curtly. "You were lucky I was able to intervene with Röhm, or things might not have gone so well."

"You're very welcome, Mr. Blanshard."

"Don't be smart, Mr. Negus. You and your friends seem to think this is some lark…a schoolboy prank."

Rowland walked on to the next painting. "Is there some reason you wanted to meet with me, Mr. Blanshard?"

After a short time, Blanshard followed. "I have another job for you."

"Capital…it'll be a lark." Rowland smiled as Blanshard glowered at the painting before him. They stood there for a couple of minutes. Finally Rowland sighed. "What is it you would like me to do?"

Blanshard exhaled, and waited for the young couple looking at a painting beside them to move on. "I need you to befriend a young lady."

"That sounds a little less onerous than your last request." Rowland moved on to another painting. "Why?"

"We need to undermine Campbell's standing among the international fascists. The Honourable Unity Mitford is a way to do that."

"And why is that?"

"The young lady is a committed fascist, and an English

aristocrat with the highest connections. I'm afraid Oswald Mosley has been somewhat indiscreet with her sister, Diana."

"I see."

"If you convince her that Campbell's shirt is not quite black, then she will spread a distrust of him."

"Why would she believe me?"

"No idea. Flatter her. Woo her. Do whatever you have to."

Rowland stared at Blanshard for a moment before he remembered that they were not supposed to know one another and averted his gaze. It was a rather extraordinary request, vaguely unseemly. He rubbed the back of his neck. "And how do you propose I gain an introduction to Miss Mitford?"

They stepped over to the next painting, but not together, so it was a few moments before Blanshard could answer.

"You will find her at the Osteria Bavaria on Schellingstrasse every morning at around eleven."

Rowland knew the restaurant. "She's fond of their sticky buns, then?" He recalled the café's advertised specialty.

Blanshard almost smiled. "The Chancellor calls in there regularly. I am reliably informed that Miss Mitford goes there in the hope of catching his eye, should he appear."

"Good Lord." Rowland shook his head. "How will I know this woman?"

"Don't worry, you will."

Chapter Twenty-three

SWASTIKA EMBLEM
ENRAGES LONDON CROWD
WOMAN WEARER ATTACKED

London, April 10

Enraged by the wearing of the swastika emblem, a crowd
in Hyde Park attacked the Hon. Unity Freeman Mitford,
daughter of Lord Redesdale, who was hit and kicked before
she was rescued by the police. Thousands of people took up
the cry of "Kill the Fascists."

—*Geraldton Guardian and Express*, 1938

Edna hitched up the skirt of her gown as she ran down the
sweeping staircase to where the men were waiting.

"Do not hurry, *dandschig Deandl*," Richter cautioned.
"Allow us to savour the splendour of your entrance."

Edna laughed and indulged him, slowing to an elegant
descent with her hand poised gracefully on the polished
banister. Milton tapped his chin to remind her to lift her own.
Clyde tapped his watch to remind her to not to waste time
being too splendid. Rowland looked at her as though he was
planning a painting.

She did feel elegant. The gown, which had been packed neatly in Millicent Greenway's trunk, had been a little big when she'd first tried it on, but Alois Richter had adjusted it with a dart here and a tuck there. She'd explained the fact that her clothes did not fit by telling him she had lost weight since it was purchased. He had tsked and tutted about the seams and the quality of the stitching, but Edna was delighted with the deep purple evening dress. She was quite enjoying Millicent's wardrobe.

She took the hand Richter offered her at the base of the stairs.

"I am certain that even if this play at the Kammerspiele proves a good one, no man will be looking at the stage with Miss Greenway in the audience," Richter said, clasping her hand in both of his.

"That would make the actors a bit cross, I imagine," Edna replied, smiling at the tailor. "Are you sure you will not come with us, Mr. Richter?"

"Alas, my dear, I have business affairs which demand my attention. Stasi and I will have a quiet evening, with brandy and paperwork. You go and enjoy yourself...Make these gentlemen the envy of every man in Munich."

"You are a flatterer, Mr. Richter," Edna said, kissing the tailor on the cheek. "Do not wait up for us...we might be quite late."

It was not until they were alone in the car that Rowland was finally able to recount his conversation with Blanshard and the latest task that he had been set.

Milton laughed. "She's loitering in bun shops hoping Hitler will walk in? She sounds crackers!"

"The English aristocracy tends to be," Rowland sighed. "Apparently she's quite well connected, albeit scandalously, with Oswald Mosley and his crowd."

"So you're to become chummy with this Miss Mitford and then defame Colonel Campbell?" Edna asked. It seemed absurdly simple.

"That's about the size of it."

"It's only really defamation if you're a fascist," Milton pointed out. "In reality, Rowly will be complimenting the Nazi-loving lunatic."

"Lying outright is probably closer to the truth," Rowland replied. "I've got to make it seem as though he's not really made of the right stuff."

"What are you going to say?" Clyde asked. "You can't really claim he's a Communist plant."

Rowland's brow rose. "That might be hard to sustain. I'll just have to fabricate some sort of skeleton."

They parked Richter's Mercedes and walked into the Kammerspiele with a stream of theatregoers. Rowland searched the foyer for cigarette girls. There were two. A petite brunette—barely twenty—who smiled at and chatted with every customer, and an older blonde, perhaps thirty. She barely looked up from her tray as she dispensed cigarettes and took money.

Rowland nodded towards the blonde. "I expect that's her."

"We can only ask, I suppose," Clyde said.

Rowland glanced at Edna. "Milt, why don't you and Ed go in and find our seats? Clyde and I will hang back and buy cigarettes."

Milton bowed extravagantly to Edna and offered her his arm. "Shall we, old girl?"

"Good luck," Edna whispered over her shoulder, as she took Milton's arm.

Rowland and Clyde waited until almost everybody else had entered the theatre before they approached the cigarette girl.

Rowland bought a box of cigarettes, although he didn't smoke and Clyde always rolled his own. "*Entschuldigung, Fräulein,*" he said, looking directly into her face as he handed her the money. "Didn't I see you on stage a couple of months ago?…What was it?"

"*Macbeth,*" she said smiling slightly. "I played Lady Macbeth. You saw it, *mein Herr?*"

"Yes. I am honoured to make your acquaintance, Fräulein…?"

"Werner, Helga Werner." She said, smiling broadly now.

Rowland introduced himself. "Robert Negus, Fräulein Werner."

Clyde lit a cigarette and wandered off to smoke leaving them alone.

"I came to see the show a second time but it had closed," Rowland said, hoping he sounded regretful.

"I was only Lady Macbeth for two days," she replied quietly. "I was the understudy…too young for the part, really."

"Of course," Rowland said, smiling. "It is only your talent that made you so believable."

Helga Werner blushed. "The critics did not think so, I fear. Perhaps the show would not have closed if Fräulein Niemann had not left."

"Fräulein Niemann?"

"I was her understudy. She was a big star in Vienna. This was her first role in Munich."

"I see. It was fortunate that she chose to leave the show so that at least a few audiences had the happy opportunity to see you as Lady Macbeth."

"But she didn't choose to leave," Helga said. "At least, I don't think she did."

"Did she fall ill, then?" Rowland asked.

"No, she simply disappeared one day. All her things were still in the dressing room…her makeup, her brush, even her jewellery. It was very upsetting for the theatre."

"Her family must be very worried."

"I don't think she had any. There were two men who brought her flowers once, but they didn't come back or ask after her."

"Robbie!" Clyde signalled to the theatre door, which was being closed.

"It was a pleasure to meet you, Fräulein Werner." Rowland smiled warmly at the struggling actress. "I do hope we will be seeing you on the stage again soon."

The production of *Romeo and Juliet* at the Kammerspiele was unexpectedly good. The story was so familiar, and the performances so visually moving, that Rowland's companions did not require German to follow the play. A modern interpretation, it was set to the background of a live jazz band and the cast wore spats and flapper beads.

Rowland noticed a number of people leave as the music started, but his attention was soon wholly on the stage.

They had come primarily to speak with the cigarette girl, but they left talking about the show and, for a while, politics, conspiracies, and spies were forgotten.

"It was inspired!" Edna said, as they found a table in a smoky bar. "The way the players connected to the audience… it's something you don't get in film. It's exhilarating! Perhaps I'll audition for the stage when we get home."

They all laughed at her, without restraint, accustomed to the sculptress' ability to find glory in the merest whim. She ignored them. Rowland told them then what he had learned from Helga Werner.

"That's odd." Milton frowned. "I wonder what happened to Miss Niemann."

"Well, considering she left her possessions behind, it seems to me that either she did not leave of her own accord or that she fled in fear."

"Rowly's right," Edna agreed. "If she was simply quitting the show, why wouldn't she just tell them?"

"I wonder what exactly was her connection to Bothwell," Clyde mused.

"Richter would know," Milton said, leaning back with his hands behind his head.

Rowland shook his head. "We can't ask him without giving away why we're really here."

"Perhaps we should just tell him," Edna suggested.

"No!" Milton slapped the table. "We cannot take everybody

we meet into our confidence." He leaned between Edna and Rowland and whispered, "Do you two remember that we are spies?"

Rowland laughed. He, too, was loath to involve the generous tailor, though unlike Milton, he was not concerned with being clandestine for its own sake. What they were doing could be seen as an act against the German government. It would not be a good idea to involve a German citizen in their plans.

The club's singer began to croon a gentle swing.

"I'll work out how to ask Richter tomorrow," he said, standing. He grabbed Edna's hand. "I'd better dance with you before you become too big a star, I suppose."

The next morning Rowland excused himself from a picnic organised by their host, on the pretence that he was meeting with another art dealer.

Richter murmured disapprovingly. "You work too hard, Mr. Negus. Young men like you shouldn't be passing up good food, let alone fine Bavarian beer and excellent company, to talk business with some withered old businessman."

"I'm afraid I must see him, Mr. Richter," Rowland replied. "Perhaps I can catch up with you afterwards? Where will you be?"

"We are going to visit the Schleissheim Palace in Oberschleissheim. Your friends will find the gardens pleasing, I think, and the paintings in the palace galleries will be of interest also."

"I'll join you there as soon as I'm finished," Rowland promised. He looked at his host a little uncomfortably. "There was something I wished to speak to you about, if you don't mind."

"Of course not, my boy. Is there something the matter?"

"No…well, perhaps. There is something I have omitted to tell you, Mr. Richter."

Richter sat down, hauling Stasi onto his lap. "Please go on."

"As you know, Peter Bothwell's widow is my cousin."

"Yes, of course."

"Apparently, Peter wrote home on a number of occasions about an actress he'd seen in a play…an Anna Niemann. Mrs. Bothwell became convinced that there was something between them."

"But Peter is dead now…surely—"

Rowland shrugged. "My dear cousin can be quite fixated about these things. She refuses to let it go. She made me promise to find Miss Niemann and speak with her."

"Oh dear, my poor Mr. Negus. To be caught between a jealous woman and her dead husband!"

"I'll say—it's rather awkward. I was hoping you might know Anna Niemann. Then I could speak with her and be done with it."

Richter shook his head. "I wish I could help you, Mr. Negus, but I am afraid I don't know her."

"Did Peter Bothwell never mention her?"

"Not that I recall…Perhaps he admired her performances." He wagged a finger at Rowland. "You tell Mrs. Bothwell that she has no reason to concern herself. Revenge converts a little right into a great wrong. It is best we remember Peter as the noble man that he was."

Rowland looked searchingly at the tailor, wondering if he was lying just to protect his friend's reputation. Richter returned his gaze with equal scrutiny.

Rowland sighed. "Perhaps you're right, Mr. Richter."

"I am, my boy. We have all made mistakes. They should be allowed to be forgotten. A clear conscience is a soft pillow, but few men sleep so."

Rowland nodded. "I'd better be off, I suppose. I'll see you all at Schleissheim Palace."

Chapter Twenty-four

NEW GUARD LEADER BACK,
WIFE ATTENDS ROYAL COURT

The Court ceremony, said Mrs. Campbell, was the most beautiful that she attended during her seven months' trip abroad. She met the late Lady Cynthia Mosley several times in England. Lady Cynthia, who was the wife of the British 'Blackshirt' leader, was prominent in the Fascist movement. "She was a woman of great charm and simplicity," said Mrs. Campbell. Commenting on the craze for blond hair in London, Mrs. Campbell said that every woman who wished to be smart appeared with fair hair, at all costs. Of course this extreme faddism was not indulged in by the people who really mattered.

—*The Sydney Morning Herald*, 1933

The Osteria Restaurant exuded a distinctly Bavarian charm. The walls were wood-panelled and painted with classical scenes. The dining room was dark and cosy. As Blanshard had predicted, Rowland recognised Unity Mitford quite easily.

Seated at a table at the front of the restaurant, she was broad-shouldered and long-limbed. Rowland wouldn't have called her pretty but there was a defensive haughtiness, a certain iron resolve about her face that he found artistically interesting. She wore a black button-down shirt and she watched the entrance like a hungry hawk.

Rowland took the table next to hers and when the waiter arrived, he tried to order in English before reverting to German. When the waiter left to bring his coffee, the black-shirted woman leaned over from her table.

"I say, are you English?" Her accent was distinctly that of the British privileged classes.

"Australian, actually."

"Oh, the colonies."

"Robert Negus," Rowland said. "How do you do?"

She turned her chair around and thrust out her hand. "Unity Mitford." She shook his hand vigorously, pumping it up and down.

"Pleased to make your acquaintance, Miss Mitford."

"I haven't seen you here before," she said. "I would have noticed another Brit, even if it was a Colonial."

"This is my first visit to this establishment," Rowland said, finally pulling his hand from her grasp.

"I've been here simply loads of times."

"Is the food particularly good?"

"No, I'm waiting for someone."

"I see. I shouldn't ask you to join me, then?"

She glanced at her watch. It was by then nearly noon. "Perhaps he's not coming today."

Rowland stood as she rose to move to his table.

"I am a direct sort of gel, Mr. Negus, so I must tell you at the outset that I am not available."

"For lunch?" Rowland asked, wondering why she was moving to his table if that was the case.

"No, I'd be rather delighted to join you for a spot of luncheon, but it must go no further. I am spoken for, as it were."

Rowland pulled out her chair. "I see. It is impertinent of me to enquire as we are barely introduced, Miss Mitford, but who is the lucky gentleman?"

She sat and beckoned him to do so too before she whispered, "Chancellor Hitler."

"Indeed."

"Do you believe in destiny, Mr. Negus?"

"Destiny?"

"I do. And destiny has brought me here."

"To the Osteria?"

"No, to Adolf Hitler. Where were you conceived, Mr. Negus?"

"I assure you, I have no idea."

"Well, I was conceived in Canada. In a place called Swastika. Don't you think that could be a sign, Mr. Negus?"

"Unless Swastika is the name of a nunnery, Miss Mitford, I am sure many people were conceived there. They can't all be destined for Mr. Hitler. "

"My middle name is Valkyrie…handmaiden to the Nordic god Odin. It's quite simply meant to be. Once we meet, the Chancellor will know it too."

"I see."

"So you and I cannot possibly be anything more than acquaintances, friends at the most."

"I'll bear that in mind." Rowland tried to steer the conversation in a less awkward direction. "Would you care to order?"

Unity gave the waiter her selection without needing to even glance at the menu. Her German was halting, but she had a healthy appetite and a fondness for Bavarian beer.

"What brings you to Munich, Miss Mitford?" Rowland asked, as the food arrived.

"I'm on an educational tour sponsored by the British Union of Fascists," she said proudly. "I'm a member, you know."

Rowland glanced at Unity's black shirt. "I had guessed."

"Of course the Germans are ahead of Britain on the path to proper government. England is still being choked by Jews and Communists."

"Choked?"

"A Jewish Bolshevik invasion, Mr. Negus. Australia's been saved from that, I suppose, being so far away. But Britain and Europe are in peril. It's time to fight back. 'Britain for the British,' I say!"

Rowland kept his face unreadable. This was going to be harder than he'd first assumed. Blanshard hadn't mentioned the woman was mad.

"I'm travelling with Australians, you know." Unity sipped her beer. "Perhaps you know them? Colonel and Mrs. Eric Campbell."

"I know *of* them," Rowland said cautiously, pleased that it was she who had raised the subject of Campbell. "The Colonel is a friend of friends, so to speak."

He watched as Unity cut vigorously into her food. There was something quite mannish about her manner. Her movements were expansive and somehow indiscreet. Everything about her was beginning to irritate him.

"He's quite an impressive sort of chap," Miss Mitford continued. "In fact, Sir Oswald Mosley, who's a personal friend of mine, is quite taken with him. He thinks Australia may be in good hands with Campbell at the helm."

"But Colonel Campbell is not at the helm, Miss Mitford."

"Not yet, but Sir Oswald thinks that will change soon. The revolution that we have seen in Germany will happen in Australia and Britain, and then right through the Empire and America. Democracy has failed, Mr. Negus. We are on the brink of being crushed beneath the heels of Zionism and Communism. The Jewish problem is real and if we do not act now, we risk compromising our racial purity forever. Fascism shall be the world's salvation."

Rowland wished to God he'd ordered something stronger than beer. He suspected he would need hard spirits to get through this conversation.

"But…" he began. He shook his head and said nothing further.

"But what, Mr. Negus?"

"Nothing…perhaps I'm mistaken."

"I must insist you tell me what you were going to say!" Unity demanded. "It's too bad to begin and not finish."

Rowland sighed, a cautious show of reluctance. "I would have thought Colonel Campbell's personal connections would have been problematic."

Unity Mitford stiffened. "Whatever do you mean?"

Rowland pushed the hair back from his face. He was conflicted. He wasn't sure how he was going to explain to Milton what he was about to say.

"Campbell's movement has never been against Jews, Miss Mitford. Rumour has it that there's a very good reason for that."

Unity gasped and put down her knife and fork. "You don't mean…?"

"It would be a hard thing to prove one way or another, I suppose," Rowland said carefully, "but it is generally known that the 'Campbell fortune' actually came from Colonel Campbell's mother's side…if you know what I mean."

Unity leaned forward, her eyes wide with horror, and whispered, "What? A Jewess? Are you suggesting she was a Jewess?"

"Of course, this could be just scurrilous gossip…and I assume if asked, he would deny it outright…but, then, I have never heard of Campbell speaking out against the Jews, just the Communists."

"Doesn't he understand that Communism is simply a Jewish conspiracy? Doesn't he see how they have plundered the civilised world?"

"Who knows what he understands? Who knows why he has never spoken of the link." Rowland felt vaguely unwell. He was not happy with the words that were coming out of his mouth. They tasted bitter.

Unity sat back. "You know, I never did trust the Campbells. Mrs. Campbell made such a fuss over Lady Mosley…ignored poor Nardy quite awfully."

"Nardy?"

"My sister, Diana. She's mad for Oswald and he for her, but he won't leave Cimmie…even though she's one of those dreadful Americans. Of course, she's terribly ill…and as soon as she's dead, Nardy will be the new Lady Mosley."

It took a second for Rowland to work out that "Cimmie" was Sir Oswald Mosley's wife. Apparently "Nardy" was his mistress. Rowland was startled by the cold callousness of Unity Mitford's declaration.

"Do you have many siblings, Miss Mitford?" he asked, hoping to direct the conversation away from the convenience of Lady Mosley's illness.

"Five sisters: Nardy, of course, then there's Steake, Soo, Hen, and Woomling, and our brother, Tudemy." She laughed at the expression on his face. "We Mitfords are rather fond of nicknames…Christian names can be so boring! Why, not one of them calls me Unity…it's Bobo or Birdie…sometimes Boud."

"Rather tiresome for your parents, I expect, having gone to the trouble of giving you all names."

"Muv and Farve? It's hard to tell…they're both stark, staring bonkers. I say, what do they call you?"

"Robert Negus," Rowland said firmly.

"Well, that won't do! I've virtually told you my life story. If we're going to be friends, we must find something a great deal more jolly. I believe I shall call you Thumper…or, I know—Bobsy!"

Rowland stared at her. The woman was a lunatic, from what appeared to be a family of lunatics.

"I've got it," she crowed. "What about Chains?…Your being Australian and all?"

Rowland looked into her enthusiastic face as she clapped her hands with joy at her own wit. He waited until she'd stopped squealing. "What about Robert?"

Rowland had been wandering the Baroque pleasure gardens around Schleissheim Palace for only a few minutes before he spotted his friends. Edna's dark auburn tresses drew his eye. Almost every other woman in the park seemed to be blond. Apparently, fair hair was the fashion of the moment. Rowland had always preferred red.

Edna waved and came to meet him, leaving the gentlemen in the gazebo they had commandeered for their picnic.

"I was worried you wouldn't see us." She took his hand and led him to the others.

"Where's Richter?" Rowland asked, seeing that it was only Milton and Clyde who were stretched out on deck chairs inside the small domed pavilion.

"He was called away at the last moment…something about a chap called Boss." Clyde stretched lazily. "Insisted we go on without him."

Edna sighed. "I'm afraid Mr. Richter is convinced that this other tailor is conspiring to ruin him. He ran off to counteract some sort of subterfuge. He'll try to join us later once he's dealt with this Boss character."

"Richter should shoot him and be done with it," Milton muttered, with his arms behind his head.

Edna laughed at the thought. It was just like Milton to let the role of spy go to his head.

Clyde leaned forward, his elbows on his knees. "Well, Rowly, how was your meeting with Lady What's-Her-Name?"

Rowland sat down, placing his hat on the bench beside him. "Unity Mitford. Arduous."

"Really?" Edna sat on the table at the centre of the gazebo, resting her feet on the bench by Rowland. "What was she like?"

Rowland groaned. "She's appalling."

Milton squinted at him. "You're serious." He sat up. "Better tell us all about it, Rowly."

So Rowland recounted his meeting with the young Englishwoman at the Osteria, where she was lying in wait for

Adolf Hitler. He began with the girl's conviction that she was destined for the German Chancellor, and her obsession with ridiculous nicknames.

"She wanted to call you what?" Milton laughed hard.

"Chains. Some allusion to convicts, I believe. Poor fool seems to think she's a real wit."

Edna tousled his hair fondly. "Poor Rowly. Imagine what Wilfred would have said if you went about known as Chains."

"It does sound a bit common for a Sinclair," Milton agreed. "He mightn't object if she called you 'Blueblood' or 'Polo' or something."

"He mightn't, but I'd be forced to respond rather impolitely," Rowland said tersely.

Milton chuckled. "I think I should like to be introduced to this young lady."

"Believe me, Milt, you don't."

"So did you manage to defame Campbell?" Milton said, still grinning.

Rowland shifted uncomfortably. "Yes, I'm afraid I did."

"Whatever's the matter, Rowly?" Edna asked softly, sensing something in his manner.

Rowland glanced guiltily at Milton. He had used Unity Mitford's prejudice against Campbell...perhaps in doing so he had given it some kind of implicit support. He wouldn't blame Milton if he was offended. "I implied Campbell was Jewish," he blurted.

"You did what?" Milton said startled.

Rowland explained himself, apologising even as he did so. He felt complicit and embarrassed.

Milton looked down, shaking his head. He smiled. "That's genius! Even if she was to ask him outright, he won't be able to prove otherwise with all the records back home."

"Yes, but—"

"Don't worry about it, Rowly...I'd happily call Campbell a Protestant, if I thought it would help get rid of him."

"Campbell is a Protestant, Milt."

"Well, there you go...and I thought it was the Catholics who were the troublemakers."

Clyde grunted. "No, it's always been the Protestants."

Rowland smiled, relieved but still uneasy.

"What's bothering you, Rowly?" Edna asked gently.

Rowland winced. "It's ridiculous, I suppose....The one good thing about our fascists is that they don't seem to have anything against Jews...and I've used that fact against Campbell."

"I wouldn't go that far, Rowly," Clyde murmured.

"What do you mean?"

"Campbell's here," Clyde replied. "He's been in Europe for months. He can't be unaware of what's been going on...and still he wants to be Hitler's mate."

Milton nodded. "Clyde's right, Rowly, old mate. If Campbell wants to bring Nazism to Australia, let him try doing it as a Jew."

Chapter Twenty-five

NAZI MOVEMENT APPROVED

The New Guard leader, sportily clad in tweed and a cap, pooh-poohed the idea of German 'atrocities' against Jews. "All I saw of Jews in Germany five weeks ago was a crowd of fat, well-dressed men eating well at expensive restaurants," he said. "To talk of 'persecution' is laughable."
—*The Sydney Morning Herald*, 1933

The afternoon was passed pleasantly, viewing the Schleissheim Palaces, of which there were actually three. They spent the most time in the eighteenth-century New Palace. A monumental structure, it was by far the largest and grandest of the complex. Its festival rooms were magnificently decorated with carved panelling and stucco work. It was, however, the large allegorical ceiling frescoes that intrigued them most, and much of their time was spent with their eyes cast upwards. Admittedly, they did occasionally find the subject matter of the overhead paintings a little odd.

"Good Lord," Rowland said his arms folded as he gazed up at what appeared to be St. Peter disciplining cherubs over his knee.

"That's the Lutherans for you," Clyde agreed quietly.

Milton shook his head. "What chance have we got if he's laying into cherubs?"

They had returned to the car park, when Rowland first noticed the lone Stormtrooper. He was walking briskly between the cars. Obviously preoccupied, he all but ran into them.

"*Entschuldigung,*" he said, glancing over his shoulder.

"No problem," Rowland replied in German.

The man walked on for a couple of paces and then returned. "Do you have a car, *mein Herr?*"

"Yes," Rowland answered carefully.

"Would you mind giving me a ride into Munich?" The Brownshirt smiled nervously. "I seem to have been left behind by my regiment, and there will be hell to pay if I'm not at tonight's parade."

Rowland glanced at his companions. He was more surprised by the Brownshirt's civility than the request. "I can take you back to Munich," he said. Excusing himself, he turned and explained to his companions in English. "He seems harmless enough...I'll take him in the 380S."

"I'll come with you," Clyde volunteered, with a sideways glance at the hitchhiking Stormtrooper.

Rowland nodded. It was probably overcautious, but they were wary of the SA. "We'll see you both back at Richter's," he said to Edna and Milton.

And so they parted for their separate cars.

"I'm Robert Negus," Rowland said, as he indicated Richter's Mercedes parked a short distance away. "This is Joe Ryan, who I am afraid does not speak German."

"You are not German?"

"Australian," Rowland confirmed.

The Brownshirt stuck out his hand. "Hans Beimler."

They each shook his hand in turn, pleased he did not feel the need to click his heels and "Heil Hitler!" at them.

Rowland had just opened the door to the motor car when there was a shout from the far end of the parking area and suddenly the place seemed to flood with Stormtroopers.

The Brownshirts ran among the cars, barking at passers-by. A rotund couple about to climb into their car pointed at Rowland, when questioned.

"What the devil—?" Clyde began.

"They're looking for someone," Rowland said as the Stormtroopers headed their way. He turned briefly. Beimler was gone.

"Name?" A young Brownshirt stood before Rowland with his chest thrust out.

"Robert Negus," Rowland said calmly.

"Have you come across a man in the uniform of the SA this afternoon, Herr Negus?"

"Yes," Rowland replied, knowing full well that he had been reported as having done so. "Are you in his regiment? He said he had lost them."

"That man is not a member of the SA!" the young officer roared, spittle flying in his fury. "He is a filthy Communist dog! A prisoner! An escapee!"

"I see. I'm afraid in the uniform I assumed he was a member of the SA."

"Where is he?" The Brownshirt took the truncheon from his belt.

"I regret to say, I don't know." Rowland spoke pleasantly but he held his ground. "He accepted a lift in another car after I told him we were going back to Munich…apparently he did not wish to go that way."

"Where did he want to go?"

Rowland shrugged. "I recall he said something about meeting up with his regiment in Nuremberg."

The Brownshirt's eyes moved to Clyde. "*Du!* Is this so?"

"My friend is Australian. He does not speak German….He saw your Communist, but he did not speak with him."

"The car! Describe it!"

"Black…a Mercedes…but an older model. Pre-1925 would be my guess."

"So you did not help him?" The truncheon was poised under Rowland's chin.

"If he had wanted to go to Munich, I might have…I thought he was one of you, after all. But he did seem rather desperate to get to Nuremberg."

The officer shouted to his fellow Stormtroopers and, amidst a great deal of cursing and bellowing, the SA departed.

"Where are they going?" Clyde asked quietly.

"Nuremberg, I hope. Where do you think Beimler went? I daresay he couldn't have got far."

Clyde glanced around the parking area. The Brownshirts were gone. A few curious onlookers lingered in the car park. Milton and Edna had driven out just before the Stormtroopers had arrived. "He's under the car, Rowly. If you open the back door, he can probably slip in without anyone seeing him."

Rowland nodded and walked round to open the rear door on the far side.

"We're helping this chap escape, then?" Clyde asked.

"So it seems."

"Good show."

Clyde opened the hood as if he was checking the engine and under that cover, Rowland was able to bend and instruct the escaped Communist to climb into the motor car and stay down. When he had done so, they wasted no further time leaving Oberschleissheim for Munich.

For a time, nobody said anything. And then from the floor in the rear, "*Dankeschön.*"

Clyde glanced back. "No problem, mate."

"Where exactly did you escape from, Herr Beimler?" Rowland asked.

"Dachau."

"The re-education camp?"

"A place where the domestic enemies of Germany are to be concentrated, according to Herr Himmler."

Rowland translated quickly for Clyde, and then asked,

"Where would you like us to take you, Herr Beimler?"

"Just leave me anywhere in Munich. I will find my way."

"I don't think that's such a good idea," Rowland said. "Do you have somewhere safe we could take you?"

"Anywhere in Munich," Beimler insisted.

"What's the matter?" Clyde asked.

"I think he's still a bit worried about trusting us," Rowland murmured. "If they're rounding up Communists, it's no wonder he doesn't want to tell perfect strangers where his friends live."

Clyde shook his head. "Fair enough, I suppose."

Again there was silence and then Clyde began to hum "The Red Flag".

After a few bars, Beimler joined him…and then they sang, Clyde in English and Beimler in German. It finished rather raucously.

"Why does your friend sing the Communist anthem?" Beimler asked Rowland.

"He's a member back home," Rowland replied, "and he doesn't speak German. I think he's trying to tell you that you can trust us."

"I see." Beimler peered over the seat, still staying well down. "And you, Herr Negus, are you a Communist?"

"No." Rowland replied. "But I am not a Nazi, either."

"There are many people who are not Nazis who are denouncing their neighbours."

"If I was going to do that, I would have done so when the Stormtrooper questioned me, Herr Beimler." Rowland glanced at the escapee in the rear-vision mirror.

Beimler nodded thoughtfully. "Yes, I can see that."

"Do you have friends in Munich, Herr Beimler?"

"Yes."

"It would be less dangerous for you if we could take you directly there. The authorities in Munich will have been alerted by now."

"You understand, Herr Negus, I do not wish to risk the safety of my comrades for my own sake."

"If we take you there we will not return or speak of it again," Rowland promised. "If you wish, my friend here will swear on the Red Flag, or *Das Kapital* or whatever it is you Communists do."

Beimler laughed softly. "Generally, we shake hands."

It was getting dark when they turned into the narrow street. The area was semi-industrial—warehouses and dilapidated town houses, with peeling paint and grimy stone. There were few other cars. Even so, the window boxes overflowed with geraniums of all colours.

Clyde removed his jacket and handed it to Beimler, who nodded his thanks and pulled it over the brown shirt in which he had escaped Dachau.

They drove into an alley between two buildings as Beimler directed, then brought the Mercedes to a stop. Half a dozen men in flat caps emerged from the buildings on both sides.

"*Dankeschön, meine freunde,*" Beimler said, as he opened the rear door to alight. The men in the alley seemed to recognise him, clasping his shoulder and greeting him with silent warmth.

Rowland started the engine again as Beimler and his comrades spoke, happy that the stray escapee was among friends. Then one man bent in through the door that Beimler had left open.

Wondering what he wanted, Rowland turned. The muzzle of the gun was just inches from his face.

Chapter Twenty-six

HITLER'S
OAK TREE

Planted by the German Chancellor—Herr Hitler—on the Tempelhof Field, Berlin, on May 1, the oak tree was cut down, and on suspicion that the perpetrator was a Communist, it was ordered that 18,000 Communist prisoners in Prussia should go dinnerless for three days.

—*The West Australian*, 1933

The front doors of the vehicle were pulled open and Rowland and Clyde dragged out.

Rowland was slammed against the brick wall of the alley and held there. For a moment he was dazed, vaguely aware of the crushing weight of the forearm against his throat.

Beimler intervened. "Eisen, stop! Are you mad? These men helped me."

"They could be spies, allowing you to lead them to the Underground…to us," he hissed, though he loosened the stranglehold.

Rowland focussed. The man called Eisen was simply enormous, a hulking, furious figure with a gun.

"Don't be a fool!" Beimler snapped. "They're not even German."

A scuffle as Clyde wrested free for a moment. Almost instantly he was punched to the ground, where he lay gasping. Rowland tried to go to his friend's aid, but Eisen would have none of it, throwing him back against the wall with the pistol's barrel pressed to his temple.

"I tell you, they're with us!" Beimler grabbed Eisen's arm. "We can't risk it!"

"You...I know you!" Rowland blanched as a torch was shone directly into his face. "You're the man who scrubbed the platz with Herr Göring."

Rowland squinted at the bearer of the torch. The man was small, his hair cropped close to his head. He wore wire-rimmed spectacles, the left lens of which was cracked—the Dachau inmate whose brush he'd borrowed in Königsplatz.

The torch beam was lowered. "Put the gun down, Comrade. This man is no Nazi."

The gun was eased away.

"Are you all right?" Rowland asked, glancing at Clyde, who was still doubled over.

Clyde nodded, straightening, though he was clearly still winded.

Beimler stepped up to the door and knocked three times. It opened, a crack at first and then wide. Still holding the gun, Eisen barked, "Inside!"

With no other option apparent, they followed Beimler in. Their eyes adjusted quickly to the darkness within. The torch beam finished in a yellow circle on the wooden floor, the walls and around the interior, as it was shone in a wide, searching sweep. The space was huge, a disused factory of some kind. Old looms and defunct machinery were still bolted to the floor. A narrow staircase led to a mezzanine and from there a ladder took them into a large attic space. There were several rudimentary beds in the eaves, and chairs surrounding a small table on which lay the remains of a hastily abandoned card game. A small, stocky man with a luxuriant moustache sat in a tattered armchair, scribbling in a notebook. He glanced up when they entered and then carried on with his writing.

The bespectacled man who had recognised Rowland from Königsplatz stuck out his hand. "*Grüss Gott.* I am Heinrich, Frank Heinrich."

"Robert Negus," Rowland replied, taking the handshake.

"Well, Herr Negus," Heinrich said, "it seems you have befriended our Comrade Beimler."

Beimler sat on a creaking bentwood chair. "I have not brought foxes into our hole, comrades. These men saved my life. I would be in the hands of the Stormtroopers if they had not helped me."

Rowland translated quietly for Clyde.

"What did you just say?" Eisen demanded, rearing suspiciously.

"My friend does not speak German," Rowland replied evenly.

The man in the dilapidated armchair looked up from his notebook and nodded. "That is the truth…he did nothing but repeat Comrade Beimler's claims in English." He sighed, closing his notebook reluctantly, and came over to join them. "Egon Kisch," he said. "Welcome to Purgatory."

Eisen pushed past Kisch to poke Rowland in the chest. "One stray word, and Kisch will know. He speaks many languages."

Rowland was now more than a little irritated. "Look, we brought Herr Beimler back…"

"He should not have allowed you to bring him here!" Eisen snapped. "He has put us all at risk of discovery."

"You are not at risk…yet, anyway. But if you don't allow us to leave now, there are people who will start looking for us. I assume you'd rather that didn't happen."

Eisen turned to Beimler. "Who else knows they brought you here?"

Beimler shook his head. "No one. I directed as Herr Negus drove. We didn't stop."

"So if they were to disappear, there is nothing to bring anyone here."

Rowland glared at him, angry now. He interpreted for Clyde without taking his eyes from Eisen. "The fat chap seems to think it's too risky to allow us to walk away. He doesn't seem too bright...appears rather eager to shoot us, I'm afraid."

Egon Kisch started. "No," he said in heavy English, glancing from Rowland to Clyde. "Eisen is overzealous. We are all..."—he hesitated looking for the correct word—"...worried."

"I'm not sure, Mr. Kisch, what we could do to allay your concerns," Rowland said.

"Perhaps you could tell us who you are, Mr. Negus. What you are doing in Munich." He nodded at an empty chair, indicating that Rowland should sit.

Rowland maintained the cover story that they had used since they left Sydney, but he added a little truth about their pasts, though he ascribed that truth to Robert Negus and Joseph Ryan: Clyde's membership in both the Communist Party and the trade unions, his own clashes with Australian fascists. "We have no intention of betraying you to the SA or anyone else, Herr Kisch."

For a while their captors formed a huddle and argued and muttered about what to do next. Rowland spoke quietly to Clyde, telling him what had been exchanged in German.

Finally Beimler turned back to them.

"You and Herr Ryan may go. Comrade Eisen's brother has an automobile. We will follow you."

"Why?"

"So we know where to find you," Eisen replied coldly. "If anybody comes for us, then we will come for you, Herr Negus. Do not be deceived by the fact that we hide like rats. We have many friends and we will find you."

Rowland was unperturbed. "You will not need to."

Eisen left then, presumably to borrow his brother's car. While he was gone, Beimler and Heinrich spoke of Dachau, initially to each other and their comrades, but when Rowland asked questions, they responded openly. It appeared the distrust was mostly the fat man's.

Beimler had, of course, escaped the camp, but Heinrich had been released, ransomed somehow by moneyed friends. Egon Kisch, too, had been imprisoned, though at a place called Spandau, in Berlin, and then deported to his native Czechoslovakia. A journalist by profession, he had returned to Germany illicitly to report on what he called the daily atrocities of the Nazi regime. Beimler and Heinrich spoke of the work details, the brutality, and the daily humiliations of the Dachau camp...and the men who were still incarcerated there.

"Is it just the Communists they've imprisoned?" Rowland asked. He had forgotten now that they were themselves prisoners.

Kisch shook his head. "Most are Communists, Social Democrats, or trade unionists, but there are also Jehovah's Witnesses. Their religious beliefs preclude them from swearing allegiance to the Fatherland, you see. There are some gypsies— gypsies are classed as asocial— a few indiscreet Freemasons, and anyone who speaks against the Nazis."

"Surely the law does not allow them to hold people on such grounds?"

"We are 'taken into protective custody in the interest of public security and order,'" Beimler said bitterly. "We are suspected of 'activities inimical to the State.'" He laughed, leaning over to Rowland. "That, my friend, is true. My activities oppose the Reich, my heart opposes the Reich. We begin with Hitler a steady march towards our own destruction."

"Sadly," Kisch added, "many Germans are too distracted by parades and uniforms to realise that our country is being wrested from us. We are cheering the man who enslaves us while the world watches on admiringly."

Nearly an hour passed before Eisen returned and told them to go.

"Good luck, gentlemen," Rowland said, as he and Clyde climbed back into the Mercedes.

"And you," Kisch said gravely. "I fear that our fight will become more than a German one. The fascists are not just here."

Eisen followed them back to Richter's house in Schellingstrasse in what appeared to be an old baker's van. He waited just beyond the driveway. They heard the van start again only when porch lights came on and the door was opened.

The relief was apparent on the faces of Milton and Edna as they entered.

Even Richter rose enthusiastically. "*Danke Gott*, you have returned."

"Yes…sorry…" Rowland hesitated, unsure of how much they'd told their host.

"I was about to telephone Himmler," Richter declared. "How dare those SA thugs use you and Herr Ryan as a taxi service! And to detain you so long! It is unacceptable…unacceptable."

"Actually, the poor fellow didn't detain us," Rowland said, glancing quickly at Clyde. "I'm afraid we took a wrong turn on the way back and found ourselves lost."

Richter frowned. "Miss Greenway was very concerned." He wagged his finger. "You have worried her."

"Don't scold them, Alois," Edna said, rubbing Richter's arm. "They couldn't help getting lost."

Richter looked at her and smiled. "Of course, *mein Kind*." He patted her hand. "I am sorry, gentlemen. I am a foolish old man who can't bear to see Miss Greenway distressed."

"You're exaggerating," Edna said laughing. "I barely cared at all!"

"We're sorry, Millie," Clyde said. "I told Robbie to turn left, but he just won't take directions."

Rowland opened his eyes, unsure if he had actually heard or just imagined the soft click of the door handle. He rolled over towards the sound, though he could see almost nothing in the darkness.

A whisper. "Rowly?"

He sat up. His eyes adjusted quickly and he could make out the familiar silhouette. "Ed."

Edna closed the door behind her.

Rowland waited until she'd made her way over to his bed. He was a little surprised, but not unduly alarmed. Edna lived with him. The four of them had some time ago, fallen into a familial informality with respect to each other. Back in Sydney, Edna often wandered into their rooms in the middle of the night to talk about some matter that couldn't wait till morning. They were not scandalised by the sight of each other in pyjamas. But still, Edna usually conducted herself properly when they were guests elsewhere.

"What are you doing here?" He pulled at the curtain which cloaked the window above his bed, allowing the moon to cast Edna in colourless light.

"I want to know what really happened today. I presume it's something you don't want Alois to know."

Rowland nodded. Richter had been home that evening and they had been unable to talk alone.

"You're cold," he said, noticing that she was shivering. He got out of bed and, slipping on his robe, pulled up a chair for himself, so that she could climb under the bedcovers. In whispers he told her of Beimler, of what they had done to ensure his escape, and of Frank Heinrich, Egon Kisch, and the Communists hiding in the factory attic.

She listened, hugging the quilted bedclothes around her. "They wanted to shoot you?" she breathed, aghast.

"I think that Eisen fellow is just a bit of a hothead," he said on reflection. "Though I can't say I'd blame them for doing whatever necessary to stay out of Dachau."

"What will they do? How long can they possibly hide?"

"I suppose they'll get out of the country...They didn't really tell us. Understandably, they're a mite paranoid."

"Alois was dreadfully upset when he heard you went with the SA. He was so worried, it made me scared."

He smiled. "There were two of us, Ed, and Beimler was alone...initially, at least. Richter's probably right to be worried about the SA...but Beimler wasn't SA, as it turns out."

"It was more than that. Alois was really distressed."

Rowland rubbed the back of his neck. He trusted Edna's instincts. "You suspect there's more to it?"

"I'm worried about him, Rowly. He seems scared." She had stopped shivering now and she let her hands emerge from under the covers. "If we come to the attention of the authorities, he might be in a lot of trouble for harbouring us. He could lose his business....What if they send him to Dachau?"

Rowland stared at the sculptress. She was right. They had entered into this knowingly and willingly. Richter was just a bystander, but if their plans went wrong, he could be more than ruined. "We should leave."

"Germany?"

"No—we can't leave Munich until Eric Campbell does. But we could go back to the Vier Jahreszeiten."

"That would hurt him terribly, Rowly. He's become so fond of us."

"He'll have to face it someday. You're not his daughter, Ed."

Edna laughed softly. "He does remind me of Papa, though Papa never made such a ridiculous fuss of me." She lowered her pitch to mimic her father's, which was not easy while speaking in a half-whisper. "'Pretty is as pretty does, my girl. Empires were not built by silly young things in fashionable frocks.'"

"Selwyn wanted you to build an empire?" Rowland asked, bemused. He'd always found Edna's father eccentric, but the expectation seemed unreasonable, even for him.

"I believe he must have been teaching ancient Rome at the time," Edna giggled. Selwyn Higgins lectured in Classics at the University of Sydney. "Poor Papa's always wanted me to fulfil my mother's potential, to be the artist Mama might have been if she hadn't married him."

"But your mother was happy with Selwyn, wasn't she, Ed?" Rowland asked wistfully.

Edna stopped. She bit her lip and shook her head. "Oh, Rowly, I thought Milt had told you."

"Told me…"

"How my mother died. She took her life when I was thirteen."

Rowland stopped breathing for a moment. Milton hadn't told him. Of course, Rowland had known Edna's mother had passed away, but the sculptress had never before spoken of the manner of her death.

"My God, Ed, I'm sorry." He wanted to wrap his arms around her, to hold her, but aware that she was in his bed, he refrained. Instead, he took her hand in both of his, and kissed it.

"I thought you knew, Rowly—I wasn't keeping it from you." Somehow her laugh was sadder than tears. "Who would have thought Milt was so discreet?"

Rowland said nothing, not sure what he could say. He had always admired Edna's independence, as much as he wished she would forsake it for him. It was a part of her vibrancy, the indomitable spirit which had bewitched him from the first. Her commitment to freedom had always appeared joyous. She laughed off the devotion she inspired, danced away from proposals of marriage like some merry, seductive nymph, and yet now it seemed there was tragedy at the core of the liberty she cherished.

It was Edna who broke the silence. "Don't feel badly for me, Rowly. It was a long time ago. I don't want to think about Mama right now. Can we not talk about it for a while?"

"Of course."

"We have to do something to protect Alois," Edna continued, turning her mind determinedly from her mother. "Something other than going back to the Vier Jahreszeiten. It would hurt him too deeply."

"I don't see what else we can do."

"Can't we make Campbell leave? Then we can go home before the authorities notice us and without upsetting Alois."

Rowland dragged a hand through his hair and regarded her dubiously. "How exactly are we supposed to make Campbell leave, Ed?"

"I don't know. Couldn't you talk to Mr. Blanshard? You've done everything he's asked…He probably wants to go home too."

"I can't imagine Blanshard having a home, to tell you the truth. He's not really a family dinner sort of chap."

"Rowly…please."

He looked at her. Rowland could see that she was really frightened for Richter; conflicted by the possible consequences of what they were doing. He felt ashamed that it had not even occurred to him. Edna was right. They had had no business dragging Richter into this, and now that they had, they would have to ensure that he was not going to suffer for it. "Do you think Richter has any idea we are not who we say we are?"

"I do wonder sometimes," she said. "Rowly, I know what we're doing is important, but let's face it, we don't really know what we're doing. I'm just afraid we're going to leave Alois in a terrible mess." She took Rowland's hand. "Speak to Mr. Blanshard…please, Rowly."

Rowland smiled. He wondered if she was aware that he was unable to refuse her anything. If she'd asked him for the moon, he would try to pull it from the sky. "I shall speak to Blanshard," he promised. "Don't worry about Richter…we'll make sure he's all right, even if we have to take him and that bloody dog back to Sydney with us."

Edna laughed quietly. "I wonder what Lenin would make of poor Stasi."

Rowland's brow rose as he considered it. "I fear Len may try to eat him."

They talked long into that night, and though neither mentioned Edna's mother again, there was a new closeness to their conversation, an understanding where there had only been acceptance before. When she eventually returned to her own room, Rowland lay awake, conscious of the faint, lingering smell of rose perfume on the sheets.

Chapter Twenty-seven

"The function of the so-called liberal Press was to dig the grave for the German people and the Reich. No mention need be made of the lying Marxist Press. To them the spreading of falsehood is as much a vital necessity as the mouse is to a cat. Their sole task is to break the national backbone of the people, thus preparing the nation to become the slaves of international finance and its masters, the Jews...

Certainly in days to come the Jews will raise a tremendous cry throughout their newspapers once a hand is laid on their favourite nest, once a move is made to put an end to this scandalous Press and once this instrument which shapes public opinion is brought under State control and no longer left in the hands of aliens and enemies of the people. I am certain that this will be easier for us than it was for our fathers. The scream of the twelve-inch shrapnel is more penetrating than the hiss from a thousand Jewish newspaper vipers. Therefore let them go on with their hissing..."

—Adolf Hitler, *Mein Kampf*

Rowland's next conversation with Alastair Blanshard was tenser than usual. For one thing, Blanshard was irritated by the fact that Rowland had demanded the meeting as a matter of urgency. The agent was at pains to clarify the nature of their relationship.

"Understand this, Mr. Negus," he growled, as they stood

under umbrellas, staring into the lion cage at the Munich Zoo. "You do not summon me. I am not here to solve *your* problems. You are here on the off-chance you can be of use to me." Of course, this was all said while he was smiling and nodding as if recounting some hilarious anecdote.

Having become accustomed to the agent's contrary gestures as well as his ill-humour, Rowland ignored him and repeated his question. "How long is Campbell planning to stay?"

"He's determined to remain until he meets the Chancellor, until he has some tangible proof of Hitler's esteem and endorsement to take back to the New Guard…and since the entire purpose of your presence and mine is to prevent such an eventuality, you'd better buckle down, Negus." He fumbled in his jacket for a cigarette case. "I knew you wouldn't stay the distance…I told those fools—"

"I assure you, Mr. Blanshard, we will not leave till Campbell does," Rowland said tightly. "I would just like to explore the possibility of encouraging him to leave."

"Well, unless you believe you can impersonate Hitler, Mr. Negus, I don't expect there is anything you can do."

Rowland gazed sullenly at the caged felines.

Blanshard pulled a cigarette from the case and lit it, drawing on it a couple of times before speaking again. "Unity Mitford asked me if I knew anything about Campbell's family."

"Oh, yes, Miss Mitford." Rowland muttered resentfully. "You might have mentioned that she was crackers."

Blanshard grunted. "Why is she asking about Colonel Campbell's family?"

"I may have implied that he was Jewish."

"I see. That explains it, I suppose."

"It's worked, then?"

"She's certainly curious about Campbell's connections, though I don't know that she's entirely convinced. Perhaps after your next rendezvous…"

Rowland stiffened. "Next…? Surely that's unnecessary?"

"You want Campbell to go home, Mr. Negus? Well, how about you do what you were sent here to do?"

"Very well." Rowland tried to keep from flaring. Blanshard was insufferable. "I will try to run into Miss Mitford again in the next day or two." He turned to face Blanshard. "But there must be a way to give Campbell a nudge home."

Blanshard's teeth were clenched into an alarming smile. "There isn't! If Campbell gets the slightest whiff that anyone is trying to sabotage his tour, he will use it to his advantage both over here and back home. You, Mr. Negus, need to pull your head in or you may just find that someone knocks it off!"

The beer garden was small and, but for three Australian men who drank together, deserted. Perhaps it was the steady drizzle, or the fact that the bar was in a less salubrious part of Munich.

Still, the paved courtyard was clean, even if the chairs were rickety and the table linen patched repeatedly. The proprietor had attempted to compensate for the general shabbiness with a small vase of dandelions placed at the centre of each table.

Clyde sighed. "Ed's got a point. We've had a couple of close shaves already. If things go wrong, it could get very ugly for Richter."

"Won't be particularly pretty for us, either, mate," Milton observed.

Rowland sipped his beer. "Maybe Campbell will give up soon."

Milton studied the froth which floated atop the amber fluid in his own glass. "Perhaps impersonating Hitler's not such a bad idea."

Clyde grunted. "It's a very bad idea…Don't even think about it."

"We've managed it once," Milton rubbed his lip. "We could…"

Rowland smiled. "You'll need more than a bad German

accent to pass as the Chancellor, Milt." He stared out at nothing in particular.

"What are you thinking, Rowly?" Clyde asked cautiously.

Rowland leaned back, glancing casually around the beer garden to ensure it was still empty. "We've managed somehow to keep Campbell from meeting anyone of consequence to date. Ironically, it's that which is keeping him here. Our best chance is to figure out what would make Campbell abandon his plan to meet Hitler."

Clyde frowned. "I suppose it's too much to hope he'll come to his senses?"

"Yes, probably."

"Perhaps we're looking at this all wrong," Milton said, drumming his fingers on the arm of his chair. "Perhaps we shouldn't be trying to push Campbell out of Germany. Perhaps we simply need to lure him back to Sydney."

"How do you mean?" Clyde asked.

"Give him a reason to go home that's more important than hobnobbing with the fascists over here."

Rowland looked sharply at the poet. "You're right."

Milton smiled. "I tend to be. What about a family illness?"

Rowland shook his head. "Too easy to verify, I should think." His eyes glinted. "But what if Campbell were to receive word that there was trouble in the New Guard...in-fighting, that sort of thing?"

"Yes!" Milton slapped the table enthusiastically. "*A coup d' état* within his beloved militia! Even before he left, there were rumours of dissension in the ranks—guardsmen who thought Campbell was becoming too fascist."

Rowland smiled. "That might just work."

"Of course it'll work," Milton replied. "We're brilliant!"

"Steady on," Clyde cautioned. "Before you jokers get carried away with your own genius, how on Earth do you propose to convince Campbell of this supposed coup?"

"Easy." Milton would not be dissuaded. "We'll get Blanshard to tell him."

Rowland frowned. "I don't know that Blanshard will be in it. In fact, I don't think we can rely on any help from the Old Guard. I doubt very much that they're going to let us take the lead."

"We could telegram Campbell," Milton persisted.

Rowland groaned. "No, it wouldn't work. He'd be able to see that the telegram was sent from within Germany...He's not a stupid man."

Milton topped up his beer glass from the jug on the table. "There's got to be some way to—"

"What if we enlist Miss Wake?" Rowland interrupted.

"Nancy? Enlist her to do what, exactly?"

Rowland spoke quickly now. His eyes narrowed as the plan unfolded in his mind's eye. "She could interview Campbell, ask him questions about the reported in-fighting within the New Guard—the rumours that the man he left in charge is preparing to stage a coup rather soon. It's perfectly feasible that she would hear things through her contacts in the press."

Milton grinned, nodding slowly. "Do you think she'd be willing, Rowly?"

Rowland shrugged. "She seems rather a good sport. It can't hurt to ask."

Clyde agreed cautiously. "Are you going to give Blanshard a heads-up?"

"I'm inclined not. I seriously doubt it would be a good idea," Rowland said, his face darkening. "Apparently, we are here to do his bidding and nothing else." He laughed softly. "The Old Guard is displeased as it is. I'm afraid Mr. Blanshard's received another telegram about our appalling lack of frugality, from that chap Munroe."

"Sounds like a Scot," Milton said in disgust. "Scots are always unreasonably thrifty...We're dealing in art, not parsnips—you can't buy it by the pound."

Clyde shook his head. "Just wait till Milton's purchases start arriving in Sydney. We'll be lucky if Hardy doesn't have our passports revoked."

"Hopefully, we'll be on a liner home by the time *Backwards Mona Lisa* or the deformed duck painting reach the good Senator."

Clyde laughed.

Milton studied them sadly. "I've always known Clyde was a traditionalist…but you, Rowly? I had hope for you."

"Get off!" Clyde retorted. "You only bought those pieces because you thought they'd offend Hardy."

Milton sighed. "I admit that may have been the basis of my initial purchase, but there's something about handing over a rather large sum of money that makes you recognise a certain merit you might initially have missed."

Rowland raised his glass. "I'm sure the Graziers' Association will be immensely grateful for your astute investments on their behalf, old mate."

They returned to Richter's mansion in Schellingstrasse that afternoon in good spirits. The plan to have Nancy Wake panic Campbell into leaving had introduced a sense of purpose to their sojourn in Germany, which had otherwise threatened to extend into endless months of simply interfering with the dealings of the New Guard leader.

Munich had its charm, but the idea of staying for an indefinite period was beginning to exasperate them more than they realised.

Two artists from whom Milton had purchased paintings the previous week had fled to London. Even Hans von Eidelsöhn was contemplating a strategic retreat to Austria, if only Millicent Greenway would consent to go with him. For her part, Edna seemed fond of the melancholy artist, but no more so than any of the other men who had caught her interest for a time.

Richter and Edna were both out that afternoon. They may have been together. Richter's fondness for the sculptress bothered Rowland a little. He did not think there was anything untoward about it, but he did wonder whether the doting tailor would be too cruelly grieved when they left. Clearly Richter's regard was tied up with memories of his own daughter, although Edna was being nothing but herself. That alone was enough to enslave most men.

Rowland left a message at the telephone number Nancy Wake had given him, and then returned to his easel. Clyde was already in the makeshift studio, working on a still life. Milton was ensconced in an armchair with a volume of *Ashenden* by William Somerset Maugham, which he apparently had found among the books in Richter's library. Rowland had not yet set out his palette when Mrs. Schuler beckoned to him from the door. When he'd come close enough she whispered that there was a very distraught young woman on the porch who, she supposed, had come to see him.

Not entirely sure if that was some kind of censure, Rowland hastened to the front door.

Though he'd been prepared by the housekeeper, Rowland was nevertheless startled by the sobbing which reached his ears before he stepped out. Eva threw herself into his arms and continued to weep into his chest.

"Good Lord, Eva…Whatever's the matter?"

She was unable to speak, gulping and crying anew as she tried. He just stood there and let her be for a while. It was perhaps because she took so long to compose herself that Rowland had time to notice the car full of uniform-clad SA officers on the street at the end of Richter's cobbled driveway.

He wasn't particularly disconcerted—the Brownshirts seemed to be everywhere these days—but he did note it.

"Fräulein Eva," he said gently, "shall we go inside? We can get you a cup of tea and you can tell me precisely what is the matter."

Eva nodded, wiping uselessly at the sodden patch she'd left on his jacket. He took her into the formal sitting room and asked Mrs. Schuler to bring tea. Clyde stuck his head in, but seeing Eva weeping on the settee, disappeared again, presumably to hide in the studio until the drama was over.

When the tea service had been wheeled in and a tray placed upon the parlour table, Rowland stood by the door till Frau Schuler realised he wished her to leave. She did so reluctantly. Rowland closed the door firmly behind the housekeeper and took a seat beside Eva. He poured her a cup of tea, and handed her his handkerchief.

"What has happened, Eva?"

She shook her head and for a moment he thought she might cry again. "Do you think I'm pretty, Herr Negus?"

Rowland's brow rose, but he said, "Yes, of course."

"When you are in love with a woman, how would you show it?"

Rowland shifted uncomfortably. "It depends on the woman, I suppose," he said uncertainly. "Has something happened, Eva?"

She rummaged in her purse and then handed an envelope to Rowland. It contained a thick wad of banknotes—Reichsmarks. "Herr Wolf took me for a picnic today…He said he had something to give me." She wiped her eyes. "I thought he might present me with a dachshund, or a bracelet—I would have liked a bracelet—or even flowers." She broke down again. "But instead he hands me this envelope, without a word of kindness. He treats me like some *schlampen* from the street!"

Rowland wasn't quite sure what to say. The envelope of money did strike him as a little cold and unseemly.

"What would you give Fräulein Greenway, Herr Negus?"

Rowland hesitated, and then he answered honestly. "Anything she wants."

That seemed to wound Eva anew, and she disintegrated into an anguished keening wail.

Rowland was becoming quite alarmed by the depth of her despair, not to mention the noise. He tried to comfort her.

"Eva…please stop crying."

She clung to him and eventually the sobs subsided. Then, pressing against him, Eva raised her face, her lips parted slightly. She closed her eyes and waited.

Rowland realised suddenly that she wanted him to kiss her. He decided quite quickly against it. Putting his hands on her shoulders, he pushed her back gently. "Eva, perhaps you should find someone other than your Herr Wolf."

She started and pulled back from him. "No, that is not possible."

"Why?"

"You do not understand. I love him. God help me, I love him. I would happily stop breathing before I was without him. If he discards me, I shall die!" Eva threw herself onto the arm of the settee, calling the name of her lover. "Wolf, my darling Wolf…"

Rowland was unsure what to do. The girl seemed on the verge of a breakdown of some sort.

Just at that point, the door was opened. Alois Richter had returned to find his houseguest entertaining a young woman who seemed to be hysterical. The moment was excruciatingly awkward, but Rowland could not help but be relieved that there was someone—anyone—to intervene, as he was clearly doing an inadequate job of comforting the poor girl.

He left Eva to her grief and, taking his bewildered host aside, explained its cause quickly.

"Her gentleman friend seems to have disappointed her, I'm afraid," Rowland said quietly. "She's quite inconsolable."

"What did he do?" Richter asked, his eyes bright, his tone hushed.

"He's made her an inappropriate gift that seems to have left her doubting his esteem."

"Oh, dear, the poor child," Richter said. "Pour her a glass of sherry, Mr. Negus. Stasi and I shall see if we cannot comfort her a little."

Chapter Twenty-eight

OUR MISTRESSES: THE PRESS

...In June 1933, having read in the English Press of the riots in Germany, and of the slaughter of the Jews and of general acts of lawlessness, I crossed the Rhine fearing the worst. I found cities and countrysides orderly and peaceable as in England. I found a courteous, industrious people, absurdly like ourselves, a little resentful, but generally highly amused at the misrepresentation of the Foreign Press. I even met Jews in Berlin trading under their own names, who hardly knew whether to be indignant or scornful of the Semitic atrocities they read about. In Berlin there were fewer traffic police than in Sydney.

Then the deliberate misrepresentation as regards alleged "breakaways" in the New Guard, proves the unreliability of the Press to demonstration...

It is when a newspaper, for its own purposes, seeks to mould public opinion that it ceases to be a public utility and becomes a sinister menace. As an industry, a newspaper is but a marshalling of machinery, paper, and ink, plus a few operatives and technicians.

What right has such an undemocratic minority to influence the opinions and control the thought of the majority?

—Eric Campbell, *The New Road*, 1934

To Rowland's surprise, Alois Richter was able to calm Eva much more effectively than he. The tailor was patient and kind, sitting in an armchair making soothing noises and plying the girl with sherry.

"Alcohol," Milton murmured, as the three of them watched from the doorway. "You should have thought of that."

Rowland nodded. It seemed to be doing the trick. Eva was now sitting quietly with Stasi occupying her lap and a glass of sherry in her hand as Richter rambled about love and loss and hats. He spoke most confidently of the last.

Rowland motioned his friends into the hallway and explained the anguished commotion that they had heard, but from which they had assiduously kept their distance.

"Perhaps he didn't mean to offend her," Clyde suggested, glancing back towards the sitting room. "Some blokes are just not good at buying presents. My old Dad gave Mum a cross-cut saw for her birthday one year."

Rowland exhaled slowly. "Who knows? It's all rather unfortunate."

"So what do we do now?" Milton asked.

"I'll drive her home when she's ready, I suppose," Rowland replied.

"Don't get too involved, Rowly," Clyde advised. "It won't be good if she switches this obsession of hers to you."

"She won't do that," Rowland said, with a great deal more confidence than he felt.

"Don't you believe it, mate," Clyde replied. "I like Eva and I feel sorry for the poor kid, but she's as silly as a wet hen."

Rowland folded his arms across his chest, leaning back against the wall. Clyde had a point.

After supper, Rowland drove Eva home. She took with her the second, more traditional nude which he'd painted when he'd realised the first revealed too much. The painting cheered her somewhat, and she talked excitedly about how she would present it to Herr Wolf.

"Do not be angry with me, Herr Negus," she pleaded, when she noticed his silence.

"I'm not angry, Eva."

"You do not want me to give my painting to Herr Wolf."

"I just wish you didn't want to, Eva. It seems to me that he makes you quite desperately unhappy."

"When he sees the painting, Herr Negus, he will be happy and that will make me happy. He is all I live for."

Rowland left it. She wasn't about to be talked out of her loyalty to the man.

He carried the painting into her apartment, where she introduced him awkwardly to her family. They were polite but cold and he wondered if perhaps they assumed he was the married man with whom their daughter was involved.

Rowland arrived back at Richter's not long before Edna finally returned.

Hans von Eidelsöhn walked Edna to the door, but it was there that she left him.

The sculptress joined them as they were sipping brandy by the fireplace.

"What on Earth is around your neck?" Milton asked the moment he saw her.

Edna smiled as she put her hand to the string of typewriter keys and pen nibs that hung around her throat. "It's Hans' latest creation. Isn't it delightful?"

Rowland smiled. "It's interesting. Another gift?"

"Of course it is. Nobody's going to pay for that," Clyde said flatly.

"I don't know," Milton said, standing to study it more closely. "What does he call it?"

"*Writer's Folly.*"

"Figures," Clyde observed. "Doubt his typewriter will be much good for anything now."

"Stop laughing," Edna admonished Rowland. "It was a parting gift." She sat down beside him, playing absently with the lettered keys.

"Parting?" Rowland asked. "Where's he going?"

Edna frowned. "Apparently the SS visited the gallery yesterday. They took some of his paintings."

"So?" Clyde shrugged. "A sale's a sale."

"They didn't purchase them," Edna said. "They confiscated them. Apparently they have been deemed degenerate."

Milton sat up. "Von Eidelsöhn's work is dread—*unconventional*, but who're the flaming SS to say it's degenerate?"

"Well, they did. Hans is worried he'll end up in Dachau, so he's leaving…He's going to Vienna." She sighed, her eyes misting slightly. "Silly boy thought I might come with him. I think I'll miss him rather dreadfully."

Rowland suppressed an irrational surge of irritation that the artist had even suggested such a thing. He had made a practice of ignoring Edna's various suitors and it rarely occurred to him that she would leave with one. The thought did not sit comfortably.

"He was silly to think he could entice you away from us," Richter soothed, pouring her a glass of brandy. "But it is sad that he should have to go when you were so fond of him."

"Indeed," Rowland murmured, hoping he sounded sincere.

Edna looked at him and smiled. Obviously, he had not.

"Were you aware that there are Brownshirts watching the house?" she said suddenly.

"Brownshirts?" Richter flushed immediately. "Watching *my* house?"

Edna nodded. "Yes…they're not terribly subtle. Hans was quite unnerved."

Rowland scowled. "I noticed them earlier, but I thought it was just a passing patrol or something of the like."

"So!" Richter stood and went to the window. Of course, it was dark now and he could see nothing. "This can only be Hugo Boss. He thinks he can send the SA to spy on me...to discredit me so he can steal my contracts!"

Rowland glanced at Edna. Could what she feared be coming to pass?

"Perhaps it is us, Alois." Edna stood and joining him by the window.

"But why would it be you?"

"Perhaps it's because of the art we're buying, the artists with whom we're meeting. Hans and the others. We should go back to the Vier Jahreszeiten...There's no reason you should have to endure this."

"I will not hear of it!" Richter said vehemently. "You should not have to endure it, either! I will speak to Himmler...He will call off Röhm and his dogs or I will interfere with the seat of the trousers in every uniform that comes out of my factories!"

For a moment there was silence as they absorbed the startling threat. Then Edna began to giggle. Rowland smiled, unable to prevent the extraordinary images that came to mind. Milton laughed outright and Clyde adjusted the belt of his own trousers.

Edna kissed the tailor on the cheek. "Alois, I adore you," she said.

Nancy Wake was waiting in the same café to which she had taken them on the night of the book-burning. She sat at a table near a trio of fiddlers, and she hummed along as she waited. It was nearly midnight.

Rowland had slipped out after she'd called and arranged this meeting. A little concerned that the SA might still be watching, he had come alone, hailing a motor cab after walking a little way from Schellingstrasse. And so it was that he was a little late. He launched straight into an apology as he removed his overcoat and hat.

She waved his words away. "That's all right, I like it here."

Rowland ordered drinks. "It's a pleasure to see you again, Miss Wake," he said sincerely.

She rolled her eyes. "For pity's sake, call me Nancy—we've been far too familiar for such formalities."

Rowland smiled. "Yes, I daresay that's true."

"Now what can I do for you, Rowly?"

Rowland recounted his conversation with the actress-cum-cigarette girl at the Kammerspiele.

"You believe this woman, Anna Niemann, was having an affair with Peter?"

"Not necessarily, but I would like to know what happened to her. I was hoping you might…"

"Be able to dig around?"

"Yes, if you'd be so kind."

She considered momentarily. "I think I shall. I'd like to know what happened to Peter myself."

"There is something else," Rowland began, a little embarrassed to be asking so much.

She regarded him curiously. "Go on, then. You'd best spit it out."

Rowland took a deep breath. This would take some explaining. "We'd like to encourage Colonel Campbell to return to Australia," he began. Nancy listened carefully as he outlined the plan to plant in Campbell's mind the idea that his army was disintegrating in his absence, that his second-in-command was on the brink of succeeding him. "If you were to tell him all this in the course of an interview, he would not doubt it," Rowland said, watching the young journalist's face carefully. "He would assume the information was coming through your contacts in the press."

Nancy grabbed his hands and squeezed them excitedly. "Why, that's marvellous! What a wonderful plan!" She laughed delightedly.

"Then, you'll…?"

"Of course! It's a fabulous caper. We don't need Hitler's nonsense getting back home. I say, I have a friend with a printing press…I may be able to mock up some articles to show him." She raised her glass. "To subterfuge, Rowly-Robbie Sinclair-Negus."

Rowland amended the toast. "To you, Nancy. I will be in your debt for many years, I suspect."

The fiddlers picked up their tempo and she stood with his hand still in hers. "I think we'd better dance, don't you?"

Rowland yawned. He had got in at dawn, which had left him just two hours to sleep. Immediately after breakfast, Alois Richter had stormed off to threaten Himmler in his indignation over the SA surveillance.

With the exception of the domestic staff, they were alone. Once the housekeeper retreated to attend to her duties, Rowland told his friends of his meeting with Nancy Wake.

"So she'll do it?" Milton asked.

"She's rather keen."

Clyde chuckled. "She's forgiven you for the liberties you took, then?"

Rowland smiled. "I believe she has."

Milton studied him. "Miss Wake is a bloody good sport."

Rowland rubbed his neck drowsily. "I think she's splendid."

For a moment, Edna looked at him strangely. "Nancy's very beautiful," she said wistfully.

Rowland glanced up, a little surprised.

Edna folded her arms. She smiled now, her eyes teasing again. "Alois won't be back for a couple of hours, Rowly. You should get some sleep while he's not here to wonder why you're so tired."

"No, I'm fine," he replied, sitting up.

It wasn't more than a few minutes, however, before he drifted off in the chair. His companions let him be, passing the time playing cards. At some point Edna slipped a cushion between his head and the wing of the chair, but otherwise they left him undisturbed.

It was past eleven when he stirred. Groggily, Rowland checked his watch.

"Damn it," he groaned.

"What's wrong?" Clyde asked, discarding a pair of cards.

"I promised to try running into Unity Mitford again to keep Blanshard happy. If Hitler doesn't arrive at the restaurant by twelve, I presume she won't wait." He stood and straightened his tie. "I'd better chuff off."

Milton folded his hand. "I might go with you."

"What?"

"It'll look suspicious if she encounters you on your own again. She'll assume you're madly in love with her...following her around. It could get awkward."

"And it'll be less awkward if I bring you?" Rowland's eyes rose from the poet's emerald green cravat to the burgundy beret he wore on his head.

"What's more natural than two old friends having a spot of lunch? You can tell her I'm an old school chum. Pip, pip, smashing wot!"

Rowland sighed. He could tell Milton was, for some reason, eager to meet Unity Mitford. Having met her once, he couldn't fathom why, but the poet had always had an acute sense of the perverse. "Very well, then...but for God's sake, don't speak like that!" He grimaced. "Bear in mind that you cannot tell her what a vapid lunatic she is."

Milton looked affronted. "Why would I do that?"

"Believe me, mate, you'll want to...but it might make things difficult."

Milton smiled. "Of vernal growth, oft quickens in the heart thoughts all too deep for words."

"Coleridge." Rowland shook his head. "There are words... they're just not very polite."

Chapter Twenty-nine

MR. ERIC CAMPBELL
Denies Persecution of Jews
SAYS FASCISM IS DEMOCRATIC

Mr. Eric Campbell expressed the opinion, however, that the New Guard movement could learn a number of things from the European movements. He said that he had found that his position as leader of the New Guard was a passport throughout Europe and Great Britain. In Rome, although he did not meet Signor Mussolini, he met other leaders of the Fascist movement. He found the Nazi and Fascist movements more democratic than any Labour Government ever was.

In Germany, he had made it his business to investigate the alleged persecution of Jews, and, from his personal observation, he would say that there was definitely no persecution. Jews had lost their position only where they were Communists.

—*The Sydney Morning Herald*, 1933

They reached the Osteria Bavaria just as Unity Mitford was leaving.

"Miss Mitford!" Rowland called out as they approached.

She recognised him. Her arm shot into the air and she shouted, "Heil Hitler!"

"Quite," Rowland muttered, conscious of the curious eyes of passers-by. Even in Munich, women rarely used the Nazi greeting socially, and never so loudly. Unity Mitford had a way of drawing attention to herself. She maintained the fascist salute until it became painfully clear that neither Rowland nor Milton were inclined to return it. For his part, Rowland dealt with the discomfiture by introducing Albert Greenway, an old friend from his school days, as if this were a perfectly normal and casual meeting.

"I say, have you and your chum come for lunch?" Unity said, finally dropping her arm.

Rowland nodded. "I enjoyed such a pleasant meal here the other day that I thought I might come again," he lied. "I don't suppose you'd care to join us?"

Unity looked back at the restaurant. "You know what, I do believe I might. It'll be rather fun to speak English for a while. I've been here since eleven and I must say I'm famished."

"You didn't order?" Milton enquired.

"Oh, no…I don't, generally. If Herr Hitler should invite me to his table, I don't want to be full, you know."

"Of course."

And so they took a table in the Osteria.

"I'm returning to take lunch with my friends," Unity announced to no one in particular, using her arms in wide, almost choreographed gestures. "You know what Australians are like…They simply would not allow me to leave without dining with them." She laughed loudly.

Milton glanced at Rowland. His brow was slightly furrowed but otherwise his face revealed little.

"I assume the Chancellor did not come in today," Rowland said, as he studied the menu.

"Not today," Unity replied. "But, you know, he's nodded to me on two previous occasions. He's noticed me, you see. It's only a matter of time before he invites me to sit with him."

"It must be quite an imposition on your time having to lunch here every day, Miss Mitford," Milton ventured.

"Oh, yes, and dreadfully expensive," Unity said, nodding ferociously. "That's why I didn't order before. Farve is already positively explosive about my expenses...but I said to him that I did not wish to be finished in silly old France. I've made my debut and now it's Germany for me! I only wish Cord might have come with me...I'm wretched without her."

"Well said, old thing!" Milton declared, though Rowland was sure that he'd understood barely a word.

"Is Cord one of your sisters?" Rowland asked.

"Yes, Diana, with whom Oswald Mosley is hopelessly in love. I believe I spoke to you of Cord when we last dined, Mr. Negus."

"I beg your pardon, Miss Mitford. For some reason I thought you spoke of that particular sister as *Nardy*."

"Oh, we do...and Cord and Bodley and Honks. We gels each have several names. It's such fun!" She laughed to demonstrate that, indeed, it was. "And don't think I've forgotten that you need a name, Mr. Negus. I simply will not call you Robbie—it's so unbearably pedestrian!"

"I'm afraid Robbie is crushingly boring about such things," Milton said, leaning back in his chair. "Won't answer to anything but Robbie...believe me, the chaps and I have tried."

"And what have you been doing with yourself, Miss Mitford?" Rowland attempted to change the subject. "Are you enjoying Munich?"

"Oh, I've been having an entirely splendid time. Those of us travelling under the banner of the British Union of Fascists have been taken on some quite extraordinary tours. Why, just yesterday we were shown around the camp to which they take those Commie vermin for their own protection."

"And from what exactly are the Nazis protecting the Communists, Miss Mitford?" Milton asked.

"From the people, of course," she replied. "They hate

the beastly Communists over here—see them for the rotten wreckers that they are. I really wish the English were more like the Germans. Oh, if only Mr. Hitler were an Englishman!"

Rowland couldn't help himself. "So you didn't see anything disturbing at the Dachau camp?"

"Oh, the horror, yes. The Communists are quite unnerving to look at, even behind barbed wire. Of course, they're treated perfectly well…The guards are not supposed to harm them physically, though I don't know how they can resist the occasional swipe to keep the wicked creatures in order. Some of them are rather fat," she added, puffing up her cheeks to demonstrate. "I'm sure the foreign press will criticise the government for overfeeding them!" She giggled. "We did see something rather fun." Unity leaned towards them quite conspiratorially. "The inmates were all made to line up on parade for exercises. One of the Kommandants, a particularly handsome chap with very pale hair, ordered them each to raise his right leg, which they all did…and then…"—she paused, sniggering again—"they were ordered to raise the left leg…without putting the right down." Unity threw her head back, her mirth unrestrained. "It was such sport to see them all come crashing down! Oh, how we laughed!"

"Indeed." Rowland forced a smile.

Milton's laugh seemed brittle. He glanced quickly at Rowland as they both checked their growing distaste. "Hitler certainly is a barrel of laughs."

Unity was now laughing so hard she could only nod her agreement.

Rowland and Milton drank while they waited for her to calm herself. Experience had led Rowland to order spirits rather than beer.

"I say, you may have been right about that chap Campbell and his priggish wife."

"How so?" Rowland asked cautiously.

"Well, I heard him say he means to meet Herr Hitler

and ask him directly what he has against the Jews! Isn't that preposterous?"

"Quite. Did he say why he would make such an enquiry?"

"He says it's to address the concerns of the Australian people. Apparently, the foreign press has been publishing ridiculous stories about Jews being mistreated. Jewish reporters, no doubt. Still, I think that perhaps there may be something to that secret you shared with me, Mr. Negus." She winked at Rowland as if they had been party to some deep and valuable confidence.

"About Campbell's mother?" Milton asked.

"You know?" Unity sat back, surprised.

"Of course. Everybody in Australia knows about Campbell's mother…One doesn't really like to talk about it. He can't help who his mother is, after all."

Rowland noticed the tiniest hint of challenge in Milton's tone, but Unity Mitford was oblivious.

"I suppose he can't, but it does say a great deal about his character. The Jew can only be what he is. Anyhow, your Mr. Campbell will not be meeting Mr. Hitler, if there's anything I can do about it. I'm making it my personal mission to protect the Chancellor from Campbell's kind. I'll speak to Putzi Hanfstaengl—he's a capital fellow, not quite an Oxford man, but he did go to Harvard. Putzi'll make sure this fellow, Campbell, doesn't worm his way into the Chancellor's esteem."

"Good for you!" Milton said, with an entirely convincing show of approval. "Someone's got to look out for the poor chap."

And so the meal continued. The Australians ate quickly because they had no wish to prolong the encounter. Unity dominated, for the most part, enlightening them with her views on world politics and trade and recounting childhood pranks played on victims ranging from servants to the Queen Mother. Milton occasionally amused himself by reflecting her manner, inventing terms with aplomb in a way that seemed to endear him to their guest.

Unity tried again to bestow Robert Negus with a nickname, and eventually Rowland gave in. He hoped never to see her again, anyway, so what she chose to call him was irrelevant. Delighted, she dubbed him "Kanga," which, it seemed, was all she knew of Australia. Albert Greenway, she decided to call "Golf," and he appeared to be well pleased with the title, launching into an improbable story about his familial connections to the great fairways of Scotland. She used the monikers repeatedly, stamping them clumsily into every possible sentence.

Rowland checked his watch. "Good Lord, Albert, we'd better get on, or we'll be late." He signalled for the bill.

"Making your acquaintance has been quite unforgettable, Bobo," Milton said, shaking Unity Mitford's hand as Rowland settled the account.

"Yes, my dear Golf, it's been simply scrumptious. We must do this again. I'm here most days, though you must understand that I will abandon you if Mr. Hitler comes in."

"I do understand, Bobo," Milton assured her. "I wouldn't dream of keeping you from Mr. Hitler."

Rowland smiled now, as parting seemed imminent. "Good afternoon, Miss Mitford," he said, still refusing to participate in the ludicrous exchange of nicknames.

And so it was with considerable relief that they left The Honourable Unity Mitford at the steps of the Osteria Bavaria.

They walked in a kind of stunned, uneasy silence and it was not until they were well away that they spoke of the encounter.

"I've gotta admit, mate, you weren't exaggerating," Milton said eventually. "That girl is a very unsavoury kind of mad."

"I wonder if Hitler's noticed she's following him about. I should think he'd find that a little disconcerting."

"Certainly ought to."

Rowland removed his hat and rubbed his hair. For some reason he felt vaguely embarrassed by Unity Mitford. She was the epitome of the ruthless and puerile upper classes of which the Communists spoke, which he had always laughed off as a political caricature. But there she was, and spending any more time in her company could very well turn him into a Bolshevik.

"It's all right, Rowly." Milton elbowed his friend. "It's not as if she's related to you."

Rowland sighed. "If she were, I could at least have her committed."

Milton laughed. "The asylums might get a bit overcrowded if you were committing people for hating Jews," he said quietly. "That's not a new thing, Rowly."

Rowland looked at him. Milton smiled, but his dark eyes flashed angrily...and there was something else. "Milt..."

"She makes me sick, Rowly. And what's worse, she scares me. What's happening here terrifies me in a way that you'll never know."

"I understand."

"No, you don't, mate." Milton shook his head firmly. "How could you understand? You're a member of the ruling class in every way...money and breeding. How could you possibly know what it's like to be despised for the blood that runs in your veins? To be excluded before you say hello? To have neither the money nor the connections to change it? I'm not saying you don't care, mate, or that you don't want to understand, but you just can't know!"

Rowland faltered. "I'm sorry, Milt...I didn't mean..."

Milton groaned. His smile was abashed, apologetic. He placed his hand companionably on Rowland's shoulder. "No, Rowly, don't be sorry. I didn't mean to bite your head off." The poet met his eye. "I'm pleased life's given you a leg-up. You're a good bloke...the best mate I've ever had. That woman's just unnerved me a bit."

Rowland chewed his lip, scowling. Unity Mitford troubled him beyond the irritation of their contact. Perhaps it was that she expressed her bigotry so blithely, as if she were talking about hats or the latest film. As if hating Jews was just the latest fashion.

Milton hooked his thumbs into the pockets of the luridly striped waistcoat he had borrowed from Alois Richter. He sighed, resigned. "If Lady Bobo manages to cause a rift between Campbell and the Nazis, it'll be worth it."

Rowland glanced at his watch. "Come on, then, we'd better hurry."

"For what?" Milton asked. "I thought you'd simply made up an appointment to get us out of there."

"I certainly would have if we didn't actually have one. But as it is, we're meeting Nancy at the Bismarck."

Milton grinned, his anger now forgotten. "What of soul was left, I wonder, when the kissing had to stop?" He nudged Rowland. "I could head back to Richter's, if you like."

"Browning," Rowland said, rolling his eyes. "Don't be daft, we're nearly there. Nancy was going to see what she could find out about this actress, Fräulein Niemann, the woman Bothwell called on before he died."

"Oh." Milton was clearly disappointed. "I had hoped you might finally have gotten over Ed."

"Ed? Oh, I see," Rowland said, now following Milton's line of thought. He laughed. "I am afraid one doesn't get over Ed— one simply learns to live with it."

Nancy Wake was waiting at a table by the window, writing in a small journalist's notebook. She looked up as they approached and smiled warmly. Indeed, Milton was sure there was something in her eyes as she looked at Rowland that he had not seen before.

"Hello, Nancy," Rowland said, aware that Milton was watching him carefully. "Have you been waiting long?"

"No, not at all," she said. "Do sit down…I have a great deal to tell you."

Rowland and Milton took seats at the little table, and signalled the waiter. They made small talk until their drinks arrived, and once the waiter had left them, Nancy began excitedly.

"Anna Niemann is quite a big star…She had her heyday during the war, but she could still attract big crowds." Nancy flipped back a few pages in her notebook. "She's lived in Vienna since 1920, but before that she was working in Munich as a cabaret singer. Her father was some kind of professor and she attended boarding school in England. It was quite a scandal for her to take to the stage. Apparently her family disapproved of her acting." Nancy glanced mischievously at Rowland. "I suppose you'd understand all about that."

Rowland laughed, and waited for her to go on.

"That's the official biography…and then I came across something really interesting." She smiled, building the suspense. "I spoke to a colleague who's been freelancing here for twenty years. He can't be certain, but he's pretty sure that Anna Niemann was accused of spying during the war."

"Spying?"

"It seems she had a British passport, and travelled a great deal on her own…and so she fell under suspicion."

"What happened?"

Nancy shook her head. "Not really sure. My friend recalls she was arrested, but this was after the war had been won. There wasn't really a great will to prosecute, I expect."

Rowland tapped the rim of his glass as he thought. Anna Niemann might have been a spy for the British. Perhaps that was the connection between the actress and Bothwell.

"So what about her disappearance?"

"It was investigated," Nancy said. "Theatregoers complained, for one thing, and of course when the show was cancelled, investors lost money. The official line is that she returned to Vienna, but nobody has heard from or seen her since. She's disappeared."

"What about the SA or the SS? Could she have ended up in a camp?"

"They only hold men," Nancy replied. "And there's nothing on record to indicate she was a Communist, or Jewish, or even just critical of the Nazis." She pulled a photograph from her bag. "I managed to find one of her most recent publicity shots."

Rowland took the picture. Anna Niemann seemed to be between forty and fifty. She was a handsome woman, with heavy eyebrows and an aquiline nose. Her eyes were light and piercing and her mouth expressive. She had the kind of face he would have liked to paint. Her features were not perfect, but there was a vivacity and strength to them. "May I keep this?" he asked.

Nancy nodded. "Yes, of course."

Rowland slipped the photograph into his pocket as he thanked her.

"My pleasure," she replied. "In fact, I wrote a piece on her for *The Tribune* so the research was very useful."

"As long as we're not imposing intolerably."

"Not at all," she laughed. "Now this interview...I called and spoke with Mrs. Campbell. She promised to pass on my request—said Colonel Campbell was always happy to talk to the press."

"That much is true," Rowland replied. Eric Campbell had always courted the spotlight. "You're still sure you want to do this, Nancy?"

She put her hand on his and smiled. "Don't worry, Rowly. Nothing will go wrong. And who knows? I might just write a story about Colonel Campbell."

Chapter Thirty

The psyche of the broad masses is accessible only to what is strong and uncompromising. Like a woman whose inner sensibilities are not so much under the sway of abstract reasoning but are always subject to the influence of a vague emotional longing for the strength that completes her being, and who would rather bow to the strong man than dominate the weakling—in like manner the masses of the people prefer the ruler to the suppliant and are filled with a stronger sense of mental security by a teaching that brooks no rival than by a teaching which offers them a liberal choice.

—Adolf Hitler, *Mein Kampf*

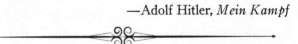

The business district was lively when Milton and Rowland finally left the Bismarck. Munich's hard-working citizens conducted last-minute business, and bought bread and sausage before returning to their homes for the evening. The spring air was tinged with the scent of limes and geraniums. Rowland was thoughtful. Anna Niemann had disappeared almost immediately after Bothwell and Richter had gone to see her. Bothwell was dead. It occurred to him that he should speak to Alois Richter. He couldn't imagine that their kind host was involved, but he had been there.

"Missing her already?" Milton smiled, misinterpreting his mood.

"Who? Oh, Nancy. I was thinking about Richter, actually."

"What the hell's wrong with you, Rowly?"

Rowland ignored the reproof. "I might have to talk to him about Bothwell, and Anna Niemann."

"How are you going to do that without giving the whole game away?"

"I'm not certain, but Richter's the only avenue we haven't yet exhausted. At the very least, he might be able to tell us what passed between Bothwell and Fräulein Niemann."

Milton frowned. "Ed's very fond of him and he's completely wrapped around her little finger. Be careful, mate. He might feel a bit put upon if he suspects you're not really Peter Bothwell's grieving cousin…not to mention that he does business with the Reich, so he could be skittish about harbouring spies."

Rowland turned up his collar as the wind rose briskly. "I'll come up with something."

The Brownshirts who'd been haunting Schellingstrasse outside the mansion when they'd left appeared to have departed. Rowland glanced at Milton. "Perhaps Richter's got more clout with the Reich than we thought," he murmured.

"Or perhaps they've just decided to be less obvious," Milton countered sceptically.

Rowland let his eyes search the street. The light was fading and the shadows were deepening. The tall, closely set buildings with their decorative alcoves would make covert surveillance quite easy. "Let's go in," he said, feeling suddenly exposed.

Edna met them at the door, opening it before they could knock. She slipped out and shut the front door behind her. "I've been watching for you," she whispered urgently. "I didn't want Alois to overhear."

"What's the matter?" Rowland asked, noting the uneasiness in her voice, the largeness of her eyes.

"After you left today, some men from the SA called by."

Rowland tensed. "Are you all right?" He studied her anxiously. "Where's Clyde?"

Edna touched his arm. "He's fine, we're both fine."

"What did the bastards want?" Milton asked angrily.

"I don't know...they didn't speak English. They asked us some questions, but of course Clyde and I had no idea what they were saying. We just showed them our passports."

"What about Mrs. Schuler?"

"She spoke to them, but I don't think she's said anything to Alois about it...and we couldn't speak to her to ask why."

Rowland put his arm around the sculptress. He could see she was unsettled. "I'll talk to Mrs. Schuler. I take it you haven't said anything to Richter either?"

"We didn't want him to go marching off to shout at Himmler..."

Rowland nodded. "Probably wise. Perhaps that's what Mrs. Schuler is worried about."

"We'd better go in," Edna said, glancing back at the door.

As they stepped into the entrance foyer, they found Mrs. Schuler watching furtively as she wiped the balustrade of the winding staircase. Rowland glanced at his companions. The housekeeper was obviously waiting. "You both go keep Richter happy," he said quietly. "I'll speak with her now."

He waited until Edna and Milton had disappeared into the formal parlour where it appeared were Richter and Clyde. "*Entschuldigung sie mir, bitte, Frau Schuler,*" he began. "My companions mentioned there was a visit today from the SA. What did they want?"

"They were looking for the girl, Herr Negus," she replied sourly.

"Fräulein Greenway?"

"That is what I assumed, but when they saw her they lost interest. They said they had made a mistake."

"You didn't mention this to Herr Richter?"

"They insisted that I do not. I thought since it was just a

mistake, then there was no purpose upsetting him." She made a sound a little like a hiss. "He is already making a fool enough of himself over Fräulein Greenway."

"He sees her as a daughter," Rowland said carefully.

Again, the hiss-like sound. "He would not allow his own child to always be so shamelessly in the company of men! If he thought her a daughter, Herr Negus, he would not tolerate you!"

Rowland stared at the old woman, shocked less by the fact that a servant was addressing him so, as by the resentment and vitriol in her voice. "I can assure you, Frau Schuler, there is nothing improper about my relationship with Fräulein Greenway."

She turned her back on him. "I have duties to attend to. It is I who run his house while he laughs and carries on like a giddy girl. You can tell Herr Richter if you like…let him become the laughing stock of the Nazis, being led round by the nose by a foreigner!" The housekeeper stormed out.

Rowland paused for a moment, watching the bent figure walk away in undisguised disgust before he moved to find his friends.

"Mr. Negus…what kept you?" Richter asked when Rowland joined them in the parlour. "Did you stop to polish my doorhandle?"

Rowland smiled. "I see you have banished the SA from outside your home, Mr. Richter," he said, opting to simply change the subject rather than come up with a reason for why he had loitered in the foyer.

Richter puffed up smugly and raised his forefinger. "Yes, Himmler tried to tell me there was nothing he could do, as the SA is Röhm's, but clearly that is not the case and the wrath of Alois Richter is something to be feared!"

Edna laughed at him. "Steady on, Alois dear. You're frightening poor Stasi."

Rowland glanced at the completely inert dog, as it dozed on the couch. Perhaps it was frightened—who could tell? He sat down and stroked the unresponsive creature, missing Lenin. His one-eared greyhound would have by now climbed onto his lap and sent everything, including his master, flying with his exuberance.

Richter detailed his encounter with Himmler in extravagant and heroic detail until Mrs. Schuler called them in for dinner. The housekeeper was once again an unspeaking, impassive presence. Rowland noted that she did not look at Edna, even when she was serving her meal, but otherwise, there was nothing.

After dinner they returned to the parlour to play cards. It was relatively early when Milton informed Edna that she looked tired and should have an early night. It was such an unusual suggestion coming from Milton that Edna agreed.

"I think I may turn in too," Milton murmured, stifling a yawn.

"But I was just about to put Wagner on the gramophone," Richter protested.

That was enough for Clyde, who yawned and made his excuses hastily.

Rowland stayed where he was with his glass of brandy. He had no particular love of Wagner either, but guessed that Milton was giving him the chance to speak with Richter alone.

He and the tailor simply sat for a while. Richter waved his hands occasionally, conducting some imaginary orchestra through the more dramatic movements, the tassel of his fez flinging from side to side.

Rowland waited until the record had finished. "Mr. Richter," he said, before the other could change or restart it, "I'd like to show you something, if I may."

"Of course, my dear Mr. Negus. Since we are alone, do you mind if we speak German? I am happy to speak English for Miss Greenway and the gentlemen, but occasionally I get sentimental for my native tongue…"

"Of course," Rowland said, slipping easily into the Bavarian dialect. He pulled the photograph Nancy Wake had procured for him from the inside breast pocket of his jacket. "Do you know this woman, by any chance, Herr Richter?" he asked, handing it to his host.

Richter rose to study the picture in the light. "Where did you get this, Herr Negus?"

"It was in Peter Bothwell's trunk," Rowland replied. "I was checking…in case there was something in it that Frau Bothwell should not see. I came across this photograph in a lining pocket, and of course I wondered if it might be of the woman whom she suspected had won her husband's affections."

Richter stared at the picture, his lower lip pressing against the upper in a tense curve.

"You found it in Peter's trunk?"

"Yes, I'm afraid I did."

"The woman in this picture is the actress we went to see perform Shakespeare. Peter took her flowers. I thought it was just an artistic admiration."

"Did he speak to her?"

"For just a few moments after the performance…not longer," Richter said, handing him back the picture. "I believe he called her Anna."

Rowland placed the photograph back in his pocket. "You will tell us, Herr Richter, if our being here in your home becomes inconvenient or problematic for you, won't you?"

Richter stared at him. "How could it be a problem? You are my guests…I have a big house…How could it be a problem?"

"I only meant that the government seems to frown on the Modernist movement at the moment and we are dealing in surrealist pieces, for the most part."

"What do I care what the government thinks?" Richter was becoming agitated.

"You do business with the Reich, Herr Richter. You have been the epitome of generosity and hospitality…We don't want to be the cause of trouble for you. We could always move back to—"

"No! I will not hear of it!" Richter slammed down his glass. Brandy splashed onto the polished surface of the low table.

Rowland sat forward. His voice was calm. "If you do not wish us to go, Herr Richter, then of course, we will not. I just wanted to make sure we had not outstayed our welcome."

Richter stared at the spilled brandy. He pulled at the silk handkerchief which protruded jauntily from his breast pocket and used it to wipe his hands and then the table. "Oh…excuse me, I apologise," he said quietly. "My dear young friend, I did not mean to be so abrupt." He moved to sit opposite Rowland. "It is not a natural thing to bury your child," he said. "Over the years I became rich, a man of influence…and yet I wondered what my beloved Helena's laughter would have sounded like in this great house that I have bought with my lonely wealth." Richter dabbed at his face with his brandy-soaked cloth, flinching as the alcohol stung his eyes. "Then Fräulein Greenway came into this cold place, with her beauty, her warmth, and while she is here, my loss is lessened."

"We will have to go, eventually," Rowland reminded him, as gently as he could.

"Of course." Richter smiled. "And when it is necessary, I will say good-bye sadly and always I will have a memory of this time."

"Your business…"

"My business will not suffer, I will make sure of that." Richter reached over and patted Rowland's shoulder. "Hugo Boss is underhanded and clever, but I am wily like the old fox…He will not get the best of me, no matter what tricks he tries!"

Chapter Thirty-one

GERMANY
Monarchist Tendencies
BAVARIA'S RELATIONS
WITH THE REICH

LONDON, February 22

Commenting on recent statements by the Bavarian Premier (Dr. Held), to the effect that if Germany secures a new monarch Bavaria will not submit to the Hohenzollerns, and "if Berlin makes further attempts to deprive Bavaria of her rights, we shall know what to do," the Daily Telegraph says: "The ex-Crown Prince Rupprecht has for long lived in his palace at Munich in much the same style as the last crowned King of Bavaria. He has always enjoyed popularity, and has never renounced his dynastic claims. He maintains his court and is treated with royal honours wherever he goes.

"There can be little doubt that the leader of the Bavarian monarchists was justified in saying recently that the accession of the Prince would be the most popular event imaginable. It would be a strange turn if Germany was suddenly required to adjust itself to a restored monarchy within the Reich. The Bavarians are quite likely to establish their king before Hitler's monarchist allies are ready to bring back the Hohenzollerns."

—*The Sydney Morning Herald*, 1933

Alois Richter walked into the dining room, waving the invitation.

"What is this, Alois?" Edna asked, as he handed her the gilt-edged card.

"This, young people, is an invitation to the social occasion of the year. A royal ball in the Hall of Antiquities at the residence of the Bavarian Kings!"

"Royal?" Rowland looked up. "Bavaria is part of the Weimar Republic, isn't it?"

Richter snorted. "The Prussians and their Republic! We Bavarians remember who our King is, even now." He pointed to one of the paintings in the opulent dining room—a formal portrait of an elderly man with a long, white beard. "Behold, Ludwig III, the last King of Bavaria—Rupprecht is his eldest son. He may yet be recognised as King. If the Nazis hadn't come to power they say the Bavarian Government would have restored the monarchy."

"And has this almost-King given the Chancellor his support?" Milton asked.

"No, my friends. King Rupprecht has little time for Hitler. Even during the Beer Hall Putsch, Rupprecht refused to join him, but that is not of any consequence…Rupprecht is giving a ball at the Leuchtenberg Palace! It will be a simply magnificent, elegant affair."

"And we're invited?" Edna said surprised. "All of us?"

"Of course…the guest list is prepared by a man called Kraus. Five-foot eight, narrow shoulders, thirty-six-inch waist. Years ago, I made his wedding suit…velvet lapels, tortoiseshell buttons…very smart. He remembers this and when I ask for a small favour, he happily obliges!" Richter sat down, beaming triumphantly.

Edna handed the invitation to Rowland. It was printed on heavy card, its edges scalloped and gilded. Embossed at the top of the page were the arms of the House of Wittelsbach.

"Finally, an occasion fit for the gown I have made for you.

And when they ask who dressed the most beautiful woman in the room, it shall be Alois Richter!"

"Alois, surely you don't propose to use me as an advertisement?" Edna said with mock horror.

"There will be no greater testament to my work, *dandschig Deandl*...Munich will know without a doubt that Alois Richter is the premier tailor in Germany."

"Will there be many people there, do you think?" Milton asked, carefully casual.

"Of course...every person of substance—or who aspires to be of substance— in Munich will attend in their finest garments!"

"I suppose the Nazi hierarchy will be there in their Sunday best too," Milton said warily.

Richter shrugged. "Perhaps not. Rupprecht refuses to join the Nazis. I suspect he does not like them. I would be surprised if he invited them to the palace. Göring, possibly, and von Ribbentrop if he is in Munich, but they are unlikely to attend. The Nazis wish Hitler to be the only king in Germany."

Rowland glanced at Edna. It would be difficult to refuse without offending their host, and yet to attend such a function would be insanely risky.

"I have already taken the liberty of sending word, accepting for us all," Richter announced, before Rowland could raise an objection. "Now, gentlemen, if you require attire, remember you are living with a tailor."

"Thank you, Mr. Richter, but I'm not sure—"

"Of what are you not sure?" Richter asked immediately.

Rowland struggled for some plausible reason they could not attend. There was nothing.

"We have a very important meeting at the Kunst Haus the following morning," Edna said, peering over Rowland's shoulder to look again at the invitation. "Dealers from England and America." She smiled reassuringly at Richter. "We cannot dance all night, as much as I would love to do so."

Richter nodded emphatically. "I understand *mein Kind*, business must be done. I am not a wealthy man because I neglected my business to dance. We will return to our beds by midnight and Herr Negus shall be refreshed for his meeting."

Rowland glanced helplessly at his companions. It did not seem they would be allowed to recuse themselves...not yet, anyway. Rowland noted the date on the invitation. They had a week to find some excuse.

The four of them set out together that morning, ostensibly for the galleries. Richter had disappeared to finalise Edna's gown and to ensure that his own tailcoat was adjusted to accommodate any recent expansions in his torso.

"Perhaps we'll get away with it," Clyde murmured, as Rowland parked the Mercedes. "The three of us could just stay in the background, keep an eye out for Campbell. It's only Ed that Richter wants to use as a billboard."

"Ed's pretty recognisable," Rowland said. "Campbell's met her too."

"That was over a year ago," Milton said. He turned to Edna. "Couldn't you do something with your hair or your face to make yourself look different?"

"I can hardly grow a moustache," Edna replied.

Milton grinned. "Look, Rowly, I don't think it'll be so bad. It sounds as if the Nazi hierarchy is unlikely to be on the guest list. If Hitler and King Rupert have fallen out, then surely Campbell's not going to risk offending Hitler by going to the King's party."

"He's got a point," Clyde agreed. "Perhaps we're swinging at shadows."

Milton continued. "If, for some reason, Campbell is invited, and does attend, and then comes across Ed while Richter is parading her around, he'll probably note that she looks remarkably like the girl who shot a man in his study, but he's unlikely to assume it is the self-same girl. How many times do you see someone that you think looks just like someone else? If Ed continues to insist she's Millicent Greenway, I doubt he'll find the familiarity enough to investigate."

On this point Rowland was sceptical. "I don't know, Milt. As you said, Ed shot a man in his study. You would think he might remember her."

Clyde raised his brows as he recalled that night. "She was splattered with blood and screaming bloody murder…With any luck, she'll look a bit different all scrubbed up."

"I am sitting right here, you know," Edna said, smacking Clyde indignantly.

Rowland smiled. "Campbell didn't only see Ed on the night she shot me, though. She came to a party at the Campbells' posing as my fiancée, if you remember."

Edna rolled her eyes. "Good Lord, it's not that difficult. If we see Campbell at the ball I will simply get a headache and slip home before anybody thinks to introduce us."

For a few awkward seconds nobody replied, as they considered what seemed too simple a solution.

"I suppose that might work," Rowland said finally.

"Of course it'll work," Edna said. Her eyes glinted. "I know you fellows are getting fond of dressing up and pretending to be God knows what—"

"Yes, all right, that's enough," Clyde interrupted.

Rowland swung open his door. They were parked outside a modern apartment building, a structure of simples lines and occasional curves in classic Art Deco style, located in an expensive neighbourhood. Chic couples strolled the pavements arm in arm. Rowland's eye was caught momentarily by a pair of glossy dachshunds holding their leads in their mouths as they trotted sedately beside an elderly gentleman.

"Well-trained," he murmured, thinking of Eva and her desperation for a dachshund.

"You couldn't get Lenin to do that," Clyde agreed.

Rowland smiled. Lenin didn't like leads. The war-torn grey-hound was hard enough to control with a grown man holding onto the lead for dear life.

"Len's an Australian dog," Milton said glancing disdainfully at the dachshunds. "There's something rather perverse about a hound that restrains itself."

Rowland was inclined to agree. He missed Lenin.

"Where are we, Rowly?" Edna asked.

"Anna Niemann lived here," Rowland told them quietly. "I thought there might be a caretaker or a building manager about, to whom I could speak. See if she had her things sent on anywhere…that sort of thing." He climbed out of the Mercedes and opened Edna's door. "You lot don't have to come with me…In fact, it might be counterproductive if you did."

Clyde checked his watch. He looked at Milton. "I suppose it's too early for a beer."

Milton smiled contentedly. "Not in Bavaria, old mate."

"I'll see you back here in about an hour, then," Rowland said, tossing the keys to Clyde.

"I'll stay with Rowly," Edna said, adjusting her hat in the reflection of the Mercedes' windscreen.

Leaving Clyde and the poet to find a beer hall, Edna and Rowland walked together towards Anna Niemann's last known address.

Rowland spoke first with the doorman, making enquiries about the building's manager and requesting an audience with the same.

The doorman directed them through a door behind the polished counter in the foyer. The office was small and clean, though cluttered. The walls were hidden by bookshelves and boards of hooks on which hung keys with brass tags. An extraordinarily short gentleman with a neat white beard stood behind a massive pedestal desk which made him seem smaller still. The manager's name was Handel. He greeted them politely and invited them to sit.

Rowland introduced himself and Edna as Mr. and Mrs. Marcel. He hadn't discussed this with Edna, and he wasn't entirely sure why he adopted the guise in this case. Perhaps he just liked the idea of introducing Edna as his wife.

"I am with Film Fransçois, Herr Handel," Rowland began, making it up as he went. "Perhaps you know this woman?" He handed the photograph of Anna Niemann to the manager. "We would like to offer her a major role in one of our upcoming productions, but we are having a little trouble locating her. Fräulein Niemann gave this as her last address, but we are told she is no longer here."

Handel nodded. "That is true, I am afraid. We have not seen Fräulein Niemann in over a month."

"Did she leave a forwarding address?"

"No, but she left everything else." Handel sat back in his chair with his hands folded over his belly. "Fräulein Niemann left in haste…My wife and I packed up her things when it was clear she would not return. Why, if it was not for her brother, her personal items would still be here in boxes."

"Her brother—?"

"Herr Niemann. He came about a week after she left, settled the outstanding rent account and took her possessions away."

"I wasn't aware Fräulein Niemann had a brother…are you sure—?" Rowland began.

"Yes, yes." Handel was emphatic. "I was surprised at first, too, as Fräulein Niemann had never mentioned a brother and he had not visited before. We do not give the goods and chattels of our residents to any person that walks in off the street!"

"Forgive me, Herr Handel, I did not mean to imply such a thing," Rowland said quickly. "It's just that I have known Fräulein Niemann for many years and I have never met this brother. What did he look like? Perhaps we have been introduced and I have just forgotten."

Handel shrugged. "Tall…about forty-five, I'd say…red hair…He spoke with an accent, though I could not place it. He was polite, but his face did not match his words. He showed me a photo taken just after the war…They were younger, of course, but the likeness was unmistakable.

Rowland frowned. He pulled the notebook from the lining pocket of his jacket and, opening to a clean page, drew quickly. "Is this the man, Herr Handel?" he asked, handing the notebook over the desk.

Handel took a pair of spectacles from his breast pocket and peered at the sketch of Alastair Blanshard curiously. "*Mein Gott!* That is him…with so few lines you have drawn him… You know him then, Herr Marcel?"

Rowland nodded. "I do…I had forgotten he was Fräulein Niemann's brother until you described him just now." He took the notebook back from Handel. "I don't suppose he left a forwarding address."

Handel raised a finger. "Yes, yes, he did…for mail and such, though there has been nothing." He opened a drawer and rummaged through it to find the note he sought. Painstakingly he copied the address onto a card which he handed to Rowland. "Perhaps you will find her there, Herr Marcel, or at least Herr Niemann. She is a fine actress…My wife and I went to one of her shows."

"We'll do our best to find her, Herr Handel." Rowland stood and thanked the manager for his time and assistance.

As their companions had not yet returned, Rowland and Edna took tea in a small but fashionable café near the apartment block. Rowland informed Edna then that it was Alastair Blanshard who had collected Anna Niemann's belongings and paid her rent.

Edna gasped. "But why?…Do you think Mr. Blanshard knows where she is now?"

"I'm beginning to wonder what precisely Blanshard knows and what exactly he's doing," Rowland replied tersely. He shook his head, remembering that when he first asked Blanshard about the mystery woman, the agent had pointed him towards Nancy. It seemed an intentional misdirection now.

"Rowly?" Edna prompted him. "What are we going to do?"

Rowland smiled, noticing that Edna had finished her cake and had duly started on his. "If we can't trust Blanshard, we're fairly vulnerable, Ed…Are you going to leave me any of that?"

Edna took another forkful of cake before returning it. "It's simply delicious," she assured him.

"Wil said that Bothwell may have been betrayed by someone within the Old Guard…Perhaps it was Blanshard."

"Are we going to confront him?" Edna asked, adding another lump of sugar to her tea.

"No, we are not," he replied quietly. "But *I* might."

Chapter Thirty-two

...It seemed a good opportunity so I asked him [Putzi Hanfstaengl] why the Nazi Party were so bitterly opposed to the Jews. His answer was surprising.

"We do not interfere with Jews. You have been around Berlin? Yes? Well you would have seen plenty of Jews with big shops looking fat and happy. I tell you, if Hitler did not want any Jews in Berlin, it would be all over in twenty minutes including the burial service." He then burst into laughter the way Germans so often do.

As I was taking my leave, three men came into Putzi's room and I was introduced. They were Ribbentrop, Alfred Rosenberg, and a Major Schmidt. The latter spoke English with a strong American accent...

—Eric Campbell, *The Rallying Point*, 1965

Rowland stopped in his tracks. Ahead of him was the parterre which ran down the centre of the park. It was here he had arranged to meet Blanshard. But the agent was not alone.

Alastair Blanshard stood with his hat in his hand, in conversation with a tall blonde in a herringbone skirt. Unity Mitford.

Rowland's impulse was to turn on his heel and walk away, but it was too late.

Unity waved, her long arm flailing in a wide, excited arc. "Kanga! Why, it's Kanga Negus!" She ran over to him dragging Blanshard with her.

"Hullo there." She smiled broadly. "I say, it must be my day for bumping into people. First Biddles Blanshard and now you!"

"Miss Mitford," Rowland said, forcing himself to smile. He offered Blanshard his hand. "Robert Negus, Mr. Blanshard. How do you do?"

Blanshard, apparently relieved that Rowland did not feel the need to call him "Biddles," responded in kind. Rowland turned back to Unity as he checked his watch. "What a surprise to find you here, Miss Mitford. I would have expected you—"

"To be at the Osteria?" she finished for him. "Not today. Mr. Hitler is in Berlin today...as is Mr. Campbell." She burst into an uncontrollable fit of giggles.

Rowland watched on uncertainly. The woman was quite mad.

Blanshard cleared his throat. "Are you acquainted with Colonel Campbell, Mr. Negus?"

"I know of him…" Rowland replied, bewildered as to where the conversation was going.

"Well, it appears Miss Mitford has played a rather amusing prank on Colonel Campbell."

Unity slapped Blanshard's arm. "No...stop!" she gasped, trying to control her laughter. "You must let me tell it...it's just too much." She hooked one arm through Rowland's and the other through Blanshard's. "Shall we walk? It'll help me control myself…" She giggled again.

And so they strolled down the parterre.

Unity did nothing but giggle for a while, and then finally she began to explain her extraordinary mirth.

"I was speaking to my friend, Putzi Hanfstaengl…that's his real name, by the way; it's so ridiculous I can't call him anything else. Anyway, I was telling Putzi 'bout Colonel Campbell and, you know,"—she lowered her voice to a scandalised whisper— "*his mother*. Of course, Putzi was as outraged as I that Campbell would presume to form an association with our beloved Mr. Hitler and we thought how jolly it would be if we could make him think he'd actually met someone important...They're like that, the Jews, always trying to insinuate themselves with their betters."

"Do you play poker, Mr. Negus?" Blanshard said loudly, glancing at Rowland over the top of Unity's head.

"What has that got to do with anything, Biddles?" Unity said, looking at Blanshard.

Rowland took heed and tried to relax his face. Apparently, his distaste was showing.

"Nothing at all, Miss Mitford...I do beg your pardon," Blanshard apologised. "Do go on."

"Well, Putzi—he's the Chancellor's secretary or some such thing—invited Colonel Campbell up to Berlin to meet Mr. Hitler at the Chancellery. As you would expect, Colonel Campbell was tremendously pleased and accepted most enthusiastically."

Rowland looked at her with growing disquiet. Was everything they had done to keep Campbell away from Nazis of note about to be undermined by this idiotic English woman?

"But of course he won't actually see Mr. Hitler...who, Putzi will tell him, has been called away at the last moment. Instead, Putzi will introduce him to Mr. Von Ribbentrop, Mr. Rosenberg, and Major Schmidt. Only it won't be Mr. Von Ribbentrop, Mr. Rosenberg, or Major Schmidt.... but two office boys and an American friend of Putzi's, all dressed up!" Unity positively screeched with laughter. Indeed, if her arms had not been firmly entwined with her companions' she might have collapsed with hilarity at what seemed to Rowland a somewhat bizarre joke.

"I take it that Mr. Hanfstaengl's American friend speaks German?" Rowland asked.

"No...not at all! He just wanted to be part of the joke. I'll say this for Americans, they're always ready for a lark. Putzi's going to dress an American in an SS uniform and tell Colonel Campbell that he's an important Nazi. Oh, how we laughed planning it!"

It did occur to Rowland that Unity Mitford and Hanfstaengl might just have orchestrated the meeting that would allow Campbell to leave Germany satisfied that he had met enough significant Nazis to justify his trip.

Blanshard, too, did not look displeased. The agent took a pocket watch from his waistcoat pocket and, after consulting it, shook his head with a studied show of regret. "As much as I'd like to stay, I'm afraid I have a previous engagement, so if you'll excuse me, Miss Mitford, I'll have to leave Mr. Negus to walk you back to your hotel."

Unity wiped the tears of laughter from her eyes. "Don't mention it, Biddles. Kanga and I will carry on."

Rowland glared at Blanshard, infuriated by this last act of bastardry. The man was capable of anything.

Blanshard smiled, looking amused for the first time. "Let me give you my card, Mr. Negus. No doubt you'll wish to write to me with thanks for facilitating this time with the charming Miss Mitford." He handed Rowland a calling card.

"Oh, Biddles, you do go on!" Unity smiled coyly. "Mr. Negus is well aware that I am spoken for."

"A man can but try," Blanshard said, tipping his hat as he left them to it.

Rowland glanced at the card before slipping it into his pocket. Scribbled in pencil on the underside was "Back Wednesday."

When he looked up again, Unity Mitford was studying him. "Do you want to do something a little bit naughty, Kanga?"

Rowland just wanted to leave.

She pulled at his arm. "Come on, then, we'll have a smashing time!"

"I'm afraid I—"

"It won't take terribly long," she interrupted. "You simply must come…I shall be most put out if you don't." She folded her arms and pouted.

"Where exactly do you wish me to accompany you, Miss Mitford?"

"To the stadium at the end of Wilhelmstrasse. I want you to see why Germany is going to become the greatest nation in the world."

Rowland relaxed. A stadium. The Nazis had a fondness for epic, classical architecture. He relented.

They took a motor cab to Wilhelmstrasse, which was located outside the central business district. The stadium he saw as they approached was not particularly spectacular. Hardly worthy of the hyperbole of Unity's description.

They alighted near the entrance and Rowland paid the driver, who Unity instructed not to wait.

The main entrance to the stadium was shut, guarded by two SA officers who stood talking about their plans for the evening and smoking.

"This way," Unity said, hooking her arm through Rowland's and pulling him away as if they intended to stroll about the outside perimeter of the stadium. About two hundred feet from the entrance was another door…small and unassuming, obviously a service or utility access of some sort.

"The lock is rusted," Unity whispered. "If you give it a decent push, it'll open. Putzi showed me a week ago."

Rowland stepped up to the door and shouldered it sharply. As Unity had predicted, it gave and opened.

"Quick, before anyone sees us." Unity pushed past Rowland and into the stairwell on the other side of the door. Rowland closed the door behind them. The stairs were dark and narrow and smelled of mildew. They came up between the rows of tiered seating which surrounded the grassed oval of the stadium.

"Stay down," Unity warned, as they slipped into the wooden seats.

Rowland wasn't listening to her, staring instead at the thousands of men parading on the oval in perfect formation. They wore the brown trousers and boots of the SA, but their upper bodies were bare.

"What the devil are they doing?" he murmured.

"They're practising for the victory rally in Nuremberg at the end of August," Unity said, squirming in delight. "Aren't they simply magnificent? A breathtaking display of Aryan manhood."

Rowland's brow rose. "And will Aryan womanhood be similarly displayed?"

"The girls league does a gymnastics show, I believe," Unity said dismissively. Clearly the women did not interest her.

They watched for several minutes, Unity pointing out the precision, the discipline, and the sheer beauty of so many honed male bodies moving in concert. Rowland found it interesting, though the performance of military manoeuvres while half-naked seemed a little odd.

The lines of men goosestepped, eight abreast, past the empty grandstand, perfecting a precisely timed fascist salute while maintaining the rhythm of the straight-legged stride. Rowland wondered for a moment what had possessed the Germans to adopt the goosestep as a method of marching. Surely it was not a sensible way to move troops from one point to another? He remembered Richter's threat to interfere with the trousers of the SA uniform. It would explain the goosestep, he supposed.

"It is a demonstration of Aryan superiority," Unity explained, when he suggested the parade might look better if the SA had not forgotten to get dressed. "Mr. Hitler is adamant that the body must be exercised and ready to serve the Fatherland."

The parade now stood in perfectly spaced lines and rows, and in unison began to sing. Rowland frowned. Campbell's New Guard had also been fond of parading. He had seen several thousand New Guardsmen drill in a farm paddock the previous year. They had been less polished, and completely dressed, but the show of potential force was similar.

"We'd better go before someone notices us and asks awkward questions," Rowland said firmly.

Unity sighed. "You really are a bit of a bore, Kanga."

He did not reply, moving so that she had little choice but to be ushered back into the stairwell, and out of the stadium.

Unity Mitford chatted loudly about the shirtless display, giggling in a manner that irritated him to distraction. She pointed out the features of Rowland's face that she was sure were indicative of his Aryan breeding. "Your eyes are very blue, Kanga. It's rather a shame you're not blond, really."

Rowland hailed a motor cab, relieved when it pulled up. He gave the driver the name of the young Englishwoman's hotel and ample fare to take her back.

Unity farewelled Rowland with the fascist salute, shouting "Heil Hitler!" at a volume that made him wince, and then lamented that he was not free to take her to dinner that evening. It seemed she was completely unaware that he would gladly have done anything to get away.

Rowland walked back to Schellingstrasse. It was not a trivial distance and it had started to drizzle, but he needed to think. So far, all he had been able to discover about Bothwell's death was that it was probably not an accident. The actress Anna Niemann seemed to have disappeared and, for some reason, all her belongings had been claimed by Blanshard. Rowland wondered about the book Bothwell had been writing…the one about which he'd spoken to Nancy Wake. Could he have been killed to prevent its revelations? If so, was it just Röhm who stood to be exposed? Suddenly, it occurred to him that perhaps the manuscript was among the papers in Bothwell's trunk. He had never opened it.

Rowland was, by the time he reached Schellingstrasse, soaked and quite chilled by the cold mist-like rain. Even so, he called in at Hoffman's Studio to check on Eva, rather than walking on towards home. It had now been a few days since she'd arrived at Richter's in tears, and left with the portrait he'd painted. He hoped the absence meant that she was happy.

Eva smiled delightedly when he walked in. "*Grüss Gott*, Robbie. What are you doing here?"

"I was just passing by," he replied. "I thought I'd say hello. We haven't seen you in a while."

Eva sighed and rolled her eyes. "My sister," she said. "It's difficult to get away without her questions."

"And Herr Wolf?"

Her face fell. "He has business away. I have not even been able to give him your beautiful painting."

"Perhaps you shouldn't—" Rowland stopped as Eva stiffened, startled.

"Of course, Herr Negus," she said loudly. "We do sell official prints of the Chancellor. How many would you like?"

Rowland turned. A tall thin man stood at the door into the studio proper. His face was long and severe, his hair combed tightly back from a receding hairline.

"I'd better take two of the most recent," Rowland said, guessing that the man was Hoffman, Eva's employer and Hitler's personal photographer.

Hoffman strode over to stand at the counter beside Eva. "I will serve this gentleman, Fräulein Eva," he said. "There are some accounts that need filing in the office."

Eva nodded. "Of course, Herr Hoffman." She paused at the door to glance hesitantly at Rowland before she left them alone.

Hoffman silently placed the photographs into embossed folders before slipping them into envelopes and handing them over the counter. "Will you be staying in Munich much longer, Herr Negus?" he asked coldly, as he took payment from Rowland.

"Sadly not, Herr Hoffman," Rowland replied. "I shall be sorry to leave."

"Sometimes it is best to go without delay."

"Indeed."

For a moment longer than necessary they eyed each other, and then Rowland tipped his hat to the photographer and left.

Chapter Thirty-three

INFANT ZEAL FOR HITLER

Even the kindergarten schools in Germany come under the influence of the Hitler regime. In a picture, received by air mail, young children—scarcely more than babies—are shown giving the Nazi salute as they march past their school master.

—*Courier Mail*, 1933

"Whatever are you doing, Rowly?" Edna asked, shutting the bedroom door quietly behind her.

Rowland was kneeling on the floor with the contents of Peter Bothwell's trunk strewn around him. His sodden jacket and tie were slung over the back of a tapestry-covered stocking chair, and the sleeves of his still-damp shirt rolled up to the elbows.

He looked up and smiled. "You're back," he said. "I was beginning to wonder where you'd all gotten to."

Edna stepped over a pile of clothing as she moved towards him. "Did you miss us?"

"Terribly…give me a hand to clear this up, will you, Ed?"

"Of course." She kneeled beside him as he repacked Peter Bothwell's trunk. "What are you doing?" she asked again.

"I was hoping to find something connected with this book Bothwell was supposed to be writing."

"And you didn't?"

"No, I'm afraid not. In fact, there's nothing here but clothes and such. No documents or letters of any kind. It's odd."

Edna peered into the large trunk. "Nothing at all? Not even letters, or a photograph?"

Rowland shrugged. He had found nothing.

Edna frowned. "That is rather peculiar. Perhaps it's because he was…you know…spying."

"Perhaps."

"Did you manage to speak to Mr. Blanshard about Anna Niemann, Rowly?"

Rowland sat back on his heels and dragged both hands through his hair. He told Edna of his bizarre afternoon with Unity Mitford.

The sculptress shook her head, smiling. "Oh, Rowly, you do know how to pick them."

"I did not pick Miss Mitford, she was foisted upon me," he retorted tensely.

Edna laughed now, leaning against him companionably. "We'll have to get even with Mr. Blanshard later. He cannot be allowed to inflict that woman on the unsuspecting public."

What Rowland wished to voice on the subject of Alastair Blanshard could not be said in the presence of a lady, and so he did not reply.

Edna stood up and sat on the bed. "Why, what's this?" she said, noticing the folders which he had discarded there when he'd come in earlier.

"Our beloved Chancellor," Rowland said, getting off his knees and sitting beside her.

"You called in to see Eva," Edna guessed, running her hand over the embossed name of Hoffman's Photographic Studio.

"I did. Can't say I took to Hoffman."

Edna opened the folder and studied the portrait of Adolf

Hitler, considering the photographer's use of light and shadow. "It's hard to believe he's an artist, you know."

"Who, Hoffman? It's not that bad a photograph, is it?"

"No, not Mr. Hoffman—Mr. Hitler. His face is so fierce… rigid…not at all an artist's face."

Rowland smiled. Hitler did look more like an angry book-keeper than a painter. "I suppose one doesn't really smile for political portraits, Ed."

She closed the folder firmly and reached over to check his watch. "I did come to fetch you for dinner," she said standing. "But you should probably change before you catch your death."

The red standards of the Nazis seemed to have multiplied in the weeks they had been in Munich. They hung as vertical banners on the façades of buildings, flew from flag poles, and occasionally fluttered from the hoods of official cars. They marked the territory and dominion of the Nazi Party, celebratory, ominous. The colour was striking and stark and somehow violent.

Silently Milton took in the crimson swathes of fabric which hung from the gallery as they stood in the Königsplatz. Rowland watched the people, the strange exuberance that seemed to have taken hold of the citizens of Munich. A year ago, when they had visited Berlin, there had been overt dissent. Unionists and Communists had clashed with the Brownshirts. Now resistance had been driven underground. Every now and then Rowland thought he saw it in the eyes of a passer-by, but that was all. The trade unions had been routed, their leadership thrown into Dachau, the membership forced into hiding.

Why the four of them had stopped at the site of the book-burning was a mystery even to them. They were not due at the Bismarck for another hour, but there were other places to pass the time.

Rowland had told his companions of the rehearsal in the

Wilhelmstrasse Stadium after Richter had left that morning, as well as the practical joke Unity had orchestrated with the assistance of Putzi Hanfstaengl.

Milton had laughed.

"Do you think they'll manage to carry it off, Rowly?" Clyde mused.

Rowland shook his head. "I don't know. Campbell is nobody's fool…but then we managed to convince Röhm that we were the SS."

"And," Milton said on consideration, "who would expect the Chancellor's Secretary to be playing pranks like a bored schoolboy? If this Hang-and-strangle bloke says 'This is Herr von so-and-so, he's a very important Nazi', why would Campbell doubt him?"

Rowland nodded. Milton had a point.

"Schlampen!" Edna turned to them excited, though she kept her voice down. "By the statue…quickly."

Milton spotted him. "Right." He pushed his hat more firmly onto his head. "You blokes stay here….I'm going to go around."

"Milt…" Rowland began, but the poet had already walked into the crowd.

The boy Edna called Schlampen was standing by the window of a small eatery, peering into the restaurant. It was possibly why he did not notice Milton. The poet walked up quietly and seized the child by the shoulders.

The gypsy boy shouted and fought blindly. Milton held on grimly. "Settle down!" He locked his arm around the boy's chest. Clyde and Rowland strode over to help. Edna got to them first.

"Careful, Milt," she pleaded. "Don't hurt him."

At that point the boy bit the poet. Milton swore and Clyde grabbed the boy.

"We're not going to hurt you, Schlampen," Edna said, grabbing the boy's hands.

Rowland bent to the boy's level and translated, speaking to the boy in Bavarian German.

The child replied, shouting at first, but as Rowland persisted, his responses became less belligerent, and longer. They spoke for a while.

"What did he say, Rowly?"

"I asked him where his parents were…if he needed help to get home."

"And?"

"His mother and sisters are in Vienna. He ran away to visit his father who is apparently interned at Dachau. Incidentally, his name is Sasha."

"Oh, the poor little mite," Edna said, placing her hand gently on the boy's sunken cheek.

He gazed at her startled, his black eyes large in the thin, peaked face.

"What did you do with my watch?" Milton said, still scowling as he nursed the hand which been bitten.

"I'd say it's well and truly gone by now, Milt," Clyde murmured, relaxing his hold on the boy. "The little scoundrel's probably pawned it."

Sasha stared at Milton and thrust his hand into the pocket of his ragged trousers. Then suddenly, panic seized the boy and he twisted to escape again. Clyde reacted quickly and caught him.

"*Was ist das problem hier?*"

Rowland turned to the voice and saw what had terrified Sasha. Brownshirts—at least six—had been bored enough to investigate the minor disturbance in the Platz.

"There is no problem," Rowland replied.

"Who is this boy?"

"Kurt Heidler," Rowland said, speaking loudly enough to ensure Sasha heard him. "He is the son of an old friend."

"Why, then, is he trying to get away from you?"

"He ran away from home a week ago…to join the SA. No

one could convince him that he was too young." Rowland smiled. "High spirits and patriotism...His father is worried sick. We'll take him home and sign him up to the Hitler Youth until he is old enough to join you gentlemen."

The SA officer stared at Sasha. The boy was unkempt and undernourished, but that was consistent with Rowland's story. He noticed then the boy's right hand, clenched in his pocket. The Brownshirt signalled his compatriots and the child was taken from Clyde and searched. Aside from a small knife and a few coins, a gold watch was taken from his pocket.

"Hey, that's my watch!" Milton exclaimed.

The watch was handed to the officer. He turned it over, studying the inscription on the back. A date: 7th September 1918—the date of Milton's bar mitzvah—and the name Elias Isaacs. The Brownshirt stiffened, his lip curled.

"You are Elias Isaacs?" he barked.

Rowland did not need to interpret. Milton had realised that his name might give them all away.

"No, I am Albert Greenway. I won the watch from a man called Isaacs in a game of poker."

Rowland repeated the explanation in German.

The boy, Sasha, watched, listening intently.

The SA officer looked suspiciously at both Milton and Sasha. They were both dark-featured. He had been trained to detect non-Aryan features.

Rowland sensed the Nazi's line of thought. He introduced his friends quickly, explaining that they did not speak German. He made a point of introducing Edna as Albert Greenway's sister.

"How did the boy come to have this watch that Herr Greenway won from a Jew?" the man demanded, his nostrils flaring upwards.

Rowland translated even as he assessed their chances of escape. Sasha was now with Edna, shaking as she enveloped him protectively in her arms. The rest of the Brownshirts had circled them.

Bystanders glanced in their direction but did not turn their heads, continuing determinedly about their business.

"I must have dropped it," Milton said. "The boy was probably trying to return it to me."

Rowland repeated the lie in German.

"It does not look like the boy was trying to return the watch to Herr Greenway." The trooper glared at Sasha.

"*Mein Herr*," Rowland began, speaking directly and quietly to the hostile Brownshirt. "As you can imagine, Kurt is a handful, but he is not a bad boy. He admires the SA, and wished only to be a part of Germany's rise. His transgressions are a misjudgement of youth." Rowland could see Sasha's face, the black eyes glittering beneath a bewildered scowl. If the boy contradicted him, the situation could become ugly for them all. He pressed on. "Kurt's father will no doubt give him a good hiding when we return, and show him a stronger hand from now on. Until then, I will personally see that he causes no further trouble."

The Brownshirt wavered.

The boy then came to the aid of his own cause. He broke free from Edna, throwing his arm into the fascist salute. "Heil Hilter!" he shouted, in a young, tremulous voice.

The Brownshirt smiled. "Heil Hitler, *jungen*." He turned to Rowland. "You tell his father to keep a closer eye on him, but not to beat him. German boys should have a sense of adventure." He tossed the watch at Milton and signalling his fellow Brownshirts, left the foreigners to deal with the runaway.

Edna held tightly to Sasha's hand as they watched them depart.

"What do we do now?" Clyde murmured.

"We take him home and feed him," Edna replied.

"For pity's sake, Ed, he's not a stray cat," Clyde muttered. "We can't very well take him home and give him a bowl of milk."

Milton laughed. "Ed's quite good with cats," he said, though whether he intended to defend or mock her was hard to tell. "Clueless with children, but cats love her."

Rowland considered the Romany boy. There was nothing more to him than skin and bone. "We'll start out by feeding him," he decided. "We'll work something out after that."

They found a restaurant that was willing to admit them with a small, dirty child in tow. It was a basic little eatery, sandwiched between two much larger buildings which blocked almost all the natural light. The wooden dining booths were lit by overhead kerosene lanterns and candles. The menu was short, but the business was clean and almost empty.

"Steady on, mate!" Rowland put his hand on Sasha's bony shoulder as the child launched into the basket of bread on the table and tried to cram an entire roll into his mouth. "You'll choke." He checked the time and turned to the others. "What say I go meet Nancy and bring her back here? Don't wait to order," he added, glancing at the boy, who was now on his third roll.

The Bismarck was only a five-minute walk away and so it was not long before Rowland returned with Nancy Wake. On the way back he had apprised her of the unexpected addition to their party.

"He came all the way from Vienna by himself?" Nancy asked, shocked.

"The little scamp was probably stowed away on the *Orient Express* when we first came over. He seems a rather resourceful chap."

"But he's just a child."

"He is." Rowland shook his head. "It appears the poor lad's been in Munich all this time, entirely on his own."

"He's lucky he didn't come to the attention of the SA before now," Nancy said. "The gypsies have always been blamed for the petty crime that occurred in Munich. And the Nazis pledged to restore law and order."

"It would be just like the SA to do so by bullying a child," Rowland said tersely.

"If you can get him back to Vienna, at least he'll be safe," Nancy replied.

When they walked into the restaurant, young Sasha was devouring sausage. Although he was no longer trying to fit as much into his mouth as possible, he hunched over the food as if he were afraid it would escape. Edna had somehow managed to procure a large glass of milk for him as well. She stroked his hair and observed as he ate, entirely ignoring Milton, who was making purring sounds.

"How long has it been since you last ate something, Sasha?" Rowland asked, as he sat down.

Unwilling to stop chewing, the boy held up five fingers.

"What are we going to do with him?" Clyde asked. "We can't leave him on his own."

Rowland studied Sasha for a moment. The child could not have been ten. "We'll have to take him back to Richter's until we determine a way to send him back to his mother."

"What are we going to tell Richter?"

"That we found a little boy who needs help," Edna said firmly. "Alois is too kind not to be glad. He'll understand that we couldn't just leave him to the SA."

And so it was agreed. They did not question the boy further, allowing him to eat as they spoke with Nancy Wake.

The young journalist was excited. "Colonel Campbell returns from Berlin today," she said. "I have an appointment to interview him tomorrow afternoon." She took an envelope out of her handbag. "My friend from the *Guardian* helped me mock these up," she said, showing them what appeared to be media despatches from Australian correspondents.

Milton scanned through them. He laughed suddenly. "Look at this, Rowly," he said, sliding the sheaf across the table.

Rowland's eyes moved quickly over the page. "De Groot? By George, that's brilliant!" He looked up at Nancy, who laughed proudly. "Campbell will completely lose his rag if thinks De Groot is staging a coup."

Captain Francis De Groot was Eric Campbell's deputy of sorts. A slight, retiring man, who had, by a single act the previous year, gained a notoriety that eclipsed that of his media-courting Commander-in-Chief. During the official opening of the Sydney Harbour Bridge, De Groot had charged in on horseback and slashed the ribbon ahead of the then-Premier of New South Wales. Overnight, he had become a hero of the right wing and Rowland suspected that fact irked Campbell.

They spent the afternoon going through the questions Nancy had prepared, making suggestions and laughing as they anticipated Campbell's reaction. They spoke in English so Sasha could understand none of it. They kept him distracted for a while with food. When he'd eaten more than seemed humanly possible for such a small boy, he curled up on the bench and slept. They let him be. Every now and then Edna reached over and patted the boy.

Chapter Thirty-four

ART PILLORY
A NAZI SHOW

BY ELLA A. DOYLE
(of Sydney, writing from Munich)

There are two specimens of Dadaism —framed compositions of bits of wire-netting and string and galvanised wire and linoleum and post-cards.

Underneath every picture in the exhibition the price paid for it is given, together with the name of the gallery which bought it, and on a red placard in white lettering one reads "Paid for out of the taxes imposed on the German workers!"

—The Sydney Morning Herald, 1937

Alois Richter had not yet returned from the business which had taken him temporarily out of Munich, and so Rowland was forced to explain Sasha to Mrs. Schuler. The housekeeper was clearly unhappy and not predisposed to making the boy welcome.

"He can sleep on the chaise lounge in my bedroom," Rowland said, when she moved to assign the child to the servants' quarters under her charge. "It's only for a night or two, until we can get him back to his mother."

"Very well, Herr Negus." She glared at Sasha. "I have counted the silverware," she said, wagging her finger at the boy. "I know *everything* in this house. If anything is so much as moved one inch, I will know!"

"He is not a thief, Frau Schuler," Rowland lied. "You need not worry."

They took charge of Sasha themselves, seeing that he was fed once more, and bathed. Mrs. Schuler burned the ragged clothes, insisting that they were infested with parasites, and so one of Milton's shirts served to clothe the boy as an interim measure. Rowland bypassed the housekeeper and sent one of the housemaids to procure some clothes for the child. When Sasha had been settled under blankets on the chaise lounge in Rowland's room, Edna braved Mrs. Schuler's hostility, venturing into the kitchen and returning triumphantly with milk.

Rowland spoke to the boy again. No longer afraid of them, Sasha answered his questions.

"What are we going to do with the cheeky blighter?" Milton asked finally, falling back on Rowland's bed. "We can't very well just put him on a train."

Rowland loosened his tie. "Ed, that Dadaist chap— von Eidelsöhn—has he left yet?"

"For Austria? Hans is going tomorrow or the day after…He didn't want me to see him off," Edna replied.

"Of course, he wouldn't," Rowland said, glancing at the sculptress. The presence of Edna could well undermine both the will and the ability of any man to leave with dignity. "But we might have to go see him tonight, regardless. He could take Sasha back to Vienna with him and see that the boy's returned to his family."

Milton sat up. "That could work."

Rowland grabbed his jacket from the back of a chair. "Right, then—Ed and I will go speak with him now. You two best stay here and protect the poor little chap from that Schuler woman."

Hans von Eidelsöhn was living in his studio. His work and equipment had already been packed and shipped and all that remained in the generous space was an iron bed and a large suitcase. Given the lateness of the hour he answered their knock cautiously, looking out through a barely cracked door before admitting them. Clearly bewildered, he greeted Rowland with his eyes on Edna. He kissed her hand tenderly and then both cheeks, embracing her as he did so. Rowland cleared his throat.

Edna told him why they had come.

Von Eidelsöhn seemed to collapse a little. "I thought you'd changed your mind," he stammered. "I hoped that you had decided to come with me."

"Oh, Hans," Edna said softly. "That is just not possible."

Rowland stared out of the uncurtained window, giving them what privacy he could. He had no wish to witness any sign of intimacy between the two, in any case. It was how Rowland had always borne his regard for Edna.

It was perhaps because he was looking so determinedly at the street outside the studio that he saw them: a fleeting glimpse as the men walked through the edges of the yellow cast of a streetlight. Stormtroopers.

"Mr. von Eidelsöhn," he asked, without turning from the window. "Are you aware that you are being watched?"

Von Eidelsöhn was startled, releasing Edna quickly to switch off the studio's solitary lamp. Rowland waited until the artist was standing beside him before he pointed out the figures of the men who stood across the street and the commercial van parked a few buildings away.

"*Meine liebe Gott*," von Eidelsöhn said grimly. "I have not seen them before."

"Have you ever looked?" Rowland asked, wondering if the surveillance had just begun or whether von Eidelsöhn was not particularly observant.

"I have not," von Eidelsöhn admitted. He smiled wryly. "I suppose it is a compliment to be considered so subversive."

"But why?" Edna asked, pressing her face to the window pane. "What have you done?"

"My work," von Eidelsöhn replied. "Dictatorship and oppression rely on a conspiracy of society and tradition. My art challenges the apathy of the masses."

Rowland's brow twitched upwards. Apathy-challenging was not the way Clyde had described von Eidelsöhn's work, but then surely the SA were not vigilante art critics. Perhaps they had read some political message into the piles of old hats and empty pails.

"What do you think they're up to, Robbie?" Edna asked.

"I don't know." Rowland frowned. "Perhaps they're just making sure Mr. von Eidelsöhn leaves...or taking note of who visits him." He glanced at the suitcase and addressed the artist. "Is that all you have?"

"Yes, I'm catching the train to Vienna tomorrow. The rest of my things have been sent on already."

"Perhaps you should leave with us...Is there a back way to this place?"

"Yes, there's an alley from the street behind. It's a little awkward..."

"We'll leave that way, then, and hail a motor cab a couple of streets away. I'll come back for the car tomorrow when you and Sasha are safely on the train."

Von Eidelsöhn looked at them, alarmed. "Do you think it's really necessary?"

Rowland shrugged. "I don't know, but I'm inclined to be cautious."

"Very well." Von Eidelsöhn fumbled about the dark room, throwing a few last items into the suitcase and making up the bed, ensuring the covers were taut and smooth.

Rowland thought the last a little odd, but he let the man be. They were in no particular hurry, though he did wonder what the watching Brownshirts thought the three of them were doing up here in the dark.

When von Eidelsöhn was finally ready, they slipped out of the apartment and onto a small balcony at the rear of the building. From there, von Eidelsöhn tossed his suitcase onto the balcony of an adjoining building. There were about three feet between the two. Obviously well accustomed to using this exit, von Eidelsöhn climbed onto the iron railing and leaped across. Edna removed her shoes. Rowland helped her up on the railing as she too prepared to jump. She glanced down and took a deep breath. He had not yet released her hand when she slipped.

Edna stifled a scream. It came out as a strangled gasp. Rowland held her with one hand. Her shoes clattered to the ground below. She looked up into Rowland's face, fixed her gaze on his dark blue eyes, and hoped he would not let her go. Rowland had no intention of doing so. He bent over the railing and secured her with his arm around her waist. For a moment they did not move, all straining for any sounds that the Stormtroopers at the front of the building had heard, that they were coming to investigate. Rowland could feel Edna's heart beating against him as he held her, his feet firmly on the balcony floor, hers in mid-air. There was nothing but the sounds of warring cats in the alley.

Now von Eidelsöhn reached across and grabbed the sculptress. Edna put her arms around his neck. Rowland did not release her until he was certain von Eidelsöhn's grip was sure, and then he relinquished her to the German artist's arms.

Von Eidelsöhn dragged Edna onto the second balcony and embraced her silently.

Rowland stopped to catch his breath before he climbed onto the railing himself and jumped across.

Edna pulled away from von Eidelsöhn and reached up to kiss Rowland's cheek. "Thank you, Rowly," she whispered.

He smiled. "We'd best go find your shoes."

They climbed down the narrow stairs into the alley, but in the darkness they found only one shoe.

"Leave it," Edna decided. "We won't be walking far."

And so two men and a barefoot woman stepped out into the night. They walked several blocks. Occasionally, a passer-by did notice Edna's naked feet, but other than a few disapproving glares, they were unmolested. Rowland hailed the first motor cab he saw and directed the driver to Richter's.

Mrs. Schuler was clearly livid. "I remind you, Herr Richter's home is not a hotel," she spat at Rowland, when they returned with yet another houseguest.

Fortunately their host had returned. "Frau Schuler," Richter said pleasantly, "I will deal with this, thank you…Perhaps you could make up a bed for Herr von Eidelsöhn in the room the gentlemen use as a studio."

She sniffed and, glowering at Rowland, shuffled off to see to the request.

"Please forgive her, my young friends," Richter pressed his palms together apologetically. "She has been looking after me for so many years."

"Not at all," Rowland replied. "We realise that we are imposing on your hospitality."

Richter shook von Eidelsöhn's hand warmly. "You are very welcome, my boy. I am only sorry of the circumstances." He looked sternly at Edna's feet. "You will make yourself ill, *Leibchen*. The pavements are cold and dirty. I have already told one of the maids to draw you a bath." And thus, with fatherly concern, he sent her off.

The gentlemen gathered in the drawing room to drink brandy.

"Stasi and I have missed much excitement, it seems," Richter said, stroking the dog who, as always, seemed incapable of excitement. "Mr. Greenway and Mr. Ryan told me of your latest encounter with the SA. You acted wisely, gentlemen. It is not becoming for the State to bully children, however mischievous they may be."

"I just hope Mr. von Eidelsöhn will be able to find Sasha's mother in Vienna," Clyde said, as he swirled his brandy.

"My family is not without means and contacts in Austria," von Eidelsöhn said quietly. "I give you my word that I shall find the boy's mother and until then I will see that he is well cared for."

Rowland nodded, aware that the prefix "von" indicated some kind of aristocratic lineage. He assessed von Eidelsöhn silently. The man was in love with Edna, but otherwise he had no reason to dislike him. Indeed, he could hardly blame von Eidelsöhn for being enamoured of the sculptress. "Miss Greenway has become very fond of the boy," he said.

Milton nodded gravely. "She thinks he's a cat."

Both Richter and von Eidelsöhn looked strangely at the poet, but Milton simply smiled.

"Then whatever I can do for the boy will be a demonstration of my regard for Millicent," von Eidelsöhn declared sincerely and earnestly. "You can rest assured, Mr. Negus, that the boy will be well."

"What about the SA?" Clyde asked. "If they're following von Eidelsöhn, perhaps we shouldn't—"

"I will accompany you to the train myself," Richter said firmly. "Röhm and his thugs will not bother you!"

Rowland glanced at his friends. They had not seen the SA outside the mansion since Richter had complained to Himmler. Perhaps the Reich's tailor had more power than they thought.

"Righto, then," Rowland said. "That's the plan."

"What's the plan?" Edna came in at that moment. She had changed, her feet were once again clad, and she held onto the hand of the boy whose fate they were discussing. "Sasha woke up," she said. "I thought I should bring him down to meet Alois and Hans."

Richter spoke first, approaching the boy and speaking softly. Sasha climbed onto the couch beside Stasi, pressing his face against the glossy black coat. The dog moved one ear.

Rowland looked at the tailor curiously. "That wasn't German."

"I speak a little Romany," Richter said. "Picked it up as a young man."

Von Eidelsöhn shook Sasha's hand solemnly and explained in Bavarian that he would take him back to Vienna and his mother. The boy considered him for a moment and nodded.

Rowland was relieved. He wasn't sure what they could have done if Sasha had refused to go, but as it was, the child seemed eager to return to his mother.

Richter played Wagner on the gramophone and summoned Mrs. Schuler, asking the housekeeper to bring sweets for the boy. Edna reminded her to also bring milk.

Von Eidelsöhn asked Sasha about his family, where they had last stopped their caravans. The child answered with directions that seemed familiar to the artist. Sasha's father had crossed the border on some sort of business, which Rowland assumed was not entirely legal. He had fallen foul of the SA, and been sent to Dachau.

Richter put his arm around the boy and spoke to him in Romany. Rowland could not understand, of course, but Sasha seemed to respond to the gentle tailor.

Von Eidelsöhn came over to where Rowland stood by the mantel. He spoke German. "Your friend Herr Richter is very kind," he said. "Many Germans these days have forgotten what it is to be kind."

Rowland nodded. "He's a good man."

"I have asked Millicent to be my wife."

Rowland nearly choked on his brandy. "I see."

"She has refused me."

The silence stretched awkwardly. Rowland wasn't sure if the man was looking to him for some kind of commiseration. It really wasn't something he could give with any sincerity. He tried. "Fräulein Greenway has always known what she wants."

"Sadly, it is not me."

Rowland smiled faintly. "In that you are not alone, Herr von Eidelsöhn."

Von Eidelsöhn seemed to find some camaraderie in that. He remained at the mantel with Rowland, looking idly at the framed photographs which stood upon it. He stopped, staring closely and long at the picture of Richter's wife and child. "You know," he said, "I'm sure I know this lady…I just cannot remember from where."

"That was Frau Richter."

"Was?"

"She's passed away, I believe."

"Oh, I am sorry. I do wish I could place her…it'll come to me…"

"*Du liebe Zeit!* It is nearly midnight!" Richter exclaimed. "Herr von Eidelsöhn and the boy have an early train to catch in the morning. Good fortune does not wait for those who lie abed!"

Rowland agreed. "We should probably turn in."

And so they said their goodnights. Milton and Edna took von Eidelsöhn to the studio, where a bed had been made up, and Clyde, who had always had a way with children, hoisted Sasha onto his shoulder to carry him upstairs. Rowland followed them but, remembering that he had left his notebook in the drawing room, returned to retrieve it.

He stopped at the doorway, seeing that Richter was still there, holding the picture of his wife and daughter on which von Eidelsöhn had commented. Richter pressed the frame to his breast, shuddering slightly as he wept. Rowland hesitated, reluctant to intrude. He turned and retreated without a word, allowing the tailor privacy in a grief that was obviously still raw.

Chapter Thirty-five

HEARD THIS ONE?

"I'm sorry, madam," said the passport official, "but there is
a mistake in your application form."

"What is it?" she asked.

"You are described as a brunette instead of a blonde."

"Dear me. Well," with an obliging smile, "will you alter
it—or shall I?"

—*The Advocate*, 1933

Rowland kept his eyes on the bobbing tassel atop Alois Richter's
purple fez, in the press of milling travellers before him. The
tailor led the way to the platform from which the *Orient Express*
would soon embark, cleaving apart the crowd with determined
swipes of his walking stick. Von Eidelsöhn walked behind him
with Edna. Clyde carried Sasha on his shoulders above the
crush as they made their way to the first-class carriages.

The SA was a visible presence at the station, arrogantly strut-
ting the platforms, demanding to see papers from time to time.

The *Orient Express* was ready for boarding. They moved
up the platform to the head of the train and there they said
their good-byes. Von Eidelsöhn, as they had come to expect,
was solemn and earnest with gratitude and assurances that he
would see Sasha safely into the arms of his mother.

Rowland beckoned the artist aside and gave him two cash-filled envelopes, one to cover the boy's expenses, the other to be given to Sasha's mother when she was found.

"It is unnecessary," von Eidelsöhn protested. "I will—"

"Take it," Rowland insisted. "It will make me feel better that I am not accompanying him myself. If you hit any trouble, you know where to reach us."

Von Eidelsöhn nodded and placed the envelopes into the pocket inside his jacket. "I remembered last night why I knew the lady in the photograph on Herr Richter's mantel," he said.

"That picture was taken many years ago, during the war," Rowland said, sceptically.

"It was many years ago when I saw her, not long after the war. I was just a young man, attending my first cabaret." He smiled at the memory. "She was magnificent...In time, she became famous, but then she was another struggling German artist."

"Famous?"

"Yes. The woman in that picture is a young Anna Niemann... she is celebrated now." Von Eidelsöhn glanced at Richter, who was singing some sort of ditty for Sasha's amusement. "I did not mention it earlier because I assume she and Herr Richter parted, and I did not think—"

"Of course," Rowland agreed. "It is best that you do not mention this to Herr Richter." He looked carefully at von Eidelsöhn. There was only an inch or so between them in height. The artist's hair was dark, though he wore it quite long, and his eyes could definitely be called blue. Rowland turned around so that his back was to everybody but von Eidelsöhn, and from his breast pocket he took the identification papers and passport which described Robert Negus as six foot one, with dark hair and blue eyes.

"May I borrow your pen?" he asked von Eidelsöhn. The artist obliged.

Rowland removed the cap and broke the nib. He allowed

the ink to drip onto his passport photograph and blotted it. It obscured just enough detail that the resultant photograph might have been von Eidelsöhn. He put the cap back on the fountain pen and returned it with the documents to the Dadaist.

"Look, Hans, let's be cautious...Just in case the SA is looking for you. These are my papers...if the Brownshirts do approach you and Sasha, use them. If they ask what happened to the photograph, tell them your pen leaked."

"But how will you—?"

"Send them back to me when you reach Vienna. I should have thought of this earlier, but it only just occurred to me that you and I have similar features...at least on paper. You might not need it, but just in case."

The whistle blew to announce the *Express'* imminent departure.

Von Eidelsöhn looked distinctly panicked, but he placed the papers into his jacket and offered Rowland his hand. "Good luck, Herr Negus."

"And you." Rowland slapped the man's shoulder as he accepted the handshake.

Alois Richter decided that they should celebrate the safe despatch of von Eidelsöhn and Sasha with ice-cream, and led them to an appropriate purveyor, where he demanded the establishment's best. Rowland watched as Edna chose a strawberry confection and then, changing her mind, attempted to convince Milton to trade. The poet would have none of it, declaring that she was fickle and needed some sort of instruction in the value of constancy. Clyde had a beer with his ice-cream, more because the fact that he could do so amused him than because he really wanted a beer at nine o'clock in the morning. Milton joined him, on the grounds that it would be rude not to observe the customs of Munich, particularly when the custom was so agreeable.

Rowland glanced at his watch, and switched his ice-cream with Edna's.

Milton accused him of undermining the lesson in character which he had been trying to teach the sculptress.

"I don't have time to eat it, anyway," Rowland said, smiling. "I have an appointment in about ten minutes."

"You're leaving us, Mr. Negus?" Alois Richter asked, wiping ice-cream from his chin.

"I shouldn't be too long," Rowland replied. "There is a gentleman I must see."

"You young people and your appointments," Richter said, shaking his head. "Always meeting this one and that one…"

Rowland stood. "I'd better get on."

Richter sighed. "I was going to take you all to luncheon…Is this meeting absolutely necessary?"

"I'm afraid it is rather important," Rowland apologised, as he signalled a waiter for his hat. "And it's well overdue."

"That's it, Mr. Negus!" Alastair Blanshard was businesslike. "The Graziers' Association is no longer willing to fund your shenanigans. I have been instructed to inform you that you should consider your association with the Old Guard finished. What you choose to do forthwith will be on your own account and therefore at your own expense."

"I beg your pardon?" Rowland said, astounded.

"I warned you, Mr. Negus. The organisation will not allow the funds of members to be squandered in this way. The excesses of you and your friends will no longer be met."

"What do you expect us to do?" Rowland demanded furiously.

"Return to Sydney. Go home."

"I can't," Rowland said angrily. "I've given Robert Negus' passport away."

"Well, that was a damn fool thing to do, Mr. Negus, but I am afraid I cannot help you. This is our last meeting."

Rowland tried to keep his temper. He had expected to confront Blanshard today, but over Anna Niemann, not bookkeeping. The money was in any case not an issue: Wilfred had pre-empted this and they still had a small fortune secreted in Richter's Mercedes. He didn't even really care about the loss of Robert Negus' papers. On Wilfred's advice, they had brought their actual passports and papers with them. He would just have to leave as Rowland Sinclair, somehow. What did incense him, though, was the timing of this renunciation by the Old Guard, and he had to wonder if it was anything to do with his discovery of Alastair Blanshard's claim to be Anna Niemann's brother. He said as much.

"You would do well to forget your tin-pot investigation into Peter Bothwell's death!" Blanshard hissed. "This is not a game, boy! Leave the matter to men who know what they're doing and take your friends and run along."

Rowland longed to punch Blanshard in the nose, but he resisted. They were standing in a museum and without Robert Negus' identification papers, arrest could be very awkward.

Blanshard glared at him, and then seemed to relent a little. "Where is this chap to whom you gave your papers?"

"Vienna…he's in Vienna." Rowland had received a telegram that morning which informed him not only that von Eidelsöhn and Sasha had reached Vienna, but that his "gift" had proved invaluable.

"Get him to send it back to you. You'll receive the passport in a day or two, I expect…and once you get it, don't delay. Leave. At the moment, nobody suspects Robert Negus and his entourage of anything. It's time to go."

"And Campbell?"

"I'll just have to deal with him myself."

Rowland stiffened. What did Blanshard mean to do? What had he already done? "What happened to Anna Niemann?"

Blanshard sighed. "I expect she's dead."

"Why?"

"Because if she were in trouble and alive she would have contacted us."

"Then it's true she was a spy?"

Blanshard ignored the question. He grabbed Rowland by the shoulders and kissed him on both cheeks.

Rowland was too startled to pull away. The Continental way of greeting was not new to him, but it was not something he expected from Blanshard.

"I have slipped a parting gift into the pocket of your coat," Blanshard said tightly. "You may need it at some point. Now, walk away, Mr. Negus. I shall neither see nor acknowledge you again."

Rowland put his hands into his pockets. His right hand closed upon the hard barrel of a revolver.

Blanshard nodded and turned away.

Mrs. Schuler opened the door to Rowland and admitted him sullenly.

"Herr Richter is in the drawing room," she said, showing him her back.

Preoccupied, Rowland barely noticed the housekeeper's hostility. He followed Mrs. Schuler into the drawing room.

His friends were there as well. Clyde and Milton were playing cards while Richter made some final adjustments to the gown he'd made for Edna. The sculptress stood on a stool as he fussed about the hem and fitted the soft fabric to the curves of her figure. She smiled as Rowland walked in, and for the briefest moment he forgot everything else. Unconsciously, he reached for his notebook, moved by a sudden impulse to draw her, to capture the delight in her face as she shimmied, showing off the dress.

"*Leibchen*, you must hold still," Richter chided, laughing. "There will be enough time for dancing tonight, when you dance with the King."

"Tonight?" Rowland said, leaning against the mantel. "That's tonight?"

Edna laughed, knowing he had not forgotten. Alois Richter had spoken of little else since the evening before.

"I suppose we should go up and check that our tails are in order," Rowland said, glancing at Milton and Clyde.

Milton picked the signal immediately. "You could be right. I recall my waistcoat's missing a button."

"A fallen button!" Richter's head snapped around. "Investigate, gentlemen! I will not have you stepping out looking as though you had been dressed by that scoundrel Hugo Boss!"

"We'll look into it at once," Milton assured him as they made their exit.

In the privacy of his bedroom, Rowland told them everything: von Eidelsöhn's rather perplexing recognition of Richter's wife, that he had given the artist his papers and about the final meeting with Blanshard.

"Why didn't you say anything, Rowly?" Clyde demanded, clearly unhappy that Rowland had kept von Eidelsöhn's revelation to himself.

Rowland shook his head. "I'm sorry. It seemed so terribly ungrateful to doubt Richter, and I had already begun to have serious concerns about Blanshard's involvement..."

"Doubt Richter?" Clyde asked.

"The man said his wife died in the Great War, and yet von Eidelsöhn saw her perform in Vienna in the twenties."

"Perhaps von Eidelsöhn is mistaken." Milton was also reluctant to think ill of their host.

"Perhaps," Rowland conceded, "But the photo of Richter's wife and child is no longer on the mantel. Why would he suddenly remove it after noticing von Eidelsöhn looking at it?"

"There are many men who won't admit their wives left them, Rowly. It's probably just pride."

"I showed Richter the photograph of Anna Niemann—he acted as though she was a stranger."

"Again, Rowly, that may not be anything but wounded feelings," Milton insisted. "The old guy has done nothing but help us since we arrived."

Clyde stood with Rowland. "No, Rowly's right. You're not seeing it straight, Milt, because you like the man." He rubbed his brow. "Perhaps Richter discovered his wife was a spy?"

Milton folded his arms and looked hard at them both. He did like Richter. But it was not in Rowland's nature to jump to conclusions…If anything, Milton considered his friend naive. "Ed's not going to like this," he said finally.

Rowland nodded. Telling Edna of his suspicions was going to be awkward.

"So what do we do, Rowly?"

"We leave as soon as possible."

Clyde agreed. "Your papers should be here with the morning mail if von Eidelsöhn got them away on time. We can concoct some family emergency and leave."

"And Campbell?" Milton asked.

Rowland glanced at his watch. "Nancy's interviewing him as we speak. With any luck, he'll be leaving soon too."

"We'll tell Ed after the ball," Milton decided. He shrugged. "We could still be wrong, you know."

Rowland frowned, aware that they still knew nothing definitive about how and why Bothwell died.

"Look," he said, "I'm going to fabricate a reason not to go to this royal reception, or at least to hang back and join you chaps later."

"Why?"

"With you all out of the house I might be able to look around. There are no papers in Bothwell's trunk. Perhaps Richter has them."

"I don't know, Rowly." Milton was doubtful.

Rowland put his hand into his pocket and pulled out the revolver Blanshard had given him. He pressed it into Clyde's hand. "An insurance policy, just in case Richter turns out to be dangerous."

"What about you?"

"Most of the servants don't live in…there's only Mrs. Schuler." Rowland smiled. "I'm sure I can handle her…I used to box, remember?"

Chapter Thirty-six

NEW RECORDS
(BY L. DE NOSKOWSKI.)

The British Symphony Orchestra, conducted by Bruno Walter, plays "Siegfried's Journey to the Rhine," one of the few cheerful pages from the otherwise gloomy atmosphere of Wagner's "Twilight of the Gods." Walter, one of Germany's most prominent conductors, has been excluded from Germany, because of his Jewish origin. His great work and fame do not preclude him from being on the "verboten" list, which, incidentally, makes one wonder whether the performance of Mendelssohn's works in Germany will also be prohibited?

Siegfried's *Journey to the Rhine* opens with the "Fate" motive, followed by several of the most important motives of the "Ring" cycle, including that of the "horn," the "Twilight of the Gods," "Rhinegold." "Woe," and Brunhilde's beautiful love motive, introduced by the wood winds.

As Siegfried proceeds down the Rhine in search of new adventures, the music becomes brighter, but towards the end the "Rhinegold" and the "Woe" motives recall the sinister curse of the fatal ring which will eventually spell death to the hero.

"Siegfried's Journey" is one of the few Wagnerian orchestral excerpts which could have well done with an up-to-date modern recording, and in this respect Bruno Walter's new version is splendidly recorded and should become very popular. (Columbia.)

—*The Sydney Morning Herald*, 1933

———————————⚬⚭———————————

Rowland left it until the last possible second, when they were all just about to walk out of the door.

Edna was enchanting in Richter's gown, and the tailor was clearly looking forward to displaying both his creation and its wearer to Munich's social elite. The gentlemen were immaculate in white tie. Even Clyde, whose brawny build was not suited to formality, looked particularly elegant.

It was a disaster, then, when Rowland spilled a glass of sherry on his waistcoat and shirt.

Richter stared at the spreading stain in horror.

"Good Lord!" Rowland said, mopping at it with his handkerchief. "What a mess." He looked up. "I'll have to change… see if I can clean this up…You chaps go on without me. I'll join you later if I can manage to look respectable again."

Richter was clearly upset, but he agreed. "I shall have Mrs. Schuler look at your waistcoat, Mr. Negus…She has rescued many garments for me over the years with the judicious application of lemon juice and soda water."

Edna regarded Rowland a little strangely, but she said nothing.

"Mr. Greenway, please take your sister and Mr. Ryan to the car. I'll just find Mrs. Schuler and telephone the palace that one in our party may be a little late—protocol, you see…I shall only be a minute."

Clyde nodded at Rowland. "Good luck, mate."

Richter made his telephone call and then returned to fuss and moan and flap. Rowland waited, trying to look contrite.

Mrs. Schuler shuffled into the drawing room just moments after Richter had eventually walked out of the door. She stood silently as he removed his tailcoat and then his waistcoat. In shirtsleeves, he handed her the ruined garment and she hobbled off, presumably to resurrect it, leaving him alone but for Stasi, who was, according to his custom, lying immobile on the couch.

Rowland waited until he heard the door to the kitchen scullery close, and then he slipped out of the drawing room into Richter's study. Like the rest of the house, it was decorated according to the tailor's florid taste, lit with chandeliers and papered in crimson and yellow. The desk was inlaid with acorns and woodland leaves, and a dressmaker's manikin served as a coat stand. Rowland started at the desk, going through each of the drawers in turn. There was nothing of interest. He opened the filing cabinet and rummaged through the files, hoping one would jump out at him, though he knew it was futile to expect to find something among the hundreds of papers.

The photograph of Richter's wife and daughter which had gone missing from the drawing room was on the desk. Rowland looked closely at the sepia image, studying the face of Mrs. Richter for a time. He pulled the photograph of Anna Niemann from inside his notebook and compared the two. Von Eidelsohn had been right. It was Anna Niemann. He considered the composition of the photograph. Anna Niemann was at the picture's edge…there was a shadow that wasn't hers. Rowland fished out his pocketknife and used the blade to unscrew the frame. The picture inside had been partially obscured by the bevelled matt of the frame. He pulled the frame away. There were two other figures beside Anna: Alois Richter and Peter Bothwell. The three had their arms about each other, laughing. The picture had been dated on the back: 1915.

So Bothwell had known Richter during the war, when their countries had been enemies. Bothwell had been a spy even then. Anna had possibly spied against Germany. Could Richter have also been a traitor to his country? Despite his reservations about the SA, and the dress sense of Himmler, the tailor had always seemed proudly nationalistic.

Rowland checked his watch. He had been searching Richter's study for nearly forty minutes. Wondering what had become of

Mrs. Schuler, he placed the photograph into his notebook and hid the frame behind some books on the shelf.

He stiffened as the silence was disturbed by a pounding at the front door. Hastily, Rowland put the study back in order and slipped out into the hallway. The pounding continued. Again he wondered what had become of the housekeeper. Perhaps she could not hear the knocking from the kitchen.

Deciding he'd best answer it himself, Rowland lifted the latch. He'd barely turned the handle when the door was forced sharply from without and he was thrown back.

"What the devil—?"

The Brownshirts barged in. Rowland froze as a gun was pointed at his forehead.

The man who stood before him was pugnacious. Deep scars marked his cheek and chin; his eyes were small and porcine. Ernst Röhm.

Rowland checked his panic, assessing what he faced. There were eight men, or men of sorts. Three seemed very young, their shoulders still narrow and slender. Two others were of Röhm's vintage and, like him, in bloated decline. The remaining two were physically between the fresh-faced adolescents and the battle-scarred veterans. Regardless, Rowland was grossly outnumbered.

Hitler's deputy sneered at him. "So this is Herr Negus, the artist."

Rowland did not allow the surprise to show on his face. He had assumed this was about their subterfuge on the night of the book-burning. How would Röhm even know he was an artist?

They dragged him into the drawing room. Stasi jumped off the couch and crawled beneath it. Rowland noticed, because it was the first time he had seen the terrier move of its own accord. It was probably a bad sign.

"What do you want?" Rowland demanded in German, as a young officer searched him, taking his notebook and handing it to Ernst Röhm.

Röhm pulled out a chair at the card table and invited Rowland to sit. "I have questions, Herr Negus. When they are answered adequately, you will be free to go."

Rowland took the seat. The SA Commander went to the gramophone and placed a record on the turntable. Wagner. Röhm closed his eyes, inhaling deeply before he returned to sit opposite his prisoner. "We are told that you have been conducting an affair with a young German woman." Röhm spoke slowly, precisely.

Rowland's brow rose. "I'm sure I don't know who you mean."

Röhm signalled to his men. Two stepped forward. One dragged Rowland up and the other punched him repeatedly in the stomach, and then they sat him down again.

"Let us not begin by being uncooperative, Herr Negus," Röhm warned, as Rowland clutched the table, gasping.

"I don't know what you're talking about," Rowland repeated angrily, as he forced the air back into his lungs.

Röhm's face darkened. Rowland braced himself. Then suddenly, the Nazi veteran grinned, leaning forward to slap the Australian on the back. "We are all men here, Herr Negus. We all understand sexual appetite, even if we do not all eat from the same trough." He laughed. "Fräulein Eva Braun. She has been satisfying you, yes?"

Rowland straightened painfully, startled. This interrogation was about Eva. His mind worked feverishly to make sense of the question. For some reason, Röhm wished to shame Eva. He looked the Nazi in the eye. "No…Fräulein Eva is a child. We have never been unchaperoned. I only painted her portrait."

At that point one of the Stormtroopers whom Röhm had sent to search the house returned, dragging the canvasses he'd found in the studio: Clyde's landscapes and Rowland's first painting of Eva.

Röhm glanced at the blue nude and laughed. "So, Herr Negus, you are a Modernist…with neither talent nor respect! The Reich does not take kindly to the defilement and slander of

German womanhood. We'll teach you that." Again he signalled his men.

This time Rowland struggled, but there were too many of them. Three held him down and a fourth forced his right arm out straight over the table.

Röhm stood and walked over to the mantel. He took the fire iron from its stand and tested its weight. The movement of music now playing on the gramophone was rising and he waited until it reached the crescendo. Rowland swore, twisting desperately as he realised what the SA Commander was about to do. A hand slammed his head against the table so that all he could do was watch. It took Ernst Röhm three swings to break Rowland's arm.

For a while, Rowland couldn't comprehend anything but pain. Released, he slid off the table onto the floor.

Leaving him to his agony, Röhm studied the nude of Eva. "So this is the painting." He traced his finger lewdly over the figure, poking as if he expected the image to react. "You painted her after you had her, yes?"

Rowland fought for focus through a haze of pain and fear. Instinctively, protectively, he knew he must deny absolutely any improper contact with Eva, for her sake, if not his.

"That is not Fräulein Eva," he managed to get out. "It's Fräulein Greenway…she has been my model for many years." He stopped, closing his eyes to shut out the spinning of the room. "The painting I did of Fräulein Eva is a study of her face which she wished to give her father." Rowland held his arm against his chest, hoping to God that Röhm had not seen the other portrait.

It seemed he had not.

The Nazi picked up Rowland's notebook and flicked through it, searching. Luck sided with the artist now. Rowland had never sketched Eva—he'd painted her image directly onto canvas. There were many pencil studies in the artist's sketchbook, many of Edna, but none of Eva.

Röhm stopped as the photo Rowland had taken from Richter's study fell out and onto the floor. He stooped to retrieve it, studying the image as he straightened again. "So the old fox has secrets," he said, slipping the photo into his pocket and tossing the notebook aside.

Rowland watched helplessly.

Squatting, Röhm placed his rubber truncheon under Rowland's chin, and scrutinised his face. The Nazi's smile was smug and cruel. "I wonder. What exactly were you doing in the Königsplatz in the uniform of the *Leibstandarte* SS, Herr Negus?"

Rowland didn't reply. He had almost dared to hope that Röhm wouldn't recognise him from the night of the bookburning.

Röhm struck him personally this time, kicking him repeatedly as he lay on the ground. "Answer me!"

"For God's sake...it was a joke," Rowland choked. "We thought we'd test the power of an SS uniform."

"So, you make a fool of Ernst Röhm," the SA Commander said coldly. He bent over and tore open Rowland's shirt.

Even through the torture of having his injured arm wrenched away from his chest Rowland wondered what the hell Röhm was doing. Stories of the Nazis' perversions came too easily to mind, and the greedy excitement of his assailant did nothing to allay his fears. He tried in vain to pull away.

Hitler's deputy dragged on his cigarette, and then, smiling, ground it into Rowland's chest.

For a moment Rowland thought he might lose consciousness. He began to hope he would.

"Wilhelm." Röhm summoned a young Stormtrooper, who looked at Rowland with wide, frightened eyes. There was a glistening shadow of golden fluff on the boy's chin and cheeks and Rowland realised the Brownshirt had not yet begun to shave.

Röhm put his arm around the youth and kissed his forehead. He lit a new cigarette and gave it to the boy.

Wilhelm hesitated and Röhm rubbed his shoulder encouragingly.

The boy closed his eyes as he held the glowing cigarette hesitantly to Rowland's skin. Röhm nodded approvingly, shouting "Heil Hitler!" as Wilhelm twisted it in. Rowland swore in English and then German as he tried to writhe away. He lost count of how many times the cigarette was relit and stubbed out on his chest in what seemed to be some bizarre initiation of young Wilhelm into Röhm's inner circle. They asked him again and again about Eva, promising a confession would end the ordeal.

Finally, with Rowland barely conscious, Röhm turned away in disgust. He instructed his Stormtroopers to leave...all but Wilhelm. When the two of them were alone with Rowland, Röhm took the revolver from his holster and gave it to the boy.

"Shoot him," he said. "Richter will bring in the others and they will tell us about the liaisons of Fräulein Braun."

The words brought Rowland out of his exhausted, tortured haze to full and desperate awareness.

Wilhelm looked down at him and as their eyes met, each saw the terror in the other's.

The boy's voice shook as he spoke to his superior. "You may want to stand back, *mein Herr*, lest blood splatter your uniform."

Röhm smiled broadly, stroking the back of the boy's neck before retreating several paces to the doorway.

"*Don't move,*" Wilhelm mouthed silently at Rowland before he pointed the barrel of the gun at his head.

Chapter Thirty-seven

THE FATHERLAND UNDER FASCISM
Reign of Persecution and Terror, Brutality and Bloodshed

...an artist friend. I had better call him Walther—he still has one eye to lose! Last summer he was the gayest person I met in grim Germany, as advanced in his art as in his politics; a daring experimenter in colour and line. Now his paintings are ashes, his face a pulp, one eye has gone, and the other in danger.

—*The Worker*, 1933

Wilhelm fired two shots and then stepped away from the body and vomited.

Röhm laughed as the boy pushed past him out of the room, sobbing, "I want to go now."

Straightening his cap, Röhm followed his young charge.

Rowland gasped, breathing again when the front door was slammed. Whoever Wilhelm might become, he was not yet a murderer. The bullets had hit the floor just a few inches from Rowland's head.

Setting his jaw, Rowland used his left arm to manoeuvre his right across his chest. He flinched as it made contact with the cigarette burns and then for several minutes he lay there as he tried to summon the energy and will to sit up. He had to get to the hallway and phone for help, though he had no idea who he could call.

He wondered what had happened to Mrs. Schuler...Where was she? Surely they hadn't murdered the old woman? She could be calling for help, but he couldn't hear anything over Wagner.

What had Röhm meant when he said that Richter would bring the others in? He needed to warn them somehow. The record played out and the house fell into silence. Rowland closed his eyes, trying to think clearly.

Perhaps he'd fainted—he wasn't sure. He knew only that when he opened his eyes again, Alois Richter was standing over him. Rowland blinked, suspecting that the figure was a hallucination. But Richter remained.

The tailor was angry. "What have they done?" he lamented, looking over Rowland. "They left you like this...?"

"Herr Richter," Rowland interrupted him. "Where are my friends? We must leave Germany now."

"They are at the ball...under the impression that I have gone back to fetch you, Herr Negus. I am very disappointed to find you like this."

Rowland winced as he tried to sit up. "I'm not exactly happy about it myself." Stasi emerged from under the couch and whined. Strangely, Richter ignored his dog. "Have you found Frau Schuler?" Rowland asked. "Is she all right?"

"I instructed her to leave before the SA arrived. She will return tomorrow to put things in order. Do not trouble yourself to get up." Richter pulled a pistol from his pocket and trained it on Rowland. "It will be of no purpose."

Somehow Rowland was not surprised. "You killed Peter Bothwell."

"Yes. I did not want to, but Peter was about to betray my secret."

"That you spied for the Allies in the Great War?" Rowland watched the gun. It was unlikely Richter would miss at this range.

"I have rebuilt my life!" Richter spat. "Back then I was young and in love. For Anna and the future of our child, I became a traitor. Now I clothe the Reich…and nothing of that past can be revealed."

"Peter Bothwell had no intention of betraying you, Herr Richter." Rowland tried to play for time with what he was sure was the truth.

"I am not a fool, Herr Negus!" Richter said. "I know Peter was here for a purpose…secret meetings…telegrams… telephone calls…and he would tell me none of it. And then he takes me to see Anna!"

"Perhaps he thought you might like to see your wife again."

"He wished to destroy me!"

Rowland began to shiver.

Richter looked at him impassively. "Shock," he said. He waved the gun. "Do not worry, it will be over soon."

"Where is Anna Niemann?"

"She is dead. I buried her with all Peter's coded documents—his so-called book. Now there is no one but you who knows that Alois Richter ever betrayed his country."

"What are you planning to do?"

"Is it not obvious? I plan to kill you. It should have been done…but Röhm and his trained monkeys never do anything properly."

Desperately, Rowland sought some leverage. He clutched at Richter's affection for Edna, hoping it was genuine. "Millicent will never forgive you."

"She will suspect me of nothing but finding your body. She will stay to nurse me through the shock of discovering you in such a state. And I, too, will comfort her."

Rowland pushed himself back as if he were trying to get away. He slid over the bullet holes in the floor. It was getting dark and he didn't think Richter had noticed them. "How are you going to explain the shooting of a man in your home?"

Richter shrugged. "You died of your wounds after an interrogation by those SA ruffians. Their brutality is well known, and certainly you have the look of a man who has been beaten to death." He smiled, pleased with the neatness of his plan. "Always the SA goes too far. Himmler and Göring have become concerned about Röhm's power. They will be happy to have the SA blamed."

"The bullet hole in my head is going to make it hard to believe I've been beaten to death," Rowland retorted.

Richter considered it. He spied the fire iron that Röhm had used to break Rowland's arm on the card table. He took it in one hand, the pistol still in the other.

Rowland felt a glimmer of hope and with it a rush of blood and strength. Richter was not a young man, and his build was slight…He would need two hands to beat a man to death with the fire iron. He would have to put down the gun and then, Rowland thought, he might have a slim chance.

With the pistol still aimed, Richter stepped over to the gramophone and reset the record. Once again, Wagner became a backdrop to violence.

Rowland braced himself…despite his injuries, he was certain he could overcome Richter if the man would just put down the gun.

But Richter swung the fire iron first with a single hand. The blow was weak but it was well aimed. Rowland cried out in agony as the iron bounced against his broken arm, and he fell back incapacitated by pain. Only then did the tailor place the gun on the card table so that he could grip the rod in both hands. He heaved the fire iron above his head while Rowland lay helpless beneath him. Stasi barked suddenly, and for a breath, the tailor hesitated.

The shot entered Richter's back and exploded out of his chest in a bloody splatter. He fell forward onto Rowland.

Rowland wasn't sure what had happened. Just faintly over the music, he could hear someone crying—a woman—but it was not Edna. Richter spasmed and gurgled before he fell still. Rowland felt the warm moist spread of the tailor's blood as it soaked his chest.

He assumed Richter was dead…he was certainly a dead weight. The body was slippery with blood and Rowland was able to slide out from under it, though the effort was excruciating. As he lay gagging on the floor, he could just make out the figure by the card table. A woman. She held Richter's gun in both hands.

"Eva?" he said.

She looked at him, her eyes wild and glassy. The revolver shook in her hands, but she didn't let the barrel drop. It was pointed at him now.

"Eva…no…" Rowland stared at her, confused and finally beaten. A cold certainty that he was about to die pressed heavily on his ribs.

Eva looked down at the revolver and then back at him. Slowly, gradually she placed the weapon on the card table and then dropped to her knees beside him. At first her lips moved without sound. "Robbie," she rasped in the end.

Rowland's chest heaved, and he realised he'd been holding his breath. "I thought…" He didn't finish. Eva stroked his face.

Rowland groaned. "Would you mind turning off that blessed gramophone?" He was beginning to despise Wagner as much as Clyde did.

Eva did so, switching on a lamp before she returned to him. She was bewildered, crying. She spoke in a stumbling outpour. "The door was not locked and I heard the music so I came in. It was dark, but I saw him hit you…and put down the gun…He was going kill you. There wasn't time to do anything else…"

"Eva," Rowland said as he reached out with his good hand

and grabbed hers. "We have to get out of here…We must leave Germany before they—"

Eva interrupted, distraught. "*Mein Gott*, I have killed a man. He'll never be with me now."

"Eva," Rowland said again. "We cannot stay. Herr Richter had powerful friends…"

Eva stopped crying. She looked at him in horror. "I cannot go. I cannot leave my Wolf. Not now, not ever."

"Eva, if he loved you, surely he would marry you," he said, more harshly than he intended in his desperation to snap her out of her mindless devotion. "He would not let anything stop him."

"That is not true!" She turned on him angrily, striking him with her fist. "If it were, you would be married to Millicent Greenway."

Rowland pulled away, cursing, not because the blow had of itself been hard but because it had landed on his arm. Eva was immediately sorry.

"Oh, Robbie…I did not mean to hurt you."

Rowland almost laughed. Röhm had broken his arm and burned him, Richter had tried to smash his skull, and Eva was sorry. He tried again to convince her that she should leave with him, begged her to do so, but the girl was resolute. She would not leave her Herr Wolf.

Rowland dragged himself upright and away from Richter's body as he tried to think. The SA had intended to kill him. Even with Richter now dead, they needed to leave. But how could he abandon Eva to the consequences of having saved his life? He looked at her. Smeared with blood and tears, she could not even leave the house.

"Take off your clothes, Eva," he said.

She stared at him.

"Put them into the fire and burn them. Go upstairs to the second floor. The first door on the right is Miss Greenway's room—her clothes should fit you. There's a bathroom at the end of the hallway…shower and get dressed. He glanced at her blood-splattered feet. "You'd best take a pair of her shoes, too."

"But why?"

"You're going to go home and forget you were ever here. You must burn the painting I did of you and deny it ever existed. I don't know who your Herr Wolf is among the Nazis, but Röhm seemed rather keen to make an improper connection between us."

"*Gott, meine leiber Gott*…What did they make you say?"

"Nothing, Eva. Really. If you go, they will have no reason to accuse you of anything."

Eva looked at the cigarette burns on his chest, visible despite the blood, and hesitated. He followed her gaze, blanching though he knew what was there.

"I didn't say anything that could be misconstrued, Eva," he said again. "You have my word. Nobody need know that we're anything more than passing acquaintances, or that you were here tonight."

"But what about you, Robbie?"

"All the buildings around here are commercial offices… empty at this time. I'm hoping no one will discover Herr Richter's body until the morning, when the servants return. When they find him, they will assume I killed him…and with luck, I will be long gone."

Eva stared at him mutely.

"Eva, please, hurry. If you insist on staying, this must be done."

She nodded and unbuttoned her dress, letting it drop to the floor, as she stepped out of her slip. Naked, she stoked the fire and threw the garments into the flames. She left Rowland then, to do as he asked.

Rowland used the back of the armchair to struggle to his feet, and then, staggering over to the front door, he bolted it shut. He made his way back to the drawing room and, with one arm, fumbled with the decanters to pour himself a drink.

He drained the glass and resisted the urge to pour a second. He would need his wits about him.

He coaxed Stasi out from under the couch. The terrier sniffed the body of his master, whining and pawing at the corpse. Rowland felt sick.

Eva descended the stairs wearing the green-spotted sundress that Edna had last worn when they were at the Starnberger See. Her hair, still wet from bathing, had been pulled into a coif and she'd reapplied her makeup.

Rowland backed away as she approached him. "Be careful, Eva. You don't want to soil your clothes again."

"But you are so terribly hurt," she said. "I cannot leave you like this."

"The Greenways and Herr Ryan will return in a couple of hours," Rowland said firmly. "I'll be all right till then. Will you not change your mind and come with us, Eva? If you don't wish to go to Australia, I could take you to London or Paris…"

Eva shook her head. "My place is here with Herr Wolf. I cannot breathe without him."

Rowland exhaled. "Then remember, you must never talk of us or Herr Richter. You must deny knowing me other than as a vague acquaintance and you must destroy that painting. Promise me you'll do that, Eva."

Her eyes welled again, but she nodded.

"Don't cry," he said gently.

"I'll never see you again."

"Not unless things go rather badly from here." He was aware that he was shivering again. He smiled, not wanting to distress her, lest she try to stay and help him.

Stasi whimpered and she looked down at the confused hound who sat by his master's body.

"Shall I take him?" she whispered. "May I take him?"

Rowland hesitated.

"Please…"

"If anyone asks, you found him in the street," Rowland said, relenting. He could feel himself fading and he needed to get Eva away while he still had the strength and will to do so. He motioned towards the hat rack where Richter had always kept the dog's lead.

Eva found it, and, coaxing Stasi away from the body, secured it to his collar. Despite everything, her misery seemed to lift with a simple childlike glee that she had a dog of her own.

Rowland unbolted the door, with a single unsteady hand. "Walk down to Hoffman's and catch a taxi from there. It will look as though you've simply worked rather late."

She nodded.

"Eva."

She looked up into his face.

"Thank you. You saved my life."

She smiled. "*Pfüat di*, Robbie."

He locked the door after her and, stumbling to the chair by the fire, collapsed into it to wait.

Chapter Thirty-eight

DRIVEN UNDERGROUND
GERMAN COMMUNISTS
WHOLESALE ARRESTS

(Australian Cable Service)

BERLIN, July 30

In spite of the ferocious measures taken to suppress the Communists, the secret police declare that the movement has only been driven underground and that the Reds are plotting throughout Germany. Stormtroops at Niochsen, in the Ruhr, discovered an organisation with 40,000 to 50,000 members resulting in arrests and seizures of explosives, ammunition and weapons. Thirty were caught practising military exercises and will be charged with high treason.

—The Cairns Post, 1933

Milton slipped behind the wheel of the Mercedes and started the engine, screeching away from the parking valet who'd brought the car around.

Alois Richter had been determined that his young guests should enjoy every minute of the reception, and so had insisted on taking a motor cab back alone to determine what was delaying Robert Negus. When after an hour neither had returned, Joseph Ryan and the Greenway siblings had decided to abandon the ball. Leaving, however, had not been easy. Millicent Greenway had caught the eye of many gentlemen who had done everything civilly possible to prevent her departure.

In the end, Edna's concern outweighed any obligation she felt to fulfil the social contract of a full dance card, or be gracious to Richter's potential clients, and she simply walked out with Clyde and Milton.

The chauffeur, not expecting to be required for several hours, was nowhere to be found, and so they left without him. In his style, the poet drove without any pretence of patience.

But as they neared the mansion, Milton slowed suddenly and pulled over. "Isn't that Eva?" he said, pointing out the figure that hurried down Schellingstrasse. "Good Lord—she's walking that bloody dog."

"Stasi doesn't walk," Clyde murmured, twisting to see.

Edna leaned out of the window and called out.

Eva stopped. She seemed relieved.

"Eva, darling," Edna said. "What are you doing out here on your own?" She opened the car door. "Come on, we'll drive you home."

Eva looked at the open door. She shook her head, smiling and pointing.

"Are you meeting someone?" Edna asked, looking carefully at the girl.

Eva pointed in the direction she was going, and waved.

Edna shut the door slowly, her brow furrowed as she watched Eva walk towards Hoffman's Photographic Studio with Stasi on a lead. Suddenly Edna was cold, her mouth dry with a creeping dread. "Drive home quickly," she said.

Milton obliged.

The house was quiet and dark when they pulled up. "Something's not right," Clyde muttered. "They wouldn't have just decided to go to bed."

"Let's see if there's anyone home." Milton ran up the stairs and knocked on the door. There was no response and he pounded again. After a couple of minutes he turned back to Clyde and Edna, perplexed. "Where the dickens is everybody?"

And then they heard the bolts being moved. The door opened.

"Rowly…Bloody hell!"

Rowland grabbed Milton's shoulder and used it to steady himself. The poet moved in to help him. Edna and Clyde followed.

"Close the door and lock it." Rowland said, before they could ask anything.

Clyde complied without hesitation. "What the hell happened?"

Rowland wasn't sure where to begin.

"Rowly, where's Alois?" Edna asked. "Didn't he come back?"

Rowland leaned heavily on Milton.

"Give him a chance, Ed," the poet muttered. "Come on, mate, you'd better sit down."

If Rowland's mind hadn't been exhausted by pain he might have stopped them going into the drawing room.

Edna didn't scream. She didn't make a sound, but simply stared in horror and grief at the body of Alois Richter, lying in a pool of blood which had been smeared across the floor when Rowland had slid out from under it. Clyde pulled her away and she pressed her face into his broad chest, her breath rasping as she tried to obscure the image with darkness.

Milton eased Rowland back into the armchair, his eyes stopping on the revolver which lay on the table beside it. "We need to find you a doctor, mate."

Rowland shook his head as he attempted to stand again. "We have to get out of here."

"Suppose you tell us what happened, Rowly," Milton said, pushing him down firmly.

Rowland closed his eyes. He tried, beginning with the photograph he had found in Richter's study, and Röhm. And then Richter's arrival, his murderous intent. He wasn't sure he was making sense. He said nothing of Eva.

Edna left Clyde's protective embrace to go to Rowland. Her eyes were still dry, wide with shock in a face that was so ashen that her lips appeared blood red. Her hand seemed unsteady as she smoothed his hair. Rowland wondered whether she was shaking; aware that it might instead be him. For what seemed like a long time she said nothing. Then, "My God, Rowly... what...Eva was here."

Rowland did not reply.

"She was wearing my dress and she had Stasi. It wasn't you... you didn't shoot Alois."

"Does it matter who actually shot him, Ed?"

She looked at him, biting her lip to stop it trembling. "No... I'm just glad someone stopped him...that you're alive. We need to call a doctor, Rowly—you're covered in blood."

He shook his head. "It's not mine," he said, trying not to look towards Richter's body. "We're in serious trouble, Ed. We must get out of here before the servants return in the morning or Röhm begins to wonder why Richter hasn't reported the murder of Robert Negus."

Clyde stood. "Rowly's right, we may only have a couple of hours." He was calm and practical. "Ed, you and Milt go up and pack a trunk."

"A trunk?"

"We can't very well escape Germany dressed in white tie and tails. Get enough clothes for all of us and don't forget our papers and overcoats...they'll cover these get-ups initially at least. The money Rowly withdrew is still hidden in the car." He glanced back at Rowland. "I'll look after Rowly."

Edna bent down and kissed Rowland's forehead. The tears had come now.

He smiled weakly. "I'm all right, Ed...really."

She touched his arm gently, her eyes lingering on his chest, where Röhm's cigarettes had burned a blistered swastika. Edna swallowed, struggling to believe what had happened.

"Ed," Clyde said sternly, as he poured Rowland a drink, "go, quickly."

She followed Milton up the stairs and Clyde placed the welcome glass into Rowland's left hand. "Here, get this into you… it'll take the edge off. How does your arm feel?"

"Wretched…it hurts like the blazes…I can't move my flaming fingers." He let his head fall back against the chair. "God."

"We'll find someone who can help, Rowly," Clyde promised. "I'm going to duck into the kitchen to see if I can find something for those burns…Look at me…can you hang on for a while—honestly?"

Rowland nodded. "I think so." Perhaps it was Clyde's calm that allowed him to let down his guard. He permitted the panic to creep audibly into his voice. "What the hell are we going to do, Clyde?"

"We'll have to find somewhere to hide until we work out how to get out of this godforsaken country."

Rowland groaned. "Where could we possibly hide?"

Clyde tapped the glass in Rowland's hand. "Drink," he instructed. "And chin up, old mate. I have an idea."

It was just past midnight when they pulled into the decrepit street. In the light of day, the window boxes had given the grimy buildings an incongruous appearance of life, but at night the geraniums were not visible. It seemed a forgotten place, empty and abandoned. But Clyde had not forgotten it.

He instructed Milton to park the Mercedes in the alleyway between two factories and he got out alone. Praying that the Underground had not relocated, he replicated the knock that they'd heard when he and Rowland had come here before.

The gun was trained through the door before it was fully opened. Clyde had expected that. Eisen's bulk filled the doorway. He spoke in furious German.

"We need help," Clyde said, hoping the man understood at least that. "Please."

Egon Kisch squeezed past Eisen. "Mr. Ryan," he said quietly, "what are you doing here?"

Clyde told him quickly. "We have nowhere else to go, Kisch. We need somewhere to hide."

Kisch translated for his comrades. Eisen frowned and protested, but Kisch seemed to wield greater authority and spoke for them.

"Where are your friends?"

"In the car."

Kisch nodded. "Bring them in. Eisen will get rid of the motor car."

Clyde took the trunk and the cash from the vehicle before relinquishing the Mercedes' keys to Eisen.

Any doubts the men of the Underground may have had about the veracity of Clyde's story were set to rest by the physical state of Rowland Sinclair.

They took them up to the concealed attic. Beimler, who had escaped Dachau, had now fled Germany, but Heinrich remained in hiding. Kisch shook his head grimly as he examined Rowland. "If that arm isn't set correctly you may never use it properly again, or you may lose it altogether," he said. "Just two days ago, we had a doctor, but he has escaped to Vienna now."

"Well, we'd better find another one," Milton said tensely. "Just look at him…"

"That is not possible."

"Rowly needs his arm," Clyde insisted. "Can't we—?"

"We cannot risk taking him to a doctor…So many are with the Nazis, and the Jewish physicians are watched…It is too much of a risk."

Rowland pulled his arm away from his chest slowly. "Nancy," he said quietly. "She trained as a nurse."

"You need a doctor," Clyde replied.

"I'm not expecting her to operate." Rowland flinched as Edna held a soaked cloth to the burns on his chest. "She just needs to pull a bone into place…Surely they teach you that in the first week."

Milton glanced at the men in the room. "Will they allow us to bring her here?"

"Who is she, this Nancy?" Kisch asked.

"Nancy Wake," Rowland replied. "She was the girl who scrubbed the Königsplatz with me and Heinrich. She's Australian originally, now French. She can be trusted."

"And she's a journalist," Milton added. "It mightn't be a bad idea for you to tell her what's really going on in Germany."

Egon Kisch put it to his comrades and for a while they debated the idea of allowing Nancy into their sanctuary. Though he could understand, Rowland did not interfere to argue on his own behalf. Considering what was at stake, he could understand their reluctance to take such a chance on another stranger. Heinrich argued for the idea, recounted the public stance in the Königsplatz with nothing to gain and much to lose. Kisch, too, seemed inclined to take the risk.

Eventually they all gathered around Rowland again. "We must know exactly what happened with the SA." Kisch pointed at Rowland's arm. "Why this was done to you."

Rowland nodded though he was not entirely clear on the incident himself. He took a chance and told the band of fugitives who they really were and why they had come. He spoke slowly, stumbling frequently when pain challenged his coherence. Kisch translated into English so that the Australians could follow the conversation. Rowland explained what they had done at the book-burning. Then he recounted the intrusion of the SA at Richter's mansion, the exception the Brownshirts had taken to his painting. "They broke my arm to make that point."

"And the cigarette burns?" Kisch asked, as spokesman for his comrades. "The SA uses such tortures to coerce information. What did they wish you to reveal?"

Rowland shook his head. "Röhm recognised me from the night of the book-burning. He was angry that we had made a fool of him."

"And then they just left?" Kisch prompted.

"They thought I was dead." Rowland rubbed his face. He was suddenly unbelievably tired. And dizzy. "Of course, Herr Richter tried rather hard to finish the job...but I got hold of his gun." Rowland did not see any reason to mention Eva. It was essentially the truth.

Kisch and his comrades conferred. One man suggested they try to set the bone themselves, contending that if they pulled hard enough it should all snap back into place. To Rowland's relief, the proposal was not popular. Heinrich, who remembered the young woman who had joined Rowland and Göring in the Königsplatz, argued for allowing Nancy Wake into the abandoned factory to help.

Kisch concurred strenuously. "If we allow this man—who put himself in danger to save Comrade Beimler—to lose his limb or worse, what then are we fighting for, Comrades? Is there any point to resistance if we are too frightened to help one another? If we cannot aid a comrade for fear, then Hitler is already the master of our souls!" The writer's oratory moved the men in hiding and soon helping Rowland Sinclair became a statement of their own resistance. Possibly, it helped that Eisen had not yet returned.

Kisch turned to Milton. "Do you know where to find Miss Wake?"

Milton stood immediately. "Yes. It might take me a little while without the motor."

Kisch frowned. "We have a bicycle. Can you operate one?"

Milton nodded. He'd had a job delivering telegrams during the Great War. He'd lasted a week, but he'd learned to ride a bicycle.

"It is better you should change clothes," Kisch said, looking the poet up and down. "You are a little overdressed for cycling...I find coat-tails can get caught in the chain."

Chapter Thirty-nine

FIRST AID AT HOME: BROKEN BONES

...Splints can be improvised from almost anything long enough, but they must be well padded, especially where they bear on bony points. Cut the splint material to the length required and pad with newspapers and tie round twice, using triangular bandages. Keep the patient warm. Get in touch with a doctor as soon as possible and do not omit to tell him the nature of the injury, so that he may come prepared and not lose time.

—*The West Australian*, 1933

It took Milton about two hours to return with Nancy Wake sitting on the handlebars. He had found her asleep in the small flat she shared with another journalist, and pretended he was a suitor inviting her out for a moonlit tryst. She had recognised him and agreed without hesitation. They had meandered back like a young couple on a joy-ride, just in case they were noticed.

She gasped when she first saw Rowland, and then, gathering herself, she smiled. "Kissed the wrong girl this time, did you, Rowly?"

He smiled weakly, and made a valiant but vain effort to stand. "Hello, Nancy."

She looked dubiously at his arm. "It's been a while since I've even watched anyone set a bone."

"We don't have many options, I'm afraid."

She pushed up her sleeves. "We'd best get started before the bones begin to knit, I suppose." Nancy borrowed Clyde's pocketknife and cut off the blood-stained remains of Rowland's shirt. She stared for a moment at the bruises and burns on his body, before she said, "You'd better remove your belt too, Rowly."

"Whatever for?"

"You might need something to bite down on while we do this."

"Oh, right…" Rowland fumbled with the buckle.

Bruised and swollen, the site of the break was obvious though the bone had not come through the skin. Nancy started at the elbow, encircling Rowland's arm with her hands and manipulating the bone. As she got near the tender lump about halfway down his forearm she asked Clyde to grip Rowland's hand and pull. Under this tension, she aligned the bone. Egon Kisch and the men in hiding watched closely, offering encouragement and groaning in sympathy. It was not a pleasant process; by the end, Rowland was damp with cold sweat and his belt had seen better days, but once the bone was set in place the relief was significant.

There was, unfortunately, no way to immobilise the limb in a plaster cast, and so after a brief search around the factory, Rowland's arm was crudely splinted with wooden rulers and secured with packing tape. Nancy was quite pleased with the end result. "It's quite straight, isn't it?"

Edna considered it. "It looks a little longer than the other arm."

Nancy tilted her head, comparing. "Hopefully, that's just the swelling. If not," she laughed, addressing Rowland fondly, "you might need to roll up your shirtsleeves, my darling, so no one notices that one sleeve's too short!"

"I'll do that." Gingerly, Rowland tested the movement in his fingers. "Thank you, Nancy."

Briefly she caught his eye and, for a glance, the moment was theirs alone. She kissed his cheek quickly. "You did well," she whispered. "Rest, now."

Then Nancy Wake sat down on the cot opposite, and held court, much as she had been doing when Rowland first met her. She told the fugitive gathering then what had happened at her interview with Campbell. Egon Kisch translated for his comrades. Quite proudly she recounted how she led and hinted and finally outright asked the leader of the New Guard about the supposed rise of Francis De Groot in his absence.

"Colonel Campbell laughed it off at first. He was rather cocksure and full of himself…boasting that he'd just come from a meeting with the most important men in the Nazi leadership."

Not quite yet able to laugh, Rowland smiled.

Nancy continued. "But then I showed him the false despatches and he became remarkably quiet. He decided very quickly that he had to get on and, when I asked for another interview, he declined." She smiled triumphantly. "He said he's leaving Germany."

Edna applauded, Milton cheered, and approval was voiced in both German and English. Nancy stood and curtseyed deeply.

Rowland lay back on the worn mattress as the loft buzzed with excitement. The men who spent their days in hiding seized and celebrated this small success, though it meant little to them. Rowland was certainly pleased, but Campbell seemed the least of their worries now. It was nearly dawn. Richter's body would soon be found and they would be the quarry of a manhunt. If Campbell was leaving, Blanshard would most likely depart with him. They could expect no further help from the Old Guard, anyway. He shook his head….It was a frightful mess.

Edna took his left hand and whispered, "Does it hurt terribly?"

He turned his head to look at her and smiled. "No."

She seemed sceptical and scared, and so he continued in an effort to reassure her that he was not in excessive pain. "I'm just not sure what we're going to do, Ed. If they aren't already doing so, I expect the Munich police and the SA will soon be hunting us. Robert Negus will be wanted for murder and, somewhat inconveniently, the poor chap doesn't have his passport."

Edna smiled wistfully. "Well, it's rather fortunate, then, that you're Rowland Sinclair."

Sensing her mood, Rowland squeezed the sculptress' hand gently. "I'm sorry about Richter, Ed. I know you were fond of him."

Her eyes grew moist and she shook her head. "I was wrong... How could I have been so wrong, Rowly?"

"We all liked him, Ed."

"I should have known. I let him treat me like Stasi, a passive pet to be indulged." Her brow descended angrily. "I can't believe I was so fooled by him...Oh God..." Her eyes traced the red and blistered line of the burned swastika which seemed to pulsate as he breathed. She swallowed, her throat tightening. "Rowly, they...he might have killed you...if not for Eva..."

Rowland frowned as he thought of Eva. "Damn! " He stroked Edna's hand absently. "I wish I'd got through to her...I hope she'll be all right."

Edna nodded slowly. "Eva's Herr Wolf—who do you suppose he is?"

"Some prominent Nazi, would be my guess," Rowland said, thinking of Röhm's questions, his determination to exact an admission of a liaison with Eva Braun.

"You don't suppose it is Mr. Röhm himself?"

"Ed, I got the distinct impression that women do not particularly interest him."

"Oh, I see." She bit her lip as she tried to piece together a picture of the SA leader from Rowland's account. "He's like Gerald Haxton, then?"

Rowland almost laughed. "Nothing like him, Ed. I don't suppose either would take to the other. Röhm is a different animal altogether." He struggled up on the elbow of his good arm. "Richter simply used Eva to summon Röhm like some flaming attack dog."

Edna sighed. "Alois must have guessed Herr Wolf's identity. I wonder if Eva realised…"

Rowland looked at the sculptress sharply. The thought had not occurred to him. He had never asked Eva why she'd actually come to Richter's that night. Closing his eyes, he remembered that moment when he thought she might shoot him, but then her horror at what she had done…No, he was sure Eva had shot Alois Richter only to save him.

"Do you suppose Mr. Bothwell was about to expose Alois?" Edna asked.

Rowland shook his head. "That's the tragedy of it. Richter seems to have mistaken Bothwell's spying for the Old Guard as some plot against him. I doubt Peter Bothwell was anything but a friend to the man…Perhaps he tried to reunite him with Anna Niemann…Richter misinterpreted it all."

Egon Kisch shuffled over to them with two tin enamelled cups of tea and passed out the steaming brews. "We must consider, Comrades, how we are going to get you all out of Germany. In some ways, the Nazis are happy for us to escape, to leave the beloved Fatherland so they can say the Communists have been expelled. But you…they will be looking for you."

"Can't we just drive across the border somewhere?" Edna asked.

Kisch laughed. "You come from a great flat country, Comrade Higgins. The borders of Germany are mountainous; the passes through them will be guarded. We could avoid the passes, of course, and cut across, but Comrade Sinclair is in no condition for such a trek."

"We'll just have to wait until he is, then," Milton said joining them.

Kisch leaned in, speaking quietly though his comrades could not understand English. "Comrades, if your friends— those who sent you here—are able to help you…"

Rowland groaned.

"Whatever your falling-out," Kisch persisted, "it is your best chance. Those of us who have escaped have had friends to help us."

"We have a friend." Edna stood. "I've got to change. Egon, would you ask your comrades to turn away, please?"

"Pardon me, Comrade Higgins?"

"I'm going to ride that contraption back with Nancy."

Milton looked up sharply. "No, you're not."

"No one will look twice at two girls on a bike," Edna said, pulling a pair of breeches from the bag she had packed.

Rowland tried to reason with her. "Blanshard was adamant, Ed…He will not help us."

"I'm not going to see Mr. Blanshard, darling," she said, bending over to push the hair back out of his eyes. "I'm going to find Mr. Göring."

Instantly, all sound died in the loft at the mention of the Göring name.

"She means Herr *Albert* Göring," Rowland said loudly in German, before suspicion could take hold. And then in English, "Ed, no…"

Edna ignored him and spoke to Kisch and Heinrich. "Mr. Göring has proved his colours, has he not?"

"He was the man who led your protest in the Königsplatz?" Kisch looked to Nancy, who was listening with interest.

She nodded. "Yes, he was truly splendid."

Kisch translated for Heinrich, who agreed wholeheartedly. "It is a good idea, but you must be careful. The SA will be watching him."

"I'll go with you," Clyde said, putting down his tea.

"No, Clyde, I'll be less conspicuous alone…or with Nancy. And Mr. Göring knows me and Nancy."

"It's a positively smashing idea," Nancy said, clapping her hands. "And it's still early. If we hurry, we'll catch him before breakfast."

"It's settled, then," Edna announced. "Now gentlemen, if you'd all kindly turn away so I can change…"

Edna slipped the black beaded cocktail dress on over her head. She studied herself in the cracked mirror in Nancy Wake's tiny two-roomed apartment. The dress would have been quite chic, worn in the evening. At this time of day, however, it made her look like a certain kind of woman.

They had reached Göring's hotel in Ludwigstrasse to find that word of the brutal murder of Alois Richter had hit the newsstands. The papers speculated on a foreign conspiracy to assassinate citizens invaluable to the Reich…apparently beginning with the execution of tailors. Magda Goebbels, wife of the Minister for Propaganda, was calling for a ban on the sale of imported garments. Röhm declared that Munich would be scoured and every port checked until Robert Negus was found and brought to justice.

The foyer of the hotel had been posted with guards, in a show of protection. Simply walking in and requesting an interview would not be possible.

And then an idea had begun to glimmer in Edna, the flame of which had been stoked by Nancy, and the sculptress and the journalist had retreated to Nancy's apartment to prepare.

Nancy Wake's housemate was fortunately out…possibly reporting on Alois Richter's murder. Nancy had pulled out the black dress for Edna and a red one for herself which was equally inappropriate for the morning. They applied rouge and scarlet lipstick and blackened their lashes.

Then they caught a motor cab back to Ludwigstrasse.

"Ready?" Edna asked, as they alighted from the car.

Nancy winked and they walked into the hotel foyer arm in arm.

The manager stared as they walked in. Edna braced herself. Would the man recognise her as Mme. Marcel, the demonstrative newlywed?

They spoke to him exclusively in French, telling him that they were there for Monsieur Göring.

Edna put her hand on the manager's as he reached for the phone. "Please, *Monsieur*, we are a gift...a special surprise. Monsieur Göring is not to be expecting us."

The manager turned crimson very quickly. "This will not do...this is not that kind of establishment! The good name of—"

Nancy interrupted him before he could add volume to his outrage. "Reichsmarschall Hermann Göring is determined that we surprise his baby brother," she crooned.

Edna leaned over the counter and whispered. "Hermann feels Albert is too shy, you understand...he wishes us to bring him out of himself. We are a generous gift, don't you think?"

The manager stared at her. His eyes narrowed. "I know you."

Edna smiled. "Yes, I have been here before...with *Monsieur* Marcel. He was a handsome one, was he not?"

"He said you were his wife!"

Edna shrugged. "He liked to pretend. Many men do." She laughed and glanced at Nancy. "Let me tell you in confidence, *Monsieur*, my friend and I specialise...in the particular fantasies of men."

Nancy winked. "It is why the Reichsmarschall is sending us to his brother...he will be disappointed if his gift is not received."

At each mention of Hermann Göring, the manager sweated a little more. The flamboyant Nazi minister was renowned for his extravagant perversions and his fondness for his brother. It would not do to displease him.

"Top floor," he muttered. "Suite two." He looked at them so beseechingly they were stabbed with unexpected guilt. "You will be discreet, won't you, *Mesdemoiselles*? This is a respectable establishment."

Nancy raised her chin loftily. "Monsieur, we are professionals!"

Taking care to appear unhurried, they sauntered with emphasised sway to the polished doors of the hotel lift. The young attendant fumbled with levers and conveyed them to the top floor. As they stepped out, Edna blew the bellboy a kiss and laughed as he blushed and stumbled as if knocked back by the impact of it. She noticed that he waited with the doors open, watching, waiting to report their reception to his manager.

Nancy knocked.

Albert Göring opened the door in his smoking jacket, an open book in his hands, an ebony cigarette holder clenched between his teeth. He gazed at them, alarmed. He squinted and peered more closely, and then stepped aside to admit them.

After they'd entered, Göring stuck his head into the hallway and caught sight of the lift attendant watching the proceedings with an excited, salacious grin. He nodded and closed the door.

"Well, well," Göring said, turning to smile upon them. "Monsieur Sinclair's beautiful young starlets…"

Edna didn't waste any time. She sat Göring down and told him everything.

He listened with unfolding horror. "They broke his arm?"

Edna nodded. Her eyes brimmed as she remembered the state in which they'd found Rowland. "To punish him for the painting," she said. "They only left because they thought the boy had shot him."

"And Monsieur Richter?"

"Rowly believes he telephoned Monsieur Röhm that evening."

Göring clicked his tongue and shook his head. "Poor Monsieur Sinclair. Perhaps he is no longer so naive a spy."

He took Edna's hand. "But you did not come here to tell me stories, *ma chère*. What can I do to help?"

Edna nearly wept at his unthinking kindness. "We have to leave Germany, Monsieur Göring."

"Of course."

Edna pulled from her purse four passports…their actual passports, rather than those which had been supplied by the Old Guard. The men had secreted them in the lining of their jackets, just in case.

Göring took them from her, shuffling through them. "And you, Mademoiselle Wake…do you not want to return home?"

"One day," she smiled. "But for the present, the authorities are not seeking me and there is much to be done in Europe."

"Indeed, Mademoiselle, indeed." Göring puffed intently on the cigarette in its Bakelite holder as he thought. "Are Mr. Sinclair and the two gentlemen in a place of safety right now?"

"They are in hiding," Edna replied. "They are as safe as they can be."

"Good, it may take me a day or so to make the necessary arrangements."

"What are you going to do?"

"I shall give your passports to my brother, Hermann."

Edna recoiled. "You're turning us in?"

He looked at her gravely. "I hope not…I think not. Hermann can grant safe passage out of Germany. I am hoping he will do so because I ask him…but there is always the risk that his love for the Nazi Party is greater than the bonds of brotherhood. That he will betray both me and you."

"How great a chance?" Edna asked, swallowing.

"I will do my very best for you," Göring replied. "I will play every card of fraternal loyalty and brotherly love. I will remind him of the games we used to play, of the toys we shared, and we shall see."

Edna hesitated. And then for some reason, Wilfred Sinclair came to mind. Wilfred, who at times seemed to disapprove of his brother's very existence. They were so different, Wilfred and Rowland, and so committed to being so, and yet their loyalty to each other was unwavering…unspoken but absolute. Edna had no doubt that Rowland would die for his elder brother, and Wilfred had never failed to arrive when all seemed lost. But he couldn't help them now. She decided. "We will hope with you then, Monsieur Göring."

Chapter Forty

FRANCE WELCOMES EXILED GERMANS
Books Banned By Hitler To Be Published

LONDON

The Paris correspondent of the *Daily Express* says that the anti-Nazi demonstration by Jews in London has electrified the immense German population in Paris. France has given a home to many of Germany's former big men in science, literature, philosophy, art, and the cinema. A mass attack on Hitlerite Germany is being planned from here by her own former leaders. France, says the correspondent, is delighted at the events, as she recognises that Germany is now more isolated in Europe than any nation since Napoleon met his Waterloo. So German migrants are welcomed. They are by no means all Jews, but include many men of the liberal school of thought. A French publishing house will soon begin the publication of German books recently burned in the streets of German cities by Hitler's orders.

—The Advertiser, 1933

The bohemian café near the station was all but empty. It was early and the proprietor was still setting up for the day's trade. Four men and a noticeably beautiful woman sat nearly shoulder-to-shoulder about one of the round tables. Two of the men drank coffee silently, while the others conversed quietly in French.

"Thank you, Albert." Rowland slipped the papers the other had just given him into his jacket. He used his left hand. To those who knew him, he seemed pale and a little drawn, but otherwise he was shaven and well groomed. "I cannot repay what you have done for us, but if there is ever an opportunity, I shall try."

Göring smiled. "Regrettably, *mon ami*, there may come a time when I shall need to call in favours."

Rowland looked at him, his intense blue eyes clear and sincere. "Whatever you need, mate, whenever you need it."

Göring rested a hand on his shoulder. "Now, remember, your papers are in order, but Röhm's murderous thugs are still looking for Monsieur Negus. They will know that his arm has been broken. It is important that Rowland Sinclair has no such injury."

Rowland nodded. Still splinted with ten-inch rulers held in place with packing tape, the injury was invisible under the sleeves of his shirt and jacket. Using the limb as if it were uninjured, however, was proving a challenge. Any accidental turn of the wrist was excruciating, but he had practised the movement required. Initially, the exercise had been staggering, leaving him gasping and cursing. Then, at Milton's suggestion, he had tried a two-handed greeting, bracing the impact on his right arm by clasping his left hand over the top. It was a more intimate form of salutation than Rowland generally used—something he associated with clergy and politicians—but it did make the motion bearable. He could now shake hands without any obvious sign of the pain it caused. And Clyde and Milton were ready to curtail a prolonged handshake by offering their own greetings. As for other things, Rowland had been born left-handed. He could write quite as well with his left hand as his right.

Somehow, Albert Göring appeared to have convinced his powerful brother to grant the necessary visas and approvals, and had organised for them to take the *Orient Express* from Munich to Paris. From there, they would make their way to London, and then back to Sydney via ocean liner. That was the plan, anyway.

Of course, the train and its passengers would be checked by the police, the SA, and possibly the SS, but unless Röhm himself was searching carriages, Rowland was unlikely to be recognised as Robert Negus. The newspapers to date had not carried a photograph, just a description that could have applied to many men.

"If you are captured," Göring continued, "I will do what I can, but it will be difficult if you fall into the hands of Röhm. It is hard to tell what Himmler would do…whether he would want Röhm to bear the full force of the Chancellor's displeasure for your escape or whether he would be willing to forgo that opportunity to gloat, in order to bring you in himself."

"Best we should avoid him, then." Rowland stifled a yawn. He wondered if it was fatigue which was keeping him so calm. Perhaps he was just too tired to panic.

Göring walked with them to the platform. He kissed each of them on both cheeks in farewell. While Clyde and Milton had always found this form of Continental greeting uncalled for, they were happy to allow Albert Göring to do whatever he wanted.

To Edna, Göring said regretfully, "I could have made you a star, *ma chère*." And then, as he helped her into the carriage, he announced loudly, "Hermann sends his regards and implores you to forgive him for not being here to see you off himself. The Chancellor requires his presence, you see."

"What's he doing?" Milton whispered, startled.

Rowland glanced at the Brownshirt troops who stood ready to board the train. "He's letting the SA know we're out of bounds."

Albert Göring had done his best to badge them with the protection of his brother, including insisting upon the swastika pins they wore in their lapels. Despite the fact that the Nazi cross had been burned into his chest—or perhaps because of it—Rowland struggled with wearing the insignia visibly. Clyde and Milton were no happier, but they could all see the wisdom of adopting the guise. Of course, Hermann Göring knew nothing of this…He had, to his mind, merely approved some documents for his brother's friends. It was not the first time and would not be the last.

They climbed aboard and found their seats, listening nervously as the SA made its way through the carriages, demanding papers and asking questions.

The Brownshirt who came into their cabin was young, and so blond he appeared to have neither eyebrows nor lashes.

He stood between the facing seats, clicking his heels and raising his arm in an enthusiastic fascist salute. "Heil Hitler!"

"*Grüss Gott*," Rowland replied casually. "Is there a problem?"

The man looked closely at him. "We are searching for a foreigner named Negus…a dangerous and desperate criminal."

Rowland shook his head. "We don't know him, I'm afraid."

The Brownshirt stepped closer, scrutinising him. "I do not know him either, *mein Herr*, but a witness describes him as having dark hair and striking blue eyes."

Rowland smiled. "Your witness is describing Chancellor Hitler."

"And you, Herr…"

"Sinclair," Rowland finished. They waited as the Brownshirt dropped his eyes to their lapel pins.

"I see you are a member of the party, Herr Sinclair. Why did you not return my salute?"

Rowland cast his eyes about the small compartment. "There's not much room in here. I was afraid I'd poke someone's eye out."

The Brownshirt stepped back. "I will make room."

At first Rowland didn't move. He sensed the alarm of his companions, the tension as they silently tried to understand with the smattering of German they'd picked up.

"Shall we see your salute, Herr Sinclair?"

"I don't see that it's necessary," Rowland said coldly.

"It would be polite, Herr Sinclair, and one assumes you do not wish to offend a member of the SA."

Rowland stood slowly, bracing himself. He wasn't sure he could force his right arm into the fascist salute, but he wasn't sure how he could refuse.

At that moment, the compartment's door was opened and another Brownshirt walked in. He was older, a man of authority.

"*Was ist los?*" he demanded. "What is the problem here?"

Rowland decided to take the offensive. "Your man here seems to think I look like Herr Hitler. The fool's so overcome by the supposed resemblance that he wants me to perform the salute so he can fantasise that the Chancellor is saluting him!"

The young Brownshirt stuttered in protest, but Rowland spoke over him. "Really, this is outrageous! I will be speaking to someone about this."

"You don't look like Herr Hitler!" The officer looked at the first Brownshirt incredulously.

"That's what I said. I suspect your man has been drinking!" Rowland took his papers from his pocket and handed them over. "Perhaps you should tell me your name, and the name of your insubordinate inferior."

The SA officer perused the documents, flushing deeply when he recognised the personal endorsement of Hermann Göring. He glared at his younger colleague and flicked his head towards the door.

"*Dummkopf!* Idiot! Get out." He handed the papers back to Rowland. "My apologies, Herr Sinclair. Some of the new recruits are overzealous. It will not happen again." He proffered his hand and smiled.

If Rowland hesitated, it was imperceptible. He accepted the handshake and smiled tightly as the officer pumped his hand vigorously.

"Enjoy your journey, Herr Sinclair." The man's eyes were watchful and did not leave Rowland's face. By sheer force of will, Rowland maintained his grip and the Brownshirt released first.

"Again, my apologies," he said as he left.

Rowland waited until Edna had locked the door before he collapsed into his seat, clutching his arm and cursing quietly.

Rowland stepped from the carriage onto the platform. Paris. He wanted to laugh. It seemed absurd that they had managed to escape. That they had managed any of it.

Edna grabbed his left hand as she, too, stepped down. Clyde and Milton were close behind her.

For a while they stood, enjoying the background cacophony of spoken French, taking in the posters which advertised shows banned in Germany, in styles that would have been considered degenerate. There was an uninhibited life to Paris that seemed a world removed from the darkening order of Germany under Nazi rule. They relished it. Eventually, they found their way to a motor cab and Rowland instructed the driver to take them to the Hôtel de Crillon on Place de la Concorde.

In the extravagant gilded grandeur of the Louis XV foyer, Rowland organised to send three telegrams. The first two were addressed to Albert Göring and Nancy Wake. They advised simply, "ARRIVED SAFELY STOP THANK YOU STOP R". The third he despatched to Wilfred. It read, "COMING HOME".

They barely said a word to each other until they were alone in the suite, and even then there seemed little to say.

"Bloody hell, Rowly!" Clyde muttered finally, unable to put into words the realisation of what they had witnessed, what they had escaped. "What in God's name is happening to the world?"

Milton braced Clyde's shoulder reassuringly. "Once meek, and in a perilous path, the just man kept his course…"

"'…along the Vale of Death'." Rowland smiled. "If you must steal something can't you find a cheerier victim than Blake?"

"Well, it didn't sound so bad until you added that last bit," Milton grumbled.

Edna pulled off her long scarf, slipping it around Rowland's neck and securing it as a sling for his arm. And then she curled up on the settee beside him, unsure of whether to laugh or cry.

Rowland loosened his tie as Milton poured and distributed drinks.

The poet raised his glass. "In the hope that we have done enough."

Rowland drank. "For the moment, at least, we've done what we can. It's nowhere near enough."

Epilogue

FASCISM
Mr. Eric Campbell Supports
BUT IS NOT ANTI-SEMITIC

SYDNEY, Tuesday

"There is nothing incompatible in treating the Jewish section of the community justly, fairly and honourably and being wholeheartedly behind the principle of Fascism reform," said Mr. Eric Campbell today.

Mr. Campbell will tell young men of the Jewish Association in Sydney tomorrow that he believes in Fascism but that he is not anti-Semitic.

He stated today that when he talked of Fascism he did not believe in the revolutionary side of it, which was purely incidental.

Expressing the utmost contempt for democracy, Mr. Campbell said that Australians had fought during the war for an ideal, but democracy had given them a raw deal.

—*The Canberra Times*, 1939

Rowland Sinclair, Clyde Watson Jones, Milton Isaacs, and Edna Higgins returned to Sydney by ocean liner arriving sometime after Colonel and Mrs. Eric Campbell made port on the *Oronsay*.

Although he was never found and tried for the crime, it was widely accepted that Robert Negus murdered Alois Richter. The Lyons UAP–UCP Government strenuously denied any knowledge of the supposedly Australian art dealer. *Der Stürmer* printed an article claiming a Zionist conspiracy to dominate the fashion industry by assassinating the competition.

Rowland Sinclair maintained a correspondence with both Albert Göring and Egon Kisch. The arm broken by Ernst Röhm healed surprisingly well, though he bore the Nazi symbol burned into his chest for the rest of his life. For the first time, the determinedly disinterested Rowland Sinclair began to take an active interest in international politics.

In 1934, Egon Kisch boarded the *Strathaird* to visit Australia as a delegate to an anti-fascist conference. Refused entry by the Lyons Government, he jumped from the ship onto the quayside at Melbourne, breaking his leg in the process. On 17th February 1935, Egon Kisch addressed a crowd of 18,000 in Sydney's Domain, where he spoke passionately about the evils of the Nazi regime, the danger of another war and of concentration camps. He was welcomed warmly at Rowland Sinclair's Woodlands House.

After escaping Dachau and Germany, Hans Beimler joined the first contingent of International Brigades volunteers as a commissar, defending Madrid from the Nationalists during the Spanish Civil War. He was killed in battle in 1936 and was buried in Barcelona.

Albert Göring continued to oppose the Nazi Government, using his brother's position to help many dissidents escape

Germany. During the war he only increased his anti-Nazi activity, encouraging minor acts of sabotage, and forging his brother's signature on documents when necessary. By 1944 a death warrant demanding execution on sight was issued for Albert. Hermann, as always, dropped everything to save him, asking Himmler personally to smooth over the matter. The Göring brothers met for the last time in 1945. Hermann was the Allies' most prized Nazi prisoner, while it seemed Albert was detained simply for being Hermann Göring's brother. In 1946, Hermann committed suicide shortly before he was due to be hanged, and Albert was freed.

Nancy Wake interviewed Adolf Hitler in 1933. Having witnessed the ruthless treatment of the Jews in Germany, she returned to Paris adamant that she would do whatever she could to fight the Nazis.

Adolf Hitler eventually noticed the young, black-shirted Englishwoman who seemed to be at the Osteria Bavaria every time he visited the restaurant. He invited Unity Mitford to his table and came to consider her the perfect example of Nordic womanhood.

In October 1933, Sir Charles Kingsford Smith flew solo from London to Wyndham, Western Australia, in just over seven days. The feat brightened his flagging prospects following the bankruptcy of Australian National Airlines, which he had jointly established with Charles Ulm. The celebrated airman opened a flying training school—the Kingsford Smith Air Service—in Sydney. Rowland Sinclair was among his first students.

The authorities never officially connected Eva Braun with either Robert Negus or Rowland Sinclair. She acquired another Scottish terrier to keep her beloved Stasi company, naming this second hound Negus. Eva remained loyal to her Herr Wolf, though the relationship continued to cause her much heartache. She attempted to take her own life again in 1934, and then in 1945, just one day after she'd married the object of her obsession, and become Mrs. Adolf Hitler. This third suicide attempt was successful.

In the absence of competition from Alois Richter, Hugo Boss became the primary supplier of uniforms to the Reich.

Senator Charles Hardy took shipment from Germany of several objects d'art in the later months of 1933. *Backwards Mona Lisa* by Hans von Eidelsöhn ended up hanging in a shearing shed near Yass, where it was said to have had a calming effect on penned sheep. Two other works by von Eidelsöhn form part of the Australian Club's private collection. Joán Miró's deformed duck painting, otherwise known as *Paysage*, passed through many hands before it was eventually acquired by the National Gallery of Australia in 1983. There is no record of what became of the pile of old hats or the empty pail titled *Drought*.

In 1937, the Nazis mounted an exhibition of "Degenerate Art" in Munich, consisting of Modernist works hung chaotically beside deriding labels. Positioned between a Van Gogh and a Picasso, under the slogan "madness becomes method," was the painting of a blue nude by a little known artist called Robert Negus. The accompanying label stated that the work was displayed as an example of art by the criminally insane.

Delighted with what he believed a successful tour, Eric Campbell was lavish in his praise of the fascist regimes of Europe. His return to the New Guard was marked with an increased autocracy during which he attempted to instigate the heel-clicking salute of the fascists, and a uniform. Campbell entertained an increasingly familiar association with Nazi representatives in Australia.

In 1934, Briton Press published *The New Road* by Eric Campbell, an argument for what the writer called a "corporate state" in which, he contended, that "the spiritual and moral inspiration of Fascism is the Hope of Civilisation," and condemned the press for censuring "either Italy or Germany for asserting their rights by force against the continued misgovernment of the sectional minorities."

In December 1933, Eric Campbell launched a formal political party, the Centre Party, to contest all State and Commonwealth elections. Despite his sycophantic praise of the German Government, there remained no public show of friendship or endorsement from the Nazi Regime, other than an autographed photograph of Adolf Hitler, procured through the German Consul-General. Unlike Hitler's National Socialist German Workers' Party, the Centre Party failed to gain popular support and the rise of Eric Campbell was curtailed. The "New Road" was not taken. It seemed Australians preferred the well-worn route of democracy.

About Sulari Gentill

A reformed lawyer, Sulari Gentill is the author of the Rowland Sinclair Mysteries, eight historical crime novels (thus far) chronicling the life and adventures of her 1930s Australian gentleman artist; the *Hero Trilogy*, based on the myths and epics of the ancient world; and a standalone mystery called *Crossing the Lines*. She lives with her husband, Michael, and their boys, Edmund and Atticus, on a small farm in the foothills of the Snowy Mountains in Australia, where she grows French black truffles and writes.

Sulari has been shortlisted for the Commonwealth Writers' Prize—Best First Book, won the 2012 Davitt Award for Crime Fiction, been shortlisted in 2013 and the 2015 Davitt Award, the 2015 Ned Kelly Award, the 2015 and 2016 Australian Book In-dustry Award for Best Adult Book, the NSW Genre Fiction Award, commended in the FAW Jim Hamilton Award and offered a Varuna Fellowship. She was the inaugural Eminent Writer in Residence at the Museum of Australian Democracy.

She remains in love with art of writing.

To see more Poisoned Pen Press titles:

Visit our website:
poisonedpenpress.com
Request a digital catalog:
info@poisonedpenpress.com